Death by Equine

Annette Dashofy

Published by Annette Dashofy, 2021.

DEATH BY EQUINE

First edition. May 11, 2021.

ISBN: 978-1638485322

Written by Annette Dashofy.

Also by Annette Dashofy

Death by Equine

Watch for more at www.annettedashofy.com.

In memory of Ramona DeFelice Long

I miss you, my friend.

One

Doc Lewis smiled into the tunnel of light created by his high beams. The stillness surrounding a barn call at three in the morning appealed to him. No one looking over his shoulder. No one questioning why the hell he was so damned happy, even though he'd been dragged out of bed, away from the warm body next to him, to venture into the damp chill of a spring night in western Pennsylvania.

Tomorrow morning he'd be out of here. Two solid weeks in Maui sounded awfully good right about now. In over twelve years at Riverview Park Racetrack, he hadn't had a vacation, hadn't missed a day of work. He'd balked at first, like one of his equine patients, but Amelia had insisted. He had to admit, he owed her this. The last few days had been nothing but one long headache. Five hours and some odd minutes from now, he'd be on a plane headed for paradise.

Doc pulled his battered Dodge Ram off the road at the sign marked "Stable Gate" and braked to a halt at the guardhouse. He half expected the idiot kid keeping watch at this hour to be asleep in his shack, but the scrawny figure in a uniform suited for a much larger man stepped out of the small building and approached. Doc shifted out of gear and rolled down the window.

"Evening, Doc." The guard's accent told of a Southern upbringing.

"Butch." Doc nodded with forced civility.

"What brings you out tonight? I thought you were on vacation and that Cameron gal was filling in for you."

"She is, but she's out on an emergency call of her own." Sometimes he wished his former protégé wasn't so dedicated to her patients. Made it hard to be mad when she couldn't jump at his beck and call. "I got a call from someone in Zelda Peterson's stable saying Clown looked colicky. I wasn't sure how long Dr. Cameron would be delayed. Figured I'd better check on him myself."

"Clown, huh?" Butch scratched the stubble on his upper lip. "I ain't seen anyone from that crew around here all night." He craned his bony neck to look beyond Doc to the empty seat beside him. "Where's that cute assistant of yours?" His lip curled into a sneer.

Doc resisted the urge to wrap a hand around Butch's skinny throat. Not worth dirtying his fingers. Doc reminded himself, *Maui*. "I get called out to treat this horse for colic every few months. No big deal. I didn't see any reason to wake her for this one."

"Too bad. She's a real babe, that's for sure. Once we get our little business matter settled, I think I might just ask her out."

The thought of Butch's grubby paws on Sherry sent a stabbing pain through Doc's jaw. He realized he was gritting his teeth.

"Well, I'll get the gate. You have a good trip, you hear?" Butch turned and shuffled back to his shack.

Doc dropped the truck into gear. The yellow and white striped arm swung into the air, and he drove into the racetrack's barn area.

The night air carried the distant rumble of the Monongahela River and the chirp of spring peepers. Doc steered around the potholes dotting the pavement. He slowed as he approached the veterinary clinic. It didn't look like much from the outside—just a long, gray block structure with a sliding metal door big enough to back a semi through in front and a matching one in the back. No sign hung on the exterior to declare the building's purpose. It didn't need one. Everyone at the track knew. It was this clinic—*his* clinic—that kept him hanging around an otherwise second-rate racing operation. The only way he'd find better surgical facilities would be to throw in with another vet—or two—at some university or equine care center. Here, he ran things the way he wanted. Not to mention the prestige of having an indoor therapeutic equine swimming pool on the premises.

Yes, he could put up with all the other crap in order to maintain bragging rights to his practice at Riverview Park.

This night, however, he would not examine his patient at the clinic. He ticked through a mental inventory of the supplies stashed in the truck's Bowie storage unit. He had what he needed.

Doc made the next left and drove between the long rows of stables, dark save for the halogen lights set high on poles scattered about the backside. He breathed in the fragrances of horses and hay and hoped treating Clown's colic wouldn't take too long. There was still packing to be done before the flight.

He parked beside Barn E, cut the engine, and climbed out of the truck, expecting Zelda or one of her hirelings to meet him. But the place appeared deserted. Only the light streaming from one of the stalls indicated anyone had been around.

He opened a compartment of the Bowie unit and filled a syringe with the painkiller, Banamine. Capping the hypodermic needle, he dropped the syringe into his shirt pocket and looped his stethoscope around his neck before strolling toward the barn.

"Yo, Zelda," he called out. "Hello? Anybody around?"

The clomp of his boots against the pavement echoed against the stillness. Where the hell was everyone? Zelda's groom had sounded half tanked on the phone. Probably got tired of waiting and went to get coffee. By the time he returned, Doc would have the horse well on his way to recovery, and he'd be on his way back to his warm bed.

He entered the shedrow. A gray with soft, dark eyes and a black with a wide blaze down his face hung their heads over the stall webbings and eyed him warily as he passed. He noted the numbers above each door. Twenty-four, twenty-three, twenty-two. Twenty-two. That was it. A lone, naked bulb lit the twelve-by-twelve box stall. Inside, the angular chestnut stallion cringed against the far wall. The stall reeked of sweat and manure.

This didn't smell right. Literally. "Hello?" he called out again. Again, no answer, except for Clown, whose explosive snort sounded like the detonation of a small bomb.

"Whoa, boy." Doc's voice usually soothed the horse, but not tonight. Clown tossed his head. One front leg struck out, the hoof pounding into the stall's bedding, digging a hole in the straw.

Clown had a knack for pawing. His stall had been victim to it for so long the dirt floor sloped toward the center, like a crater. No, it wasn't the pawing that triggered Doc's internal alarm. It was the smell. Fresh manure...something he certainly didn't expect to find in the stall of a colicky horse.

Doc lifted a lead shank from a hook on the open top half of the stall door and unlatched the lower half. He stepped into the stall and pulled the door closed behind him, too hard. Clown flinched. Doc studied the horse as it paced back and forth along the back wall, head low, ears pinned. He caught a glimpse of white-ringed eyes.

"Easy, fella," he cooed. "What's wrong there, old boy?"

The horse had a tendency to act aggressive, but Doc knew it was all for show. Clown believed if he scared you off, you might leave him alone. When the ploy didn't work, he'd give up and behave more gentlemanly.

Doc stepped toward Clown, keeping up an easy patter to relax the horse. Clown stopped pacing and tipped his head toward Doc. Good. But when he reached for the horse's head, Clown squatted back onto his haunches and reared. The animal struck out with one front foot. Doc tried to dodge the blow, but it came too quick and grazed the side of his skull. Stunned, he staggered back. Pain seared his head. He raised a hand to his ear. Touched a chunk of loose cartilage where the appendage had once been. The hand came away warm and sticky. And red.

"Damn—" He stared at the big horse. Tried to think. Entering the stall alone had been a huge mistake. He prayed he had time to correct it. "Easy, big guy. No one's gonna hurt you. Steady there." He drew the words out, keeping his voice soft. One small step back. No quick movements.

Clown flung his head, showing Doc his teeth. With a ferocious, deep-throated roar, the stallion again went up on his hind legs, lashing out with both front feet. The aluminum racing plates he wore slammed into Doc's chest, driving him down in the straw. The syringe sailed from his pocket in one direction. His straw hat flew the other.

Doc struggled for breath. A million flashbulbs burst behind his eyes. "Son of a bitch," he wheezed through the pain and the panic. He lay there for a moment, clutching at his chest, his gaze riveted on Clown. Doc had to get out of the stall and do it quickly, but without further aggravating the stallion. When he was finally able to catch his breath, he began to crawl backwards on his elbows, propelling himself with the heels of his work boots, in one last effort to reach the stall door.

Head lowered, the horse advanced on him. Teeth gleamed between curled lips. He raised one front leg and rammed the hoof down on Doc's thigh. The bone snapped. The sound of it screamed through Doc's head, meeting with the explosion of pain that raced up from his leg to nearly push him into the encroaching darkness. A shriek tore from his throat.

"Help! Someone!" He wasn't sure if his thoughts formed words or if the words made sound. As he sprawled in the crater in the center of the stall, it occurred to him that Clown had dug Doc's grave.

The horse retreated for a moment against the back wall. Doc looked toward the stall door, searching for some sign of rescue. Was that movement he saw? A shadow? Or was he hallucinating? He called again for help. Believed he saw the shadow move. His heart leaped. But imagined or not, the source of the shadow was not coming to his aid. A rustle from the back of the stall drew his attention once more to Clown. Something—some *one*—had driven the horse to react this way. Doc had only seen such rage in this animal's eyes once before. He should have recognized the signs sooner. Now it was too late. Clown went up on his hind legs, and Doc knew the last thing he would ever see was the underbelly of this chestnut stallion.

Clown's front feet thrust down on him and all went silent and still.

Two

Dr. Jessie Cameron's first inkling of something amiss was the abandoned guard shack and the raised gate at the stable entrance. Even at three o'clock in the morning, security never left the place unattended. Never. The red and blue flashing lights of several police vehicles, including two Pennsylvania State Police SUVs, and an ambulance positioned in the roadway between barns confirmed her sense of foreboding. A swarm of uniforms around the stall to which she'd been summoned completed the trifecta of bad vibes.

She left her Chevy pickup next to one of the state trooper's vehicles and struggled to maintain a calm exterior. *Don't spook the horses.* It was a lesson drilled into her from as far back as she could remember, but at the same time, her gut prodded her into a run for the barn.

She recognized the trooper who cut her off before she reached the first stall. "Greg, what's going on?" Any other time, the sight of the man who'd ripped her soul to shreds would've driven her to either head the other way or want to slug him. Tonight, all she wanted to hear was this emergency response was a false alarm.

He caught her by her shoulders and held her firm. "Jess, don't get any closer." The words sounded gruff, as if he was fighting a cold.

They only fed her apprehension. "Tell me what happened."

Greg's face was set in deep lines. She'd known him long enough to recognize the look. This was bad. Real bad. "There's been an accident. It's Doc. He's dead."

His words hit her with the force of a sucker punch. "Dead?" she echoed. "Doc? No. He wasn't supposed to be here."

"What do you mean?"

"He's supposed to be on vacation. I'm covering for him." She struggled to make sense of what Greg had just told her. Doc was home in bed. His flight would take off in a few hours. It was the only reality she could accept. "There must be some mistake."

"There's no mistake. We found him in the stall. Horse must've trampled him. There wasn't anything any of us could've done for him."

"No. It must be someone else. Doc's too smart. Too careful." She searched Greg's face for some hint of uncertainty, but he avoided her gaze. Seizing the moment, she spun from his grasp, ducked under his arm, and dodged the guy in the county police uniform, tripping to a stop in front of the stall. She immediately wished she'd heeded Greg's warning.

Doc's broken and bloodied body sprawled in the center of the stall. One leg was obviously shattered at the femur. His chest, unnaturally concave. And his head...

The metallic stench of blood...lots of blood...smacked her in the face and overpowered the more soothing smells of straw and manure.

Gagging, she wheeled away and closed her eyes against the sight. Closing her mind to it was harder. She sagged against the cool block wall and tried to breathe in the spring night air. But her lungs constricted as if her own chest had been crushed.

This couldn't be happening. Not Doc. Not the man who'd been more of a father to her than her own had ever been.

A second state trooper, every bit as tall as Greg but twice his weight, appeared in front of Jessie. "Get her the hell out of here," Trooper Larry Popovich said, his voice gruff and no-nonsense.

A gentle hand closed around her arm. "Sorry about that, Larry." Greg tugged her away.

Once they were out of the shedrow, away from the cops and the helpless medics, Jessie managed to find her breath. Doc was dead. There was no going back, no undoing what had happened. But she couldn't go to pieces. Not now. *Focus.* "Have you notified Amelia?" God, this was going to devastate Doc's wife.

"I called Daniel Shumway. He offered to go over to their house and break the news."

"Good." As Riverview's CEO, Daniel possessed a quiet strength that served him well in business. Jessie felt certain it would also serve him well while delivering the news that would destroy Amelia Lewis's world.

Greg steered Jessie toward their vehicles, but she stopped and pulled free of his grasp. She wasn't about to be sent home. There was work to be done. Questions she needed answered. "Where's the horse from that stall? Did you guys shoot him?"

"No. The trainer moved it to another stall." Greg pointed to the far end of the shedrow. "The horse's name is Clown Around Town. Trainer's a woman by the name of Zelda Peterson."

Jessie thought of the phone call from Doc only a few short hours ago. Clown Around Town was the name of the horse he'd asked her to treat for colic. But she'd been on another emergency. If only she hadn't told Doc she'd be delayed, he wouldn't be laying in that stall. He wouldn't be dead.

She brushed a hand across her face, fending off the guilt and the rush of tears searing her eyes. "I have to check on him."

"Him? Who?" Greg's eyes widened. "Not the horse."

"Yes, the horse. I'm a veterinarian. Doc called me about this animal. I have to find out why."

Greg stepped in front of her. Again. "No, Jess."

She started to point out it was a little late for him to show concern for her wellbeing, but the arrival of a van marked Monongahela County Coroner shut her up. Her vision blurred at the realization she wasn't going to awaken from this nightmare.

"I have to go talk to the coroner," Greg said.

She battled the rising hysteria. Fought to hold it together.

Greg shook a finger at her. "Stay away from that horse until I can go with you. We don't need another body here tonight."

She watched him walk away. Under different circumstances, she might have found his protective act touching. Tonight, it only further reminded her of all she'd lost. She had no intention of being the next body with or without Greg playing security guard. Shrugging the tension from her shoulders, she headed for the far end of the shedrow.

A gray-haired woman with the physique of a linebacker paced the narrow end of the barn, her phone pressed to her ear. Jessie remembered meeting Zelda years earlier when she'd worked as Doc's assistant. When the woman spotted Jessie's approach, she ended her call.

"I'm not sure you remember me. I'm Dr. Cameron."

The woman extended her hand and Jessie grasped it. "You're filling in for Doc." As soon as Zelda said it, her eyes filled with tears.

"He called me to treat Clown. He said the horse was colicking."

Zelda appeared confused. "Really?"

"Isn't that why you called Doc?"

With a trembling hand, the woman held out her phone. "I didn't call him."

"What do you mean, you didn't call him? Who did?"

"I don't know."

Jessie tamped down her frustration. "Then what are you doing here?"

"The police contacted me at home. Told me my horse had been involved in an accident. I thought Clown was hurt, but when I got here, it was Doc." Zelda turned the device over and over in her hand. "I've called all my employees. So far none of them say they were here tonight. I can't get hold of one of my grooms, but I can't imagine why he'd have been here either."

Jessie massaged her temples. "What about Clown? Is he colicky?"

"No. He's acting spooked, but no colic."

"Spooked?"

"I mean, he does colic. Doc's here all the time treating him for it. But right now, Clown's fine."

Except he'd just killed a man. Jessie glanced down the shedrow toward the crowd gathered around the stall and forced her attention back to her work. "Can I see him?"

"Clown? Sure." Zelda hoisted a thumb. "He's in the first one."

Jessie drew a breath, hoping it would alleviate the dull ache in her chest, and edged toward the stall. A metal grate barricaded the door. Inside, a tall, muscular chestnut leaned into the back corner. He flipped his head at her, ears pinned flat to his neck.

Jessie reached for the clip securing the grate.

"What are you doing?" A note of panic rang in Zelda's voice.

"We may not know who, but someone called Doc about this horse. I need to examine him to make sure he's okay." Greg's words about not needing another body echoed in her brain.

"Dr. Cameron, I appreciate this, but he's really high-strung tonight. All this excitement. I'm afraid you might get hurt."

"How about if I sedate him?"

Zelda's eyes widened. "Oh, no. You don't want to do that. Clown becomes completely uncontrollable when you tranquilize him. Especially when he's already aggravated. We found out the hard way a couple of years ago."

Greg stormed down the shedrow toward them. "Jess!" In the poor lighting, she couldn't tell if the urgency in his voice was from anger or fear. "I told you to stay away from that horse."

"Fine," she snapped at him and turned to Zelda. "This horse needs to be looked at. I want him shipped to Ohio State University for a complete workup."

Zelda cast her eyes downward. "Okay."

"They'll draw blood and do a urinalysis for every medication they can think of. He's going to be tested from stem to stern, and if he has a hair out of place, they'll find it, and I'll hear about it." Jessie knew the prospect of that kind of scrutiny would throw a great many trainers into panic.

But Zelda gave a resigned nod. "I'll arrange transportation first thing in the morning."

"No. Tonight. I'll contact them so they'll be expecting him."

The woman's shoulders sagged. "I'll go home and get my trailer."

"Before you go," Greg said to Zelda, "we have a few more questions." As he escorted her toward the other cops, he shot a look at Jessie.

She raised both hands in exhausted surrender. Let him think she was obeying his orders. In truth, the horse looked fit and healthy. His coat was shiny and his eyes bright. She saw no reason to risk her life treating a horse that wasn't in distress.

Instead of trailing behind Greg and Zelda, Jessie slipped out of the barn and walked the road back to her pickup. She noticed Doc's truck and changed course, heading for the dented Dodge Ram. Doc kept the tools of his trade immaculate. Except for his vehicle.

The driver's window was down. She rested her arms on the edge of the door and inhaled the smell of stale cigarette smoke. Not her favorite aroma, but closing her eyes and drinking it in, she could almost pretend Doc was sitting behind the wheel, cracking off-color jokes and making her blush.

Doc always said he'd seen something in Jessie all those years ago when she'd hung around the old farm, mucking stalls in exchange for riding privileges. He'd taken her under his wing—and into his home—given her veterinary books to read, helped her earn her scholarship to Ohio State. She wouldn't be here, wouldn't be a vet, if not for Doc.

A burst of tinny music interrupted her memories. She opened her eyes and spotted Doc's phone on the passenger seat, the screen lit up with an incoming call. She glanced around, but the cops were all gathered in the barn, and the paramedics were inside their ambulance, paying no attention to her.

Jessie climbed into the truck and picked up the phone. Caller ID showed the incoming call was from Amelia. Doc's wife. Doc's widow. Jessie swore under her breath. Her thumb hovered over the answer button. What should she say? What words could she use to soften the blow?

While Jessie deliberated, the music stopped, and the call went to voicemail. A thought struck her. She had a million questions about what had happened here tonight. Doc's phone might provide the answer to one of them.

She pressed the button to wake the device, grateful he'd never bothered to set up a lock screen. She pulled up the list of recent incoming calls. There was Amelia's unanswered one. The last call that had been picked up revealed only a number. No name. Disappointed, Jessie looked around for Greg and spotted him with Zelda, the other trooper, and two of the township cops not far from the stall where the coroner was now at work.

Jessie crooked a finger at Greg. They exchanged a few hand signals, his saying "in a minute" and hers saying "now." He gave her his evil eye and excused himself.

"What?" he demanded.

She held up the phone. "I have the number of whoever called Doc about the horse."

"That's Doc's phone? Where did you get it?"

"In his truck."

Greg let out a growl. "Have I taught you nothing about evidence?"

"You mean like don't touch it?" At the moment, she didn't care about proper procedure. "By the way, Amelia is trying to reach him. Shouldn't Daniel be there by now? Maybe you should call him again."

Greg retrieved a nitrile glove from his pants pocket and wiggled his fingers into it. "Just give me the phone."

She handed it over, realizing with a pang that Doc would never call her from it again.

Greg read the number on the screen aloud as he scribbled in his notebook.

"Wait." Zelda Peterson approached them. "How'd you get that number?"

Jessie looked up at her. "You know it?"

"It's the one I've been calling since I got here. That's the number for my groom. The one who isn't answering my calls."

Greg pulled out his own phone. "Maybe he'll answer for me."

Zelda gave him a puzzled look.

"Ever consider he might be trying to dodge his employer?" he said as he waited for the call to connect.

"Oh."

Greg swore and put the phone away. "It went straight to voice-mail. What's his name?"

"Miguel Diaz. He's just a kid. And not very ambitious. I can't imagine he checked on the horses without being ordered to."

Jessie looked around. Patches of light spilled on roof and pavement from halogen bulbs overhead, but the shedrows lay in deep shadow. She shivered at the thought of someone lurking there.

"You can go make those transportation arrangements," Greg told Zelda. "Thanks for your help."

As the trainer walked away, Jessie frowned at Doc's phone, still nestled in Greg's palm. "Who called it in?"

"Pardon me?"

"Who dialed 911? Doc wasn't in any shape to call for help. Besides, he left his phone in the truck."

A sad smile crept across Greg's face. "I guess ten years as a state trooper's wife did teach you something."

She winced, still trying to accept ten years as Greg Cameron's wife would never become eleven years.

"Let me make a call." He pulled out his phone again. "And you're forgiven for the lapse of judgment where handling evidence is concerned."

The grumble of an engine snatched her attention back from her momentary wallow in self-pity. She recognized the track CEO's white Ford Expedition as it rolled toward them. She left her soon-to-be ex-husband to his detective work and headed for the car.

Jessie hadn't seen Daniel Shumway in ages, even though their farms backed up to one another. One of the reasons she'd been looking forward to these two weeks at the track was the opportunity it offered to possibly bump into him. But not this way.

Both the driver's and passenger's doors flew open. A tiny woman with curly flame-red hair bolted from the passenger seat, making a run for the barn. Daniel Shumway, blond, rugged, and slightly disheveled, charged after Amelia Lewis, catching her around the waist before she could reach the barn. She flailed and screamed, but he turned her toward him, and she collapsed against his chest.

Jessie jogged to them. Daniel met her gaze over Amelia's head. He wore the helpless expression most men exhibit when faced with a sobbing female.

Jessie touched Amelia's shoulder and tried to say her name, but words refused to come.

Amelia wheeled from Daniel, crumpling into Jessie's arms, babbling something unintelligible against Jessie's shoulder.

Amelia's anguish fed Jessie's. "I'm so sorry," Jessie whispered against her hair, fighting back her own tears. Not now. Amelia needed her to be strong.

Jessie glared at Daniel.

He obviously caught the meaning of Jessie's scowl. "I didn't want to bring her here, but she said she'd drive herself if I didn't."

Jessie knew she would have too. Doc had always called Amelia his little spitfire. The red hair came with a temper. Amelia took no guff from anyone. Not Doc. Not their two kids. And not Jessie during the years she'd lived with them.

If Amelia Lewis set her mind to something, heaven help the person who got in her way.

Amelia sniffled and pushed away from Jessie. "I need to see him."

"No, you don't." Jessie lowered her head to look Amelia square in the eyes. "I thought I did too. Now I wish I hadn't."

"He's my husband." Amelia tried to wrest free of Jessie's hold. "I need to be with him."

Jessie held firm. "He's gone, Amelia. There's nothing any of us can do for him now."

Amelia's face contorted. "You've seen him?"

"Yes."

"It's—it's really him? You're sure?"

"There's no doubt. But you don't want that picture of him frozen in your mind. Believe me."

"But what happened?" Amelia wailed. "How did he—die?"

"He—" Jessie choked on the words. "He was trampled. By a horse he was treating."

A commotion in the shedrow drew their attention. Two guys wearing jackets emblazoned with Monongahela County Coroner carted a stretcher into the barn and disappeared into the stall.

Greg, the other trooper, and several uniformed officers huddled and compared notes. Trooper Popovich broke away from the group, climbed into his SUV, and drove away.

Jessie watched his taillights disappear at the end of the shedrow while wondering how much Daniel knew about what had happened. She didn't want to catch him up on the details with Amelia standing there.

The coroner guys wheeled the stretcher, now carrying a blue body bag, out of the stall. When they draped a black shroud over it, Amelia let out a cry that sounded like a wounded animal. Jessie held her tight. Daniel wrapped his arms around both of them, as if they might keep the widow from breaking into little pieces.

By the time Doc's body had been loaded into the Medical Examiner's van, Amelia's weeping had subsided. "I need—" She hiccupped. "—to sit down."

Jessie looked at Daniel. "Let's get her back in your car."

"I can't believe this is happening," Amelia said as Jessie assisted her into the passenger seat. "None of it feels real. We're supposed to leave for Hawaii in the morning."

Jessie held Amelia's hand. What could she say? *I know. I'm sorry. If there's anything I can do...*

None of it sounded adequate.

"Doc just couldn't stop working," Amelia went on. "Even when he's supposed to be on vacation. He was out on calls all night."

"But—" Jessie stopped, puzzled. On the phone, Doc had told Jessie he didn't want to get out of bed to drive to the track in the middle of the night. Or had she misunderstood?

Jessie ran the conversation through her head. Tried to remember each word. Each detail.

It had been a little after one a.m. when he'd called her and said he was on vacation as of midnight. Doc's words rang in her memory. "I'm dumping this one on you so I can get some sleep before catching my flight." She'd told him of the emergency she was dealing with and said she'd get there as soon as she could.

"His last words to me," Amelia said, "were, 'I'll be home as soon as I finish a couple of emergency calls.' That was right after we had dinner."

Daniel climbed behind the wheel of his Expedition and touched Amelia's arm. "There's nothing we can do here. Let me take you home. We'll call your kids and ask them to come stay with you."

She took a shuddering breath. "Yes. I suppose that's best. I have to cancel our flight..."

"I'll come over in the morning in case you need anything." Jessie gave her hand a squeeze.

"Wait." Amelia suddenly clutched Jessie's arm. "There is something you can do for me."

"Anything."

Amelia gazed hard into Jessie's eyes. "Find out what took place here tonight. You and I both know how careful Doc always was. I can't believe he'd put himself in a position to let something like this happen." She touched Jessie's cheek. "He loved you like you were one of our own. I do too. Find out why he died. For me. Will you do that?"

Jessie's vision blurred. Doc had always taught her to be alert around these beautiful, graceful, but high-strung animals. She placed her hand over Amelia's. "I promise."

Amelia gave her a tearful smile and leaned back into the seat.

Jessie watched the Expedition drive away until its taillights disappeared. A spring breeze carried a fishy whiff of the nearby river. She closed her eyes. Maybe when she opened them again, she'd be in her bed, and it would have all been nothing more than a bad dream.

Instead, when she opened them, the emergency lights from the police vehicles continued to sweep and flicker, painting the shedrows in splashes of red and blue.

Jessie found Greg standing next to the coroner's van.

"I'll do the autopsy in the morning," the coroner was saying. "Toxicology will take a week or so, but it looks to be fairly cut and dried. We get one or two of these a year. People getting careless around large animals." He climbed into the driver's seat. "I'll get my report to you fellows ASAP."

Once the coroner had driven away, Greg eyed Jessie. "How's Amelia?"

"Distraught." Jessie rolled her shoulders until a knot of tension popped. "Did you find out who called 911?"

"As a matter of fact, yes. Dispatch said the caller didn't give a name. But would you like to guess the phone number?"

Greg's grim expression gave her a pretty good idea. "Zelda Peterson's missing groom?"

"You got it. Larry Popovich is headed over to the kid's house right now. Maybe he got scared and beat it out of here after seeing what that horse did to Doc. At least he called for help first."

"A little too late." But Jessie couldn't completely blame him for running away. Not after what she'd seen in that stall.

Greg's phone rang. He glanced at the screen. "That's Larry now."

She waited and listened, learning nothing from the one-sided conversation. After several *uh-huhs* and *okays*, Greg hung up.

"Well?"

Greg waved the county officers over to include them in the update. "Popovich just called. No sign of Diaz at his apartment. We'll let you guys know once we catch up to him."

The taller cop glanced around. "I guess we're done here for now."

Jessie choked. "Done? That's all you're going to do?"

One of the other officers spread his arms wide. "Look around. There's no one to question tonight. And if the coroner declares the death accidental, there won't be anything to investigate." He extended a hand to Greg. "Thanks for your help tonight, Trooper."

The county cops pulled out, leaving Jessie's and Doc's trucks and Greg's SUV. And a long silence.

Until Greg broke it. "Are you finished for the night?"

"Almost. I'll wait until Zelda gets back with her trailer. In case she needs help loading Clown."

"I'll wait with you."

"You don't have to." Jessie would prefer he leave. This business of moving on from their marriage was a strain on a good day. Tonight, after losing yet another man in her life, she felt too overwhelmed for the whole "just friends" routine.

"Actually, I do," he said. "I called for a tow truck for Doc's pickup. I'll stay until they get here."

"Don't you think you ought to wait for him by the stable gate, so you can direct him back here?"

"I suppose you're right." Greg gave her shoulder an awkward pat. "Good night."

Jessie watched him stroll away. She pried her eyes away from his ass—old habits die hard—and took another long look at the shedrow from which Doc's body had been removed.

She checked her watch. Doc should've been on his way to the airport by now. Amelia's words echoed in Jessie's mind. Doc had loved her like one of his own.

He'd never asked her for anything. Just this one small favor. Fill in for him so he could take Amelia to Hawaii. The very first time he passed along an emergency call to her, she'd failed him. Now he was dead.

The agony Jessie had been stuffing down all night finally tore from her throat in a strangled moan.

It should have been her.

Three

F ive days later, Jessie leaned on the wood rail fence surrounding Riverview Park's outdoor paddock and scrutinized the movements of her patient. Inside the oval, ten Thoroughbreds in various states of nerves paraded, led around the circle by handlers wearing brightly colored numbered vests, waiting for the next race. But the only one concerning her at the moment was the sleek black two-year-old named Risky Ridge. The colt's owner, Catherine Dodd, stood at her side.

"Don't you just love all this excitement?" Catherine didn't take her eyes off her horse. "I'll bet you've been over here every night watching the races."

Jessie freed her unruly hair from the elastic band that had held it, captured a few errant strands, and rebound her long ponytail. "To tell you the truth, this is the first time."

Catherine looked at her, astonished. "Really?"

"I don't know how Doc kept up the pace." Jessie had long ago become accustomed to the frantic emergency calls in the middle of the night. But for the last five days, she'd been arriving at Riverview each morning by seven and was still treating patients until well after the last race. Other than Wednesday and Thursday when the track was closed, she hadn't collapsed into bed earlier than midnight.

Catherine lowered her head. "I still can't believe Doc's gone." She returned her gaze to the colt in the paddock. "What do you think about Risky? How's he look to you?"

The colt's sleek, dark coat, sprinkled with dapples, glistened in the sun. He carried good weight, and his muscles rippled beneath his skin. Risky Ridge showed all the evidence of being ready to run. "He looks good. In fact, I'd say he looks terrific."

Catherine smiled. With her hair caught up in a gravity-defying style, and attired in a bright pink linen jacket, skirt, and heels, the woman appeared ready for Kentucky Derby crowds as opposed to a warm Friday night at Riverview Park. "Maybe this is the one."

Jessie had known Catherine since high school and was all too aware how desperate she was to find the horse to take her to the big time. Until now she'd only encountered disappointment.

Jessie looked at her. The black colt might have been the picture of health, but the owner lacked her usual glow. "Are you all right?"

"Why do you ask?" Catherine said, perhaps too quickly.

"You seem...pale."

"Oh. That." Catherine shrugged. "I've been fighting a spring cold. I'd hoped the pink suit would brighten me up."

It didn't.

"But I couldn't miss seeing Risky in his maiden race."

The colt strutted around the circle, his long neck arched as if posing for the crowd of bettors lining the rail. Otherwise, he showed no signs of the nerves one might expect from a horse about to run in his first race.

Jessie had to admit, he had charisma. Maybe Catherine was right. Maybe this *was* the one.

The chestnut gelding in front of Risky, on the other hand, was soaked in a nervous sweat. A tall, older man, who Jessie recognized as one of the local trainers, picked up a hose and aimed a stream of water at the horse. The gelding leaped away from it, jerking his young handler off his feet. The dark-haired youth, who wore a bright red vest with the number one on it, grabbed the lead shank with both hands. The trainer flung the hose aside and stormed after them, giving the horse—and the kid—a thorough cussing out.

Ignoring the ruckus, Catherine worked a strand of her auburn hair free from the clips holding it in place and twirled it around one manicured finger. "What did you think of Doc's funeral this morning?"

The weight that settled on Jessie's shoulders every time someone mentioned Doc bore down on her again. "It was...nice." She immediately regretted her word choice.

"Yes, it was, wasn't it? Quite a crowd. I guess you never know how many people love you until you're gone." Catherine's wistful voice trailed off.

A quick riff of rock music burst from Jessie's pocket. She pulled out her phone.

Catherine glanced at her. "Duty calls?"

Jessie checked the message, then the time. "Not yet. I'll have to leave right after this race though. I have to scope a horse in Barn E, but I want him to be cooled out a bit first." She tapped on the keyboard, *Be there in 20.*

When she looked up, several of the horses, including Risky, had been led into the numbered saddling enclosures on the far side of the paddock. Valets carrying saddles and equipment approached the horses and handlers.

Catherine pointed toward the woman who held Risky's lead shank. "Zelda's done a superb job of bringing him along. Don't you agree?"

"Yeah." Jessie still had a hard time looking at Zelda Peterson without flashing back to that night with Clown.

Zelda moved with practiced precision as she placed a chamois on Risky's back, followed by the weight pad, and the pink number eight saddle towel. On top of that, the valet placed the tiny racing saddle—little more than a leather pad to hold the stirrups. The trainer buckled the under girth and topped it with the over girth.

Zelda led the black colt out of the three-sided enclosure and fell into step with the other young horses.

A loud crack made Jessie jump. The same chestnut gelding that had given the dark-haired kid a hard time wanted nothing to do with the whole saddling routine. He kicked out, striking the wall of the number one enclosure a second time. His trainer snatched the lead shank from the young handler and gave it a sharp snap, sending the animal onto his hind legs.

Catherine gasped. "What does Neil think he's doing?"

Jessie watched in scornful silence. In the few short days she'd been working there, most of the trainers had made every effort to welcome her. Neil Emerick was not one of them. And if this was any indication of his style of horsemanship, she decided his avoidance might be for the best.

After directing more harsh words at the sulking boy, Emerick led the jittery gelding across the paddock to the indoor saddling area.

Catherine continued to toy with her hair. "What did you think of Sherry Malone?"

"Who?"

"At the funeral. Sherry Malone. You know. Doc's assistant."

Jessie ran the long list of funeral attendees through her mind and came up blank. "Which one was she?"

"You never met her? She was the one with the long braid."

"So that's who that was." Jessie had wondered about the stony-faced young woman standing off to the side of the group gathered around the casket.

"What did you think of her?"

"I guess I didn't think one way or the other." There had been quite a few mourners at Doc's funeral whom Jessie didn't recognize. His circle of friends and acquaintances extended well beyond her own. As for the young woman in question, Jessie had assumed she was a friend of one of his and Amelia's kids. Or one of many track employees in attendance.

"Didn't you notice the way she looked at Amelia? And at you, for that matter."

"No." Jessie wished she'd paid closer attention. "How was she looking at us?"

"Oh, it's probably just my imagination. But you know the old saying. If looks could kill."

For a moment, all sound became muffled as Catherine's words rumbled through Jessie's head, and Sherry Malone's face, cold and stoic, floated across her mind's eye. What would Doc's assistant have against her? Or Amelia?

"Jessie?" Catherine's hand on her arm jarred her from her daze. "Jessie? Are you all right?"

"Yeah." She pulled her attention back to the horses in the paddock. Certainly Catherine was mistaken. Not everyone expressed their grief in tears.

Neil Emerick's horse was back, saddled and adorned with the red number one saddle towel.

The paddock judge called out, "Riders up!"

A procession of jockeys attired in various colorful silks poured into the ring and approached the horses, seeking their assigned mounts.

Zelda leaned down, caught her jockey's leg, and boosted him into the saddle. The black colt stepped out, disappearing into the building. Jessie turned to head for the stairs to the grandstand, but a commotion drew her attention back to the paddock in time to see the chestnut's jockey being launched into the air. The rider managed to land on his feet, as light as a cat.

The horse continued to buck. Neil Emerick gave several quick yanks on the lead shank. The animal flung its head up and reared. Emerick yanked again, spitting out curses at the horse, the young handler, who had retreated to the far side of the paddock, and the jockey.

The chestnut scrambled backwards. The number two horse and groom behind him pulled up short and scurried to get out of the way.

Reacting on impulse, Jessie ducked through the fence and charged toward the disaster in the making. She was vaguely aware of voices around her, but her focus locked onto Neil Emerick and the wild-eyed chestnut gelding.

"Stop it." She drew her voice up from the soles of her boots, a deep commanding tone that worked on frightened horses. And obstinate men. Sometimes. "Neil. Stop."

He whirled on her and snarled. "What the hell are you doing? Get away from me."

She held his gaze, but cautiously kept the colt in her peripheral vision. "Quit jerking on him and he might settle down."

Emerick towered over Jessie. The stench of his pungent breath led Jessie to doubt his familiarity with dental hygiene. "This is none of your concern. Get out of my way. I'll deal with my own damn horse any way I damned well see fit."

Jessie willed herself to stand firm. "It is my concern if your stupidity results in one of these horses getting injured."

A hand on her arm startled her. Frank Hamilton, Riverview Park's paddock judge, stood next to her. "Mr. Emerick, Dr. Cameron's right. Please tone it down. If you can't control your horse, I'll remove him from the race."

Emerick drew a hissing breath. He glared at his horse, which was standing stock still, its head in the air. It gazed down on them with white-ringed eyes. "I'm sorry, sir," Emerick said through clenched teeth. "We're good."

"All right then." Hamilton kept his grip on Jessie and escorted her to the fence.

Emerick led the riderless horse past them, glowering at Jessie. The trainer and gelding moved through the doorway to the indoor paddock where they entered the tunnel under the grandstand to the racetrack.

The jockey chose to walk.

The official gave Jessie's arm a squeeze. "Dr. Cameron, I'd appreciate it if you left the policing of the paddock to me."

Stunned at the reprimand, Jessie pulled away from him. "Someone was going to get hurt if he wasn't stopped."

"Yes, however, it's my job to keep things in line here. Not yours."

"I'm sorry," she said, even though she wasn't. "But I didn't see you doing anything about it."

His eyes narrowed.

Catherine cleared her throat behind them. "Jessie? Excuse me. Should I just meet you over there?"

Jessie held Hamilton's stern gaze. Seconds ticked away. He released a soft growl. "Get out of here. And don't step into my paddock again unless I've summoned you."

"Yes, sir." She climbed through the fence before he could change his mind.

Jessie fell into step behind Catherine and the others who'd been watching the scene in the paddock, but now moved toward the track for the race.

"Do you think that poor horse will be all right?" Catherine asked as they climbed the flight of steps to the mezzanine viewing area above the indoor paddock.

"I hope so." Jessie also hoped he'd left his antics in the paddock and didn't do anything to bring harm to himself or the other horses once they hit the track.

A tinny recorded rendition of the "Call to the Post" followed Jessie and her well-dressed client through the doors to the grandstand. They skirted the lines at the ticket windows where hopeful bettors waited their turns. Jessie glanced at the concession stand and wondered if she'd have time to grab some nachos after the race. Probably not. The last meal she'd had was french fries for lunch.

At the front of the grandstand, Jessie headed for the door, but Catherine caught her arm. "Come watch the race from my lucky box."

"No, thanks." Jessie had seen Catherine's "lucky box." It consisted of four uncomfortable chairs at a table with a small cheap TV showing a snowy live feed of the race. "But you go ahead. And good luck."

Catherine offered an anxious smile. "Thanks." She teetered up the steps in her high heels.

Jessie squeezed through the doors with the rest of the crowd heading outside to the concrete apron next to the finish line.

"*The horses are on the track,*" blared the loudspeaker. "*This will be the third race, five and a half furlongs, a maiden special weight for two-year-olds. Post time, eight minutes.*"

Jessie squinted across the track where the tote board listed Risky Ridge at fifteen to one. The horses made their way toward the backstretch where the starting gate was parked almost directly across from the finish line. Ten young hopefuls, none of whom had broken their maiden. For Risky, it was his first attempt. For a few of the others, it was a second or third try at a win.

Surveying the area in front of the grandstand, Jessie spotted an unoccupied picnic table on the nearby deck. She darted through a group of bettors studying their programs and took the two steps onto the platform with one big stride, only to see a couple of older men claim the table as their own. Muttering under her breath, she turned and slammed into the person behind her.

"Sorry," she sputtered before looking up to see her victim happened to be the track CEO.

Daniel Shumway let loose a deep laugh. "Well, hello, Jessie. I was hoping to bump into you at some point. Didn't think it would be quite so literally."

Jessie's cheeks warmed. Daniel was the kind of guy men liked to hang out with and women wanted all to themselves. His rugged outdoorsman appeal had never been lost on Jessie, even before her marriage had begun to unravel. Back then, she'd secretly rationalized any ogling by thinking, "I can still look as long as I don't touch." Not that someone with Daniel's good looks and sophistication would be even remotely interested in an awkward bookworm like her. And a full body collision didn't count as touching. More like making a total fool of herself. She stammered an apology.

He waved it off. "Where are you going in such a hurry?"

"I was looking for a place to sit." She cast a glance at the two men at the picnic table. "But I wasn't fast enough."

"How about joining me?" He motioned to another table where an attractive brunette eyed the two of them with a scowl on her face.

"No, thanks." The last thing Jessie needed was to be the third person in a party for two. "I'll just watch from the rail."

"Nonsense." He gently took her elbow and led her toward the table and the brunette. "I need to talk business with you anyway."

An embarrassed flush of heat spread down her neck.

Daniel released Jessie and leaned down to buss the woman on the cheek. "Would you mind excusing us for a few minutes?"

The brunette rose, gave Jessie the stink eye, and strutted away.

"Have a seat," Daniel said.

Instead of taking the woman's spot, Jessie perched on the table next to a pair of binoculars and braced her boots on the bench. She pointed to the field glasses. "Do you mind?"

"Be my guest." He took a seat next to her on the picnic table and bumped her with his shoulder.

Jessie scooted over to give him more room, certain the brunette was watching them.

"Are you interested in any horse in particular?" he asked.

Through the lenses, Jessie found Risky loping easily down the backstretch with his lead pony at his side. "Catherine Dodd asked me to take a look at her colt in the paddock. I have a few minutes before my next patient, so I thought I'd stick around for the race."

He squinted across the track. "Which one?"

"Number Eight. Risky Ridge." She handed him the binoculars.

"Is he any good?"

She relaxed. Horses were a topic she could handle. "You don't really expect me to comment, do you?"

"Doctor-patient confidentiality?"

"Something like that."

Daniel gave the binoculars back to her. "How've you been holding up?"

She studied the glasses without raising them to her eyes. "It's been a rough week."

"I hope no one here at Riverview has made it any tougher on you."

She decided to keep quiet about her dust-up with Neil Emerick. "Everyone's been great."

"I'm glad to hear it. That makes what I wanted to talk about a little easier."

Static crackled over the loudspeaker, interrupting him. "*The horses are approaching the gate. Soldier Bob is balking.*"

Jessie raised the binoculars and focused on the horses bunched behind the starting gate. Neil Emerick's chestnut had his head in the air again, pulling against the assistant starter who was tugging the horse toward the number one slot.

Daniel shaded his eyes. "What's going on over there?"

"One of Neil Emerick's horses. He was acting up in the paddock too."

Daniel pulled a racing program from his hip pocket and flipped a page. "Soldier Bob. From the looks of his workouts, he has some good speed."

"If he has enough energy left to show it once the race actually starts."

"Could be all this carrying on is just an indication of his spirit."

Jessie had her doubts. "Maybe."

"Soldier Bob is still refusing to go in the gate."

Three members of the gate crew worked with the horse. Finally, with one assistant starter at his head and two locking arms behind his rump, the chestnut gelding loaded.

"And Soldier Bob is in." The announcer called out each horse as it stepped into the gate without a fuss. Including Risky Ridge.

Jessie handed the binoculars back to Daniel, relieved Risky had loaded like a gentleman.

"Catherine's colt looks good." He bumped her shoulder again. "I don't suppose you had anything to do with that."

"In only a week? Hardly. Besides, the vet just keeps them sound. The trainer gets them in shape."

"And they're all in the gate," crackled over the loudspeakers. *"Wait. Soldier Bob has flipped."*

A murmur ran through the crowd.

"Soldier Bob has flipped in the gate."

Daniel swore.

Jessie's heart dropped like a brick. A horse that reared in the gate and went all the way over could suffer any number of injuries. The state vet would be right there in case the horse needed treatment, but her phone would soon ring if the horse was badly cut and needed stitches. She wiggled her fingers at Daniel, and he handed her the binoculars. But the starting gate blocked her view.

Several long moments passed. The gelding's jockey appeared behind the gate dusting himself off. He looked none the worse for having come off his mount twice. A few minutes later, the riderless chestnut appeared. He seemed fine. Jessie released a breath. An assistant starter walked the horse in circles. One by one, the other horses were backed out of the gate.

"Soldier Bob is a late scratch by order of the vet," the loudspeaker announced. *"There will be a delay."*

An outrider pony loped out to retrieve the chestnut. All good news. If he'd been seriously injured, they'd have sent the equine ambulance instead.

"Neil Emerick will be calling you to meet him back at the barn," Daniel said.

She bit back a sarcastic laugh. "Maybe. He'll check the horse out himself first." And after their confrontation in the paddock, he'd probably call Dr. McCarrell, the other vet who worked the backside.

The rest of the horses reloaded without incident.

"And they're off!"

The horses broke in one pack except for two that trailed behind. One of the stragglers was Risky Ridge. Jessie imagined she could hear Catherine's moan all the way from her box in the glass-enclosed grandstand. The announcer barked out the horses' positions as they charged down the backstretch toward the far turn. Risky held firm to the next-to-last spot.

"At least he's beating one of them," Daniel said.

As the horses swung into the far turn, Jessie lost sight of Risky for a moment and tried to follow the announcer's call of the race. Most of it was a jumble to her ear. But then the horses came around toward the stretch and she caught one line of the announcer's patter. *"Risky Ridge is making a big move at the quarter pole."*

Jessie no longer needed the field glasses. She set them down and pressed her fingers to her lips to keep from giving a yelp. With all the trainers, many of them Doc's—her—clients, gathered within earshot, it wouldn't do to show favoritism.

The horses thundered down the stretch. Two battled for the lead, several lengths ahead of the rest. But one big black colt's strides ate up the track, coming up on the outside.

"And here comes Risky Ridge!"

A squeal escaped around her fingers.

"Coming to the wire, it's Highlander Gold and Arctic Oak. Highlander Gold and Arctic Oak..."

Jessie heard someone yell, "GO!" and realized it was coming from her own throat.

Three horses pounded under the wire ahead of the pack. Less than a length separated them.

"It's Arctic Oak with Highlander Gold in second and Risky Ridge in third."

Daniel clapped her on the back. "Good work, Dr. Cameron. He was flying at the end. One more furlong and he'd have had that race."

"Catherine will be pleased." Jessie laughed at her understatement of the century. Catherine would be over the moon. "I have to go. I have a patient to scope."

"Wait. We still haven't talked."

Jessie stepped down from the picnic table. "About what?"

He stepped down too, blocking her path. "I want you to take over Doc's practice. Permanently."

Around them, bettors and racing fans filtered inside, either to cash in tickets or to check out the next race's entrants in the paddock. Jessie watched the migration for a moment, using the time to let Daniel's proposition sink in.

In the last week, there had been more than one occasion when she'd gotten past the melancholy that engulfed her and had truly enjoyed the work at the track. The hustle and bustle of life on the backside, the colorful characters, the high-spirited Thoroughbreds.

If Doc was simply away on vacation, the last few days would have been a blast. But to step into this world on a permanent basis? Doc's shoes were just too big.

"I can't."

Daniel crossed his arms in front of him. "Why not?"

"I have too many responsibilities. My own practice. Patients. Employees. A partner."

"Your partner could buy out your part of your practice." He locked her in his gaze. "Jessie, you're doing a great job here. The horsemen like you. You have a wonderful touch with the animals. You've worked with Doc in the past and you understand his way of doing things. If I had to bring in someone else, someone with no experience working at a racetrack? Let's just say the transition will be much smoother with you."

Her head spun. The transition might be smooth for Daniel and the horsemen. But not for her. She'd been uprooted so often as a child, all she wanted in her life now was stability. She was already dealing with the collapse of her marriage and the death of the man who'd been a father to her. To now be asked to abandon the only other thing that kept her grounded? It was too much. "Why don't you ask Dr. McCarrell? He's already got a practice here."

"Mac's almost seventy. He's been talking about retiring for the last five years. I already spoke to him about helping out, but he doesn't want to take on any more clients than he already has. Jessie, I need you."

Looking into his pale blue eyes, Jessie imagined this man got his way more often than not. Especially with women. She battled the urge to succumb to his charms. Somewhere in her head, she heard Doc's gruff voice saying, "*Sucker.*" It elicited a laugh from her.

"I wasn't trying to be funny."

"I know. I wasn't laughing at you. Look, I'll make you a deal."

"Okay. Let's hear it."

"I've already arranged to fill in for Doc's two-week vacation. If I can get my partner to agree to continue covering for me, I'll stay a while longer. But only until you can find someone else to buy out Doc's practice."

"But—"

She held up her hand to him. "I'll help you look for another vet. And I'll stick around long enough to show them the ropes. That's the best I can offer."

Daniel's expression swung through an array of emotions. None of them happy. Finally, his face softened. "You have me over a barrel, Dr. Cameron. If that's the best you can do..."

"It is."

He held out a hand and she took it. "Then I guess I have no choice. Deal."

Jessie excused herself and made her way through the grandstand and down the back staircase. As she burst through the doorway into the rear parking lot, a voice hailed her from behind. She glanced over her shoulder.

Zelda lumbered toward her. "Dr. Cameron, I didn't get a chance to talk to you at the funeral this morning. Have you heard anything from Ohio State on Clown?"

Jessie was fast approaching the twenty-minute window for the horse that needed to be scoped. "I have a patient to look at. Can you walk with me to my truck?"

"Of course." Zelda fell into step beside her.

"I spoke with the tech at OSU earlier today. Toxicology results won't be back until early next week. But their initial report showed nothing wrong with him."

Zelda placed a hand on her chest. "That's a relief."

"But it doesn't explain why someone felt they should call Doc Sunday night." Or who had placed the call. "Any word from your groom?"

"Miguel? No. He hasn't shown up for work all week. Hasn't called in. And he doesn't answer when I call him."

Jessie wondered if the cops'd had any better luck. She made a mental note to contact Greg. "Where's Clown now?"

"The track stewards ruled him off the property, so I have him at my farm."

"How's he been since he got back? Any signs of colic?"

"None."

They reached Jessie's truck, and she turned to face the trainer. "I'll let you know when I get the toxicology results."

"Dr. Cameron." Zelda ran her tongue over her lips. "I was hoping you could do me a favor."

Jessie unlocked the truck and opened the door. "What is it?"

"About the steward ruling Clown off the track. I intend to file an appeal. I was wondering if you'd be willing to speak with them. Maybe we—you—could get them to change their minds."

Stunned, Jessie shot a sideways glance at Zelda. "Why don't you hold off doing anything until we get the tox results."

Zelda gave her a weary smile. "I know I need to be more patient. I don't mean to sound crass, but Clown's my biggest money maker. I could ship him to Mountaineer or Presque Isle, but I'd prefer to keep him closer to home."

Jessie bristled. "I'll let you know as soon as I hear anything."

Zelda thanked her and walked away.

The last thing Jessie wanted was the horse responsible for Doc's death back at Riverview. The only thing about that night she knew for certain was Clown was the killer, but a great many questions remained. Where was the groom who'd placed the call? Why had he summoned Doc to look at the horse in the first place? Until the cops tracked down Miguel Diaz, she had no way of learning those answers.

And why would Doc enter a stall alone with an aggressive horse? Jessie thought of something Catherine had said earlier and realized she knew exactly who could help her answer that one.

Four

Bleary-eyed from another night of sleep deprivation, Jessie wrestled with the massive sliding door to Doc's clinic, careful not to spill her mug of coffee. She leaned into the door. It creaked and groaned before giving a shudder and rumbling open. Inside, the early morning sun filtered through dirty windows set too high in the cavernous exam area for easy cleaning. If she seriously considered Daniel's suggestion she take over Doc's practice, she'd have to make a list of things to change around here. A new door, maybe a garage-type one with a motorized opener, would be at the top of the list. And she'd hire someone to climb up there and scrub those windows.

She quickly dismissed the thought as absurd. Instead of a list of changes, she created a list of reasons why such a move would be ill-advised. Both the door and windows were on it.

She made her way across the space, the rubber floor mats muffling the sound of her footsteps. Every morning when she made this trek, she felt like she was walking over Doc's grave. Even a hit of coffee failed to chase away the chill.

She paused at the hallway opposite the big door. On one side of the aisle, a door held a plaque with the word *office* on it. Someone had added "Doc Lewis's" above it in black Sharpie. Across the aisle was the surgical suite—an operating room, a padded recovery stall, and a kennel room for small animals. In the years she'd worked with Doc, they'd used the facility on a horse once. Most of the time, they'd only used it to spay and neuter stray cats. Still, Doc had been proud of the potential his clinic held.

Jessie's gaze trailed down the passageway to the gaping dark cavern at the far end. For the last week she'd avoided the "spa." Simply another large room that housed the indoor equine swimming pool. Something else Doc had been proud of. To Jessie, it was another addition to the list of reasons against taking over his practice. Given her druthers, she'd have the thing pumped out and the hole filled in.

But the spa's future wasn't in her hands. Someone else would take over Doc's practice. Someone who hadn't nearly drowned when they were a kid.

Turning away from the hallway and her phobia, Jessie unlocked the office door and flipped the light switch. The fluorescent bulbs in the ceiling fixture flickered and finally took hold.

Doc's office.

His presence permeated the space in the same way the stale smell of his cigarette smoke lingered in the air. It was as if his spirit still sat at the ancient oak desk. She pictured him there, straw hat perched askew on his head, reading glasses ready to slide off the tip of his hawk-like nose. Doc always appeared frayed and disheveled, belying the sharpness of his intellect. She'd spent endless hours parked on the worn vinyl sofa that sat against the wall opposite his desk, laughing at his tales, picking his brain, astounded at the depths of his knowledge.

Jessie set her coffee on one of the rings created by years of Doc's cups, placed a rumpled copy of the overnights next to the mug, and smoothed the sheet with her palm. When she'd worked here with Doc, he'd been the one to study the information to determine which of his clients had horses running that evening and which ones needed Lasix that afternoon. Now the job fell to her.

A knock on the doorframe startled her. She whirled to find Milt Dodd, Catherine's husband, grinning at her and bumped the coffee mug in the process. Hot brew seared her hand and slopped onto the paper. She gave a yelp and licked the burn to cool it.

"Oh, for cryin' out loud. I'm sorry, darlin'." Milt whipped a bandana from his pocket and mopped up the spill. "Didn't mean to scare you."

Jessie had known Milt for years, going back to her time as Doc's assistant. One of the track's blacksmiths, Milt had the kind of face that made pinning an age on him nearly impossible. His full head of white hair and the deep creases where dimples had once framed his easy smile led Jessie to surmise he must be close to sixty. But the impish twinkle in his blue eyes made him seem much younger. Milt never changed. Never aged. She figured either Oklahoma or Texas had given birth to his drawl and his cocksure swagger, but she'd never been sure which.

She rubbed her hand dry on her jeans and held up the splattered overnights with the other. "Guess I should pick up a new copy."

Milt pulled a crumpled bundle of papers from his hip pocket and peeled one off. "Here. Take one of mine. It's my fault yours got all slopped up."

"Thanks." Jessie slid into Doc's lumpy chair, sipping from what was left of her coffee. "What can I do for you?"

Milt lowered onto the sofa and crossed an ankle over a knee. "Not a thing. I realized we haven't crossed paths all week, and I wanted to stop by and say 'howdy.'"

"That's nice. Howdy yourself."

"I think it's great you're taking over Doc's practice. We need some new blood around this stuffy old place."

Jessie choked. "I'm not—"

"Now don't get me wrong. Doc was one of my best friends. I miss him something terrible. But you're a darn sight prettier."

"I'm not taking over—"

"And..." He dragged the one short word out to almost three syllables. "I wanted to tell you how plum tickled my Catherine was with that colt's performance last night. You did a helluva job getting him ready."

"The only thing I did was inject his hocks. He's been in training long enough that he was due." Doc would have done the same thing. In fact, he was the one who helped her master the technique.

"All I know is you worked on my wife's colt, and he actually earned her some money. That makes you nothing short of a hero in my book. Look, I realize this is gonna be hell. Doc was like a daddy to you. Stepping into his boots can't be much fun. Not to mention some of these track folk can be a pain in the ass. But most of 'em are real decent." He thumped himself on the chest. "I know which are which. I can let you know which owners you can trust to bill 'em and which ones should pay you up front. In cash."

"Milt." She held up a hand to stop him. "I'm not taking over Doc's practice."

"Right." Milt winked at her.

"No, seriously. I have a practice of my own."

"But you're here now."

"Because my partner is pulling double duty covering for me. She's not going to appreciate me staying one minute longer than the two weeks I promised."

"So you'll sell her your share. You need that money to buy Doc's practice, right?"

"No." Jessie took another hit of caffeine. "I mean, yes, I would need to sell my practice in order to buy Doc's. But I'm not." Her gaze settled on the bank of mismatched metal filing cabinets lined up against the opposite wall. She waved a hand at them. "See those things?"

"What?"

"Those are Doc's patient files. On paper."

"So?"

"I loved the man, but he was a Neanderthal where computers are concerned. All of those paper files are making me crazy. His idea of high-tech was this old dinosaur." She slapped a fax machine on a cart behind her. "And he only agreed to have it here because otherwise he'd have to wait to get test results by mail. Snail mail. Ohio State actually faxed me Clown's test results the other day instead of emailing them."

"I see you've already started to update the system." Milt nodded at her laptop perched on the desk.

"That's for my own record keeping. Whoever eventually takes over this practice will have to transfer all those files onto a computer. It's not going to be me."

Milt climbed to his feet, a smug grin on his face. "You'll hire some computer savvy kid to do it for you. Trust me on this. You're gonna fall in love with this place in spite of yourself."

His comment about hiring a kid raised a thought. "Before you go, there is something you might be able to help me with."

"Name it."

"Do you happen to know Sherry Malone?"

His eyes momentarily clouded. "Sure, I know Sherry. Everyone around here does."

"I don't. Catherine told me she was Doc's assistant."

"Yep, she was. Kinda like you used to be. She's in school to be a vet, just like you were."

"Where's she been since Doc died? I haven't seen her around."

"Why are you asking? If you're looking to hire an assistant, I gotta tell you, Sherry isn't your girl."

That wasn't Jessie's reason for asking, but Milt's answer stirred her curiosity. "Why not?"

Before he had a chance to reply, a tall dark-haired whirlwind in the form of Dr. Meryl Davidson blew through the exam area and settled to a stop in the office doorway. "I should've known I'd find you hanging out with some good-looking cowboy."

Laughing, Jessie rounded the desk to throw her arms around her business partner and best friend. "What are you doing here? Is everything all right at the hospital?" They both knew she meant the Cameron Veterinary Hospital where Meryl was currently taking on both their caseloads.

But Meryl pulled away, her attention riveted on Milt. "Never mind that. Introduce me to your cowboy friend."

Jessie made the introductions and stood back to watch two hopeless flirts in action, knowing full well it was all in good fun. Milt had his beautiful younger wife, Catherine, at home, and Meryl was as happily married as they came, complete with four kids. But that never stopped either of them from enjoying the game.

"Why, Jessie, if I'd 've known you had such a pretty thing working with you, I'd 've come to visit you at that animal hospital of yours instead of going to my own doctor for my last physical."

Meryl cocked an eyebrow at him. "Mr. Dodd, are you implying you're an animal?"

"Yes, ma'am. With the right woman, that is. And I have to say, you look like my kinda woman, all right."

Meryl let loose a peal of laughter. "I do love sweet talking cowboys."

"He's no cowboy," Jessie corrected. "He's a blacksmith."

Meryl seated herself on the edge of the desk and leaned languidly toward Milt. "Close enough."

"All right already." Jessie made the hand signal for a time out. "Cool it before I have to dump a bucket of water on you two. Meryl, why are you here?"

She snapped out of flirtation mode and glowered at Jessie. "I want to know when you're coming back. Carrying your load is killing me. I haven't gotten home for dinner all week."

Jessie was about to tell her about the sixteen-hour days at the track, but Milt cut in. "Darlin', you're gonna have to get used to it, 'cause Jessie here's taking over Doc's practice permanently."

Meryl jumped to her feet. "What?"

"No, no, no. I am not."

"Then what's he talking about?"

"It's all over the backside," Milt said, as if Jessie was the only person who didn't know. "Daniel Shumway asked her to take over Doc's practice."

"I turned him down."

"That's not how I understand it."

"Then you understand wrong."

"Whatever you say." Milt gave Jessie an ornery grin and headed for the door. "Now if you ladies'll excuse me, I have a horse to shoe."

"Wait," Jessie called after him. "I need to know about Sherry Malone."

"Who the hell is Sherry Malone?" Meryl demanded.

Milt paused, his hand on the doorknob. "I told you Sherry won't want to work for you."

Meryl gave Jessie a searing look that should have caused her to spontaneously combust.

"I don't want to talk to Sherry about a job." Jessie aimed her words at Meryl as much as Milt. "I want to talk to her about Doc."

Meryl folded her arms. "What about Doc?"

Exasperated, Jessie flopped onto the battered sofa. "I promised Amelia I'd find out what happened last Sunday night. She wants to know why he died. So do I."

The fire went out of Meryl. "Anything I can do to help?"

"I don't think so." Jessie looked at Milt. "But you might. Any idea where I can find Sherry?"

"What do you expect to find out from her?"

"I have questions, that's all."

He rubbed his chin. "If I was to venture a guess, I'd say check Neil Emerick's barn."

"Neil Emerick?"

"And don't be expecting a warm welcome. Sherry's a little...well...let's say she's rough around the edges."

"Thanks for the warning." Jessie didn't mention Neil Emerick wasn't exactly the president of her fan club either.

"I'm outta here." Milt tipped his hat to Meryl. "I sure hope I'll be seeing more of you now that your former partner will be working here."

Meryl grabbed a stapler from the desk and winged it at him. It slammed into the door as Milt closed it behind him. "That man is a troublemaker."

Jessie laughed. "Yes, he is."

Meryl fixed Jessie with what she'd come to refer to as The Mom Look. "Out with it. What's this about Daniel asking you to work here?"

"That much is true. He did ask."

"And?"

Jessie hesitated.

"Oh, my God. You're really considering it."

"No."

"Yes, you are."

"Considering isn't the same as accepting."

"It better not be. I have no intention of being the sole owner of Cameron Veterinary Hospital. *Cameron.* That's you."

"I know. I have no intention of accepting the offer."

"But Daniel Shumway?" Meryl made a pained face. "He's got certain powers of persuasion. Like those blue eyes. And those dimples." She sighed dramatically.

Jessie thought of the brunette who'd reluctantly left them to talk business at the track last night. "Those powers are deeply diminished by his drop-dead gorgeous girlfriend."

"Girlfriend, huh? Well, that's good. If you don't get back to your hospital asap, I'm going to start killing people."

"Who's on your hit list now?"

"That damned ditzy receptionist you hired."

"Vanessa? She's sweet. The animals adore her. So do the clients."

Meryl thought about it. "She does have an incredible memory for clients' names and phone numbers. It's like she's some idiot savant. But something's gotten into her. She's been late for work three times in the last week."

Jessie grinned and elbowed her friend. "Are you sure you aren't just being tyrannical?"

"Tyrannical my ass. I don't mean she's been five or ten minutes late. We're talking two or three *hours*." Meryl shook her head. "I'm telling you, Jessie, I'm not the diplomat. You are. And if you don't get back soon, I'm going to kick her butt all the way to Pittsburgh."

"I'll be back. I promise."

"Good. I'm counting the days. Ten, including today."

Jessie squirmed. "About that..."

Meryl cocked her head. "Oh, don't tell me."

"I may not have accepted Daniel's offer, but I did tell him I'd stay until he finds another vet."

"Jessie," Meryl growled. "You realize he isn't going to try very hard."

"I'll help him look." In an attempt to placate her partner, Jessie added, "You can too."

With the same growl, Meryl said, "You bet I will."

"And don't fire Vanessa."

"I won't fire her. I may *kill* her."

"Call me if you need bail money."

A wicked smile crossed Meryl's face. "Maybe Greg could pull some strings and get me off."

"A murder charge isn't like a parking ticket. Besides, I don't have the same influence with him that I used to."

"True. But he's divorcing *you*. He still likes *me*."

As usual, Meryl was being her brutally honest, pull-no-punches self. She was also right.

Meryl opened the door to leave but turned back. "What's the deal with that Sherry Malone person?"

"She was Doc's assistant. I figure she might be able to shed some light on everything that happened Sunday night. Or some of it, at least."

Meryl gave a thoughtful nod. "I hope you find out how it happened. And not just for Amelia. I know how much the old guy meant to you."

With that, Meryl left Jessie alone in Doc's office. But she didn't feel alone. She faced the desk and could picture him behind it. "Not just for Amelia and me," she said to the empty chair. "For you too, Doc."

By nine thirty, Jessie had responded to half a dozen texts and another five phone calls from trainers. So far, nothing out of the ordinary.

A light drizzle speckled her windshield as she parked her pickup in the road between stables. She sipped her third cup of coffee and gazed out at Riverview Park's backside.

The rows of barns reminded her of train cars, linked by a common roof. Each housed fifty-two stalls, twenty-six per side, facing outward. Paved roads, on which she and track personnel drove, separated the shedrows. Fire hydrants and dumpsters full of manure and dirty straw created something of an obstacle course, not to mention the horses coming from and heading to the track for their morning workouts.

Most days, there were a few horses being hand-walked in the road too. Today the chilly spring rain had driven them under the cover of the shedrows, where they passed the stalls on one side, looped around the end, and then passed the stalls on the other side, counterclockwise. Always counterclockwise.

Jessie drained the last of her coffee and added the empty Styrofoam cup to the collection behind the seat. She decided to take advantage of a lull in the action.

Milt had said she might find Sherry hanging around Neil Emerick's barn. Jessie "just happened" to be parked next to it.

She studied the shedrow housing Emerick's stable and realized she'd never been inside it. Twice this week, including yesterday, she'd made stops here to administer Lasix. Both times, one of Emerick's grooms had brought the horses out to her. They'd said they were trying to do her a favor. Save her some time. But it struck her as peculiar. Especially since Emerick himself had never so much as cracked a smile in her direction.

Nor had he called about the horse that flipped in the gate last night. She didn't expect him to but hated the idea that the gelding might suffer because his trainer and vet had a falling out. Checking on the horse sounded like a reasonable excuse should anyone, including Emerick, wonder why she was there.

So far, she hadn't spotted him moving around inside the barn.

She hadn't spotted Sherry either.

As Jessie entered at the gap between barns, a voice called out, "Through the middle." She waited, and a short, stocky man with skin the texture and color of leather appeared from the other side leading a dark bay. The groom nodded to her and kept going.

She fell into step behind the pair, glancing into stalls as she went. Emerick claimed all the stalls on this side, but she wasn't sure which one held the gelding in question. What was his name? Soldier something. Bob. That was it. Soldier Bob.

The first stall held a tall black with a flashy white star and stripe on his face. The second held a dark chestnut with his front legs wrapped, snoozing in the back corner. As she approached the third stall, a lighter chestnut with a row of neat stitches angling across his face lunged at her, straining the stall webbing. For a moment, she feared he might come through, but thankfully the heavy plastic panel held firm.

He reached over it, though, showing her a mouthful of teeth.

"Hello, Soldier Bob." Jessie studied the stitches from safely out of range.

Behind her, a voice demanded, "What are you doing?"

Jessie spun to find the very person she'd hoped to run into. Sherry Malone. "I didn't think anyone was around."

"So you're just snooping." The young woman—Jessie guessed her to be in her early twenties—glared at Jessie with blue-gray eyes that sparkled like ice, only twice as cold. A scar marred a face that might otherwise have been pretty. Hair the color of an old bale of straw hung down her back in a thick braid, gathered at the top by a silver and turquoise barrette. She wore a white tank top, and the bulging muscles in her tanned arms and shoulders would put a body builder to shame. Jessie may have stood several inches taller, but she wouldn't want to take on this young woman in a fight.

"I'm not snooping. I saw this colt flip in the gate last night and wanted to make sure he was okay."

"If he wasn't, Neil would've called you."

Would he?

Soldier Bob had relaxed a bit, so Jessie leaned in for a closer look at his head. "Who stitched him up?"

Sherry rammed her hands into her jeans' pockets. "I did."

"I didn't realize you were licensed."

Sherry didn't answer. She looked toward the road.

"You aren't, are you?" A little thing like a license to practice veterinary medicine wouldn't matter to Emerick. Not if Sherry could save him some money.

"I'm waiting for the results of my boards. Then I will be."

If the stitches were any indication, she was probably right. "Nice work."

Sherry looked down but not before Jessie caught a glimpse of a proud smile.

"Do you have a minute?" Jessie asked. "I'd like to talk to you."

Any hint of a smile vanished. "About what?"

"The night Doc died."

Sherry jutted her jaw. "I don't know what there is to talk about."

Jessie leaned against the rough concrete block wall, trying to look casual. "It's been nagging at me. Why he would go in Clown's stall alone. Why weren't you with him?"

Sherry's jaw tightened. "Because he didn't call me. I'd worked with him all day, but he was supposed to be on vacation as of midnight." The look she gave Jessie was vaguely accusatory. "*You* were supposed to be on call for him. Why weren't *you* there?"

The guilt of Sunday night struck Jessie once again. *It should have been me.* "I came as soon as I finished up with another emergency." She wondered if she sounded as guilty as she felt.

Sherry's voice dropped to a growl. "But it was too late then, wasn't it?"

This wasn't going as planned. Jessie battled to regain her composure. "What do you know about Clown?"

Sherry gave a reserved shrug. "What about him?"

"Doc went into the stall alone. If you worked with him for any length of time, you know how careful he was. He never took unnecessary chances."

Sherry's expression softened. "He wouldn't have had any qualms about Clown. We treated him all the time. Oh, he acted like a bad ass, but it was all for show."

Just as Zelda had claimed. "It wasn't an act on Sunday night. Do you have any idea what happened?"

Sherry's face turned stony again. "No."

Jessie spotted something in her eyes. Sherry knew more than she was admitting. Jessie waited, holding Sherry's gaze. But whatever Jessie thought she'd seen had vanished.

A distant voice called, *"Through the middle."* A moment later Jessie heard footsteps muffled by the sandy surface of the shedrow. She and Sherry pressed closer to the wall to let the groom and horse pass.

Discouraged, Jessie asked one last question. "Don't suppose you know who placed the call to Doc, do you?"

"Not a clue."

"Thanks." Jessie made no attempt to hide her sarcasm. "You've been very helpful."

Sherry gave her a snide smile. "Anytime."

Jessie had been bested, and she knew it. Looking over Sherry's shoulder, Jessie watched the groom and his charge striding away from them. She moved to follow, but Sherry blocked her.

"You can go out that way." She nodded toward the gap where Jessie had entered.

Jessie eyed her. Why was Sherry trying to keep her from taking an innocent stroll down the shedrow? "I've never been through Emerick's barn before." Jessie gave what she hoped looked like an earnest shrug. "I'd like to see what kind of horses he's got."

A flush of red tinged Sherry's face. "You have no business in this barn unless Neil calls for you. And he hasn't."

"What's the problem? I'm not going to bill Emerick for it." Jessie sidestepped again.

Sherry moved with her. "Neil doesn't like people snooping around. Some of our stuff has been coming up missing."

"You think I'm here to steal something?"

Sherry's lips pressed into a thin line. "Maybe."

"Trust me. Neil Emerick has nothing I want."

"Why should I trust you? Besides, Neil's given orders. No one comes in his barn without his say-so."

Jessie gazed past Sherry, down the shedrow. The groom and his charge had circled to the other side and were out of sight. Emerick was nowhere to be seen. No horses looked out of the next six or seven stalls. Farther down, a lone gray head hung over the stall webbing. Jessie looked behind her. The black with the star and even the dark chestnut that'd been snoozing were watching the two women. But in the other direction, nothing until the gray. Odd. Were all those stalls empty? Empty stalls meant no income. More than likely, the horses were tied up in the back corners so they couldn't look out. But why?

"Okay," Jessie said, slowly. "I'll go."

Jessie left the way she'd come. As she approached her truck, she pondered a whole new set of questions. What exactly was going on in Neil Emerick's barn? What didn't they want her to see?

Five

The sight of Greg's Pennsylvania State Police Interceptor waiting in front of the clinic dampened Jessie's mood more thoroughly than the drenching rain.

The impending divorce weighed heavy on her soul. She and Greg had been college sweethearts. He was the basketball star. She was the studious introvert. He could have had any girl he wanted, with his dark hair, indigo eyes, and heart-melting smile. The fact that he'd pursued her had boggled her mind. They'd married. He'd used his criminal justice degree to get a job with the PSP. She'd opened the Cameron Veterinary Hospital on the farm they'd bought together. Life was bliss. Happily ever after.

Until four months ago when he announced he was moving out. No warning. At least none that she'd seen.

Or wanted to see.

Since then, Jessie had been struggling through the stages of grief, starting with denial. The night she ran into Greg and a stunning redhead holding hands at a restaurant slapped her out of stage one.

Anger followed. Meryl helped her craft a pair of wild schemes as revenge, but good sense prevailed, and the plans were aborted.

After weeks spent wrapped in a protective blanket of guilt and depression, Jessie truly believed she'd reached the final stage—acceptance.

And then Greg stepped out of the Interceptor in front of the clinic, and the grief hit her all over again.

She climbed down from the Chevy's cab slow enough to let her head regain control over her heart. Remembering the redhead always did the trick. "What are you doing here?"

"The Medical Examiner released his report on Doc's death," Greg said stiffly. "I thought you'd like to hear it."

He thought right. "Let's get out of the rain." Jessie put her shoulder to the heavy door. Greg reached over her and, with one hand, easily rolled the thing open. "Show off," she muttered, torn between annoyance and gratitude.

The rain thrummed against the tin roof. She raised her voice to be heard over it. "What's the verdict?"

Greg removed his trooper hat and held it somberly in front of him. "No big surprises. Cause of death was blood loss. He suffered massive internal injuries to several major organs."

Doc's mangled body flashed across her memory. Closing her eyes only intensified the image, so she focused on the stainless-steel counter behind Greg. The sink. The glass canister filled with swabs. Anything to blot out that picture.

"The tox screen came back clean," Greg continued in his flat, all-business voice.

She could have told them that much Sunday night. "Any word on the missing groom? Miguel Diaz?"

"He turned up in Akron. Says he had a fight with his girlfriend Sunday evening and took off. He's been staying with friends and didn't know anyone was looking for him. He didn't seem very concerned about leaving Zelda Peterson in the lurch."

A fight. Sunday evening. Sunday. Evening.

Jessie didn't give a damn about Miguel Diaz's love life. But the timing? That was another matter. "What about the call to Doc?"

"He says he didn't make it."

"How does he explain his number on Doc's phone?"

"Says he lost his phone last week. Figured he'd left it in the barn. He didn't want to pay to replace it until he was sure it wasn't gonna turn up."

"How convenient. You don't believe him, do you?"

Greg worked the brim of his hat, still hanging from his fingers. His gaze dropped away from hers.

There was more. Something he wasn't telling her. "Greg?"

"I do believe him. His story checks out. His buddies confirm he's been there since eight o'clock Sunday evening."

"Of course, they do. They're his friends. Giving your pal an alibi is part of the friends' oath, don't you know that?"

Greg gave her a tired smile. "Friends help you move. Good friends help you move bodies."

"Exactly."

"Except these same friends took Mr. Diaz out to drown his sorrows Sunday night. Bartender and several patrons remember him."

"Are they sure it was Sunday?"

"Very. Apparently, he was trying his hand at a new romance since the old one didn't work." Greg cleared his throat, and Jessie wondered if he was recalling having done the same thing. "But the girl he tried to pick up had a jealous boyfriend with her. The resulting altercation made enough of an impression that the witnesses were quite certain of the day and time. Miguel Diaz has been cleared of any connection to Doc's death."

Jessie slumped into a worn chair. "Where's his phone?"

"I don't know."

"What do we do next?"

"Nothing."

Jessie couldn't have heard him right. "What do you mean?"

"That's the other part of the Medical Examiner's report. Manner of death was determined to be accidental."

"So? What's that got to do with tracking down the missing cell phone?"

"Accidental," Greg repeated, biting off each syllable. "We don't investigate accidental deaths."

"I don't understand."

Greg knelt next to her, bringing his face close enough to hers that she couldn't avoid his stern gaze. "Doc's death was an accident. We know he was killed by a horse, but we haven't started arresting horses for homicide."

Jessie brushed aside his feeble attempt at humor. "How can he rule it an accident if we don't know why Doc was there?"

"It doesn't matter."

"It matters to me." She cringed at the shrillness of her own voice. "I was supposed to be there, Greg. It should have been me."

"But it wasn't you. Look, Jess, you're dealing with survivor's guilt. You think because Doc's dead and you're not that you have some obligation to prove it could have been avoided. Sometimes accidents are just accidents." He patted her leg awkwardly and rose.

"It's not survivor's guilt. I promised Amelia I'd find out why Doc died."

"I can answer that. He was in the wrong place at the wrong time."

"You think it's that simple?"

He gave a short, humorless laugh. "It's not simple. It's the way it is, Jess. Move on."

She stood. "You're not going to do anything else about it?"

"Nope."

"The case is officially closed?"

Greg slapped his hat back on his head. "Officially there *is* no case."

Fuming, she turned away from him.

His voice softened. "There's another reason I'm here. It's about Peanut."

Jessie spun back. "Peanut?" Their yellow Lab. The one Greg had claimed custody of when he left. "What's wrong with him?"

"Nothing's wrong. He's due for his shots. I was going to call for an appointment with Meryl, but I figured you'd want to see him. When will you be back at the vet hospital?"

Good question. "I'm not sure. Why don't you just bring him here one day next week?"

"I'll do that." He hesitated. "One other thing."

Jessie couldn't help but laugh. "You're turning into Columbo."

Greg didn't smile. "I was wondering if you'd found a divorce attorney yet."

Her own smile died as she hurdled back a few steps in those stages of grief. "Not yet. I'll get on it as soon as I finish up here."

He raised a doubtful eyebrow at her.

"I will. I promise." She thought of all the promises he'd made—and broken—to her. Like that big one. Until death do us part.

He eyed her for a moment but didn't say anything else before he ambled out into the rain.

Jessie rubbed the hint of a headache lurking at her temple. Okay, yes. It was time to accept the end of her marriage. But she was not ready to let go of her questions about the night Doc died. No matter what the coroner or the police said.

MONDAY MORNING, THE rain gave way to fog. OSU had promised to send Clown's tox results today. Jessie checked her email before leaving her house and before starting her rounds. Nothing.

She parked next to Barn M where she had a request for a Coggins test. Before getting out of her truck, she again scanned the email on her phone.

A gruff voice outside her window startled her. "Hello. You the new vet?"

She looked up to see a tall, bony man with gray hair and skin. "Yes, I am."

He grunted and pulled a ragged sheet of paper from his pocket. He handed it and a twenty-dollar bill to her through the window. "This should handle it."

Jessie looked over the tattered and expired Coggins test paper and noted the information listed. "Are you Harvey Randolph?"

"Yes, ma'am."

She picked up a pad of the Veterinary Service Equine Infectious Anemia lab test forms—more commonly referred to in horse circles as Coggins tests—from the seat next to her and reached for the door handle.

"What're you doing?" he asked, a puzzled look on his grizzled face.

"I'm going to draw blood from..." Jessie glanced at the old paper again. "Extreme Valor."

"You're gonna draw blood?" He seemed surprised.

Jessie wondered if he'd been drinking. "Drawing blood is the normal procedure for running a blood test."

"Well, yeah. But the old guy..." Randolph shook his head. "He just never bothered. You know?"

No, she didn't know. "Never bothered?"

"He was a busy man. And Valor, he don't like needles." The man's gray skin grew even paler. "But, hey. Whatever floats your boat. I just hope you brung a twitch. Or a hefty dose of tranquilizer."

The memory of Doc's body in Clown's stall flashed through her mind, but it was overshadowed by Randolph's words. *He just never bothered.* She'd heard about unethical veterinarians drawing blood from a "substitute" horse, sending it to the lab under the name of another animal. But that was one of those urban legends. Wasn't it?

True or not, she refused to believe this was something Doc would have condoned. Let alone willingly taken part in. Whether a horse was a handful or not.

"I hate to see you get hurt." Randolph tugged at his ear. "Why don't you check with that little gal that used to help Doc?"

"You mean Sherry Malone?"

"Don't recall her name. His assistant." He tapped the back of his head. "With the long braid. She took care of a lot of that stuff for him."

Jesse swung her door open and slid down. "I'll check with her later. But for now, let's go see about drawing some blood from this boy."

"Whatever you say. It's your funeral."

She wondered if he noticed her shiver.

Harvey Randolph hadn't been kidding when he said Extreme Valor didn't like needles. But she'd been prepared. Doc had trained her well on the skills of staying safe.

The sun gradually burned off the fog and warmed Jessie's skin as she drove around the shedrows with her window open and her arm hanging out. A skittish filly with an exercise boy on her back appeared from the gap between barns. Jessie braked, preferring to wait and give the young horse space in case the filly decided to test her rider's skills. The trainer trailed after the horse and rider and gave Jessie a smile and a wave.

Sitting with her foot on the brake, she watched two grooms walk their horses in the road instead of under the cover of the shedrow, soaking up the glorious sunshine. Pigeons swooped across the sky, landing on one of the roofs. A cat sauntered across the road from one barn to another. Over the PA, a monotone voice was giving the rundown on upcoming race entries. A normal, peaceful spring morning on the backside.

Inside her head was another matter entirely.

Could Doc have been taking shortcuts with Coggins tests? Randolph had to be mistaken. Or maybe it had been a one-time occurrence when Doc was extra busy. Somehow, though, she had no trouble believing Sherry might have taken the lazy way out on several occasions.

None of her barn calls this morning took her near Emerick's stable. Not that she knew what to say if she did run into her. *Hey, Sherry, are you dealing in fraudulent Coggins tests?* Jessie doubted the direct approach would get her more than a quick and venomous denial.

She picked up her phone and thumbed through her messages, texts, and emails, hoping for something from Ohio State. Nothing. The clock on the dashboard read ten thirty. Still plenty of day ahead to fidget over what those tests might reveal. Be patient.

In her mind, she heard Doc's gruff voice mutter, "Patience my ass," and smiled at the memory. Waiting hadn't been one of his strong suits either.

The cat had disappeared into its destination, and the frisky filly had rounded the far end of the shedrow on her way to the track. Jessie eased the truck toward her next appointment.

By noon, she'd completed her rounds, and her rumbling stomach demanded her attention. A full slate of farm calls promised to keep her running until the afternoon's Lasix shots required her presence back at the track. Since none of those farms took her near a fast food joint, she headed for the front side and her favorite food concession.

Five minutes later, Jessie bounded up the back stairs into the relative quiet of the grandstand. The musical drone of the slot machines mingled with the low chatter of the television monitors simulcasting races from other venues.

As she waited for her order, she became aware of footsteps behind her. She glanced over her shoulder. Wearing a white shirt unbuttoned at his neck, khakis, and boat shoes, Daniel looked like he'd taken a wrong turn at the beach. Even as a married woman, she had to admit to being attracted to the man, although she'd never act on the attraction. Then she remembered. She wasn't exactly married anymore.

Daniel offered her a bemused smile. "What's wrong?"

"Headache." She rubbed her temple to cover the lie.

"Sorry to hear that." He leaned against the counter and said to the woman behind it, "Coffee, please." Then he turned again to Jessie. "What brings you to the front side today?"

"Lunch. The rec hall was too crowded."

Daniel nodded. "Have you given any more thought to what we spoke about on Friday?"

"You mean Doc's practice? I haven't had a chance to check with other vets. Sorry."

"What about you? I still think you're the best choice for the position."

The woman behind the counter set two plastic containers in front of Jessie. "Grilled chicken salad, hold the chicken. And nachos with extra cheese. Be right back with the coffees."

Jessie dipped a corn chip into the sauce and crunched into it, savoring the salt and the clash of textures. "Sorry." She hid her mouth and her sheepish grin behind her hand. "I'm starved."

Daniel eyed her dubious meal choice. "Chicken salad, hold the chicken?"

"I'm vegetarian." She swallowed the nacho and resisted diving into another. "Never felt right about eating something that might have been a patient of mine."

"I always assumed vegetarians were..." He motioned toward the too-yellow-to-be-real cheese. "...health conscious."

"Maybe I should complain to the CEO about the shortage of menu choices."

A smile crept across Daniel's face. "Maybe you should."

The woman set two large cups of coffee on the counter.

Daniel waggled a finger at Jessie's order. "Put it on my account."

"That's not necessary."

"Consider it a bribe. I've been hearing wonderful things about you from the horsemen."

Jessie closed the lids on both plastic containers and stacked them. She shoved a plastic fork, a napkin, and a packet of ranch dressing in her jeans' pocket. Lack of dining choices aside, the idea of making the move to Riverview permanent was growing on her. But giving up her hospital? Abandoning Meryl? "I can't. I have too much invested in my own practice to jump ship."

Daniel studied her. "I hope you know I'm going to keep trying to change your mind."

"Go ahead. But it's made up." Talk of Doc's practice jogged her memory. She moved her lunch and her coffee to a nearby table and pulled out her phone. It showed no new texts or messages. However, her inbox listed the awaited email from Ohio State.

Daniel sipped his coffee. "What is it? An emergency?"

"No. It's Clown's blood work from OSU."

"And?"

"It's too hard to read. I'll check it on my computer later."

Daniel hoisted a thumb toward his office at the back corner of the grandstand. "You can use mine if you want to pull it up now."

The answer she'd been seeking might very well be in the palm of her hand. Could she stand to wait until later that afternoon, or maybe even that night, to learn the truth?

Patience my ass.

"You wouldn't mind?"

"I wouldn't have offered if I did." Daniel gathered her lunch and strode across the grandstand. Jessie followed him through the doorway and up the long staircase to Riverview Park's inner sanctum.

Daniel's private office reminded Jessie of a Thoroughbred racing museum with dozens of framed photo finishes and winner's circle portraits hanging on the wall. But there was no time to gawk at the artwork. She sunk into his cushy leather chair and logged in to her email. A few clicks later, she studied the attachment listing OSU's findings and scanned pages of test results. Normal. Normal. Normal. Until she came to the drug panel. That one brought her up short. "Son of a bitch."

"What?" Daniel peered over her shoulder at the screen.

Jessie scanned the rest of the report before answering. The tests revealed no abnormalities to explain why Doc had been called. The horse had been healthy. However...

"This shows the presence of acepromazine in Clown's blood."

Daniel shrugged. "As I understand it, Clown can be a handful. Wouldn't it be normal procedure to tranquilize him?"

"Normal, yes. Which is why nobody paid attention to this before." Jessie tapped the monitor with her finger. "But there are some horses that suffer an adverse reaction to ace. If they're high strung to start with, it can make them behave with excessive aggression."

"I've heard that."

"Clown is one of those horses."

"Why would Doc use it on him? Wasn't he aware of Clown's history?"

"That's a good question." And one she didn't have an answer for. But she intended to find out.

Six

Afternoon farm calls took longer than Jessie planned, forcing her to launch immediately into her Lasix rounds at the track. Once the races began, she had to alternate between the pre-race injections and the calls for horses coming back from the track in worse shape than when they left. A lull finally hit, and she retreated to the office. All afternoon she'd puzzled over the report from OSU. She wanted desperately to dig into Doc's files on Clown.

Jessie sensed something wrong the moment the clinic came into sight. The big door stood open a few feet. She'd completely closed it when she left. Lights blazed inside, but she knew darned well she'd turned them off.

Protective impulses took over. She slid down from the cab of the truck, slammed its door, and took two storm-trooper steps toward the building when another possibility stopped her cold.

Veterinarians carried a wide variety of narcotics that were in high demand by junkies and dealers.

She looked toward the stable gate and could see the guard on duty outside his shack. Was he close enough to hear if she screamed for help?

Jessie dug her phone from her pocket and punched in the number for security. Her thumb hovered over the send button. Was she positive she'd shut off the lights? She'd been in such a hurry, maybe she'd forgotten. She'd feel like an idiot if she summoned the guard for nothing.

She moved to the back of her truck and dug a heavy pair of hoof testers from one of the compartments in the storage unit. Armed with the false sense of bravado provided by clutching a blacksmithing tool in one hand and her phone keyed up for security in the other, she slipped inside the clinic.

Light streamed from her office. She was sure she'd locked that door too. A glance at the secured drug cabinets in the corner of the exam area revealed no obvious tampering. If the intruder was after meds, he'd either missed them or hadn't gotten there yet. A noise she recognized as the slamming of one of Doc's desk drawers echoed from the office.

"Who's in here?" she called, trying to sound fierce.

Sherry Malone swung the office door open. "About time you showed up." She turned and disappeared back into the room.

Irritation replaced fear. All day long, Jessie had hoped to cross paths with Sherry and here she was. Jessie pocketed her phone but held onto the hoof testers and crossed to her office.

Sherry sat at the desk, rifling through the drawers.

Jessie's grip on the steel tightened. "What are you doing?"

"I'm looking for something." Sherry slammed one drawer and moved to another.

For the past week, Jessie had felt like an outsider in what she still thought of as Doc's office, but at the sight of Sherry rummaging around in the desk—*Jessie's* desk—her territorial instincts kicked in.

"Excuse me." She placed a hand on the contents of the drawer Sherry was dismantling. "If you'll just tell me what you need, I'm sure I could find it."

Sherry eyed the hoof testers and smirked. "You plan on checking to see if I'm sound?"

Jessie contemplated telling her she'd planned to whack the intruder who broke into her office but kept quiet. She might still want to keep that option open. "What are you looking for?" she repeated.

"The appointment book for the equine pool."

Jessie caught her wrist and withdrew Sherry's hand before closing the drawer. "It's not in there."

Sherry wrenched free from Jessie's grasp. "It's supposed to be on the desk over in the spa."

"Not anymore. I want to keep a closer watch on it." Plus she wanted to avoid any and all reasons to enter that side of the building. Keeping an eye on Sherry, Jessie moved to one of the aging black metal filing cabinets along the far wall and set the hoof testers on top. From the bottom drawer, she removed the ledger in which horse owners and grooms signed up for swim times for their animals and handed it to Sherry.

"I prefer to keep it by the pool."

"You're not in charge. I am."

Jessie thought for a moment that Sherry might snarl at her. Instead, she thumped the book onto the desk, opened it, and snatched a pen from the old coffee mug. "Something's come up. I need to change my pool appointment from tomorrow morning to the afternoon." After scratching out her name on one line and scrawling it on another, she handed the open ledger back to Jessie. "Does that meet with your approval, Doctor?" She made the title sound like an expletive.

Jessie closed the book. "What horse are you bringing in?"

"Sullivan. He's coming back from a bowed tendon."

"He's from Emerick's stable, right?" Jessie thought of Sherry blocking her access to the shedrow.

"What difference does it make?"

"Just curious. Is Sullivan one of the horses I saw when I was in Neil's barn on Saturday?"

Sherry tilted her head slowly to one side. For a moment, Jessie didn't think she was going to answer, but then in a soft voice she said, "Maybe." She pointed at the appointment book in Jessie's hands. "You might as well put that back where it belongs. By the pool."

"I told you—"

"I heard you. But you're temporary. Before long, I'll take over, and *I* want it where it was."

"Aren't you jumping the gun? You're not even licensed yet."

"I told you before. It's only a matter of time."

"Even if you pass the testing, how do you plan to buy Doc's practice? It's not going to come cheap. I know from experience the kind of student loans you must have."

A smug smile crept across Sherry's face. "That's not going to be a problem. Just don't get too comfortable in this office. And stop changing things around. I happen to like everything where it was." She moved toward the door.

How could Sherry afford to buy an established practice like Doc's? Jessie was still wondering if *she* could swing it, even selling her share of her vet hospital to Meryl.

Sherry was almost to the door when Jessie remembered the ashen man. "Wait."

"What now?"

"I had an interesting call this morning."

"Good for you."

"One of Doc's clients was surprised when I actually intended to draw blood for a Coggins test."

Sherry's smirk dissolved. "Who?"

"Harvey Randolph."

Sherry nodded thoughtfully. "Harvey's a little strange. Don't pay attention to him. He was confused is all."

"He didn't seem confused to me."

"Forget about him. All you need to remember is that you're only temporary." Sherry sauntered out.

Jessie bristled. Sherry intended on taking over Doc's practice as if it was her God-given right. "Maybe," Jessie said to the empty office.

She caressed the worn surface of the appointment book, carried it back to the file cabinet, and replaced it in the spot *she* had chosen for it. Only then did she remember why she'd returned to her office in the first place. The file drawer rolled open with a rusty squeal that set Jessie's teeth on edge. *Note to self: invest in a can of WD-40.*

She sifted through the folders, cursing Doc's Luddite ways. It was going to take her years to transfer these to digital files. The thought brought her to a stop. Not her. Someone. It was going to take *someone* years to transfer Doc's paper to digital.

Not her.

But Sherry? Not if Jessie had anything to say about it.

She resumed her search and finally located a fat folder labeled "Zelda Peterson Stables" under "Z" instead of "P." Returning to the desk, she opened the file and flipped through the contents.

Doc had kept detailed charts on each of Zelda's horses, just like he did with all his clients. After paging through the records twice, Jessie couldn't find anything on Clown Around Town. Puzzled, she returned to the cabinet. Perhaps Doc had a second folder for Zelda. But there was nothing under "P" or "Z." Jessie even tried "C" for Clown. Nothing.

Frustrated, she flopped down in the desk chair and buried her face in her hands. A rap at the door roused her.

Milt stood in the doorway, grinning. "Hey, darlin'."

"Hey, yourself."

"You look beat."

She rubbed her eyes. "Thanks, pal. Just what a girl likes to hear."

He chuckled. Gnawing on a well-used toothpick, he pulled a ratty vinyl-upholstered chair away from the wall and sat down, propping his steel-toed work boots on the desk. "You getting settled into your new digs yet?"

"Don't start on that again."

"I know you're gonna stay, and you know you're gonna stay. You might as well quit fighting it."

She gave him her best dirty look.

He held up both hands in surrender. "Suit yourself. What's got you all riled up this evening? Rough day?"

"Yeah."

"Anything I can help you with?" he asked around the toothpick.

"Only if you can tell me what Doc did with Clown's file."

"Sorry. Can't help you there. Maybe it got misplaced. You'll probably come across it sometime when you ain't looking for it."

"Probably." She started thumbing through the records yet again. "But it's not like Doc to lose something."

Milt removed the toothpick. "Maybe Sherry lost it."

Jessie let the folder fall shut. "Now there's a possibility. She was in here right before you showed up. You weren't kidding when you said she was rough around the edges."

"She's a real piece of work, all right. What'd she do now?"

Jessie considered telling him about Harvey Randolph. And Sherry's dismissal of what could be a serious situation. But Jessie decided to keep the Coggins test thing under her hat. For now. "She was upset because I moved the appointment book for the pool into the office."

"She does have her own ways of doing things."

Jessie leaned forward, resting her arms on Zelda's folder. "Do you know anything about her?"

"Sherry? Not really."

"Does she come from a wealthy family?"

Milt gave a short laugh. "Not as I'm aware. Why do you ask?"

Jessie settled back into the desk chair again. "Sherry wants this practice."

Milt's boots hit the floor with a thud. He flicked his toothpick into the trash. A huge smile lit his face. "And you don't want her to have it." He slapped the desk triumphantly. "Because you want it. Ain't that right?"

"I didn't say that." Jessie hoped her protest didn't sound as feeble as it felt.

But Milt was laughing too hard to hear her.

Her phone's notification ping announced a text message. She checked the screen. So much for the lull in the action. "I have to go."

Milt's laughter faded to a cough. "So do I. I promised Catherine I'd join her in her box when I was done with work." He rose, wiping his eyes with a bandana. "And don't worry about Sherry. You're the one Doc would want taking over. No way Amelia would sell to her instead of you."

Jessie followed Milt out of the office. At the door she stopped and looked back at the open file on the desk—*her* desk—and recalled another of Doc's quirks.

Not only did he keep paper files. He also kept backup ones.

HOW EARLY WAS TOO EARLY for a social call? Since it wasn't entirely social, did that make a difference?

Jessie considered putting off a visit to Amelia for another day. Tomorrow—Wednesday—the track would be closed, and Jessie's workload would be considerably lighter. Not exactly a day off, but as close as she got at Riverview.

Clown's tox panel and missing records had nagged at her all night. And since Amelia had been the one to request Jessie look into Doc's death, hopefully she wouldn't mind taking visitors at the crack of Tuesday's dawn.

Doc and Amelia Lewis's sprawling ranch-style house was the closest thing to home Jessie had known. This was where she finally found roots after spending her childhood bumping from town to town with her parents. They and her brother thrived on the vagabond life. But she died a little inside every time they uprooted her from the friends she'd struggled to make. Here, in this cozy unpretentious house, she'd felt more a part of a family than she ever did with her blood relatives.

She parked in the driveway and almost expected to see Doc's bearded face at the door. She thought of his rowdy greeting. How he'd throw an arm around her and squeeze so hard she half expected to hear a rib pop.

Jessie shook off the memories and climbed down from the truck. At the front door, she hesitated. A light shone through the curtains in the window. She hoped that meant Amelia was up. Jessie knocked.

Long moments passed. As she stood there, chastising herself for calling at such an early hour, the lock scraped, and Amelia, in a worn bathrobe, swung the door open.

"Jessie?" she said, squinting.

Feeling like a jerk, Jessie sputtered. "I'm sorry to come by so early. Did I wake you?"

"No, no. Not at all."

Jessie didn't believe her.

Amelia moved to one side. "Come in. Is everything all right?"

Jessie cringed even more. The last person who woke Amelia at an ungodly hour was Daniel coming to tell her Doc was dead. "Everything's fine. I should've waited until later. Or tomorrow."

"Nonsense. I'm happy to see you anytime."

Jessie stepped inside and waited as Amelia closed the door behind her.

At first glance, the living room looked the same as always. Framed family photos filled one wall. The Lewis's kids called it the "Wall of Shame." There were faded pictures of a younger version of Doc and Amelia with two small children, senior portraits, wedding photos. Included in these last two categories were pictures of Jessie's high school and college graduations and one of her and Greg on their wedding day. She always felt humbled and honored to be given spots on that wall. She doubted her own parents even carried a picture of her in their wallets.

Copies of the *Veterinary Journal* and *JAVMA: The Journal of the American Veterinary Medical Association* covered the reading table next to Doc's favorite recliner. The stale smell of cigarettes lingered in the air, and an ashtray still filled with butts remained next to the magazines.

Then Jessie noticed the couch. A dented bed pillow graced one end. A rumpled quilt lay where it had been dumped.

Amelia must have seen Jessie looking at the makeshift bed. "I can't bring myself to sleep in our room," she said apologetically. "Not yet anyway."

Without thinking, Jessie pulled Amelia into a hug and was startled at how frail she felt. Hardly the spitfire Jessie remembered. "How are you?"

Amelia eased free from Jessie's embrace and dug into her bathrobe pocket. "I'm taking it one day at a time." She came up with a tissue and dabbed her nose. "What brings you here so early?"

"I've been doing as you asked. Looking into Doc's death."

Amelia motioned toward a chair and shuffled back to her nest on the sofa. "Have you found something?"

Jessie lowered onto the offered seat. "There are some oddities I'm checking out."

"Such as?"

"I still can't figure out why Doc was there in the first place. Clown—the horse—didn't have anything wrong with him that we can find. And the phone that placed the call is still missing."

Tears glistened in Amelia's eyes. "You haven't found anything to explain why he died?"

"The tox screen from Ohio State showed the horse had acepromazine in his blood."

"A tranquilizer." Amelia nodded. One didn't live with a vet for as long as she had and not pick up some of the terminology.

"Yes. But the horse's owner said he—the horse—had a history of bad reactions to it. I wondered if Doc knew."

"You'd have to check his records."

"I tried. They're missing. That is...the ones for that particular horse are missing."

"Oh?" Amelia looked dazed.

"But I know Doc always kept duplicate files here. Would you mind if I looked through them?"

Amelia was silent, frowning at a spot on the carpet. For a moment, Jessie wasn't sure she'd heard the request. But she blinked. Met Jessie's gaze. "I'm sorry. My mind wandered. It's been doing that ever since...ever since he died." Amelia flapped her hand as if chasing away a bothersome fly. "What did you say?"

"I'd like to look through the records Doc kept here if it's okay with you."

"Absolutely." She rose, but her knees buckled, and she flopped back down onto the couch. "You know where they are, don't you?"

"Yes." Jessie stood. "Can I get you something while I'm up?"

Amelia's gaze drifted again. "A glass of water would be lovely. Thank you, dear."

Jessie crossed the hall to the kitchen and froze in horror. Open containers of lunchmeats, salads, and casseroles—probably offerings from worried neighbors and friends—cluttered the table. The countertop and sink were piled high with dirty dishes. The trashcan overflowed onto the floor. The stench of rancid food choked her. Trying to hold her breath, she found a clean glass in the cupboard and filled it from the tap. Back in the living room, the usual odor of stale cigarette smoke came as a welcome relief in comparison.

"Amelia, where are your kids?"

"They left right after the funeral." She accepted the glass of water. "Had their lives to get back to, you know."

Jessie turned toward the disaster in the other room. She was going to be late getting to the track as it was, but she couldn't very well leave the kitchen in that condition. Bracing against the smell, she plunged in.

She located the roll of trash bags under the sink. Wishing she had brought a pair of Latex gloves with her, she gingerly picked up the scraps that had spilled onto the floor.

"What are you doing?" Amelia called from the living room.

"Just cleaning up in here." Breathing through her mouth, she shook the full bag to settle the contents. A swarm of gnats rose out of it. She clamped her lips shut and waved them away.

Jessie managed to tie off one bag and lugged it to the back door. When she returned, she found Amelia standing wide-eyed in the middle of the mess, as if she hadn't noticed it before. "I guess I let things get ahead of me a bit."

Jessie paused. She didn't think Amelia was attempting humor.

Amelia gave her a weak smile.

Maybe she *was* trying for humor after all. Jessie smiled back.

Picking up a plate with something unidentifiable dried to it, Amelia said, "I'll start loading the dishwasher."

A half an hour and three trash bags later, the kitchen was beginning to look like it might pass an inspection by the health department. Amelia was still at the sink, soaking a few of the more stubborn dishes. "Jessie, you didn't come here to clean my house. Go find what you were looking for."

Grateful for the reprieve, Jessie headed down the hall. The smell followed her. She wasn't sure if the kitchen still stank or if the odor had attached itself to the inside of her nose.

Doc had claimed the house's smallest bedroom as his home office. Jessie hesitated in the doorway. She recalled sitting on the carpeted floor of this room, struggling with one of the classes she was taking. She would come home from university on the weekends and obsess over an upcoming exam. Doc would sit her down with one of his books and a notepad. He'd take a seat at the desk, lean back in his chair, and lecture her on the difficult topic du jour. Somehow, coming from his lips, the material made sense.

Now the corner desk held sloping towers of junk mail. Two books lay forsaken on the floor. Another ashtray in need of emptying teetered on top of a stack of papers.

The same style of metal filing cabinets that inhabited the office at Riverview lined three of the walls. Yellowed tags alphabetically identified the contents. Jessie touched the cool metal and slid a finger down the drawers until she came to one listing "Pa-Pi." The drawer screeched open, but the file she wanted wasn't there. Recalling the filing system back at the clinic, she closed the drawer and moved to the one labeled "X-Z." A quick search brought her to a thick folder for Zelda Peterson Stables.

Jessie looked at the desk. There wasn't a clear spot big enough for the folder, so she carried it back to the kitchen. Amelia was spritzing something floral around the room, which now smelled like rot and lavender. Not really an improvement.

Amelia noticed Jessie's return and lowered the spray can. "Did you find what you were looking for?"

Jessie set the folder on the cleared table. "I'm not certain yet." She flopped into a chair and thumbed through the pages of records for all of Zelda's horses. Jessie couldn't determine any order to Doc's system, but finally came across a bundle of papers labeled Clown Around Town. "Here it is."

Amelia moved to Jessie's side.

Clown's chart appeared no different than any other. Jessie flipped to the back sheet. The earliest dated report showed a clean pre-purchase vet check followed by an array of minor afflictions: exam for soreness after a brisk morning workout, his first reported pulmonary bleed and the subsequent order for Lasix, and several bouts of colic all successfully treated with Banamine.

Jessie only had to read as far as the second page to find what she'd been looking for. During an otherwise routine call to have Clown's teeth floated, Doc had administered acepromazine. Not only were his notations about Clown's adverse reaction to the tranquilizer quite clear, but Doc had scrawled reminders at the top of each subsequent page, including the top, most recent one: *Drug reaction: acepromazine.*

"He knew," Jessie said.

"Knew what?"

"I was sure Doc knew Clown reacted badly to this drug." Jessie tapped the page. "I thought maybe he'd forgotten and administered it to the horse that night. But he made clear notes."

"You said OSU had found it in the horse's blood?"

"Yes."

"What's that mean?"

Jessie stared at Doc's familiar and distinctive handwriting. "It means someone else drugged Clown."

Amelia touched her fingers lightly to her lips. "Who? And why?"

"That," Jessie said, "is what I'd like to know."

Seven

J essie left Amelia Lewis's house with the woman's renewed pleas
for help ringing in her ears and Doc's backup file of Zelda's stable
stashed behind the Chevy's seat. Already late for her morning
rounds, Jessie rolled through the stable gate with the intention of
jumping right into them. The sight of Greg's personal vehicle parked
in front of the clinic changed her plans. She'd completely forgotten
about her appointment with him and Peanut.

Jessie wheeled into her usual spot and slammed the truck into
park. She managed to jump out and muscle the clinic's rebellious
door open before Greg had a chance to come to her aid.

Off duty and dressed in a black t-shirt and jeans, Greg stepped
from the car. "Where the hell have you been?"

"Good to see you too, Greg."

He gave her a wry look and folded the front seat forward. A rotund yellow Lab with a graying muzzle bounded out of the backseat.

"Peanut," Jessie called and dropped to her knees. The dog crashed
into her, and she put one hand back to keep from tumbling over. She
laughed as the Lab licked her face. His tail wagged so hard his whole
body rocked.

"I think he misses you," Greg said with a trace of a grin.

She directed her reply to the dog. "Did you miss me, sweetie? I
missed you too." She threw both arms around the wriggling mass of
fur, buried her nose in his coat and inhaled his doggy smell. Peanut.
They'd given him that name the day they'd brought him home as a
puppy. It had fit him for all of a week.

"I appreciate you taking the time to see him today. I know you're busy."

She looked up at Greg, who wore his unreadable cop face, but she knew he was mocking her. She climbed to her feet and headed into the clinic, slapping her thigh. "Come on, Peanut." The Lab happily trotted beside her. To Greg, she said, "No problem. After all, he's my dog too."

"*Was.*"

And to think she once believed this guy hung the moon and the stars. "Thanks." She made no effort to contain her scorn. She led Peanut to the corner set up for animals smaller than the equine variety and coaxed the dog onto the scale. "By the way, I found out something about Doc's death."

"Oh?" Greg wandered around the exam area, pausing to study a series of faded winner's circle photos tacked to the wall.

"The horse's toxicology report showed traces of the tranquilizer acepromazine."

"So?"

Jessie made a note of Peanut's weight. Stroking his head, she inserted a thumb between his teeth and lips, easing his mouth open for a peek at his gums. "Clown has a history of bad reactions to the drug. It makes him even more aggressive."

Greg ambled to a stainless-steel counter, where he picked up the glass jar of swabs. "That explains it then, doesn't it? That's why he attacked Doc."

"It doesn't explain anything." She moved to the dog's ears. "Doc had notations all over Clown's records about it."

Greg set the jar down and leaned one hip against the counter. "Then why would Doc give the stuff to him?"

"He wouldn't." She looked up from the exam. "Someone else drugged the horse."

Greg scowled. Jessie could almost hear the wheels grinding inside his cop brain.

She waited for a response. None came. "Doesn't that change things?"

"Change things how?"

"You said you weren't investigating Doc's death because it was ruled an accident."

"Yeah?"

She reached for the stethoscope hanging on the wall and contemplated choking Greg with it. "Well, you can't say that anymore."

"Why not? If I'm not mistaken, anyone can give that stuff, right?"

"Most horsemen around here keep some on hand to use when needed."

"There you go. Whoever called Doc probably didn't know about the horse's history and thought he was doing Doc a favor."

Jessie contemplated Greg's theory as she listened to Peanut's heart. Content with the dog's health if not with Greg's hypothesis, she draped the stethoscope around her neck. "That brings us back to the big question. Who called Doc? Have you located the phone?"

"Jess, there is no investigation."

"That means you haven't."

He fixed her with his best patronizing frown. "That means we aren't looking anymore."

Infuriated, Jessie stormed to the drug cabinet and prepared Peanut's annual shot. "There is another possibility, you know."

Her back was to Greg, but she could hear his exasperated sigh. "What possibility is that?"

"Someone knew Clown's history. Knew ace would turn him into a killer. They drugged him and then called Doc." She turned to face Greg, but his expression remained stony. "I think someone inten-

tionally—" The word stuck in her throat. "I think someone intentionally killed Doc."

For several long moments, Greg silently held her gaze. When he
finally spoke, he said, "You mean murder."

"I guess I do." Jessie returned to Peanut, who didn't appear to notice when Jessie gathered a handful of fur and skin and injected the
vaccines into him. His tail never missed a beat.

Greg pushed away from the counter and bent down to scratch
Peanut's ears. "Do you have any idea how crazy that sounds? Who on
earth would want Doc dead?"

"I don't know." She tossed the syringe into the disposal canister
she kept separate from the regular trash. "But the only thing that
sounds crazy to me is you cops not investigating a murder."

"Give it up, Jess. You're looking for monsters in the closet."

"Do you mean to tell me you don't wonder what happened to
that missing phone?"

Greg towered over her. She stubbornly refused to look up, knowing he'd give her a grin intent on making her forget how mad she
was. "Would I be happier if all the loose ends were tied up nice and
neat?" He rested his hands on her shoulders. "Of course. But in the
real world, that doesn't always happen." He gave her a gentle shake.
"Now, are we done here?"

"With Peanut? Yeah. He's healthy. A little overweight, but that's
nothing new."

Greg released her. "I know. He's been getting some table scraps."

"Greg, you know better than that. You never used to let him eat
from the table."

He gave a guilty shrug and clipped the leash to the dog's collar.
"By the way, in case you haven't heard, Miguel Diaz is back in town."

"Zelda's groom? The one the phone belongs to?"

"Yep." Greg stroked the dog's head. "Thanks for taking the time
to see us. And do me a favor. Give up these wild notions. I'm the only

cop in this family. You don't play detective, and I won't operate on any animals. Deal?"

"No deal. If you aren't going to investigate, someone has to. Besides, we aren't family anymore, remember?"

He opened his mouth. Closed it again. "Just be careful. All right?" He called to Peanut and they headed out of the clinic.

As Jessie watched them go, two things Greg had said stuck in her mind. First, if he had no interest in investigating the case, why had he bothered to find out Miguel Diaz was back in town? And second, why would he caution her to be careful if he truly believed no crime had been committed?

JESSIE THOUGHT OF A poster she'd seen once that stated: *The hurrieder I go, the behinder I get.* As the morning nudged toward noon, she began to believe her picture should have appeared on that poster. Only when the track closed following morning exercise, and trainers headed home for lunch, did she finally catch a breather.

It seemed the only trainer who hadn't needed Jessie's services was the one she wanted to talk to. Zelda should've left an hour ago, but Jessie gambled and swung by Barn E just in case.

Apparently, Jessie wasn't the only one running behind. Zelda was still there, raking the area in front of her stalls.

The trainer spotted her and stopped to lean on the rake. "Dr. Cameron. I've been hoping to see you. Did you hear anything about Clown?"

"His results came in yesterday afternoon. They didn't find anything wrong with him."

"I guess I should be pleased." Zelda's expression, however, was not one of pleasure.

"There was something else, though." Jessie told her about the tranquilizer in his blood.

As Zelda absorbed the news, her tan faded. "Are you sure?"

"Who else knew about Clown's reaction to the drug?"

"Everyone. You know how the grapevine is. Something like that happens, and word gets around."

"What exactly happened the first time he was tranquilized?"

Zelda gazed into the distance. "I'd asked Doc to come by and check Clown's teeth. They'd never been done before, and Clown wasn't too keen on letting anyone mess with his mouth. Doc was always good with him. Knew his quirks and how to calm him down. Except none of the usual tricks worked this time, so Doc injected him with ace." Zelda shuddered. "Clown went nuts. He attacked Sherry."

"Sherry?" This was news to Jessie. There hadn't been any notes about Doc's assistant in the horse's records.

Zelda gave a nod. "Clown had her down in the stall. Took three of us to drag him away from her."

Jessie flashed on Doc's body. There hadn't been anyone there that night to pull the raging stallion off him.

"We had the ambulance here. You can imagine the crowd *that* drew."

"Ambulance? How bad was she hurt?"

"She only needed stitches." Zelda traced a finger along her own cheek, and Jessie thought of the scar on Sherry's face. "As I recall, she refused transport. But there was so much blood. I didn't want to take any chances."

A young man with black hair appeared from Zelda's feed room. He had a cell phone pressed to his ear. Intent on his conversation, he seemed oblivious to the two women.

"Is someone new working for you?" Jessie asked Zelda. "Someone who wasn't here back then? Someone who might give Clown ace without knowing any better?"

Zelda kept glaring at the guy on the phone. Whoever he was, Jessie gathered he wasn't currently in Zelda's good graces. "Anyone who works in my stable knows about Clown's reaction to the stuff. I make a point of telling them. And I have a note in my feed room stating he isn't to be tranqued."

With similar warnings scrawled all over Doc's records, Jessie was having a harder and harder time believing the drugging was an accident.

The guy on the phone jabbed at its screen and flung it onto a bale of hay. It bounced and tumbled off the other side. Muttering in Spanish, he stomped across the shedrow and shoved the bale aside, searching for the phone.

"That's probably how you lost the last one," Zelda said to him.

"*Sí.*" He came up with the phone and wiped it on his shirt. "Perhaps."

To Jessie, Zelda said, "This is Miguel Diaz. He decided to honor us with his presence."

The missing groom. Jessie fought to control a flare of excitement as she introduced herself.

"*Mucho gusto,* Doctor."

Jessie fought to keep her voice light. Something in the kid's eyes led her to believe he might spook like a skittish colt. "We were searching high and low for you."

"I did not know at the time." He shot an embarrassed glance at his boss.

Jessie pointed to the phone in his hand. "That's a new one?"

"No. I borrow from *mi amigo.*"

"You didn't find the old one?"

"I did not. I think someone stole it."

"Really? Who?"

"I do not know." He crossed the shedrow to the wood railing and set his phone on it. "I am sure I put it right here. Like this."

"You should've put it in your pocket," Zelda said.

He snatched the new phone from the rail and followed her suggestion. "*Sí*. I know that now. But I was going to bathe a horse and did not want to get it wet. When I come back, the phone is gone. I look and I look, but I cannot find it. Someone must have stolen it."

Jessie looked at Zelda. "Any idea who else was in your barn that day?"

She gave a frustrated shrug. "You know how it is around here. People come and go. Grooms walking horses. Exercise boys. Owners and other trainers drop by. Anyone could've picked it up."

Miguel snapped his fingers. "I remember something. Someone who was here that day."

"Who?" Jessie asked.

"Doc Lewis's daughter."

Daughter? Doc only had one daughter and she lived in North Carolina. Miguel's grasp on English must be shakier than she realized. "Daughter, Miguel? *Hija*?"

"*Sí*." Miguel nodded enthusiastically. "*Hija*."

Jessie searched Zelda's face for an answer, but she seemed as perplexed as Jessie.

Miguel looked back and forth between them, his dark eyes eager. When neither of them responded, he frowned. Rubbed his head and appeared to be searching for another word. Finally, he snapped his fingers again. "Assistant. Doc's assistant."

"Sherry Malone?"

His face brightened. "*Sí*. Sherry Malone. Doc's daughter. Assistant. She was here the day I lost my phone."

Miguel's confusion of English was giving Jessie a headache. "Sherry was Doc's assistant, yes. But she's not his daughter."

Miguel gave Jessie a blank stare. "*Sí*. She is. She told me." Then his eyes widened. "Oh. She told me it was a secret." He slapped his forehead and burst into a stream of Spanish that was well beyond Jessie's rusty foreign language skills.

Besides, her focus had shifted from understanding his words to understanding their ramifications.

A LIGHT LOAD OF AFTERNOON farm calls allowed Jessie to make it back to the clinic by two o'clock. She wanted to talk to Sherry and find out for herself what kind of fantasy world the young woman lived in. And today, Sherry had an appointment to swim one of Emerick's horses right there at the clinic's swimming pool.

Jessie had a plan. Rather than give Sherry a chance to make up a lie, Jessie intended to blindside her. Sherry's reaction might be more revealing than her words.

Jessie glanced down the darkened hallway. No lights at the pool told her Sherry hadn't arrived yet, so Jessie nestled into her office chair and opened her laptop. She'd made it through two clinic reports when she heard the rusty screech and rumble of the back door quaking open. *Note to self: replace the back door as well as the front one.*

Jessie abandoned her office and moved down the dimly lit hall into the spa. The odor of chlorine and liniment hung in the air. As much as Doc had taken pride in the indoor equine pool, she'd avoided this part of the building. Until now.

The massive back door, a duplicate of the one on the clinic side of the building, stood wide open. Just inside, Sherry unbuckled a stable sheet from a sleek Thoroughbred who stood tall and proud, ears flicking forward and back.

"Hello," Jessie said.

Sherry glanced up, but dismissed Jessie's presence and returned her attention to the horse.

Jessie assessed the pair as she approached them. Sherry, wiry and tough. The horse's well-groomed dappled chestnut coat told her Emerick was at least doing something right. The Thoroughbred's hip and back legs looked like something straight out of a book on perfect conformation, but both front legs were wrapped from the knee down.

Whispers around the backside spoke to this horse's potential. He'd won handily in the cheaper $5,000 claiming races and moved up the ranks to the higher priced claimers. Recently, he'd shown flashes of brilliance in the pair of allowance races he'd run. Then he'd come up lame.

Jessie positioned herself in front of the horse and crossed her arms. "So this is the mighty Sullivan."

"He used to be before he bowed a tendon." Sherry hung the stable sheet on a nearby rack. Squatting beside the horse, she unwound the bandages from one front leg. "Hopefully, he will be again."

"I'm sure he will." As long as Emerick didn't rush his rehab.

Sherry tossed the leg wraps into a pile and reached across to the other leg. "I didn't realize I'd have an audience."

"Do you mind?"

"Does it matter?"

"Not really."

"That's what I figured." Sherry added the second set of bandages to the heap.

She stood and led Sullivan to the ramp that descended into the pool. The horse moved with a barely discernable limp and balked at the top of the slope. Muscles at the base of his tail twitched and tightened, and the tail lifted and cocked to one side. The whisper of gas was quickly followed by the soft *plop, plop* of manure hitting the rubber-matted floor. When the horse continued to balk, Sherry made a kissing noise at him. He responded, stepping gingerly down the ramp and into the water. Once in the twelve-foot-deep pool, he swam away on the end of his lead rope. Sherry strode after him on the catwalk. "Get the gate," she called to Jessie and nodded at the plank that was hinged open over the entrance to the pool.

Now it was Jessie's turn to balk, but the last thing she wanted was for Sherry to see her fear. Summoning her courage, Jessie approached the edge of the water. She reached up to release the gate, which was more of a bridge, closing the gap in the catwalk while also blocking the horse's exit from the pool.

Her task completed, Jessie retreated to safety outside the rail surrounding the walkway. Sullivan doggy paddled around the pool, only his head above the waterline.

Sherry lengthened her stride to keep pace. "What are you doing over here? I remember Doc mentioning how much you hate being around the spa."

Jessie had no intention of discussing her phobia of water with Sherry, and she wasn't pleased knowing Doc had either. "I remembered your appointment. Saved me tracking you down." Time to get down to business. Waiting until she had a good view of Sherry's face, she asked, "How long have you known Doc was your father?"

Jessie expected Sherry to act surprised. To respond with denial. Or at least some cagey retort. Instead, she appeared unfazed. "Always." She clucked to Sullivan and then added, "I grew up knowing."

Not the response Jessie had anticipated. "Really?"

"How did *you* find out? I was under the impression Doc didn't mention it to anyone else."

Jessie rested her elbows on the railing. "He didn't. Miguel Diaz let it slip."

"Damn him. Can't speak more than half a dozen words in English and he still can't keep a secret."

"Then why'd you tell him?"

"I didn't. He overheard Doc and me talking about it."

A theory began to take shape in Jessie's mind. What if Sherry had sprung her true identity on Doc and he'd reacted badly. Rejected her. Wouldn't that be a possible motive for foul play? "How long had he known?"

"Miguel Diaz?"

"No. Doc."

"Oh. My mother told him as soon as she knew she was pregnant." So much for that idea.

"I didn't get to spend much time with him when I was a kid. In fact, until I decided to follow in his footsteps and go into veterinary medicine, he never showed much interest in me. But then everything changed. I was 'daddy's little girl' once I started college. We've been inseparable since I started helping him here."

Jessie watched Sullivan chug around the circular pool. Every few strokes, the horse snorted. "Does Amelia know about you?"

Sherry chuckled. "Hell, no. Haven't you heard? The wife's always the last to know."

Jessie cringed. News of Doc having an illegitimate daughter was going to be yet another shock for his widow. "I suppose you plan to tell her?"

"She'll find out soon enough. As soon as the contents of his will are made known."

Jessie caught a glimpse of an icy twinkle in Sherry's eyes as she passed in front of her. "His will?" Jessie asked.

"Yep. Dear old Dad left his practice to me."

If Sherry's intention was to knock the wind out of Jessie, she succeeded. "How do you know that?"

"I just know." Sherry barked a laugh. "You should see the look on your face. I told you not to get too comfortable around here. As soon as my license to practice comes through, you're history, Dr. Cameron."

Jessie clutched the railing. She'd thought she was going to be the one to blindside Sherry. At least Meryl would be happy to learn Jessie's stint at the track truly was temporary. Jessie hadn't really wanted the clinic. Had she? But if that were true, why was she beginning to think of Doc's office as *her* office? She no longer called it "Doc's desk." It had become *her* desk. The backside felt more and more like home.

From across the pool, Sherry said, "You always thought of yourself as his shining star, didn't you? Well, you were nothing but an employee. You always wanted to be his daughter, but you weren't. I was."

"I never wanted Doc to be my father." Jessie hoped it sounded like the truth when she knew it wasn't.

"Uh-huh." The sarcasm in Sherry's voice told Jessie she'd failed.

Time to try another angle. "The night Doc died," Jessie began, keeping her voice low and controlled. "Did you know the call came from Miguel Diaz's phone?"

The startled look on Sherry's face suggested Jessie had chosen the right topic this time. "Miguel made that call?"

"He says no. But his phone is missing."

Sherry's pace slowed, but Sullivan's lead line tugged her forward. "I had Clown tested at OSU. In case you're interested in what caused your father's accident, someone administered acepromazine to Clown that night."

Sherry stumbled but caught herself and kept walking.

"I understand he went after you once when he was tranquilized."

"Went after?" Sherry fingered the scar on her face. "He tried to take my damned head off."

"Any idea who might have tranquilized him?"

"No." Sherry's voice had grown tight. "How would I know?"

"Just asking."

Sherry's circuit of the catwalk brought her toward Jessie again, and her expression took on a hard edge. "Look. My father's dead and nothing is going to change that." She came closer to Jessie. "It's a shame he didn't stay home that night like he was supposed to. Then it would've been you in that stall."

The now familiar pang of guilt hit Jessie in the gut again. *It should have been her.* The pang was joined by something darker, swirling beneath the surface of her thoughts like Sullivan's legs churning in the murky water.

"If you keep butting in where you don't belong," Sherry continued, "someone might just give you a little shove, and you might end up taking a swim like old Sullivan here." Her gaze locked on Jessie's. Then a smirk crossed her lips as she passed. "Oh, I forgot. You can't swim, can you?"

Eight

It wasn't every day that Jessie received a death threat, so she wasn't entirely sure what they looked or sounded like. Sherry's cold voice, combined with the glint of pleasure in her eyes, shook Jessie. All afternoon as she made her Lasix rounds, the poolside exchange lurked in the periphery of her thoughts. Twice, she picked up her phone and punched in Meryl's number. She wanted to dump this whole mess in Meryl's lap and let a calmer head prevail. Twice, Jessie changed her mind before the call rang through. Meryl, never known for tact, was hardly a calmer head. In fact, Jessie imagined Meryl would be ecstatic to learn someone else would be taking over Doc's practice. Jessie could almost hear Meryl shouting at her to get the hell out of there now and get back to the vet hospital where she belonged.

By six thirty, Jessie had administered her last dose of the diuretic for the day. No one had called or texted, so she decided to give in to her growling stomach. She aimed the Chevy through the stable gate, cruised toward the grandstand, and parked in the lot reserved for trainers.

She watched for a couple of minutes as grooms and their horses bustled into the indoor paddock in preparation for the next race. Hopefully, it would be a quiet night with none of them requiring her services.

She entered through the back door next to the security office and took the stairs two at a time. In the grandstand's main concourse, a cluster of eager racing enthusiasts discussed the previous race and debated the merits of the entrants for the next one. A group of well-dressed patrons of the gambling arts sat at a bank of slot machines, choosing to test their luck on mechanical beasts rather than four-footed ones.

She'd zeroed in on her favorite concession stand when the sight of a lady in too-snug orange Capri pants and knee-high nylon stockings with purple sandals distracted her. Amused, Jessie turned to make sure she wasn't imagining the outlandish fashion statement and slammed into someone coming the other way. Sputtering an apology, she reached out to steady her victim. "Catherine?"

"Jessie." Catherine Dodd primped her strawberry blond up-do. "Are you all right?"

"I'm fine. What about you?"

"Heavens, I'm not fragile. You know that." Milt's wife struck a pose. "Seriously. Do I *look* fragile? Or do I look like the owner of a world class racehorse?" In her bright yellow fitted jacket and skirt, low-cut silk blouse, string of pearls and matching earrings, and off-white pumps, Catherine stood out against the rest of the casual crowd.

"You're definitely dressed the part," Jessie said. "How's Risky doing after last Friday's race?"

"He's fine." Catherine dropped the smile and the pose. "I'm just not convinced he's the one to get me to Kentucky on the first Saturday in May."

Jessie wasn't about to point out the obvious. She didn't know what percentage of colts made it to the Derby, but she was pretty sure Risky Ridge, in spite of his bloodlines and strong third place finish, wasn't in that elite group. "You'll get there eventually. Have faith."

"Faith, I've got. It's a horse I need. I keep after Milt. I mean, he meets and greets a lot of horse people around the business, so you'd think he'd be able to find me a horse. A *good* one." She sighed. "We thought he had. Remember that big gray?"

"The one with the broken coffin bone?"

"Mexicali Blue. He was supposed to take us to Churchill Downs. Maybe Pimlico and Belmont too." Catherine's lower lip jutted out in a childlike pout. "But instead, thanks to that damned little bone in his foot, we're stuck with a three-year-old who can't do anything except eat. He's really good at that. Don't suppose you know of anyone shopping around for a smashing-looking thousand-pound house pet, do you?"

Jessie suppressed a smile. "Sorry."

Catherine clutched her hands to her chest. "Blue broke my heart. But what are you going to do? I keep hounding Milt to find me another like him. Only sound."

"Sound is good. You should let me vet check the next one before you buy it."

A fleeting scowl clouded Catherine's face. "I thought...Oh, never mind." She brightened. "Anyhow, Zelda has her eye on a colt in one of the claiming races tonight. She asked me to meet her here and watch him run. Are you planning to stay to watch?"

"Afraid not. I'm just grabbing something to eat while I have a chance."

"Oh. Too bad. You work entirely too hard."

"So I've been told."

"Doc did too. He spent way too many hours at this place." Catherine picked at an imaginary spot on her sleeve. Her voice was no more than a whisper when she said, "I still can't believe he's gone."

"Me neither."

Catherine brushed away whatever had been on her sleeve. "I'd better go find Zelda and look at that horse. You never know. It might just be my ticket to the Triple Crown."

Jessie wished her well and watched as she sauntered away with the air of a model on a runway.

The sun was hanging low on the western horizon by the time Jessie trudged back across the trainers' parking lot. She balanced a plastic tray of nachos in one hand while fumbling with the keys to the Chevy in the other. As soon as she reached for the door, her phone chimed with an incoming text, signaling the end of her respite. She set the tray on the truck's bench seat, slid it over, and started to step up into the cab when someone called her name.

"Hold up there, darlin'." Milt ambled toward her, his Texas good ol' boy swagger firmly in place.

"I've got an emergency call." Jessie tugged her phone from her pocket and checked the message. A request for x-rays over in Barn I.

Milt propped his polished boot on her pitted chrome bumper. "I won't keep you long. You looked kind of pale last time I saw you. I just wanted to make sure you weren't coming down with something."

She flashed back to the events of the afternoon. "The only thing I'm coming down with is a case of Sherry Malone-itis."

"What's that girl done now?"

"Nothing really. Except..." Did Jessie dare say it out loud? "I think she threatened me."

"She what?"

Jessie rolled her phone in her hand while replaying the conversation—or her disjointed memories of it—over in her mind. "I confronted her in the spa about something. We argued. Then she made some comment about shoving me into the pool, knowing full well I can't swim."

Troubled lines creased Milt's forehead. "What were you arguing about?"

"We weren't really *arguing*. We were talking about Doc's practice." Jessie leaned against the truck's open door. "You'll never guess what I found out today."

The lines disappeared. "Okay. Since I'll never guess, just tell me. You know I love good backside gossip."

This ought to thrill the old rumor monger to tears. "Sherry Malone is—" Jessie said and winced. "*Was* Doc's daughter."

Milt's foot slipped from the bumper. "I'll be damned. Are you sure?"

"Sherry confirmed it for me. According to her, she expects to inherit Doc's practice once the will has been read."

The look of astonishment on Milt's face faded to one of despair.

"Sorry. I know you wanted me to take over."

"Hell, yes, I did. And don't you go lying to me or to yourself. You wanted it too."

She gazed across the lot to the eager Thoroughbreds being ponied from the barns to the paddock. "It doesn't matter now. If Sherry's right—"

"I don't think she is." Milt removed his hat and ran a hand through his hair. "You said she *expects* to inherit the practice."

"Yeah."

"I don't believe it. No way would Doc leave his practice to her, daughter or not. Hell, I doubt she even passes her licensing exam."

"But—"

Milt waved a hand to shut her up. "Listen to me. Those two argued like cats and dogs all the time. I overheard Doc giving her a verbal thrashing once about her work ethic. Or lack of it. He said she doesn't have what it takes to do this kind of work. Now you tell me. Does that sound like someone he's gonna trust his life's work to?"

Jessie mulled over his words. Work ethic. It was something Doc had always stressed. And had praised her for. Others—Greg for example—had called her a workaholic. Doc had called it devotion. Passion. *A good work ethic.*

"And another thing." Milt slapped the hat back on his head. "Why would Sherry threaten you if she was so sure of herself?"

"That wasn't the reason. We were talking about OSU finding acepromazine in Clown's blood. I asked her about the time he'd attacked her and if she knew who might have administered the drug to him the night Doc was killed." Jessie paused to quell the pounding in her temples. "She told me to stay out of it. Or else."

The creases were back in Milt's forehead. "The horse had been tranquilized?"

"Didn't I tell you?"

"And you think someone did it intentionally?"

"I got my hands on Doc's records. There were notations everywhere about Clown's sensitivity to the stuff. There's no way Doc gave him ace."

"Guess not." Milt squinted across the Monongahela River at what was left of the setting sun.

Jessie's phone burst into song. A quick check revealed a second horse needing attention. "I have to go. Do you want a ride to your truck? Where are you parked?"

"That would be great. I'm over in the employees' lot by the rec hall."

Jessie pressed the button to unlock the other door.

Milt circled to the passenger side and climbed in. "There's something else I bet you didn't consider," he said as Jessie shifted into drive.

"About what?"

"Sherry. She wants Doc's practice, right?"

"Yeah."

"Maybe she's right about inheriting it. Doc was a good man. A good father. He might just leave his practice to his daughter, hoping by the time he passed, she'd be worthy of it."

"That's true. I'm sure he didn't plan on dying for quite a few years yet."

"Right." Milt turned toward Jessie, a glint in his eyes. "But Sherry doesn't strike me as the patient type. If she wanted to take over sooner rather than later...and if inheriting was the only way she could get her hands on it..."

The spring evening air suddenly took on a chill. "That would be motive." Jessie shivered. For murder.

It was after midnight by the time Jessie made the right turn off Harden Road into her farm lane. One of the lights illuminating the Cameron Veterinary Hospital sign had burned out. She made a mental note to replace it.

Burned out light bulbs. She savored the sweetness of such mundane problems.

The lane climbed the hill beside her 1850 vintage farmhouse and looped around behind it to the hospital. Jessie recognized the two vehicles in the lot. Their presence, combined with the light streaming from the newer building's windows at this hour, couldn't be good.

She parked next to the red Ford pickup and headed for the hospital's front door.

Unlike the massive two-story farmhouse, the veterinary hospital was long and all one level. Jessie maintained the farm flavor by matching the white siding and red tin roof of the house.

She entered to find the reception area was empty.

Doors to the trio of exam rooms stood open, the rooms dark. Same for the hallway to the side entrance. Loud and unhappy voices drifted from the other hallway leading to the office. Jessie followed them.

A bead of light traced the bottom edge of the closed office door. She reached for the knob and pushed through.

Meryl wheeled toward her.

Vanessa, their petite blonde receptionist, jumped to attention, her eyes so wide that white showed all the way around, like a scared colt.

Meryl's eyes were considerably narrower. "It's about time you got home."

Jessie briefly considered retreating. "What are you doing here so late?"

Meryl massaged one temple. "Philip Lombardo's Australian Shepherd broke his chain and tried to herd the traffic on Route 8. Got hit by a car."

Surrendering to exhaustion, Jessie sank into her chair. "How bad?"

"Bad enough. Fractured pelvis and femur. I called in a team, and we did surgery. Pinned and plated the old boy back together. I just wanted to stick around until he came out of the anesthesia." Meryl folded her arms. "You're going to have to add some overtime into this week's payroll."

"No problem." Jessie looked up at Vanessa, who continued to impersonate a statue. "At ease."

She swallowed hard. "Can I go now?" Her voice sounded like it belonged to a ten-year-old instead of a twenty-something.

Meryl flapped a hand at her. "Hell, yes. Shoo."

"Thanks." Her gaze darted between Meryl and Jessie before she bolted.

Meryl gave a soft growl. "I'm telling you, that girl's getting flakier by the minute. If you don't get back here soon, I really am going to have to kill her."

"What'd she do now?" Jessie raised a hand. "Never mind. I don't want to know. Come on down to the house. I'll make us some coffee."

"No coffee for me. Got any Dr. Pepper?" Meryl's beverage of choice.

"Of course."

"Let me check on my patient. I'll be right there."

Jessie retraced her steps to the parking lot. Vanessa's pastel green VW Beetle was gone. Jessie wondered what she'd done to get on Meryl's shit list. With Meryl's sour mood, it wouldn't have taken much.

A well-worn path trailed down the hill from the parking lot to the back entrance of the farmhouse. The door had been crafted to look old even though she'd had it and a new jamb installed only a few months ago. While she adored the original doors and rippled-glass windows that graced the house, last winter's heating bills had nudged her to reluctantly start modernizing.

Once inside, she pushed the door shut and tested it. The door came open without turning the knob. She slammed it and tried again. It still hadn't caught. On a third attempt, she slammed the thing so hard the windows rattled, but this time it stayed closed. New wasn't always better. She made a mental note to look up the number for the contractor who had done the job and demand he fix the problem.

Her footsteps filled the silence as she crossed the enclosed porch. She sat on a long rustic bench, a find during a Sunday afternoon yard sale treasure hunt, unlaced her work boots, tugged them off, and dumped them on the floor with a pair of thuds. Resisting the temptation to lean back and close her eyes, she climbed to her feet, opened the door into the dark kitchen, and smacked the light switch.

A plump, longhaired, black-and-white tuxedo feline sat next to the stove.

"Hello, Molly." Jessie knelt to pet the cat who purred and skimmed under her hand. She scooped up the mass of fur, and the cat nuzzled against Jessie's chin and meowed. Loudly. At seventeen, Molly was deaf and meowed loud enough to hear herself.

Jessie carried the cat into the dining room, turning on lights as she went. After months of aching from the quiet that shrouded the house since Greg and Peanut had moved out, Jessie was finally embracing the solitude. Where she'd once seen only empty chairs and heard echoes of missing voices, she now saw freedom. Autonomy. No one to answer to but herself.

And the cat.

Jessie lowered Molly to the floor and grabbed a bag of dry food, senior formula, from the antique sideboard. She topped off the bowl that hadn't been empty. The cat dived into the fresh food as if she'd been starving.

The sound of the backdoor banging shut reminded Jessie that company was coming.

"Hey," Meryl shouted. "Anybody home?"

"In here."

"THIS SHERRY MALONE sounds like a real piece of work." Meryl scowled at her can of soda as if it had offended her in some way.

Jessie sat cattycorner from her friend at a dining room table big enough to feed a farm family plus their hired hands and cradled her umpteenth cup of coffee for the day. "That's putting it lightly."

"She threatened to throw you in the pool?"

"More like she implied it could happen."

Meryl turned her scowl from the can to Jessie. "Get picky, why don't you. What exactly is it she doesn't want you digging up?"

"I wish I knew." Jessie stared across the table to the darkened living room. "Have you ever heard of anyone doing Coggins tests without drawing blood?"

Meryl choked. "Are you kidding me?"

Jessie looked at Meryl and waited.

"I remember something about counterfeit papers." Meryl grabbed a napkin from the table and pressed it to her chin. "But the department of health cracked down on it. Can't be done anymore."

"Can't?" Somehow Jessie suspected where there was a will, there was a way.

"Why on earth are you asking about this?"

Jessie told her about Harvey Randolph.

"Are you sure you understood him?"

"I understood. And he said Sherry took care of that stuff for Doc."

"What stuff? Fudging test results?"

"That'd be my guess." Jessie glanced down at Molly, who was head-butting her leg. "There's more."

Meryl gave a short laugh. "Terrific. What?"

Jessie scooped up the cat and settled her on her lap. "Sherry is Doc's daughter."

Meryl slammed a hand on the table and let loose one of her famous strings of expletives.

"Not only that, she says Doc left his practice to her in his will." Jessie expected Meryl to jump up and dance around the table.

Instead, she stared at Jessie. "Shit."

"I thought that would make you happy."

"It would if it was anyone else but her." Meryl leaned back in her chair. Picked up the can. Took a long draw on it. "How does Amelia feel about it?"

Jessie rubbed Molly's ears. The deep rumble of her purr vibrated through Jessie's fingers but did little to soothe. "As far as I know, Amelia is unaware of the situation."

"She doesn't know her husband has another child?"

"I don't believe so."

Meryl grunted. "She's gonna find out."

"I know. I saw her this morning. She's a mess. I need to call her kids and let them know the shape she's in. I'm afraid hearing about Sherry will push her over the edge." Jessie thought of the stench in that kitchen. "Further over the edge."

Meryl swirled the soda in the can. "You want to know what I think?"

"Do I have a choice?"

"I think you need to tell Shumway about the Coggins test business. And then I think you need to get the hell out of that place. Now. This Malone chick wants it so bad? Let her have it."

"But she isn't licensed yet."

"I don't care. Doc died there. You've been threatened. There's stuff going on that you have no business getting involved in. Come back to the hospital where you belong." Meryl drained the can and plunked it down. "We need you. Preferably alive."

The house phone rang. At that hour it could only mean an emergency. Jessie deposited Molly onto the floor and crossed to the table next to the window to answer it. She was right. One of her clients had returned home to find her cat unresponsive. "I'll be there as soon as I can," Jessie told her.

Meryl crossed her arms on the dining table. "You mean *I'll* be there as soon as I can."

"Go home. You've put in a long enough day. The track's closed tomorrow, so I can go in late."

"Don't expect me to argue with you. I'm outta here." Meryl rose and made it to the kitchen doorway before turning back. "Are you going to take my advice and tender your resignation?"

Jessie watched as Molly sprung onto the dining table to sniff Meryl's empty soda can. She thought of Amelia and the mess Doc's death had created. She'd been able to clean up the kitchen. How could she walk away now and leave everything else in turmoil? "I'll stay the rest of the week. I promised Doc that much."

"I guess it's better than nothing." Meryl turned and left, her footsteps clomping across the enclosed porch. The back door slammed. Slammed again. Then a third time. Jessie definitely had to get that taken care of.

After she figured out why Doc had been killed.

Even if it took longer than the rest of the week.

Nine

Wednesday mornings were normally Jessie's one chance to sleep in, but her phone blasted her awake. Groggy, she squinted at the screen. The incoming number wasn't a familiar one.

A frantic voice on the other end informed her that a horse had gotten loose on the backside, had been caught, and needed a vet. Jessie scribbled the barn number on a notepad she kept next to her bed. "I'll be right there."

Molly hadn't budged from her spot on the bed. Jessie kicked off the sheet and rolled away from the cat, who awoke with an unladylike grunt. "Sorry, baby," Jessie said, running a hand over the silky fur.

Jessie stared at the clock. It was later than she'd first thought. No sunshine brightened the room. What she'd mistaken for a tractor trailer rumbling along Harden Road turned out to be thunder.

She shuffled to the bathroom. After splashing cold water on her face and brushing her teeth, she returned to her bedroom to pull on a t-shirt and a pair of Wranglers. She winced as she worked a brush through the knots in her unruly hair before restraining the stuff with a fabric-covered elastic band. Tossing the brush back onto the dresser, she reached for the note next to the phone. The fog finally cleared from her brain, and she stared at the words on the page. Had she written down the message right? She looked again, but the barn number remained the same. Neil Emerick's.

She headed for the door, leaving the bed unmade around Molly who watched her with bored eyes.

"Come on, sweetie," she said, knowing full well the cat couldn't hear her.

But apparently, Molly could read lips. She jumped off the bed with a muffled thump and trotted after her, claws ticking against the hardwood floor.

Jessie set a bowl of canned senior formula cat food in front of Molly and eyed the empty coffee pot. Why hadn't she paid extra for the one with the automatic timer? She spent a moment watching Molly devour her breakfast before grabbing a ball cap and her oilskin duster and heading out the door.

The track was closed for training and racing, so the place was largely deserted. Unlike every other barn on the backside, Emerick's buzzed with activity. Jessie considered entering from the "forbidden" end just to see what was down there. But her snooping would have to wait.

Emerick met Jessie at the opening between barns, looking every bit as happy to see her as he had the night she'd confronted him in the paddock. "Dr. McCarrell wasn't available," he said by way of a greeting.

Jessie guessed he didn't want her to mistakenly believe she was his first choice. "What happened?"

He hitched his head toward the stalls. "Sullivan got loose. Busted through the stall webbing."

She looked in the direction he'd indicated. The same black with the star and stripe she'd seen on her previous visit peered at her from the first stall. Soldier Bob with his stitches gazed at her from the third. Otherwise, no faces greeted her. But at the far end of the shedrow, she spotted Sherry engaged in an animated conversation with a slump-shouldered man Jessie didn't recognize. Sherry threw up her arms and strode toward Jessie. The man shuffled away.

Sherry broke into a jog. "Dr. Cameron. I'm glad you could make it."

Jessie stiffened. Before she could respond, Emerick wheeled and stormed toward Sherry. Jessie noticed Sherry's eyes widen for a split second. Emerick whispered something to her that Jessie couldn't make out.

Sherry, however, made no attempt to conceal her reply. "I heard you the first time."

Jessie watched as the pair exchanged what amounted to an entire conversation with their eyes.

In a voice thick with menace, Emerick said, "You better have." Without looking at Jessie, he stomped down the shedrow.

She considered asking what that was all about but decided she didn't really want to know.

Sherry grabbed Jessie's arm and steered her toward the second stall. "I want an ultrasound of his leg. I'm afraid all the running around on the concrete might have damaged that tendon again."

They stopped outside the stall. Sullivan, appearing much less grand than he had at the spa yesterday, stood tied in the back corner, his head hanging low. The entire left side of his body exhibited a bad case of road rash.

It hurt to look at him.

Jessie lowered her gaze to the stall guard, securely latched across the stall opening. If the horse had broken through this particular webbing, someone had made a quick and thorough repair. "How'd he get loose?"

"Neil brought him out." Sherry unclipped the guard. "Sullivan's been feeling pretty good, and being cooped up in his stall all the time has turned him into a handful." She stepped inside and moved to the horse's head. "Neil should've been more patient with him. But when Sullivan started acting frisky, Neil started yanking on his head and yelling."

Jessie thought back to the incident in the paddock.

"The two of them got into a pissing contest, and Sullivan won. He broke free and took off before anyone could get a hand on him."

Jessie had no problem believing her and eased into the stall. Sullivan might have been frisky earlier, but not now. She knelt to get a better view. The front legs had been wrapped. The bandages on the left side were shredded, same as his hide. "How'd all this happen?"

Sherry stroked the horse's nose. "The guy that finally caught him said he ran into a car and went down on the pavement. He doesn't appear to be lame, but..." She swept a hand at the resulting injuries.

Jessie circled to look at his right side. "Even if he's not lame today, he's gonna be one sore pony tomorrow." She placed a hand on his hip. "Watch out," she said to Sherry. "I need to move him over so I can see."

"I'm fine."

Jessie pressed on the hip. "Over, son."

The horse took one slow step to the side.

"He looks good over here."

"I could have told you that."

Jessie resisted an urge to laugh. For a moment, she'd thought someone had pulled a body snatch on Sherry, but here was the old familiar venom she'd become accustomed to. "By the way, was that the guy who caught him?"

"Who?"

Jessie circled back to Sherry's side and nudged Sullivan over to his original spot. "I saw you talking to someone at the end of the shedrow when I got here. Was that the guy who caught Sullivan?"

Sherry's eyes shifted. "No."

"Who was he?"

Sherry dropped to her knees and began to remove the tattered leg wrap. "Just an owner. Now about that ultrasound?"

Jessie studied the silver and turquoise barrette on the top of Sherry's head. "I'll go get the equipment." Jessie fingered the stall guard. Neil Emerick had lied about Sullivan breaking through it. She also didn't believe the man Sherry had been talking to was *just* an owner.

The ultrasound revealed some new, small tears in the tendon, but Jessie and Sherry agreed the new damage wouldn't delay his healing time by more than a couple of weeks.

To help with the pain and swelling, Jessie mixed bute and Banamine in a syringe and injected it, topped with a shot of dexamethasone in the muscle. She also dispensed some Tri Hist granules to help reduce any generalized swelling. "Make sure you tell Neil the horse will definitely get a bad drug test for the next thirty days on these."

Sherry studied the label. "No problem. Sullivan won't be running on that leg anytime soon."

Jessie gazed down the shedrow. Emerick had parked a wheelbarrow near the stall where Jessie remembered seeing a gray horse last time she was here. Today, Emerick was mucking out the stall. Most trainers at Riverview jumped in and handled the grunt work alongside their hired help. They couldn't afford not to. But she hadn't pictured Emerick doing any kind of menial labor.

A short, scrawny kid with a sad excuse for a goatee charged into the barn from behind Jessie. He brushed past her without acknowledging her presence and stuck his head into Sullivan's stall. "Sherry, I did what you said. Everything's set."

Sherry glanced at Jessie and hissed at the kid through her teeth. He stiffened and turned, as if he only now realized someone else was there. "Sorry. Hi, Dr. Cameron."

Jessie studied him, certain she'd never seen him before.

He grinned. "I'm the one who called you this morning."

"Oh."

"Sherry told me to."

"Oh," Jessie repeated.

"Thank you, Jimmy." Sherry spoke the words slowly as if the kid was dimmer than the gray, rainy day.

He gave Sherry a quick nod before scurrying off toward Emerick.

Jessie concealed a smile. Grooms were quickly becoming her favorite source of information. "*You* told him to call me about Sullivan?"

Sherry's face reddened. "Yes." She lowered her head and breezed past Jessie into Emerick's feed room. She reappeared a moment later with both hands full of Vet Wrap and bandaging materials.

"*You* told him." Unlike at the pool, Jessie had regained the upper hand. "Not Emerick. You."

"Neil wouldn't call you if you were the only vet on the planet." Sherry dropped to her knees and began working on Sullivan's leg.

"He does have you, after all. His own personal vet. Unofficial. But still." Jessie shrugged. "That seems to be the case, right?"

When Sherry looked up, her lip was curled back in a snarl. "No. It's not."

"Then what exactly is it you do for him? Why are you always here?"

Sherry stopped wrapping Sullivan's leg. "It's none of your business."

"You *do* work for him. Right?"

A muscle in Sherry's jaw danced beneath the skin's surface. "Since my father died, I have to make money somehow."

"Until your inheritance comes through and you take over Doc's practice."

Sherry resumed wrapping Sullivan's leg. "Exactly."

Jessie leaned against the stall doorway. "What would you have done if Doc hadn't died?"

The roll of Vet Wrap dropped from Sherry's hands. "What?"

Jessie let the question sit there between them. Down the shedrow, Jimmy with the goatee had taken over stall cleaning duties from Emerick.

Sherry picked up the bandage and started over. "I'd have gone into practice with my father. That was my dream."

"Now you won't have to share. Convenient, huh?"

Jessie expected an explosion. Instead, Sherry lowered her head. Her shoulders shook. Jessie thought she was sobbing until she heard the laughter.

Sherry threw her head back, cackling in mirth. "You—" She gasped for breath. "You think I killed my dad?" She burst out in laughter again. "You really are clueless, aren't you?"

Not the reaction Jessie had expected.

"I didn't want my dad dead." Sherry wiped her eyes. "If you're looking for someone who wanted to kill my old man, you don't have to look very far." She held up one finger. "Butch from security? He's into, shall we say, personal banking."

"You mean loan sharking?"

"You're not so dumb after all. Yeah. Loan sharking. He and my dad had a few big blow-ups over it. Dad knew and threatened to turn him in if Butch didn't pay to keep him quiet. You can damned well bet Butch wasn't too keen about sharing his profits." She held up a second finger. "Frank Hamilton."

"The paddock judge?" Jessie could buy Butch being into illegal activities. But Frank Hamilton? "You've got to be kidding me."

Sherry swung her head like a slow pendulum. "I'm serious. Race fixing. I don't know the particulars, but my father did and was putting the screws to Frankie baby." She held up three fingers. "And then there's Daniel Shumway."

Now Jessie knew Sherry was lying through her teeth. "And I suppose you're going to tell me Daniel's a drug dealer." Jessie made no effort to mask her sarcasm.

"Maybe. I just know Shumway and my dad had a serious screaming match a few days before Dad died." Sherry curled her fingers into a fist. "You do the math."

From the far end of the shedrow came a crash. Jessie jumped. Neil Emerick had kicked the wheelbarrow of manure and straw over and was ranting at a cowering Jimmy with the goatee to clean it up. Emerick looked up and homed in on Jessie. Even at that distance, she could see his face redden. He stormed toward her.

Had Jessie given into her survival instincts, she'd have high-tailed it out of there. The barn across the road showed no signs of human life. For a fleeting moment, it occurred to her that Sherry, who'd threatened to push her into the pool, was the only witness or possible rescuer in sight.

"What the hell are you still doing here?" Emerick's face was the same color as Sullivan's road rash. "Are you done with that horse or not?"

Jessie straightened. "I'm done. You were lucky. The additional damage to the tendon is minor and shouldn't significantly delay his healing."

"Lucky, huh?" Emerick leaned in, his face only inches from hers. His stale breath ruffled the strands of her hair hanging loose from her ball cap. "If you want *your* luck to hold, you'd better get the hell out-ta here."

Jessie met his gaze, unblinking. The rage in his eyes made her think perhaps Sherry should have held up one more finger. "I'll send you my bill." Without waiting for a retort—or physical vio-lence—she sidestepped him and headed down the shedrow. Toward Jimmy with the goatee and the forbidden part of the barn.

Behind her, Jessie heard his menacing voice raised at Sherry. "I don't care what happens. Don't you ever bring that woman into my barn again."

Jessie anticipated either Emerick or Sherry stopping her as she took the scenic route out of his barn, but no one did. She glanced into each stall she passed. Each stood empty. The only sign of recent occupancy was the one Emerick had been mucking out. And it was now vacant as well.

Ten

Jessie knocked on Daniel's office door not really expecting him to be there at nine o'clock on a Wednesday morning. He called out for her to come in. Apparently track CEOs didn't get days off either.

"Jessie." He rose as she entered the room. "How nice to see you."

She doubted he'd feel the same once he heard what she had to say.

He motioned to a chair opposite his desk, which she accepted. "I hope you're here to tell me you're taking over Doc's practice."

"No. In fact, it might be out of my hands."

Daniel sank into his own chair. "What do you mean?"

Sherry's relationship with Doc wasn't part of Jessie's agenda. "Never mind. That's not why I'm here."

"Oh?" He rested his forearms on the desk. "That tranquilizer. Acepromazine. Did you ever find out why Doc gave it to Clown?"

"I don't believe he did." She told him about the records she'd tracked down at Doc's house and the notations about the horse's reaction to the drug.

"If Doc didn't administer it, who did?"

"That's what I'm trying to find out. According to Zelda, everyone knew about it, but maybe someone new to the track didn't." Jessie's throat tightened. "Otherwise, whoever gave Clown the drug did it intentionally, knowing what would happen."

"Sounds like you think someone meant for Doc to be killed."

Jessie held his gaze. And her tongue. She waited for him to tell her she was crazy.

Instead, he asked, "Any idea who?"

111

"What do you know about Butch?"

"Butch?" Daniel frowned. "From security?"

"Yeah."

"Not much. You suspect him? Why?"

"I heard he's been doing some loan sharking on the side." Sherry had made it sound viable. Coming from Jessie's mouth, it sounded lame.

"Loan sharking." The look on Daniel's face suggested he agreed with Jessie's latest assessment.

"That's what I heard. And that Doc was blackmailing him."

Daniel picked up a pencil and tapped it on the desk. "I'll look into it."

"There's also Frank Hamilton."

The pencil fell still. "What about Frank Hamilton?"

Jessie wondered if this was going to sound insane too. "I understand he's been involved in fixing some races."

"Damn it. I warned him if I ever caught him trying that again..."

Maybe Sherry wasn't so far off base after all. Which left Jessie pondering the third name on Sherry's list.

The pencil continued drumming. "But why would Hamilton have reason to harm Doc?"

"Apparently, Doc knew what was going on and was putting some pressure on him."

"I'll look into that too." Daniel used his drumstick to jot a note. "How'd you find out all this?"

Jessie wasn't sure she wanted to reveal her source. Then she thought of the pool. "Sherry Malone."

"Ah." He nodded as if he should have guessed. "She was Doc's assistant, so she would know."

"She's also his daughter."

The pencil slipped from Daniel's fingers and clattered from the desk to the floor. "You're kidding."

"I don't have a paternity test to prove it, but according to her, it's true."

Daniel swiveled his chair toward the window overlooking the outdoor paddock.

Jessie studied his profile. His strong jaw. Dimples that were aging into creases. A flush of warmth rose to her neck. She lowered her eyes and hooked a finger in her collar, giving it a tug. Good thing Meryl wasn't here.

"Jessie? Are you all right?"

She looked up to find Daniel watching her. "Sherry believes Doc left her his practice in his will."

"That's what you meant about it being out of your hands?"

"Unfortunately, yes."

He turned toward the window again, but not before she caught a glimpse of something dark in his eyes.

Jessie stood. "I should be going."

He swung around in his chair, as though he'd forgotten about her. "I'm sorry." He flashed his charming, boyish smile at her. "I'm not a very good host. You don't have to go."

"Yes, I do. I have a lot of paperwork to catch up on."

He rose and stepped around his desk. "I'll check into Frank and Butch and let you know what I find out. You'll keep me posted if you learn anything more?"

"Absolutely."

He extended a hand and she took it. His grip was warm and firm. And gentle. She found herself wondering about that argument he'd had with Doc. But now wasn't the time to ask.

It must have shown on her face. "Are you sure you're all right?" he asked.

She looked up into Daniel's concerned eyes. "Absolutely." She threw in a smile for good measure before slipping her hand from his and beating a hasty retreat.

JESSIE HAD SKIPPED breakfast, and her rumbling stomach insisted she make a detour on her way to the office. Armed with a second large coffee and a Styrofoam container of toast and scrambled eggs from the rec hall, she wrestled open the clinic door and trudged across the exam area. She set her "brunch" on the desk and popped open the lids, savoring the aromas. No sooner had she taken her first bite than a familiar voice called from outside.

"Hello? Jessie?" Catherine Dodd stood just inside the big doorway, out of the rain.

"Come in," Jessie called around a mouthful of bread. She chewed fast and managed to swallow by the time Catherine reached the office. "What brings you all the way out here?" Catherine rarely strayed into the backside.

"I hope you don't mind. I need to talk to someone." Catherine pointed at the container on the desk. "I'm sorry. I see I've interrupted your breakfast."

"Don't worry about it." Jessie flipped the lid closed and motioned toward the couch. "Have a seat."

Catherine brushed a hand across the vinyl as though that might make it acceptably clean before sitting down.

Jessie suppressed a smile. "Catherine, how do you always manage to look so put together? Not only do you look like you stepped out of the pages of *Vogue*, but you stay so...*clean*."

Catherine glanced down at her perfect pale blue skirt and jacket. "What do you mean?"

"I put on clean jeans and a t-shirt in the morning, and within an hour I'm covered in cat hair, hay, and straw."

"Maybe you should stay out of the barn."

Jessie studied Catherine's face for some sign of humor. There wasn't any. "Maybe I'll give that a try." Jessie waited for a laugh or a grin, something—anything—to show Catherine recognized the irony in her words. When none was forthcoming, Jessie cleared her throat. "What did you want to talk about?"

Catherine let out a shuddering, damp sigh. "Jessie, do you think Milt might be having an affair?"

Jessie choked. "An affair? Milt?"

Catherine extracted a tissue from her jacket pocket. She didn't reply but watched Jessie intently.

Jessie gazed into her coffee cup, imagining Milt's face with all its good ol' boy charm. She thought about how he and Meryl had been making eyes at each other a few days earlier. No doubt about it, Milt was a shameless flirt. But Jessie couldn't fathom him ever taking it further.

Catherine touched the tissue to the corner of her eye. "You know I was the one who broke up Milt's first marriage."

Jessie hadn't. Maybe he *was* capable of taking it further.

"I've heard the best predictor of future behavior is past behavior." Catherine sniffled. "This spring, I was certain Milt had a girlfriend on the side, so I decided to retaliate."

The office suddenly felt too close. Too confined. "Why are you telling me all this?"

"I can't stand it anymore. I need to talk to someone about it. We've known each other forever, and you know everyone involved. Plus, I trust you won't repeat any of this." Catherine again dabbed at her eyes, careful not to smudge the mascara. "I slept with Doc."

What? While Jessie adored the man and his brilliant mind, she couldn't picture Catherine, with her perfectly styled hair and matched suits, together with Doc and his dusty blue jeans and shabby hat.

"Doc was such a wonderful, sweet lover. Incredible really..." Catherine's face took on an ethereal smile. Jessie sensed she had drifted away to a place Jessie did not want to think about.

"Does Milt know?"

Catherine snapped out of her reverie. "Oh, Christ, no."

"You sure?"

"Absolutely. Milt would never be able to hide something like that from me. He would be crushed. I'm certain he doesn't know. And I don't want him to find out."

From experience, Jessie knew exactly how Milt would feel. Betrayed. Devastated. Heartbroken. She wouldn't wish that on her worst enemy, let alone a friend. "I won't say a word."

"Thank you." Catherine lowered the hand clutching the tissue to her lap. "Are you positive you don't know anything about him having an affair?"

"Not a thing." Nor did she want to.

Catherine nodded. "I'm probably projecting my own guilty conscience on him." She stuffed the tissue back in her pocket. "It's good to be able to talk to someone about these things." She stood and moved to leave, then hesitated. "I almost forgot. Could you take another peek at Blue sometime when you get a chance?"

Jessie rubbed her eyes, still trying to get the vision of Catherine with Doc out of her brain. "What's wrong with him?"

"Nothing really. Well, nothing *new*. I just wanted you to check him and make sure. Maybe the break has healed better than you expected. Do you think you could x-ray him again?"

"I doubt I'd have anything more to tell you than I did last time."

"I know, but I'd still like another set of x-rays."

"Sure."

"Good. I'll call you and set up an appointment." Catherine performed a flawless pirouette on four-inch heels before ambling out the door, waving one dainty hand as she went.

Jessie stared at the container of cold eggs. Even if they'd still been hot, she didn't think she could choke them down. She picked up the box and dropped it in the trash.

Jessie had started entering the first of Doc's old records on her laptop when a knock on the office door jolted her. She looked up to find Milt grinning through the glass. She waved him in.

"Hey, darlin'." Milt closed the door behind him. "What're you doing here on your day off?"

"Paperwork."

He ambled in and flopped down on the old sofa. "Anyone ever tell you that you're a workaholic?"

Jessie made a face. "Yeah. Greg." She watched Milt sprawl out, crossing his ankles as they hung off the not-quite-long-enough couch. The Dodd family were certainly making themselves comfortable in her office today. "I've got nothing better to do, so I've started computerizing Doc's files," she said.

"Why bother if you don't plan on taking over his practice?"

Jessie snorted. "I didn't think you paid attention when I told you I wasn't staying." She tried to focus on the information she was typing, but Milt's question stuck in her head. Why *was* she bothering with Doc's records? Why was the idea of Sherry inheriting his practice creating knots of tension in Jessie's shoulders? And why was Jessie hoping Milt had been right about Doc not leaving his practice to Sherry?

"Hello?"

Jessie realized Milt had been talking. "I'm sorry. What?"

"I said, I pay attention to everything you say, but I also know when you're kidding yourself."

Before Jessie had a chance to come up with a retort, the office door crashed open. She jumped, certain the glass was about to shatter. A crimson-faced Frank Hamilton stood in the doorway.

Milt jumped to his feet. "What the hell, Hamilton?"

"This has nothing to do with you, Dodd." The paddock judge didn't take his eyes off Jessie. "My business is with the doctor. You should go find a horse to shoe."

Jessie recalled her last face-to-face with Frank Hamilton in the paddock. That night he'd been stern and authoritative, dressing her down for encroaching in his territory. The man who stood before her now displayed no such self-control. She shot a pleading glance at Milt.

The blacksmith hooked his thumbs in his jeans' pockets. "I'm not going anywhere with you acting like this, Hamilton."

Jessie released a breath.

Hamilton ignored the blacksmith and took two steps toward her. "You, Dr. Cameron, are meddling in affairs that are none of your concern."

The man stood several inches taller than Jessie, but she countered his attempt at intimidation by rising slowly from her chair and stalking around the desk. Keeping her voice low, she said, "Get out of my office."

"Or what? Are you going to turn me in to Daniel Shumway again?" He took another step closer. "I don't appreciate people threatening my job. I told you before to stay out of my paddock. Now I'm telling you to stay the hell out of my business."

Milt took one long stride and grabbed Hamilton by the arm. "You wanna tell me what this is all about?"

Hamilton tried to tug free. "Stay out of this, Dodd."

Milt's grip held. "Sorry. Can't do that."

The two men glowered, fists clenched. Before they could come to blows, Jessie jumped in. "Sherry told me you've been fixing races, and Doc knew about it." Neither man blinked. "I told Daniel and got the impression he wasn't surprised by the news."

Milt and Hamilton continued to glare at each other, however a hint of a smile flickered across the blacksmith's face. "At it again, are you, Hamilton?"

The paddock judge tried to wrest his arm free. "No, I'm not. And no one can prove otherwise. Not you. Not Shumway." His gaze turned to Jessie. "Not you either. And certainly not Doc."

The tone of his voice sent a chill through her. "Certainly not Doc," she said. "Seeing as he's dead."

Hamilton lunged at Jessie. She tried to step back, but her leg hit the desk. She scrambled to keep her balance. Milt hauled Hamilton away from her, but the paddock judge swung his free arm. The fist connected with Milt's jaw with a sickening pop. Jessie yelped. Milt staggered. Caught himself. And charged.

Hamilton *oofed* as Milt's shoulder impacted his midsection. The next thing Jessie knew, Hamilton slammed into her, sending her over the desk. Something jammed into her back as she tumbled sending electrical sparks of pain screaming up her spine. Pens, veterinary reports, and notes went sailing. With Hamilton on top of her, they both skidded across the desk.

Jessie expected to go all the way over. She pictured herself landing headfirst in the office chair. But the weight of the paddock judge not only crushed the air out of her, it dragged her to a stop.

Hamilton groaned.

Jessie wished she could groan too. She hadn't realized how big a man Hamilton was until all two-hundred-pounds-plus of him flattened her. She tried to maneuver her arms in closer to her body so she could leverage him off, but he didn't budge.

Suddenly the weight lifted. Jessie gasped for air. She looked up to see that Milt had hoisted Hamilton up by his collar. "Jessie, darlin', are you all right?"

Her initial reaction was *hell no*. Something hard and sharp bit into her back. Her ribs ached. She was bent backward over her desk and still feared she might end up on her head. The only word she could muster was, "Ouch."

Milt shoved Hamilton down onto the sofa and caught Jessie's arm. She let him pull her up to sit. His gaze looked past her, and his eyes widened. "Oh, mercy."

She turned and discovered why her back stung like she'd tangled with a porcupine. Her laptop lay in shambles where she'd fallen on it. The screen's glass had shattered in a design to rival a spider's web. Instead of showing the record she'd been working on, it looked like an abstract painting complete with a rainbow of color. Several of the keys had popped from the keyboard. Jessie suspected some of them might be imbedded in her back. She swore.

Milt wiped a hand across his mouth. "Don't suppose you had that stuff backed up, did you?"

Jessie stood and winced at the pain. "Some of it. Not all. None of what I did today." She looked at the floor where all her notes and two manila folders of Doc's records lay scattered. She swore again.

Frank Hamilton staggered to his feet. Milt turned toward him, braced to take a swing. Hamilton held up both hands. "Enough, Dodd." He sidestepped to the door without taking his eyes off Milt and Jessie. "I'm filing assault charges against both of you." He pointed to Jessie. "And if you ever say one word about me again, I'll sue you for libel." Then he wheeled and stormed out.

"That would be *slander*," Jessie called after him. But he gave no indication he'd heard her. She eyed Milt. "If he's going to sue me, he should at least get the charge right."

Milt chuckled. "And he's filing assault charges against both of us?"

"I assaulted his back with my face. If the cops come after you, send them to see me. He took the first swing. I saw it." She reached around to rub the sore spot on her spine. "My poor laptop."

Milt circled the desk and bent to pick up a handful of papers. "I'll help you sort these."

She took them from him. "Don't be silly. Besides, there's no rush. I can't do much until I get a new computer. Go on. Get outta here."

He frowned at the mess and then at Jessie. "I shoulda busted him one in the jaw."

"What good would that have done? Then he'd really have grounds for assault charges."

The frown turned into an impish grin. "But it would've been fun to give him a bloody lip. That no-good jackass. Gives the rest of us track people a bad name."

She nodded in agreement. "Go home, Milt. And thanks."

He thumped her on the shoulder and walked away.

As he crossed the exam area, Jessie remembered her visit from Catherine. She'd been trying to forget it, but there was one issue she needed to address. "Hey, Milt," she called from the office door.

He turned toward her.

"Tell Catherine I'll stop by tomorrow afternoon."

A look of puzzlement crossed his face. "Why?"

"She asked me to take some new x-rays of Blue's foot."

He shook his head. "I don't know why she wants to waste more money on that boy, but she's the boss." With a wave, he left.

Jessie returned to her desk and scooped up an armload of records. She thought of Frank Hamilton and his threats of an assault charge. Dumping the papers next to the mashed laptop, she reached for the phone. If anyone was going to bring the cops into this mess, it was going to be her.

Eleven

"Damn it, Jess. How many times do I have to tell you to leave the investigating to me?"

"About as many times as it takes for you to actually do some investigating."

They stood toe-to-toe in front of Jessie's desk and demolished laptop. Greg towered over her, one hand on his hip, the other on his sidearm. He might have struck anyone else as an intimidating figure in his state trooper uniform. She was immune to it.

She calmly ran down a partial list of suspicious activities, beginning with Sherry's familial connection to Doc and her potential inheritance, touching on Butch and his personal loans side gig, and ending with Frank Hamilton's recent visit and resulting destruction of electronic equipment. At least, she started out calm. By the time she got to the part about being pinned between a large man and a smashed computer, she'd lost a considerable amount of her composure.

A muscle twitched in Greg's jaw. "Do you want to file a complaint against this Hamilton fellow?"

"Yes," she snapped. Mental images of her future flashed through her brain. Lawyers stating Hamilton hadn't done anything but had in fact been the victim of Milt Dodd's attack. Countersuits against Milt. And against her for slander. After all, she'd only been repeating what Sherry had told her. "No."

"Wise choice. You're stirring up a hornet's nest around this place. The best thing you can do is let it all drop and get out of here. Let this woman who alleges to be Doc's daughter have the damned practice if she wants it so bad."

"But what about Doc's murder?"

Greg raised both fists, clenched and shaking. "There was no murder."

A timid knock at the door interrupted them. A teenage girl with tears streaking her freckled cheeks peered at them through the glass, a bundle of towels clutched to her chest. Greg strode to the back corner of the office as Jessie opened the door. "Can I help you?"

In a shuddering voice, the girl introduced herself as Katie and said she cleaned stalls in Barn M. She gingerly unfolded one corner of the bundle to reveal a pitiful, half-grown orange and white tabby. "One of the horses stepped on him." She hiccupped. "I think his back is broke."

Jessie glanced at Greg. He waved a hand. "Go ahead. I'll wait."

She escorted the girl into the exam area, gently took the bundle from her, and set it on a stainless-steel table. Once unwrapped, the small cat made no effort to escape. He rumbled like a small gasoline engine.

"Why's he purring?" the girl asked.

"Cats don't just purr when they're happy." Jessie probed the feline's hip and pelvis. "They purr to soothe themselves too."

"Oh."

"The good news is his back isn't broken. The bad news is, I think his hip is."

"Can you save him?"

Rock music burst from Jessie's pocket. A quick check of her phone revealed a text about an emergency two barns down. "Tell you what, Katie. You leave the little guy here. I'll see what I can do to fix him up. Check back around three o'clock this afternoon. Okay?"

She flashed a smile through her tears before bolting out the door.

Jessie scooped up the kitty and the towel and carried him down the passageway between her office and the surgical suite, pausing to stick her head through the office door to tell Greg about the emergency. He followed her into the small animal kennel.

"Jess, you have to stop digging into all this stuff."

She cradled the tiny cat in one arm. "But didn't you say there was no murder? If no one has anything to hide, what difference does it make if I ask a few questions?"

"Just because Doc's death was accidental doesn't mean there's nothing shady going on. You poke the wrong sleeping bear and your death may not be so accidental. I don't want to have to investigate another murder."

"*Another* one?" She placed a heating pad into the cage before nestling the cat and its towel inside. "The first one being Doc's?"

Greg blew out an exasperated breath. "Not officially, no."

She spun to face him. "But unofficially?"

He glared at her. "I'll ask some questions. Discreetly. Which is a concept you don't seem to comprehend."

Jessie gave the cat's head a quick scratch. "I'll be back before you know it, little one. You rest." She latched the cage and motioned for Greg to follow her out. "There's one more thing you can look into if you're so inclined."

"What?"

"Besides Butch and Hamilton, Sherry mentioned Daniel had an argument with Doc a few days before he was killed." Jessie paused to lock the office door.

"Did she say what it was about?"

"No."

"It was probably nothing. People argue all the time and don't end up killing each other, but I'll see what I can find out."

She led the way outside and reached for the handle on the big outside door. Greg got there first and dragged it closed for her.

"Promise me you'll stay out of trouble." He headed for his Interceptor. "I have a feeling if you start shutting down every illegal operation going on around here, there won't be anyone left to race the horses."

Jessie made a sour face at his back and climbed into her truck.

The emergency involved a horse that had found an errant nail and had opened a bright pink gouge in his brown hide. A few stitches later, Jessie returned to the clinic and sedated the cat for its x-rays.

She eyed Doc's old film radiography equipment with trepidation. When was the last time she'd been in a dark room? Abandoning that idea, she dragged her portable digital unit in from the Chevy.

It wasn't until she finished that she realized she had no computer on which to read the digital x-rays. She watched the drugged feline from the kennel's doorway and turned the memory card over in her hand. She had two options. Stick the kitty in her truck and drive him home where she could let Meryl take over. Or find another computer on which to view the x-rays.

Ten minutes later, Jessie sat at Daniel's desk as the pictures uploaded. "I really appreciate this."

He took a seat in one of the chairs across from her. "No problem. What happened to your computer?"

Jessie tensed. The reason she was stuck using Daniel's computer was because of the last time she'd mentioned Frank Hamilton's name in this office. "What exactly did you say to Frank?"

"Hamilton? I asked him about fixing races. He denied doing anything like that here."

"Here?"

Daniel leaned back and crossed his arms. "Let's just say he's been reprimanded for his actions at another track."

Jessie clicked through the different views of the cat's hip on the monitor. "Did you believe him?"

"Maybe. Maybe not. I'll keep an eye on him. What's that have to do with your computer?"

"Did you happen to mention why you questioned him?"

"No." Daniel scowled. "Why?"

"He stormed into my office complaining that I turned him in. Milt tried to get him to leave and the two of them started pushing and shoving. My computer was collateral damage."

"That jackass. I'll have another talk with him."

"No. Please. I can't afford any more visits from disgruntled paddock judges."

"And I can't afford to have my favorite veterinarian being harassed."

She peeked around the monitor at Daniel. "Then just leave my name out of it."

He sat forward. "I did. I know full well he didn't hear from me that you were the one making accusations."

She returned her attention to the x-rays and sighed. Accusations? Spreading rumors was more like it. Perhaps Hamilton had every right to be pissed at her.

"What's the verdict on your patient?" Daniel asked.

"As I expected, his back is fine. Unfortunately, his hip isn't."

"Can you do anything?"

She gave him a grin. "Of course." As she clicked back through the pictures, her stomach emitted a loud rumble.

"What was that?"

"I guess I should grab some nachos and a salad on my way out."

"A snack?"

"Lunch."

Daniel checked his watch. "No wonder your stomach's growling. We really have to do something about your eating habits."

Jessie closed the file and removed her memory card. "Good luck with that." She stood and stepped from behind his desk.

Daniel rose as well. "I'm taking you out to dinner tonight."

"Excuse me?"

"There's no racing. As your boss, I'm ordering you to take the night off. No phones. Go home and put on your best dress."

Daniel was asking her out?

She hadn't been on a date since college. Maybe she'd fantasized more than a few times about running her fingers through Daniel's blond hair. And maybe she'd admired his California beach-boy good looks. What she'd never counted on was this. Fantasies were safe. Reality? Not so much. "That's really sweet of you, but I don't think so."

He placed one hand on his desk and leaned toward her until she could feel his breath on her face. "I *do* think so. You've had a rough couple of weeks and maybe part of your difficulties has been my fault. Let me make it up to you. Besides, boss's orders, remember?"

Jessie kept her eyes on the buttons on his shirt, afraid to meet his gaze. Afraid of getting sidetracked at his mouth. The last time she'd been this dizzy was at last year's Cameron Veterinary Hospital Christmas party when she'd discovered—and liked—chocolate wine. "First of all, you aren't my boss." She hoped she sounded flip rather than stupid. "And if you were, wouldn't this be considered sexual harassment in the workplace?"

"Yes, it would. Too bad."

Another obstacle came to mind. "What about your girlfriend?"

"Girlfriend?"

"That evening I saw you at the races?"

"Oh. Gwen." He waved a dismissive hand. "She's just someone I spend time with on occasion. Nothing serious. I'll pick you up at seven." He placed a hand at the small of Jessie's back and escorted her from the office.

"Wait a minute." She turned to face him. "Where are you taking me?"

"Lorenzo's, Mount Washington, Pittsburgh."

She had a sneaking suspicion her mouth gaped open. He flashed a dimpled smile as he stepped back and shut his door.

ALL THE WAY BACK TO the clinic, Jessie chided herself for being a moron. How in the world had she gotten herself into this? Lorenzo's? Mount Washington? There was no way she could possibly fit into a place like that. She didn't have the wardrobe for it. And she sure as hell didn't have the sophistication for it. She should've flat out told Daniel *no*.

Katie was pacing in front of the clinic looking pale and worried when Jessie pulled in. "How is he?" the girl asked as Jessie slid down from the truck's cab.

Relieved to be back in her comfort zone, Jessie said, "The kitty has a broken hip. I can do surgery and fix him up."

"When?"

"Right now. Check back in a couple of hours. If he's coming out of the anesthesia by then, you can take him home."

Katie smiled and thanked her before jogging away.

Jessie found the tabby in the same spot where she'd left him, purring in his kennel. She gently scooped him up and carried him into the adjacent operating room.

The surgery consisted of performing a femoral head ostectomy to remove the broken bone fragment. She'd done many of them and this one went flawlessly. To finish, she created a perfect line of stitches across the cat's hip. Her handiwork would never be seen once the cat's fur grew back.

Five o'clock came and went with no Katie. At five thirty, with only an hour and a half until Daniel would be picking Jessie up, she decided to track down the freckled-faced girl. She made a quick trip to Barn M only to learn that Katie had come down sick and left early.

"Looks like you're going home with me," Jessie told the sleepy cat.

She crossed the hall to the storage room where she'd seen a plastic cat carrier. Somewhere. As she searched the shelves, her phone rang. Another emergency? She dug the device from her pocket thinking at least she'd have a good excuse to cancel her date. But the text was from Greg. *Stop at my apartment on your way home.*

Maybe he'd learned something about Doc's death. She located the cat carrier and transferred the tabby into it. Before leaving, she gathered an armload of Doc's folders from her office, as well as the notes and records she'd rescued from the floor following the brawl. Loaded down with paperwork and her patient, she climbed into her truck and headed for West Cumberland.

Since moving out of their house, Greg had taken up residence above a secondhand store. Jessie turned right at the only traffic light in town, pulled into the alley, and parked behind the building next to Greg's car. She assured the groggy tabby she wouldn't be long, climbed the steep stairs to his apartment, and knocked lightly.

When the door swung open, she expected to see six-foot-four dark-haired Greg. Instead, the person who stood there was barely five feet tall and very blonde.

"Vanessa?"

Her receptionist's eyes widened. "Dr. Cameron. I—I—didn't think—"

Jessie struggled to process the scene in front of her. Everything about it was familiar. But the pieces didn't fit. What was her ditzy receptionist doing in her husband's apartment?

Vanessa turned away from Jessie. "Greg! Dr. Cameron's here."

A door squeaked elsewhere in the apartment. Greg appeared from around the corner dressed only in a brown towel wrapped around his hips. "Jess? I didn't expect you so soon."

With a thunk, the pieces fell into place. Vanessa's tardiness at work. Meryl's suspicions about a new boyfriend.

Meryl's fury at Vanessa last night.

"Oh, my God." Jessie averted her eyes from her half naked soon-to-be-ex-husband. "I'm an idiot."

Greg strode toward her. "You never head home from the track this early."

"I have a date."

He stopped. "A what?"

"A date." She looked up at him. Noticed his ripped abs. Turned away only to find herself looking into Vanessa's deer-in-headlights blue eyes.

"With whom?" Greg demanded.

"Daniel Shumway." Jessie immediately regretted it. Her social life was none of Greg's concern. "You texted me to stop here. Did you find out anything about Doc?"

Greg put his hands on his hips and must have only then remembered his current state of undress. He clutched at the towel. "No. This isn't about Doc. Excuse me while I go put on some pants."

"Please." Jessie fixed her gaze on a spider crawling across the stair's railing. Anything to avoid looking at Greg. Or Vanessa.

He disappeared into the back room. "Come on in."

Jessie stepped around Vanessa into a small but neat kitchen. The aroma of fresh coffee permeated the apartment.

Peanut rose from his bed on a rug in the living room and, tail wagging, galloped to Jessie.

Relieved to have something safe to focus her attention on, she dropped to her knees. "Hey, there, old boy." She threw her arms around the dog who greeted her as if it had been a year since he'd seen her instead of a day.

"Coffee?" Vanessa asked, her childlike voice even softer than usual.

"No, thanks. I'm kind of in a hurry." Jessie gave the dog's ears a final scratch before standing. Peanut ambled back to his rug and flopped down.

With the dog out of the way, Jessie and Vanessa stood alone and silent, awkwardly avoiding each other until Greg returned, zipping up his jeans.

Jessie cleared her throat. "What did you want?"

He reached toward Vanessa, who moved to his side and wrapped her arms around his waist. "For starters, I wanted to tell you about us."

"Okay. I got that. Can I go now?"

"We're living together," Vanessa added with a shy smile.

Jessie suddenly remembered the restaurant in West Cumberland. "What happened to the redhead?" she asked, making no attempt to hide her contempt.

Vanessa's smile faded. She looked up at Greg. "What redhead?"

His face blazed as he gave Jessie a look he usually reserved for hardened criminals. "That was a long time ago."

"Not *that* long."

She could tell he wanted to say more to her, but instead he looked down at the petite blonde, his eyes softening. "It was one date. She meant nothing to me."

Vanessa considered his words for a mere moment before forgiving him with a smile. She snuggled in closer. "Go ahead," she said. "Ask her."

Jessie eyed the pair in disbelief. Clearly, Greg had brainwashed Vanessa.

He brought his attention back to Jessie. "The other thing I've wanted to talk to you about..." For a moment the big, tough state trooper struggled to gather his nerve. "It's about our divorce settlement. We want the house."

The room started spinning.

"This apartment is too small for both of us and Peanut. He needs room to run."

"You can't be serious." Jessie reached for one of the kitchen chairs. Maybe it wasn't the room that was spinning. Maybe it was her head. Whatever it was, she wanted it to stop.

"Yeah, I'm serious."

"Our lawyer said we have as much right to that house as you do," Vanessa said. He gave her shoulder a squeeze and made a shushing sound, shaking his head at her.

Our lawyer? "Why don't you just get your own house? Why mine?"

"That house is huge, too big for one person," Greg said. "I always dreamed of starting a family there. And you're never home."

"A family?" Jessie pointed at Vanessa's tiny waist. "Are you...?" The word refused to pass her lips.

Greg filled in the blank. "Pregnant? No. Not yet anyway."

Jessie clung to the chair, willing the screaming pain in her head to shut up. "There is no way in hell I'm giving you two my house. I bought it. I paid to restore it. Hell, I did most of the restoration myself. And what about poor old Molly? She'd have a terrible time adjusting to a move."

Greg's gaze didn't waver. "I thought about that. We want you to leave her there. We'll take care of her. She'll be happy to have Peanut to harass again. And she'll get more attention from Vanessa than she does from you."

Vanessa beamed. "You know how I love cats. And they love me."

Jessie glared at the blonde. "I suppose you want to take over Cameron Veterinary Hospital too."

"Oh, no. Don't be silly," Vanessa said. "I'm not a vet."

Jessie's knuckles turned white as she gripped the chair's back. It wasn't the room or her head that was spinning. It was her life spiraling out of control.

"There is no way I'm giving you my house and *no* way you're getting Molly."

Greg pulled away from Vanessa and took a step toward her, extending a hand. "Jess—"

"No." She backed away from him. "It's not going to happen. Not in my lifetime." As she turned toward the door, she spotted the look of shock in Vanessa's eyes. Struggling to catch her breath, Jessie staggered out of the apartment.

Twelve

"I should've told you as soon as I found out." Meryl rocked back in her office chair. "But I was too damned pissed and too damned close to wringing that little bitch's skinny neck."

"Don't hold back." Sarcasm was as close to humor as Jessie could muster. "Tell me how you really feel." She checked the clock on the wall. Six fifteen. All she wanted to do was curl up on the floor, pour out her day to Meryl, and then listen as her business partner cussed out everyone from Greg and Vanessa to Sherry and Emerick. But there wasn't time for that. Dogs barked from the waiting room, reminding her that Meryl had patients to deal with. Jessie tapped the plastic cat carrier she'd placed on the desk. "Mind if I leave this little guy with you?"

"As a matter of fact, yes, I do."

Startled by the response, Jessie flinched. "Why?"

Meryl rubbed her eyes. "I just managed to clear out post-op. If you leave him here, he's going to spend the night alone in a cage. Take him down to the house with you."

Jessie looked at the small face watching her through the wire door. With his pupils still dilated, the kitten reminded her of one of those seal pups with the big eyes. "I have a date."

Meryl fixed Jessie with an incredulous stare. "You *what*?"

Jessie didn't bother to repeat the news.

"With whom?"

"Daniel."

"When?"

"Seven o'clock."

Meryl did a quick check of the clock. "Tonight?"

"Uh-huh."

"Then what the hell are you doing here?" She jumped to her feet and stuck the cat carrier in Jessie's hand. "Go get changed."

"I'm thinking about cancelling."

"You'll do no such thing. Daniel Shumway is taking you on a date. Daniel. Shumway. The hottest guy in the tri-state area."

Meryl was right, but the pressure only reinforced her nerves. "That's it. I'm definitely cancelling."

"You are not. But if you keep hanging around, it'll be a moot point." Meryl gave her a nudge. "Where's he taking you?"

"Lorenzo's. On Mount Washington."

"What are you going to wear?"

"I have no idea."

Meryl stopped, her hand resting on the office doorknob. "Jessie, do you even own any makeup?"

"Depends. Does that stuff have an expiration date?"

Meryl rolled her eyes. "Wait here." She backtracked to her desk and tugged her purse from the bottom drawer. After raking through it, she returned to Jessie and pressed several plastic tubes and compacts into her hand. "Wear that brown sarong thing. Now go."

As Jessie lugged the cat carrier through the crowded waiting room, Meryl's voice trailed after her. "I want a full report in the morning."

DRESSING UP AND ACTING sophisticated wasn't exactly Jessie's forte. All her life, she'd been happier in a barn mucking stalls than at a party or fancy dinner. Why had she agreed to this?

With a stack of Doc's files tucked under one arm and the cat carrier with the tabby in her other hand, Jessie crossed the enclosed porch. Molly greeted her inside the kitchen. When Jessie set the cat carrier down in front of her, the old cat sniffed its occupant only briefly before returning her attention to Jessie. Molly was so accustomed to the smell of the vet hospital that a post-op patient didn't draw so much as a hiss from her.

"You're a good little nurse cat, aren't you, sweetie?" Jessie cooed as she rubbed Molly's ears.

The kitten was only interested in sleeping off his hangover, and Molly was only interested in a fresh bowl of food. Jessie left them in the dining room, contented and alone.

After a glance at the mantle clock, she grabbed the bundle of folders and took the stairs two at a time.

Lorenzo's.

She had never been there but knew of the place. Anyone within a two-hundred-mile radius of Pittsburgh had no doubt heard of Lorenzo's. Famous for fine food and outrageous prices, Lorenzo's had played host to four presidents as well as Prince William during his last visit. And now Daniel Shumway—handsome, debonair Daniel Shumway—was taking her there.

In less than forty minutes.

She dumped Doc's records on the desk in her home office, stripped out of her t-shirt and jeans, and scurried into the bathroom wearing only her robe. Adjusting the water temperature to comfortably lukewarm, she stepped into the claw-foot tub. The water pelted her head, shoulders and back as sweat and dust mingled with soap and trickled down the drain. Propping one foot at a time on the rounded edge of the tub, she carefully shaved her legs. But not carefully enough. She soon drew blood. How was it that she performed flawless surgical procedures on all manner of animals, but couldn't shave her own legs without nicks?

There was no time to do anything with her incorrigible curly hair. She picked out most of the knots, wishing she'd pilfered some mane and tail conditioner from the track. At fifteen minutes to seven, she retreated to the bedroom.

Maybe Daniel would be late.

Maybe Daniel would stand her up.

The idea cheered her.

Having finished her dinner, Molly stretched out across Jessie's bed, settling in for the main attraction.

In desperation, Jessie stared into her open closet at the dismal selection of dresses hanging on the rod. All had been purchased years ago for some special occasion or other. Heeding Meryl's suggestion, she pulled a slinky sarong-style dress from the back of the closet and studied it. Moderately low cut, sleeveless with a long skirt that was slit well up the thigh, this dress, she decided, seemed to be the least objectionable of what she currently owned.

Shoes created an even bigger dilemma. Had she been searching for work boots or sneakers, there would have been a wide selection. But none of the boxes she opened contained anything that looked appropriate. From the very back of the closet, Jessie pulled a battered old shoebox covered in a layer of dust. She flipped the lid off and found a pair of beige high-heeled, open-toed shoes she'd last worn when she dated Greg in college. They had to be at least fifteen years old, but they would have to do.

Jessie turned from the closet with her old dress and her even older shoes in hand and noticed Molly watching her with an amused expression on her black and white face.

"Don't look at me like that, little Miss Molly. We can't all be naturally beautiful like you."

The cat yawned and rolled over on her back.

Bright red numbers on the bedside clock revealed it was 6:51 when Jessie sorted through the stuff Meryl had pushed on her. Years of surgical training may have paid off in steady hands under pressure, but her eyelids twitched. Mascara soon coated skin as well as lashes.

Dabbing with a tissue only spread the smudge. Jessie stared at the raccoon eyes looking back from the mirror and couldn't decide whether to scream or weep. With the aid of some Q-Tips and a reapplication of liner and mascara, she appraised her reflection. *Good enough.*

Her hair was another matter. She finally pulled it up in a twist and stuck in some tortoise-shell combs, hoping they would hold.

At five minutes after seven, she teetered down the steps in her high heels buoyed by the increasing likelihood he wasn't going to show. Molly raced downstairs, nearly tripping her. Jessie clutched the banister. She wanted an excuse to get out of the date but not due to a broken leg or neck.

The tabby with the shaved hip had begun to show interest in his new surroundings and plinked at the pet carrier's wire door with his claws.

Jessie kneeled and peered in at him. "Sorry, little one. You're confined to quarters for the night." He might think he was up to some exploring, but she didn't want to return home to find he'd fallen down the stairs or off a chair. He might be unhappy in his crate, but he would be safe.

The muffled crunch of rubber on gravel signaled a vehicle was making its way up the lane. Jessie tottered to the kitchen and peered out the window as Daniel climbed out of a vintage Corvette.

A Corvette? Lorenzo's? Makeup and a dress? Why couldn't she simply dive back into dating by having a casual lunch at the diner in West Cumberland? She shook her arms trying to release the tension in her shoulders. Drawing a breath of courage, she crossed the enclosed porch and opened the door just as Daniel lifted his hand to knock.

"Oh," he said, momentarily startled. Then he lowered his arm and let his gaze slide down to her feet and back up again. "Wow. You look great."

"Thank you." Judging by the heat in her cheeks, she must be five shades of crimson. "You look pretty good yourself." His usually tousled sun-bleached hair was styled to perfection, and in a black suit, white dress shirt, and rich red tie, he looked more elegant than any man she'd ever seen, except maybe in movies. Maybe even including the movies.

"May I come in?"

She realized she'd been staring. "Sorry. Yes, please." She stepped aside and let him enter, then closed the door. The darned thing came open when she tested it and forced her to slam it to get the latch to hold.

Daniel cast a quizzical look at her.

"I need to get someone out here to fix that." Jessie slipped past him and led the way through the kitchen into the dining room.

He surveyed the space. "Nice. I remember this house before you and Greg bought it. It was a shame to see it falling apart. You've done a hell of a job restoring it."

A flush of pride warmed her face. "Thanks."

He spotted the plastic crate on the floor. "What do we have here?" He dropped to one knee in front of the box.

"The little guy got stepped on by one of the horses. I had to do surgery, so he's spending the night here."

Daniel scratched the tabby's chin through the wire and grinned up at Jessie. "Just tonight?"

She knew what he was getting at. "That's the plan. But he'll need some special attention until he heals."

Molly announced her presence with an earsplitting meow.

"Well, hello." Daniel turned toward the black and white cat and reached out to stroke her head.

"She's deaf," Jessie said.

"She's loud," he replied.

"She has to talk loud enough that she can hear herself. That's Molly, by the way."

Daniel stood and turned to face her. "We should be going. We have reservations for eight o'clock. But a few ground rules first."

"Ground rules?"

"No phones."

"*What?*"

"And no shop talk. We're not going to discuss anything that's going on at the track including what happened to Doc."

"It could prove to be a very quiet night. But okay."

Daniel rubbed his palms together. "Ready?"

No, she thought. "Let me grab my purse." She crossed the room to pick up her handbag from one of the dining room chairs and cringed. The ragged black fabric sack didn't match her dress or her shoes or anything remotely involved with Lorenzo's. With no alternative, she hid the bag behind her as she turned to him. "Let's go."

She followed him out and slammed the back door twice before it latched. Then she double-checked to make sure it was locked before wobbling up the path behind him.

BY THE TIME PITTSBURGH traffic forced Daniel's speed into the reasonable category and the narrow, but aptly named, Grandview Avenue brought the Corvette's forward progress to little more than a crawl, Jessie's fingernails had pressed grooves into the black leather passenger seat. She peeked at the speedometer once during the trip and decided to keep her eyes closed for most of the drive.

Below them, at the bottom of Mount Washington, the Monongahela and Allegheny Rivers merged, giving birth to the Ohio. At their confluence, the fountain in Point State Park formed the centerpiece of the city. From their vantage point high above downtown, Pittsburgh looked like a child's elaborate toy village.

"Wow," Jessie said as she took in the view.

"Haven't you been up here before?"

"Once a long time ago. I'd forgotten how beautiful it was."

Jessie's view vanished behind Lorenzo's stone and cedar façade. A young man in black pants and vest and white shirt opened the car door for her.

"Wait." Daniel stopped her with a hand on her wrist. "Hand over your phone."

"You're serious?"

"Absolutely." He held up his own as proof. "If we leave them in the car, we can't break the 'no phone' pledge."

With a sigh, she dug hers from her purse. He reached in front of her, opened the glovebox, and deposited his inside. She did likewise.

"Good," he said.

She stepped out into the evening air, which had begun to redevelop a sultry tinge. The valet headed to the driver's side. Daniel accepted a claim ticket from the young man before rounding the car and placing a hand at the small of Jessie's back.

"Shall we?"

Jessie braced herself. Tucking her ugly black purse under her arm, she let Daniel guide her through the elaborately carved mahogany front doors.

She stifled a gasp. High-backed gold upholstered chairs surrounded square tables draped in white linen and set with sparkling silverware. Crystal goblets embraced perfectly folded linen napkins. Two walls of floor-to-ceiling windows overlooked Pittsburgh and the Point. Crystalline chandeliers hung from the ceiling. Jessie tried unsuccessfully not to gawk.

"Mr. Shumway, how divine to see you again." A tuxedoed maitre d' greeted them.

"Mario." Daniel tipped his head in polite acknowledgement.

"And your dinner companion is lovely this evening." The maitre d' nodded in Jessie's direction.

"Indeed, she is." Daniel smiled at her.

Her cheeks warmed again. She wondered if he was simply saying whatever Daniel wanted to hear.

"Your table is ready," Mario announced after Daniel formally introduced them. "If you'll follow me..." He ushered them to a table in front of the bank of windows with what had to be the best view in the house. Mario assisted her with her chair, then handed her a menu, which contained no prices.

Once they were settled, and Mario left them to attend to his duties, Daniel leaned across the table toward her. "What do you think?"

She tried to take everything in with only moderate success. Aromatic fragrances of roast meat and poultry, butter, onions, and garlic drifted on the air currents of the room. A small band made up of a pianist, a bass player, a violinist, and a drummer played Rodgers and Hart while elegantly attired couples swayed in each other's arms on the parquet dance floor. "Wow." Embarrassed, she laughed softly. "I'm really good with the English language, huh? Honestly, I do know other words."

"No. 'Wow' is a pretty good word for the place. And you haven't even had their food yet." Daniel picked up his menu. "What are you hungry for?"

She opened hers and scanned the options. Lorenzo's Delmonico, Lamb Shank, Seared Scallops in Champagne-Saffron Sauce, Citrus Roasted Duck...

"I could make some suggestions if you like."

"That's all right." She located Mushroom Risotto at the bottom of the page. "My choices are usually slim, but I see something that may work."

Daniel tapped the side of his head. "I forgot about you being vegetarian. I'm sure Lorenzo could make something special for you."

The idea of *the* Lorenzo whipping up a dish just for her brought a smile. "Thanks, but no."

"It won't be a problem. Really." Daniel raised a hand to summon a waiter.

Jessie reached across the table and caught his arm. "No." Amusing as the idea had been, the last thing she wanted was to draw attention to herself, her old dress, or anything else. "Please."

She hoped the expression on Daniel's face was one of puzzlement rather than pity. "All right." He lowered his hand.

Jessie released his arm, but not before poking at it. "Don't forget, I'm used to making a meal out of nachos and french fries because of limited menu choices. Mushrooms and rice sound like a delicacy to me."

Daniel was still laughing when their waiter arrived.

THE RISOTTO PROVED to be the ideal choice. Creamy, savory, and seasoned to perfection. Jessie briefly contemplated licking the plate clean.

Within the boundaries of the "no shop talk" rule, conversation with Daniel felt easy and relaxed. But conversation was the only thing that felt that way. She stole glances at the other women in the restaurant and marveled at their chic apparel. Everyone must be discreetly pointing at her and wondering what homeless shelter Daniel had rescued her from.

"The staff all seem to know you," she commented as they waited for dessert. "How often do you come here?"

"Not all that frequently." He winked at her. "I just tip well."

"I see," she said with a laugh.

Her gaze swept the room again. She'd always known he wasn't poor, but after seeing his choice of vehicle, restaurant, and custom-tailored suit, she began to wonder how well-off he really was. She'd never considered herself destitute, despite her shabby wardrobe, but a chasm the size of Texas divided their two worlds.

"Hello?"

Jessie realized Daniel had been talking to her. "I'm sorry. What did you say?"

He chuckled. "I asked how long you'd had Molly. Your cat?"

"Oh. Since she was a kitten. Her mother had been hit on the road and someone brought the litter to Doc. He found homes for all but Molly. I kept her and took her with me to Columbus when I went to college." The memory of the tiny puff of fur was sweet, but Daniel's question also stirred one of her own.

He must've noticed the change in her expression. "What's wrong?"

She rubbed the ache between her eyes. "It's Greg. I found out today that he and my receptionist from my veterinary hospital are living together."

Daniel froze, his coffee cup midway to his lips. Slowly, he returned it to its saucer. "Oh."

"And that's not the best part. They told me they want my house. And Molly."

He stared at her. "You can't be serious."

A picture of Jessie's future life flashed across the movie screen of her mind. Sleeping on a cot in the hospital's office. No. That was too close to the house Greg and Vanessa planned to share. The location changed to a generic apartment, a generic bed, and no Molly, no Peanut, no husband. No stability. She'd lived that life once, sharing furnished apartments and motel rooms with her footloose parents and younger brother. Never having anything to hold onto. Nothing to anchor her.

She'd be damned if she'd go back to that.

Something brushed the back of her hand. She flinched before realizing it was Daniel. He pulled back. "I'm sorry."

She wasn't sure if he was expressing sympathy for her marital situation or apologizing for touching her. Either way, it didn't matter. She shook her head. "That's okay." She met his troubled eyes and forced a smile. "It's not been a good day." As the understatement escaped her lips, the rush of tears took her by surprise. "I'm sorry," she said, choking. The chair almost tipped over in her haste to rise. Catching it, she spun and bolted to the restroom.

It was empty, much to her relief. She barely noticed the white marble and brass décor, the crystal light fixtures, and the gleaming exotic hardwood stalls. Instead, her focus was on deep breathing. She would not cry. Not here. Not with Daniel waiting at their table, wondering if she'd lost her senses. And definitely not because of one more insult laid upon her by Greg Cameron.

And Vanessa? Photographic memory for names and phone numbers or not, Jessie should have let Meryl fire her like she'd wanted to.

The thought of siccing Meryl on Vanessa brightened Jessie's mood. The thought of doing the firing herself brightened it more. If Vanessa believed for one minute she was going to walk to work at Jessie's vet hospital from Jessie's house, she was sorely mistaken.

Braced by the resolve to throw as big a monkey wrench into Greg and Vanessa's plans as possible, Jessie decided to enjoy the rest of her evening with Daniel even if it killed her.

She snatched several tissues from an abalone box on the marble counter and risked a look in the mirror. Not as bad as she'd feared. She pressed the tissues to the corners of her eyes then to her nose.

The door swung open. An elegant woman in a cream dress that perfectly matched the color of her hair entered. She cast a curious glance at Jessie before averting her eyes and going about her business.

Jessie took a deep breath and tossed the tissues. She charged through the door.

And slammed into Daniel.

He caught her shoulders to steady her. "I paid the check." He held out her purse, which she'd left hanging on the back of her chair. "Let's go home."

JESSIE RESTED HER FOREHEAD against the cool glass of the passenger side window and watched as the lights of houses and businesses sliced bright streaks through the darkness on the quiet drive home. She didn't dare risk a glance at Daniel's solemn profile, afraid to catch a glimpse of the disappointment she knew would be there.

Daniel made the left turn into her lane and gunned the Corvette up the hill and around to the back of the house. The hospital was dark and the parking area empty.

He cut the ignition. Steeling herself, she turned toward him.

His smile didn't reach his eyes. "Here we are."

She forced a smile back at him.

He opened his door. Not waiting for him to come around to her side, she climbed out and met him at the front of the car. He slipped an arm around her waist. If she hadn't let Greg ruin the evening, she imagined she'd have enjoyed the closeness as he walked with her down the path to the back door.

"I had a good time tonight." She hoped she sounded more convincing than she felt.

"Did you?" His voice was edged with sadness.

"Yeah, I did. Thank you."

He placed a hand high on the doorframe, leaned into it, and studied her face. "I hope so. I thought you deserved a nice evening. I'm not sure I showed you one."

"It was great. I'm just...not accustomed to places like that." She stared at her toes peeping out of her old shoes.

He leaned closer to her. "That's a shame. You belong in places like that. They suit you."

Warmth tingled her cheeks and told her she must be glowing in the dark.

Daniel's face moved closer, and she lifted hers. His lips caressed the corner of her mouth as soft as a whisper. "Good night." He turned and headed back to the Corvette.

She watched his back as he went, the broad shoulders and the narrow hips in the exquisite black suit. He disappeared into the car's interior, and the sound of the revving engine floated down to her.

Jessie fumbled in her purse for her keys. Damn it. Dinner at Lorenzo's with just about the nicest, most attractive guy she'd ever met and she'd blown it.

Her fingers touched metal, but it was her nail file. Then she found the jumble of keys and pulled them out, locating the one for the house. As she brought it up to the lock, the door drifted open.

Thirteen

H ad Jessie left the door open? No. She remembered checking to make sure it'd caught. She remembered locking it. She closed her fingers around the doorknob. It turned easily in her hand. The clammy sweat from the night's humidity turned cold.

She wheeled in time to see the Corvette's taillights disappear at the end of her lane. Daniel wasn't coming to her rescue.

She dug in her purse for her phone but found nothing. With a groan, she realized she'd been so distraught when they left the restaurant, she'd neglected to check her phone and subsequently never reclaimed it from the glovebox.

She muttered a few choice words, turned back toward the house, and stepped inside.

Jessie didn't think something was wrong. She *knew* it. The air conditioner rumbled, but the air inside the house felt as sultry as outside. A sensible person would get out. Call the police.

But the cats. She couldn't abandon Molly and the kitten.

Jessie flicked on the kitchen light and turned the corner. The illumination cut a swatch into the dining room, falling across the pet carrier, its door wide open, the interior empty. What the hell? She reached around the doorframe to hit the next switch.

The antique brass chandelier lit the dining room where the sideboard and buffet doors and drawers hung open, their contents strewn across the floor. Tablecloths, silverware, packages of paper plates and napkins had been scattered. Her stoneware plates and bowls smashed.

She spotted her cordless landline phone resting on the fireplace mantel and crossed to it. But when she punched 911 and hit send, only dead air hissed in her ear. She swore and winged it onto her upholstered reading chair.

If she had any sense, she'd run. Jog up the hill to the hospital and call for help from there.

Her gaze returned to the empty pet carrier, followed the light that feathered into the living room, and stuck on the reason the house felt so oppressive. The front window had been shattered. A small cedar table from the front porch lay in the center of the room among the shards of glass and wood.

Molly.

Where was the kitten? Where was Molly? Had the intruder harmed her cats? The idea was more hideous than Jessie could handle. No way could she leave without finding them.

"Molly," she cried out and immediately chastised herself. The old cat was deaf. But Jessie didn't know what else to do. "Molly!" she called again.

Except for the sound of the forced air battling to cool the house, only silence responded.

The know-how she'd gained from being married to a cop went out the window with the cool air. Unsteady in her high heels, she half ran, half stumbled into the living room and slammed on the light switch with no concern for fingerprints.

The entertainment center, disguised as an armoire, was open. The TV had been toppled onto the imitation Oriental carpet, its screen shattered. The DVD player and stereo system also lay in fragments. The shelf containing her DVDs and CDs had been stripped bare.

The lace curtains framing the broken window fluttered in the night breeze. Had Molly escaped? She hadn't been outdoors in years.

A coyote or other wild animal could grab her. At the very least, the poor old dear would be terrified.

"Molly!"

Jessie teetered through the house, from room to room, flipping on lights as she went. She had yet to renovate the remainder of the empty downstairs rooms, leaving nothing to trash and nowhere for a cat to hide. She started up the steps. Her heart pounded harder than if she were running a marathon.

Halfway to the top, the acrid smell of smoke touched her nostrils. She took the rest of the stairs two at a time, high heels and all. The stench grew more pungent, but no gray haze hung in the air. She tripped into her home office and slapped the switch with her hand. Light flooded the room.

Her home laptop was missing from her desk. Her printer and router lay shattered on the floor. She let out a soft wail. A plume of smoke rose up the chimney from the fireplace where the blackened remains of a stack of files smoldered. She closed the distance between the door and the remnants of the fire in three long strides and yanked out the folders, beating the still-smoking embers with the palm of her hand. She sifted through the papers—Doc's files that she had been entering into her computer. Some of the records appeared salvageable. Most were little more than char.

But in the midst of the violation of her home, the only things that mattered were Molly and the kitten.

Jessie dumped the blackened files onto the hearth and picked her way through the ruins of her printer.

She rounded the corner to her bedroom, which appeared unscathed, but she had an eerie sense that someone had gone through her things. She dropped to her knees and peered under the bed. "Molly?"

Nothing. No black and white longhaired tuxedo-marked fat cat. No small drug-addled orange and white tabby.

Frantic, she checked the rest of the rooms. The bathroom, Greg's old office, the guest room. All seemed intact. She peered under the guest bed and behind bureaus and desks and dressers. Anywhere that Molly had ever claimed as a hiding spot. Nothing.

As Jessie clumped down the stairs, none of her surgeon's training helped. Her hands trembled. She couldn't fill her lungs. After another sweep through the first floor, she wasn't sure which scared her more—the idea of never finding the cats at all or finding them in some condition she couldn't accept.

Jessie unlocked the heavy front door, which no one ever used, and stepped out onto the porch. The lawn sloped down through a thick growth of ancient pines to the road. If Molly had escaped and was out there, Jessie didn't have a clue where to start searching. She cupped her hands around her mouth and called, "Molly!"

Nothing but the chirp of spring peepers answered. What about the little guy? That little tabby. He had no name, but he could hear. Would he respond?

"Here, kitty, kitty, kitty," she called into the night.

Nothing. Of course not. He didn't know her or this place. He was terrified. Hiding.

Jessie went back into the house and closed the door behind her. She staggered to the stairs and collapsed on the second step. With trembling fingers, she unbuckled the ankle straps and peeled off the old high-heeled shoes. Then she cradled her face in her sooty hands and surrendered to the flood of tears.

Scritch, scritch, scritch.

Jessie lifted her head.

Scritch, scritch.

Swallowing her tears, she tilted her head to listen. What the hell was that? And where was it coming from?

She climbed to her feet and tiptoed up the steps, listening for the sound. But it stopped. At the top of the stairs, she paused. Waited.

Scritch, scritch, scritch, scritch, scritch.

It was coming from her office. She went to the doorway and surveyed the rubble.

Scritch.

The sound—could it be?—came from behind the closed closet door next to the fireplace. She charged across the room, ignoring the pain as her bare foot came down on something sharp, and flung open the door.

Molly and the tabby blinked as the light fell upon them. Jessie dropped to her knees. Molly let loose with one of her high-decibel meows. Jessie translated it as, *what took you so long?*

Laughter bubbled in her throat as she scooped up the old cat and held the small warm body tight, burying her nose in the silky fur. The tabby, still shaky on his feet, wobbled out. Jessie pulled him close against her thigh, rubbing his ear.

Molly gave Jessie's chin a head-butt, and a purr nearly as loud as her meow echoed through the room. It was the most beautiful sound Jessie had ever heard.

Immense relief soon gave way to intense anger. Who the hell had done this? Vanessa came to mind. Vanessa wanted her out of the house, and what better way to accomplish it than to scare her out?

Logic told Jessie the idea was preposterous. Sweet, waiflike Vanessa was incapable of such vandalism. But the alternative meant some unknown intruder had been in Jessie's house, trashing her things, messing with her cats. Setting fire to Doc's files. The notion of the break-in being related to his death started to raise the hair on the back of her neck, but she shook it off.

Blaming Vanessa felt so much easier to accept.

There was a gaping hole in the front of Jessie's house, courtesy of the shattered window. She'd already imagined the cats escaping into the night. No way was she about to let it actually happen. She packed some clothes in a bag and both cats in the carrier. Wearing work boots with her sooty dress, she loaded everything into the Chevy and got the hell out of there.

LIGHT SEEPED AROUND the curtain covering Greg's apartment window. Jessie stood on the stoop at the top of the steps and pounded on the door.

Greg jerked it open. "What the...?" He gaped at her. "Jess?"

She pushed past him into the kitchen. "Where's Vanessa?"

He closed the door behind her. "She's out with some girlfriends. What's going on? Why...?" He waved a hand up and down at her, indicating her attire or condition or both.

Jessie collapsed into one of the retro chic vinyl and chrome chairs. "Someone broke into my house."

"*What*?" He sank into the chair across from her.

Exhaustion closed in. She braced her elbows on the table and told him about her evening.

When she fell silent, he leaned back in his chair and crossed his arms. "Did you call 911?"

"No. I'm reporting it to you. I've got the cats in the truck and I'm going to stay at my office at the track for a few nights."

"Any idea who might have done this?"

Jessie tried to meet his gaze and failed. "I was thinking Vanessa."

He shot forward and slammed his palms on the table. "Come on, Jess."

"She wants me out of the house. Well, I'm out. But I'm telling you here and now, it's only temporary."

"There is no way Vanessa would break into our house and bust it up."

The "*our* house" comment didn't escape Jessie's notice. But did he mean "our" as in his and Jessie's? Or "our" as in his and Vanessa's?

"She's not here, is she? Besides, she could've hired someone else to do the dirty work."

"You've gone over the edge on this one."

She knew he was right but wasn't about to admit it. Maybe tomorrow in the rational light of day, but not tonight when her nerves were raw.

"Did you ever think that maybe this has something to do with you accusing everyone at the track of murder?"

She had, but denial was so much safer. "Explain to me why a murderer would put the cats in my closet."

"Why would Vanessa?"

"To freak me out, which is exactly what happened. And besides, you keep telling me there is no murderer."

"I don't think there is, but you're making accusations and getting people fired up. Sounds like a good way to make enemies."

She hated it when he made sense. "Look, I just wanted you to know what happened and where I'll be." She stood up. "You'd better get over to the house tonight and board up that window. I don't want any wild critters moving in. Vanessa probably wouldn't like that either."

He opened his mouth to continue the argument, but then clamped it shut. After a few moments of glaring at each other, he said, "We should go through the place together to determine if anything's missing."

Jessie headed for the door. "I can already tell you my laptop's gone."

"Okay, that's a start. I'll nail up some plywood tonight and see what I find. How about you meet me there sometime tomorrow?"

"Fine. My morning is booked, but I have time after lunch."

He rose and opened the door for her. "Are you gonna be okay at the track? Where will you sleep?"

"I've got the sofa in the office, and there's a small bathroom with a shower." She failed to mention its grungy condition.

Greg gripped her shoulders. "Be careful, okay? Call me if you need anything."

There he was, warning her to be careful again. "There is one thing you can do for me."

"What's that?"

"Tell Vanessa she's fired." Jessie jerked free of his grasp and stepped out into the night.

AT SEVEN THE NEXT MORNING, Jessie returned from an emergency coffee run to find Molly grooming herself in the middle of the desk. Next to the cat, Jessie's phone sat on a folded sheet of paper. She picked up the note and recognized Daniel's letterhead as well as his blocky printing.

You left this in my car. I thought you might need it.

No kidding. She pocketed the phone and crumpled the note.

The tabby curled into a feline doughnut on the blanket under which Jessie had slept on the sofa. At about three in the morning, she'd decided to replace the too-short tattered sofa with a new futon the first chance she got, whether she took over the practice or not.

She set the coffee down and flopped into her chair. Molly greeted her loudly while offering her head to be scratched. When the door swung open unexpectedly, Jessie jumped.

Milt swaggered in. "Good morning, darlin'." He froze in mid-stride and pointed at the cat on the desk. "Who's this?"

Jessie took a slow, deep breath to settle her jangled nerves. "This is Molly. And close the door, please."

He obliged, and then glanced around the office. His gaze settled on the blanket and pillow on the sofa and the sleeping tabby. "What's going on?"

Jessie ran her hands through her matted hair. "Someone broke into my house last night."

"Good lord. Were you home when it happened?"

"No." The thought of being there to encounter the vandals sent a chill along her spine. "I was out."

Milt pushed the blanket aside. The tabby stirred briefly. "Are you all right?" he asked as he took a seat.

"I'm fine, but they broke my front window. Greg's supposed to put up some plywood to cover it. In the meantime, the cats and I have moved in here."

"Dang. I'm sorry to hear about that. I just came in to see how your big date went with the boss man. Everyone's buzzing about it."

Terrific. At least the horror of the break-in had distracted her from thinking about the horror of the date-gone-wrong. "I'd rather not talk about it."

"Really? What happened?"

"Didn't I just say I'd rather not talk about it? Nothing happened. Nothing at all. Then I came home, and my house was trashed." She thumbed the lid off the cup. "Perfect end to a perfect evening."

Milt studied her without saying anything for a moment. "I'm really sorry, Jessie. How long before you figure on moving back into your house?"

"I don't know. Depends on a lot of things." She hoped Greg would catch whoever had done it, and then she could feel safe in her home once again. But if he made no more progress in solving the break-in than he had solving Doc's murder, she might be out of her house for a very long time.

"You could always stay with me and Catherine."

She offered him as much of a smile as she could muster. "Thanks, Milt, but I'll be fine here."

"If you change your mind, the offer stands."

"I'll remember that."

"Did they take anything?"

Jessie sipped her coffee and let the medicinal effects of the caffeine spread throughout her body. "They destroyed my TV and some other electronics. But the only thing I know they stole for sure is my laptop."

Milt stroked the tabby, who stretched and purred. "Maybe they figured it was more portable."

"I guess." She thought of her other laptop. The one that had been smashed thanks to Frank Hamilton's visit. Her shopping list was getting longer. "Something else that's odd. They burned a stack of Doc's files I'd taken home with me."

Milt stopped petting the kitten and frowned. "Why would anybody do that?"

"I don't know." Jessie rested her head on the back of the chair. "I don't know why any of this is happening."

The door swung open again, and Greg in his State Trooper uniform strolled in, carrying a nylon duffel bag.

Milt climbed to his feet. "Well, darlin', I'd best be going. Remember what I said. My offer stands." Milt shook a finger at Jessie and then let himself out.

"What offer?" Greg asked.

"To let me stay with him and Catherine."

Greg set the bag on the desk next to Molly. "I've come to take your fingerprints. I need to determine which prints at the house belong there and which ones don't."

Jessie checked her watch. "Okay, but I've got to look at a horse in fifteen minutes."

He unclipped a pair of buckles and flipped the bag open. "No problem."

"Have you found anything?"

"I haven't had a chance to do a thorough investigation yet. I did a quick walk-through before boarding up the window. I'm headed back over there as soon as I finish up with this."

Jessie considered asking if he'd taken Vanessa's fingerprints but didn't feel up to the ensuing argument. Besides, as she'd expected, in the light of day, the petite blonde looked less and less like the culprit.

"What time do you think you can meet me?" Greg asked.

"About two?"

"Good." He inked each of her fingers and rolled them from one edge to the other against a card, which he labeled and tucked back into the box. After repeating the process on her other hand, he offered her a paper towel.

She scowled at the mess. More black gunk. She still had soot under her fingernails. "Why don't you have one of those scanner things to do this?"

"It's broken."

Just like her window. Their marriage. Her life.

Greg's head tilted toward the duffel, but his gaze rested on her face. "When did you and Shumway start seeing each other?"

"Last night. Started *and* finished. I blew it." She cringed. Why confess to Greg, of all people?

His gaze shifted back to the fingerprinting kit. "If that's true, Shumway's a fool." Greg packed his gear and closed the lid. "Are you okay?"

"I'm terrific," she said without conviction.

"Maybe you should take Milt up on his invitation."

She glowered at him. "Maybe you should find out who busted up my house."

He rubbed Molly's ears before picking up the duffel bag and heading for the door. "Two o'clock, then?"

"Yep."

He pulled the door shut behind him, and Jessie felt the emptiness close in on her.

Fourteen

W alt McCutcheon, a stout red-haired man wearing a beat-up ballcap, stood outside Barn P when Jessie pulled up. The call was for a Coggins test, and when the trainer approached her truck before she had a chance to open the door, she hoped she was wrong about what was coming next.

"Dr. Cameron." He handed her a folded piece of paper through the open window. The old Coggins test with all the horse and owner's information. "I sure appreciate this. You'll put it on my bill, right?"

"Yes, sir." She kept a hand on the door handle, but he stood too close. She'd hit him if she tried to open it.

"All righty then. Thanks." McCutcheon slapped the truck and turned to leave.

Jessie seized the opportunity and opened the door. The trainer turned back to her, his face the picture of confusion. "Was there something else, Doctor?"

"I have to see the horse. Draw his blood."

"Oh." McCutcheon's eyes widened. "Oh. I just assumed...I'm sorry. Doc was always so busy. Of course. Right this way."

She tucked the pad of test forms under one arm, opened the compartment in the storage unit to retrieve the plastic bin containing empty Vacutainers and clean needles, and wondered. How could she dismiss Doc's laziness as a one-time occurrence now?

JESSIE SAT BEHIND THE wheel of the Chevy, jotting notes about a lame colt she'd just examined. He'd likely run his last race until fall at the earliest, but she had a difficult time concentrating on the paperwork.

Out of everything that had come to light about Doc in recent days, this Coggins test situation weighed heaviest on her mind. While her view of him as an honorable man had been sullied beyond repair, she'd still clung to the belief that he was a good vet who cared for the animals above all else.

Until now. Bypassing the legally required procedures for running a Coggins test potentially put all horses at risk. If EIA, the highly infectious disease the test screened for, managed to slip into the track's stables, carried by a horse with fraudulent papers, untold numbers of animals could be destroyed.

A loud metallic boom jarred her from her quandary. She lifted her head and saw Daniel standing next to her truck's front fender, his palm resting on the hood he'd just slapped, a dimpled grin on his tanned face. "Wake up."

"I am awake, thank you very much."

"I've been looking all over for you."

"That's where I've been. All over."

He moved to the door and rested his forearms on it. "I tried to call you earlier at your house but got no answer. Then I ran into Milt. He told me what happened." Daniel's expression turned grave. "I should've seen you in last night instead of just dumping you at the door."

"You didn't just dump me. I don't recall inviting you in."

"Oh, yeah." The dimples returned. "Are you sure you're okay?"

"I'm sure. But I hope you don't mind if I camp out here for a while until Greg gets this sorted out."

"Here? At the track?"

"In my office." She wondered if he noticed she didn't refer to it as *Doc's* office.

He gave no indication if he had. "I don't *mind*, but it can't be very comfortable. Why don't you stay at my house?"

Everyone wanted her to move in with them. "That's sweet, but I don't think it'd be a good idea." A warm breeze carried the smell of impending rain through the open window, and wisps of hair that had escaped her ball cap tickled her nose. She caught a strand and tucked it behind her ear. "Why were you trying to call me?"

"To tell you I had your cell phone for starters, but also, I wanted to thank you for last night."

Jessie shifted in the truck seat. "I'm surprised. I honestly didn't think you'd ever want to talk to me again."

"Why would you think that? I'm the one who messed things up."

"You?"

"I just wanted to show you a nice time. An evening out to enjoy yourself." He gave her a sad smile. "Major fail."

Before Jessie could argue, a skinny young fellow wearing a dirty plaid shirt and jeans with holes in the knees stepped in front of the truck and started toward it. When he spotted Daniel, the young man froze in midstride. He shoved his hands in his pockets and waited his turn.

Daniel eyed the guy for a moment then turned back to Jessie. "Have you come up with anything new about Doc's death?"

"I guess the ground rules from last night have expired."

"At the stroke of midnight."

Jessie thought about the Coggins tests. She started to tell him about them, but the words stuck in her throat. Doc's shortcuts were a result of laziness, not criminal intent. The horses involved had already tested negative and likely hadn't come in contact with the disease to change that. As long as Jessie didn't perpetuate the scam, once the bogus certificates expired, those horses would have to be properly re-tested. Provided Sherry didn't continue the practice.

"Hello?"

Jessie blinked. "Huh? Oh. Sorry."

"Where'd you go just now?"

"Thinking about Doc." It wasn't a lie.

"And? Anything new?"

"No."

"You don't sound too sure." Daniel shot another glance at the guy in plaid, who had done a one-eighty and now faced the other way.

Jessie set her notes from her last patient on the seat beside her. Obviously, this young man had another patient ready for her as soon as Daniel left. "I'm not sure about anything anymore. First there was this illegitimate daughter. Then there were the accusations of extortion and who knows what else. Am I crazy? I thought he was a good man. He was more of a dad to me than my own father. I thought he had a good marriage and only two kids." Heat rose behind her eyes. "Did that man ever exist? Or was he a figment of my imagination?"

Daniel reached into the cab and touched her arm. "You loved him."

She swiped a hand across her face to keep the rush of tears at bay.

"Did the man you thought you knew ever exist? He did for you. You looked up to him, cared for him, and admired him. Sometimes love clouds our judgment, and we only see the parts of a person we want to see. You saw the man you wanted Doc to be. Others saw him in a different light. Does that make you wrong?" Daniel shook his head. "I don't think so. I think it makes Doc damned lucky."

She smiled sadly. "Thanks."

Daniel inclined his head toward the young man who was now tapping one foot. "Someone's waiting to talk to you, but I have to ask you something while I've got you here."

She fumbled for a tissue in her jeans' pocket. "What is it?"

"Zelda Peterson contacted me. She wants the track stewards to lift the ban on Clown. What do you think?"

"It's not up to me."

"No, but if you don't want it to happen, I'll put a stop to it."

"Let her go to them. I'll be fine."

"Are you sure?"

"Clown was just the murder weapon. Not the murderer."

"Zelda will be happy to hear that." Daniel pushed away from the window. "And I really am sorry you didn't enjoy Lorenzo's last night."

Ill at ease, she shifted in her seat. "Last night was nice. It really was. I just felt—I don't know—out of place, I guess."

"Why? You looked great."

"I didn't feel like I looked great."

He didn't respond but waited for her to go on.

Jessie glanced at the guy now facing them again, arms folded in front of his chest, legs spread wide. "The thing is, I don't often have the opportunity to get all dressed up, so I wasn't prepared." She kept her voice low and raced through the confession. "I didn't have a nice new dress or shoes. I had to make do with what was in my closet, which wasn't much. I felt like a charity case."

"A charity case?" He snorted. "I thought you were beautiful. Still do."

The heat warming her eyes moved to her cheeks.

"Let me see if I've got this straight." He fixed her with a hard stare, but there was still a mischievous twinkle in his blue eyes. "The reason you were so uncomfortable last night was because you don't have any fancy clothes?"

She gave him a sheepish nod.

"Other than that, did you have a good time?"

"My dinner companion was nice."

"So if I were to ask you out again..."

The guy in the plaid shirt had taken a couple steps closer. Jessie opened the truck door and slid down from the seat. "If you were going to ask me out to someplace like Lorenzo's again, you'd better give me advance warning so I could go shopping."

"But if I did that, would you accept?"

She turned away from Daniel so he wouldn't see her grinning like a schoolgirl. "Maybe."

"Maybe, huh?" He caught her arm and drew her close to whisper in her ear. "Go shopping."

A PAINTING OF A LITTER of puppies stared down at Jessie as she propped her feet on her desk at the Cameron Veterinary Hospital. Meryl sat on the floor, her back against the wall, her long legs stretched out and crossed at the ankles. Scowling, she removed a slice of onion from the hoagie she was eating. "Next time you come bearing gifts of food, tell them to hold the onions, okay?"

"Picky, picky, picky," Jessie said around a mouthful of sandwich. "At least I made sure they didn't put any hot pepper rings on it."

Meryl grunted. "Are you gonna go out with him again?"

"I don't know." Jessie set her hoagie down on the waxed paper wrapping in her lap. "The worst part about getting a divorce is this dating business."

"What d'ya mean? Daniel Shumway is hot. He drives a fast car and takes you nice places. What's not to like?"

Jessie eyed her friend. "He wants me to stay on at the track permanently."

Meryl grunted. "There is that."

"And according to Sherry, he and Doc had a big argument right before Doc was killed."

"What about?"

Jessie opened the sandwich to rearrange the slices of tomato and pickles. "She didn't say, and I'm not about to ask Daniel."

"Why not? I would."

Jessie choked a laugh. "I know you would." She reassembled her hoagie and took a bite.

For several moments, the only sound in the office was soft munching and the crinkle of waxed paper. Meryl broke the silence. "What time are you supposed to meet Greg?"

Jessie glanced at the clock on the wall, which read 1:48. "Two o'clock."

"I'm coming with you."

Jessie stopped mid-chew. "Excuse me?"

"You heard me. I want to have a chat with Mr. Bad-Ass State Trooper."

"That's what worries me." Jessie swallowed. "Assaulting a police officer is frowned upon in legal circles."

"Screw him if he can't take a joke."

Jessie covered her mouth, glad she'd already swallowed. Otherwise, Meryl might be doing the Heimlich maneuver on her. "That's Vanessa's department these days."

Jessie had a feeling Meryl was gauging her sense of humor. Until recently, Jessie would spiral into a fit of despair and uncontrolled weeping at the mention of Greg's extracurricular activities. But she shot her friend a grin.

Meryl smiled back. "Better her than you."

"Amen." Maybe Jessie really had attained acceptance.

Someone knocked at the door. "Come in," Meryl called.

One of their receptionists, who was now pulling double duty since Vanessa's recent firing, poked her head in. "Dr. Cameron? Your—uh—Trooper Cameron is here."

Before Jessie could respond, Meryl flipped a dismissive hand at the bearer of bad news. "Tell him we're busy and we'll be there when we're good and ready."

The receptionist's gaze darted between the two of them. "Okay." She ducked out again.

Meryl insisted they weren't "good and ready" until five after two.

"Aren't your clients going to be mad that you're running late?" Jessie asked as they walked down the path to the backdoor of the farmhouse.

"I don't have anything scheduled until two thirty. I took a longer lunch break today since I've been working all these un-godly hours." Meryl tipped her head toward Jessie. "Which reminds me. When did you say you're coming back?"

"I wondered when you'd bring that up."

"Well?"

They'd reached the door. Jessie paused, her hand on the knob. "Meryl, I really like it there."

"Oh, no, you don't."

"Look, if what Sherry says is true, she's going to inherit the practice anyhow, so it doesn't matter."

"And if she doesn't inherit it?"

Jessie gave her an apologetic grin.

Meryl swore.

The doorknob was yanked from Jessie's hand. She looked up into the unhappy face of her estranged husband. "Glad you decided to make it."

Meryl pushed past Jessie and managed to ram a shoulder into Greg's chest as she entered.

He winced. "Good to see you again, Meryl."

She scoffed. "I bet."

Jessie stepped into the enclosed back porch and slammed the door behind her. It bounced open. Greg raised an eyebrow. She didn't respond to his silent question but turned and gave the door a solid shove. It closed and stayed that way.

Silence hung on the air. No cooling system hissing in the background. No loud meows from the absent housecat.

The living room was darker than usual with one of the windows covered in plywood. Fingerprinting powder coated many surfaces, but otherwise, nothing had been touched since Jessie left last night. The dining room floor remained littered with the contents of the buffet and sideboard. The living room floor glittered with glass shards, wood chips, and fragments of electronic equipment.

She planted her hands on her hips. "You could have cleaned it up a little."

"I'll help later, if you want," Greg said. "Right now, I'm more interested in what's missing."

Jessie looked around, the immensity of the destruction pressing down on her. "Where do I start?"

He motioned to the mess on the dining room floor. "Right here's as good a place as any."

She ran through a mental inventory of Grandma's linens and Great Aunt Rose's china, all gifts from her grandparents before they died. The closest thing she had to a family history. Dropping to her knees, she sorted through the mounds of tablecloths and napkins and scattered table service for twelve. A few smashed plates suggested it might now be a service for eight. Maybe six.

An intruder had been in her house. A stranger's hands had touched her things. Or maybe not a stranger. Which was worse?

"Nothing seems to be missing here." She climbed to her feet. "Broken, yes. Missing, no."

Greg turned to his notebook lying open on the table and jotted something down. "The living room's next. Watch your step. There's glass everywhere."

He wasn't kidding. Jessie preferred to wander the house barefoot but was glad she had kept her work boots on today. She doubted she'd ever get all the shards vacuumed out of the Oriental rug.

"All my CDs and DVDs are gone."

"Do you know how many and what titles?"

"Sure," she said. "Whatever ones you left behind."

A muscle twitched in his jaw. "I'll need a list of them whenever you get around to it."

"You two are so cute together." Meryl crunched past Greg, but not before giving him a good shot in the arm with her fist, using too much oomph for it to be mistaken as a friendly gesture.

Greg turned his head toward her. "Is there a reason why you're here?"

"To annoy the hell out of you." Meryl's laugh sounded decidedly evil. "Is it working?"

His sigh was more of a growl.

Jessie pointed out fragmented remains of the television, DVD player, and stereo. "Nothing else is missing here. But nothing's intact either."

Greg made more notes and then led them through the rest of the downstairs rooms, all untouched. "This doesn't make sense." He started up the stairs. Jessie and Meryl followed. "Someone went to a lot of trouble for a few CDs and DVDs. Why smash all the electronic stuff? Why not take it too?"

Jessie was about to offer Milt's theory about portability when Meryl spoke up. "Have you asked Vanessa?"

Greg stopped three steps shy of the landing, turned, and looked down. Not at Meryl, but at Jessie. "You just had to share your suspicions with everyone, didn't you?"

"Not everyone." She wanted to tell him she no longer believed Vanessa was the culprit, but he didn't give her a chance.

"Why would Vanessa smash all your stuff?"

Meryl stepped between them. "Maybe the fact it was Jessie's was reason enough."

This time Meryl was the recipient of Greg's angry-cop face.

"Vanessa's already got her husband. Now she wants her house." Undaunted, Meryl climbed one more step, leaving Jessie only a view of her back. But she could well imagine what her face looked like. "This seems like an effective method for getting it. I wouldn't put anything past that twit."

"Vanessa's not like that. You don't know her. She wouldn't stoop to this level."

Jessie wondered why he bothered debating the issue. Unless he was trying to convince himself. "Then who?" she asked.

Greg didn't reply. Instead he turned and continued up the stairs.

Three of the second-floor rooms were easy to assess. The guest room contained a few pieces of antique furniture, and the dresser and bureau drawers were all empty except for an extra set of sheets and a blanket. Greg's old office, likewise, was sparsely furnished and, since he'd cleared his things out, held little to interest a burglar. The bathroom remained undisturbed.

Greg and Meryl waited at the door while Jessie wandered through her bedroom. She opened drawers one at a time and noted the contents. Nothing seemed to have been displaced, but she still imagined the interloper going through her clothes.

Meryl touched her shoulder. "Are you all right?"

"Yes. No." Jessie shook her head. "I will be." From the top of the dresser, she scooped up the cosmetics Meryl had loaned her and held them out to her. "Thanks."

Meryl accepted them with a silent smile.

Jessie slammed the drawer and turned to the black lacquered jewelry box with Japanese scenes painted into the glossy finish. She lifted the lid and the music box inside began to play a tune. The contents of the box, a few pieces of costume jewelry, were just as she had left them.

"Well?" Greg asked.

"It's all here."

"That leaves your office." He stepped back, allowing her to pass.

Light shone through the large six-over-six paned windows, casting pools of sunshine on the littered remains. The room didn't look any better in the daylight than it had last night.

"My laptop's gone." She gave the desk a closer inspection. "And my external hard drive."

"What was on them?"

"Patient records." As she said it, something whispered in the back of her brain, too low to make out.

Fifteen

Greg stepped into the room, his shoes crunching against the debris, sending the whispers scurrying into the darkness. He jotted in his notebook. "Anything else?"

"My printer and router are trash." Jessie crossed to the hearth and gazed at the blackened remains of Doc's files.

"I think this had to be done by kids," Greg said. "They could unload the CDs, DVDs, and hard drive without drawing too much attention. Unlike the bigger stuff, which they probably had a grand old time smashing."

Jessie's breath slowed. Her eyes remained on the char in the fireplace. She didn't think it was kids who broke into her house. While she'd prefer to think it was Vanessa being a bitch, she didn't believe that either.

"It wasn't kids."

"Look, Jess, I'm getting tired of hearing your accusations against Vanessa."

"I'm not talking about Vanessa."

"Oh?" Greg struck his standard in-command stance.

Jessie pointed to the hearth. "Somebody started a fire in here."

"Still could have been kids. Did you check the kitchen? Maybe they made themselves a snack."

"Really? Teenage hoodlums are going to lug a package of my tofu dogs all the way up here to grill?"

The expression on his face told her he guessed not.

"Besides, there are plenty of papers on my desk they could have used. There are books. Hell, they could have torn down the curtains and torched them. No. They chose the stack of files I brought home from the track. Doc's files."

"That means what exactly?"

First, Doc turned up dead. Then his files on the horse that killed him had turned up missing. Now this. Jessie didn't like the implications. "I'm not sure," she said. "But doesn't it strike you as odd?"

Meryl crossed to stand next to Jessie and surveyed the fireplace. "It definitely does." She met Jessie's gaze, a perplexed look in her eyes. It was a look Jessie rarely saw in Meryl.

Greg's gaze shifted between the two of them. Jessie could almost hear the grinding of gears inside his head. His gaze lowered and he scribbled something in his notebook. "Anything else missing?"

Jessie did a slow three-sixty, surveying the room. "I don't think so."

"You know the drill. If you discover anything's missing later—"

"I'll be sure to let you know."

The trio tromped down the stairs in silence. Something still whispered to Jessie. She was missing something and had a feeling it was something obvious. But the nagging voice refused to speak loud enough to be heard.

"What are you going to do?" Greg's voice shattered the stillness she'd been trying to penetrate.

"Huh?"

"I don't think the house should be left vacant. If you don't feel safe, I'll stay here for a few days."

For one fleeting, off-kilter moment, she thought he meant with her.

"I gather you'll stay in your office at the track?"

Her world, as she now knew it, righted itself. "Of course," she said without missing a beat.

Meryl slung a protective arm around her shoulders. "I've already offered my house."

Jessie thought of Meryl's home with her four kids and assorted dogs, cats, fish, and occasionally a ferret or Guinea Pig. "I appreciate that. Really. I have no shortage of places to stay. Milt said I could bunk with him and Catherine. And Daniel invited me to stay at his place."

The room fell deadly silent. Jessie looked up to find both Greg and Meryl eyeing her with the same stunned expression. Meryl's morphed into a sly smile. Greg's did not.

"But for now, I'm fine at the track."

Greg cleared his throat. "I have to go. Call me if you need anything."

"Right."

Greg started toward the dining room.

"Wait up." Meryl fell into step behind him. "I'll walk you out. There's something I want to talk to you about."

Jessie smiled to herself. Poor Greg. The "something" Meryl had in mind was surely Vanessa. Jessie hoped she wasn't going to spend the rest of the day bailing her friend out of jail for assaulting an officer of the law.

Once they were gone, Jessie wandered around the living room, poking at the glass fragments with her foot. She wondered if Greg would bother cleaning up while he was there. The thought almost made her laugh. Half consciously, she dug deeper into the shimmering mound with her toe. Something in the rubble caught her eye. Using the sole of her boot, she nudged away the debris. The object caught the light coming through the other windows but didn't refract it the same way the glass did.

She squatted and brushed the broken pieces aside. Gingerly, she picked up the silver and turquoise barrette that had been buried. She didn't have to study it long to know where she'd seen the thing before.

Meryl's voice startled her. "Did you find something?"

Jessie rose, cradling the barrette in her hands. "I think my burglar left behind a calling card."

"What is that? A belt buckle?"

"No." Jessie held it up.

"A hair clip? Whose?"

Jessie stashed the barrette in her pocket and smiled. "Sherry Malone's."

JESSIE ARCHED HER ACHING back and stretched in a useless attempt to relieve the knots accumulated from a second night on the old sofa. She thought about the three offers of beds and skimmed right over Milt's and Meryl's to settle on Daniel's. She closed her eyes and toyed with a delicious daydream involving the memory of his goodnight kiss, expanding to the purely fantasized feel of his arms around her, the warmth of his body.

A fat feline jumped onto her stomach, effectively performing the Heimlich maneuver, expelling the rest of her fantasy.

Jessie sat up with a groan, gave Molly's ears a scratch, and deposited the cat on the floor. Molly ambled over to the bowl where the tabby kitten was crunching dry food, ran her rough, pink tongue over the tabby's face a couple times, and nudged him aside so she could get her own breakfast.

Jessie shuffled to the desk and flopped into the chair. She removed the silver and turquoise barrette from the center drawer and turned it over in her hand. What had been in those records that Sherry so desperately needed to hide?

A loud rap at the office door jarred her from her thoughts. She slid the barrette back into the drawer. "Come in."

As if thinking of the young woman had conjured her up, Sherry poked her head into the office. Her usual tan seemed to have washed away, and her voice had a raspy texture that hinted of a sleepless night. "We have a problem in Barn F."

Jessie tried to recall who was stabled there but couldn't. "What kind of problem?"

"You'd just better come with me."

Sherry climbed into the passenger side of Jessie's truck but refused to offer any kind of explanation. "Drive," was all she said.

Jessie was surprised to see Neil Emerick waiting in front of the barn, gnawing on a toothpick. She and Sherry slid down from opposite sides of the cab.

"What's going on?" Jessie asked.

His eyes shifted between the two women. Removing the toothpick, he turned. "This way."

Jessie followed with Sherry bringing up the rear.

At first glance, the barn appeared empty, but a small crowd gathered around one of the stalls halfway down the shedrow. Three men gazed into the stall, their conversation too low for her to understand. When Jessie approached, they grew silent and parted, giving her a clear view of the horse inside.

An emaciated gray stood in the center of the stall with his head hanging and his eyelids half closed. The horse's flesh seemed to have sunk inward with only traces of it attached to prominent withers, an angular spine and much too obvious ribs and pelvis.

Jessie had seen a pasture full of badly neglected horses once when she'd volunteered with the animal control officer during her internship. She'd hoped to never see such a heart wrenching sight again. This was worse. "My God. How could you let this happen?"

"I didn't let nothing happen," Emerick snapped. "I've been pouring the feed to the old bag of bones ever since he got here. He gets more grain than any three of my other horses combined. He just don't pick up. Then this morning *that* one insisted you look at him."

He thrust a thumb at Sherry, who leaned against the railing across the shedrow from the crowd, chewing her cuticles.

The haunted look in her eyes rattled Jessie. "He's running a fever," Sherry said and went back to chewing her fingers.

Jessie's gaze lingered on her, but she refused to meet it. Jessie sensed she had the answers to nearly all of her questions about the last couple of weeks. Right now, though, Jessie only had time to consider the skeletal gray.

"I'll be right back." Jessie excused herself to go to her truck. By the time she returned with a white plastic bucket full of supplies, someone had snapped a break-away tie hanging in one corner to the horse's halter. The tie appeared to be all that kept his nose from hitting the ground. "You said he's been like this since you got him. How long ago was that?"

"I said he's been like that since he's been *here*. He ain't mine. I'm training him for Doug Whitman." Emerick motioned toward one of the three men who now stood clustered together farther down the shedrow.

She rested a hand on the gray's pencil-thin neck and spoke softly to the horse. He didn't respond. His hair-coat felt hot and dry, almost brittle. She stroked the flat area between his eyes, slid her hand to cup his ear, rubbing a thumb against the soft hair inside. Then she moved back to pat his neck and ran her hand along his bony spine. Picking through the contents of the white bucket, she found and greased a thermometer with Vaseline and then slid it into the gray's rectum. A length of cord attached the thermometer to a spring clothespin, which she clipped to the gray's tail. "How long has he been here?"

"A month. Maybe a little less. Maybe a little more. I'd have to check my books."

Jessie bet Emerick knew to the minute how long this horse had been in his stable. She shifted her gaze to the three men, unsure which one to direct her question to. "Mr. Whitman? How long?"

The one in the center with a long face and a John Deere ball cap replied. "Like Neil said, about a month."

Jessie examined the horse starting with his head, checking his gums, his tongue and his eyes. "Mr. Whitman, how long have you owned this horse?"

"Not long. Maybe three, four months. I got him at an auction in Oklahoma."

She ran her hands down the gray's left front leg. As she knelt beside him, she saw the band of swelling that ran along his underside, from his breastbone back. She caught Sherry watching her and knew immediately why Sherry had insisted she be called.

"I assume you have health papers for this animal?" Jessie stood and looked first at Emerick, then Whitman.

They exchanged nervous glances.

"Yeah." There was a hint of a question mark in Whitman's voice.

"I'd like to see them, if you don't mind."

Emerick sent one of the other men, a younger fellow, off to fetch the papers.

Jessie moved toward the horse's hindquarters, running a hand under his belly, along the band of edema. After a check of her watch, she unclipped the clothespin and retrieved the thermometer. "One hundred and six."

Emerick muttered something under his breath.

Whitman shifted his weight from one foot to the other. "What do you think it is?"

Jessie eyed Sherry, who continued to silently chew on her nails. Sherry suspected the same thing she did—Jessie was sure of it. She didn't expect the health documents to tell her much, but she was praying the Coggins papers had been signed by any vet but Doc.

Emerick's young assistant appeared around the corner and jogged down the shedrow toward them. He clutched a dirty envelope, which he offered to Emerick. The trainer indicated he should hand it to Jessie.

Her head throbbed as she removed the papers and unfolded them. They were dated three weeks prior to Doc's death. A third of the way down, the space naming the federally accredited veterinarian responsible for drawing the blood listed Dr. Samuel Lewis, Doc's given name.

She studied the horse. The sweet, sad, dark eyes. The rough coat. She could only imagine the agony he was in. "I need to do bloodwork." Her voice sounded hollow in her ears.

Emerick shrugged. "Whatever."

Jessie shot a look at the poker-faced trainer who appeared a lot less concerned than she believed he really was. As she watched him, a puzzle piece snapped into place in the back of her mind. She swung around to Sherry, thinking of the morning Jessie had gone to Emerick's barn to check on Soldier Bob. The morning Sherry had blocked her passage. The gray head hanging over the stall webbing farther down the shedrow. The apparently empty stalls on either side of him. And later, Emerick himself cleaning out that lone stall.

Sherry finally met Jessie's gaze but just for a moment. Then she lowered her head. The glimpse had been enough for Jessie. She turned back to Emerick. "I'm also going to need to draw blood on all the horses in your barn."

Emerick's poker face dropped away like a mask. "Why?"

"That's where you had this boy stabled until recently, right? Empty stalls on either side of him. You suspected something was wrong and isolated him. Then you moved him here when you heard I was on my way to look at Sullivan."

Emerick stepped toward her, his fists balled. "So what? I figured he had a cold or something. I didn't want the other horses catching it. I don't see why you need to draw blood from them."

Sherry spoke up. "EIA." She pressed away from the rail. "Dr. Cameron thinks it's EIA. Swamp Fever." Sherry wheeled and strode away, her long blonde braid swaying side to side. No silver and turquoise barrette adorned the top of it.

Whitman's face matched the color of his sick horse.

The trainer loomed over Jessie. "EIA? Equine infect—"

Jessie refused to react to the stench of his stale breath. "Equine infectious anemia. I'm placing both barns under quarantine."

Jessie swabbed the gray's neck just under his jaw with an alcohol wipe. Then she picked up the Vacutainer she'd prepared a few minutes earlier. She probed the skin and flesh until she found the spot she wanted, inserted the needle, and popped the vacuum tube into place. He didn't flinch, didn't bat an eye. Dark blood began streaming into the tube.

The somber gathering had been joined by Tony Rizzo, known around the track as The Stall Man. Short, stocky, and bald, he controlled which trainers were assigned which stalls. Most days he appeared to take tremendous pleasure in the power he wielded. Today, he seemed even shorter than usual.

"Are you sure about this?" Tony asked from behind her. "I mean, about it being EIA. Couldn't it be something else?"

Jessie's eyes never left the Vacutainer. "Sure it could. It could be a few things."

"So this could be nothing?"

"I didn't say that."

"What are the other possibilities?"

She removed the filled tube, placed one finger at the injection site, and extracted the needle, holding pressure. "Anthrax. Equine Encephalitis, Equine Influenza..."

Tony's eyes widened. "Those are contagious, aren't they? I mean, to humans?"

She glanced over her shoulder at him. "Yep. Of the choices, EIA is probably preferable. At least as far as we humans are concerned. None of it's good for them." She released the pressure on the spot where the needle had gone in and stroked the gray's neck. One of the reasons she'd always wanted to be a veterinarian was so she could do something to help sick and injured animals. Except this time she was powerless. There was no cure. No medication. Only one way out. And it sucked.

Tony tugged a red bandana from his hip pocket and wiped a gleam of sweat from his bald head. "Christ," he muttered. "What can we do? How do we stop it from spreading?"

"Quarantine."

"I know that. Anything else?"

Jessie nodded to Emerick who slipped the halter off the horse and clipped the stall webbing to the eyehook in the doorway.

"Do all the barns have those zappers?" Jessie pointed to the blue lights enclosed in a pitted chrome wire cage hanging from the ceiling. As if on cue, a hapless horsefly flew toward the light and the thing emitted a *zzzttt*. A small spark flashed where the fly had been.

"I don't know. I doubt it."

"Flying insect control is the most we can do. Make sure each barn has a zapper or two. Or three. Close in this barn—both sides—as much as you can. That one too," she said, pointing to the adjacent stable. "Same thing up in Barn K, where Neil used to stall him."

Tony shrunk another inch. "But that's just about impossible."

"You close them in during the winter, don't you?"

"Well, sure. But trainers take weeks to get the sheets of plywood and such nailed up in the fall."

"In this case, better make it hours. Make sure the manure piles are kept cleaned up and cordon off the area around the exterior of the barns."

"How far?"

"Preferably two hundred yards—"

"*Two hundred yards?*"

Jessie understood how much space that entailed. "For now at least, take it out to the stables above and below both barns."

He rammed the bandana back in his pocket. "I'll get right on it." He turned toward Emerick and regained his normal stature, pointing one stubby finger at the trainer's face. "You. I never gave you permission to move a horse down here."

Jessie noticed Emerick dropped the superiority pretense in the face of the man who could ship his entire stable to a less well-maintained barn. Or cut the number of stalls he could use. Under different circumstances, the sight of diminutive Tony Rizzo successfully dressing down tall, obnoxious Neil Emerick would have brought her immense pleasure. Today, it only made her sad.

Word was getting out. By the time Jessie, Emerick, and Tony arrived at Barn K, a crowd had gathered on the road in front of the stable. They gazed in, worried expressions on their faces. The one face conspicuously absent was Sherry's, and for once, Jessie would have appreciated her presence. Jessie had a whole barn full of horses that needed to have blood drawn. She could use an assistant right about now. The possibility that Sherry had broken into Jessie's house was the least of her concerns.

HAVING COMPLETED THE sad task of drawing blood from every horse in Neil Emerick's barn, Jessie sat in her office, resting her head on her arms folded on top of the desk. Sherry had failed to return, leaving Jessie to manage the entire job alone. To make a bad situation worse, she'd been forced to contend with at least half a dozen owners ranting about her insistence that no horse be allowed to leave the barn. Like rats leaving a sinking ship, they wanted to get their horses out. She heard promises that they would take their animals home and keep them there for the duration. She refused to budge.

At least there had been no panic. So far. Most palpable was the resentment aimed at her, as if this were all her fault. With a moan, she sat up and rubbed her eyes. If they were as red as they felt, she must be a frightening sight.

Even if she'd spoken up the minute she learned about Doc's shortcuts with the Coggins tests, nothing would've changed. The gray would still be sick. The others would still be in danger. But if she had said something sooner, she wouldn't be burdened with the sense that, in keeping quiet, she had somehow contributed to this disaster.

A soft knock came at the door. Milt stuck his head in before she had a chance to say anything.

"Hey, darlin'. I hear you're up to your ass in alligators."

She smiled in spite of herself. "Come in, Milt."

After closing the door behind him, he sank into the sofa. "Where are your kitty cats?"

Jessie pointed toward her feet. Both Molly and the tabby had curled up together under the desk for a nap.

Milt crossed one ankle over the other knee. "What's the deal with Emerick's stable? I heard rumors you suspect Swamp Fever."

"You heard right. I hope I'm wrong, but the symptoms are all there."

"Are you really thinking of quarantining all of Riverview?"

"If any of the horses test positive for EIA virus, it may mean shutting down the entire track."

"For how long?"

"It depends on a lot of things. First, we have to do blood tests on every horse on the property. The feds will be involved—"

"The feds?"

"United States Department of Agriculture. I've already called and alerted them we may have an outbreak. I'll let them know what the initial tests show. They'll decide where we go from there."

"When will you get the tests back?"

"At least twenty-four hours, but I'll bet it won't be until the first of the week. No one wants to work in a lab on a beautiful spring weekend."

Milt swore under his breath.

There was another call she'd been avoiding. "I imagine Daniel's heard the news by now."

"Maybe not. He hasn't come in yet. At least he hadn't when I was over at the front office fifteen, twenty minutes ago."

Jessie knew the quarantine, especially if it went track-wide, would be costly. She wondered how Daniel would deal with the situation. She wondered how he would deal with her.

Milt had grown pensive.

Jessie looked around the room at the battered file cabinets, the ratty sofa, the faded winner's circle photos tacked on the wall. Her eyes settled on the framed veterinary license bearing Doc's name. "He could've prevented this, you know."

"Daniel?"

"No. Doc."

Milt's face became a portrait of perplexed amusement. "Now, Jessie, I know you think Doc was some kind of superhero, but even he couldn't have stopped this."

"That's not what I mean. He'd been falsifying Coggins tests. His signature is on the papers for that horse. If it turns out they were faked..." The ramifications made her queasy. "The blood test would've caught the presence of the virus. The horse would never have made it through the gate."

Milt remained silent, watching her. She waited for a response that didn't come.

"I've been learning a lot about Doc," she went on. "I thought I knew the man. Obviously, I didn't. Now, besides all the other nonsense, he's put the lives of his patients in jeopardy."

Milt still didn't utter a word.

She wished he'd try to argue the point, if only to make her feel better. With a sigh, she set her phone on the desk in front of her. "I have to call Daniel."

Milt drew a noisy breath in through his teeth. "What are you gonna tell him?"

"About the falsified Coggins results. That we may have more horses on the premises that haven't been properly tested."

Milt rested his elbows on his knees and stared between them at his boots. "Shumway already knows."

Sixteen

"What do you mean, he knows?"

Milt didn't meet her gaze. "Doc used blood from a ringer. He'd send it to the lab instead of bothering to draw blood from some of the horses. Especially the ones that were hard to handle. Shumway knew about it."

Jessie struggled to comprehend what she'd just heard. Daniel knew? She stared at Milt as another realization struck her. "*You* knew."

His head bobbed.

Jessie suddenly felt like a complete outsider. It was an experience she'd known all too well growing up. As if everyone was in on the joke but her. Worse, this time she felt like the joke was on her. In addition to Doc, Daniel and Milt were fast becoming total strangers.

She dug her fingernails into the surface of the desktop hoping it would somehow anchor her in the reality that was spinning out of her grasp. "How could Daniel know about this and not put a stop to it?"

"He wanted to. But Doc had the goods on him and threatened to spill if he said anything."

"What do you mean?"

Milt climbed to his feet and rammed his hands into his jeans' pockets. He paced to the file cabinets and stood there, his back to her. "Daniel Shumway isn't his real name. I don't know what it is, but Doc did. Just like Doc knew he'd spent time in prison. Shumway, or whoever he is, killed a man. It was years ago, mind you, but the fact of the matter is he's a convict." Milt turned, meeting her eyes for the first time since the topic of Daniel had come up. "He's got a criminal record, you see. No way should he be able to hold a gaming license and run a racetrack. When Shumway caught wind of Doc swapping blood samples for Coggins tests and threatened to go to the authorities, Doc told him two could do that dance. If Shumway turned him in, Doc would go to the racing commission. This track is all Shumway's got and he'd lose all of it. So he kept quiet, and Doc went right on doing what he'd been doing."

Jessie closed her eyes and wished she could shut out her thoughts as easily. "Daniel killed a man?"

"Afraid so."

"When? Where? What happened?"

"I wish I could tell you more, but as far as I know, Doc took Shumway's secret to his grave."

"How'd Doc find out?" She opened her eyes to see Milt shaking his head.

"He never told me the details, and I never asked."

"That's how you know about all this? Doc told you?"

Milt lowered his head. He didn't reply. He didn't need to.

Jessie buried her face in her hands. "No. This is a mistake. You misunderstood. Or Doc was lying. I don't believe Daniel's a murderer."

Milt moved to her side. He put a hand on her shoulder. Gave a gentle squeeze. Then he left without another word.

WHEN JESSIE WAS GROWING up, her parents' response to adversity involved packing up her and her brother and leaving town. She'd hated it. Hated running. Hated being on the move. But after talking to Milt, she wanted more than anything to climb into her truck and just drive.

Daniel? A murderer?

She stuffed her phone in her pocket and made it halfway across the exam area before coming to a stop. Where did she think she'd go? To her trashed house? She wheeled and returned to the office where Molly had climbed onto the desk and sat looking at her with big yellow eyes.

Jessie closed the door and leaned against it, watching the cat watch her. "Don't look at me like that. I'm not going anywhere without you."

She removed the phone again and slid into her chair before keying in Greg's number. When his voicemail answered, she let out a disgusted growl and left a message to call her.

She stroked Molly as the seed of an idea sprouted.

According to Milt, Daniel had already served time for his crime. She'd known him as "Daniel Shumway," upstanding citizen, for just shy of ten years. Whatever he'd done had to be ancient history. It wasn't like he was a serial killer lurking in their midst.

Jessie almost talked herself into leaving Daniel's past buried. Except if Doc had threatened Daniel, would the charming and handsome racetrack CEO revert to old ways?

Just like Jessie almost reverted to running away?

The idea bloomed, and her gaze settled on the file cabinets. Steeling for whatever she might find, she rose and approached them.

The files she'd taken home, now largely ash, had only been from "A" to "H." *Shumway* should still be here. Although, knowing Doc's odd filing system, she couldn't be sure. She dove into the drawer marked "S" and was relieved to find a folder with Daniel's name scrawled across the tab. She carried it back to the desk. What did she expect to find in there? What she hoped to find was nothing. Nothing incriminating, nothing out of the ordinary. She might not be able to prove him guilty or innocent by strict legal standards, but perhaps she could put her mind at ease. She flipped the folder open.

Daniel didn't own any racehorses. Conflict of interest, she imagined. He did, however, own two Appaloosas, which were used as lead ponies to escort the racehorses to the track and starting gate. She thumbed through the stack of paperwork and noted the usual assortment of minor emergencies and standard inoculations and tests. Nothing abnormal.

Until the last page. A notation dated a week before Doc's death listed a vial of acepromazine had been dispensed to Daniel. But the handwriting didn't match the rest of the entries.

Jessie closed the file. Sherry had given Daniel the same drug responsible for Doc's death. Or had she? Maybe she'd penned the notation to set Daniel up to take the fall for her own crime.

The word *premeditation* screamed inside Jessie's head.

She picked up her phone. Tried Greg's number again, and again she got his voicemail. Maybe he was at the house. She tried that number. Her voice on the answering machine greeted her. At least the phone line had been repaired. She hung up without leaving a message. "Where are you when I need you?" she asked Greg and slapped the phone down on the desk.

She opened the desk's top drawer and removed the silver and turquoise barrette. Rubbing the smooth stone with her thumb, she contemplated what to do next. No doubt the wisest choice would be to wait until Greg returned her call. Let him play connect the dots with all her new information.

The barrette stared up at her.

She picked up the phone again and entered a different number. This time the phone at the other end picked up.

"Milt?" she said. "I need your help."

"ARE YOU SURE ABOUT this?" Milt waved away a fly buzzing around his head.

Jessie gazed doubtfully at the front of the rec hall. They'd asked five or six different people before someone reported seeing Sherry there. "I'm not sure about anything anymore."

Milt and Jessie weaved around a crowd gathered outside the building. He paused and let her climb the wooden steps ahead of him.

"Maybe you oughta hold off a while. Think this through." He swatted at the fly again.

She was tired of thinking. She wanted to *do* something—anything—to disprove her suspicions about Daniel.

The weathered wood and screen door screeched open. Milt let it slam behind him once they were inside. Four wiry-looking men sat in a huddle at one table discussing the day's events or yesterday's race results or maybe the threat of quarantine. Two young women in dirty sleeveless t-shirts and blue jeans occupied another table. A TV perched high in one corner aired televised races from another track. As Jessie's eyes adjusted to the dim light, she spotted Sherry at the back of the room, alone, playing pinball.

The treads of Jessie's boots squished against the tacky floor as she headed toward Doc's daughter.

"About time you showed up." Sherry kept her eyes on the game.

Milt grabbed a chair, turned it around, and straddled the back.

Jessie walked around the machine and shouldered the scoreboard. She wanted to see Sherry's face. "You were expecting us?"

"You anyway." She tipped her head in Milt's direction. "Didn't expect you'd bring reinforcements to help rub salt in my wounds."

"What are you talking about?"

"You haven't heard? I got a call today from my dad's attorney. It seems he changed his will before he died." Sherry bumped the machine hard with her hip. "He didn't leave me his practice after all."

"Oh?" Jessie realized her voice carried too much pleasure. She noticed one corner of Milt's mouth slanting upward.

"Don't get too excited. He didn't leave it to you either."

Had he left his illegitimate daughter anything at all, or had killing her father netted her absolutely nothing?

Sherry must've had mindreading skills. "He left me money instead." She rocked the machine. "Not enough to buy his practice from Amelia, as if she'd ever sell it to me. But enough to repay some money I owe."

Jessie pondered the source of those loans, but then she spotted the plain brown leather clip in Sherry's hair. She fingered the silver and turquoise one in her pocket, regaining her focus. "I notice you're not wearing that pretty barrette you usually have in your hair."

Sherry removed a hand from the button on the side of the pinball machine to touch the back of her head. "I lost it the other day."

Jessie considered revealing where she'd lost it but decided to keep her ace in the hole concealed for now. Instead, she shifted topics. "How long have you known about Doc falsifying Coggins tests?"

Sherry slammed her hip into the machine again. "Yes," she hissed at the metal ball hurtling from flipper to bumper beneath the glass. To Jessie, she said, "Does it really matter?"

"You knew the gray was sick. You suspected EIA. I'd say it matters."

Sherry jiggled the machine like a pro, keeping the ball in action. "I don't know how long. It was just something Doc would do every so often if he knew the horse was healthy."

"*Healthy?*" Jessie exclaimed. "You think that gray was healthy?"

Sherry didn't reply.

"And you covered for him."

A muscle in Sherry's jaw twitched, but she didn't respond.

Time to change direction. "Tell me about Daniel Shumway."

Sherry glanced up just long enough for the pinball to get kicked into the oblivion between the flippers. "Goddamn it," she muttered when the machine's electronic music spiraled downward. Then she stepped back and met Jessie's gaze for the first time since she'd arrived. "What about Shumway?"

"According to Doc's records, a vial of acepromazine was dispensed to Shumway a week before Doc's death." Jessie's fingers traced the shape of the barrette in her jeans' pocket. "Except it wasn't Doc's handwriting. It was yours."

Sherry's face remained impassive. "So?"

"You admit giving it to him?"

Sherry gave a one-shouldered shrug. "He runs the place. If he wanted the stuff, I gave it to him. Lots of people use ace, you know. Most of the time it's no big deal."

Most of the time. Not this time.

Back at their trucks, Milt parked a hand on Jessie's door, keeping her from opening it. "What was that all about?" he asked incredulously. "I thought you said you needed a bodyguard."

"I thought I might," Jessie said. "But since Sherry's playing things close to the vest, I decided I should too."

He narrowed his eyes. "I get the feeling you're fixin' to do something stupid."

"Probably." The plan started to form the moment Sherry hadn't reacted when Jessie accused her of dispensing the ace to Daniel. Jessie preferred to give it more thought, but from the look on Milt's face, he clearly wasn't about to back down. "Every other notation in Daniel's records was made by Doc, except that one. That one was made by Sherry."

Milt didn't budge.

"Either Daniel did request a vial of ace from Sherry and she gave it to him..."

"Or?"

"Or she made it up. Wrote it in the records to throw suspicion in Daniel's direction." Jessie lowered her voice, thinking out loud. "Sherry knows about Doc falsifying the Coggins tests. Heck, she helped him. He'd have shared with her what he knew about Daniel. She knew he had a motive, and if he didn't come under suspicion on his own, she could easily point the police in his direction."

Milt looked like he'd caught a whiff of something foul. "I hate to tell you, darlin'. You might be trying to play your cards close to your vest, but you just showed your king, asking her about Shumway. Her giving him the drug and all. She won't have to tell the police anything. She knows *you* will."

Jessie flinched. Milt was right about showing too much of her hand. If Daniel was innocent, Jessie might've set herself up to be part of the frame job.

Seventeen

The hour before dawn suggested a gray day ahead with clouds blocking the stars. The air carried a promise of rain.

The reality of Jessie's plan set in, making her queasy as she drove past the clinic. A few of the shedrows displayed lights and activity—horses being saddled and prepared for their early morning exercise. But most remained dark and still.

Jessie kept the truck at a crawl all the way to the chain-link fence at the edge of the Monongahela River. She braked to a stop at the corner of Barn A where Daniel stabled his horses. It was deserted. She exhaled a relieved sigh.

An idea struck her. She shifted into reverse, backed up, and swung the truck into the road above the barn, even though Daniel's stalls were located on the lower side. As an afterthought, she pulled closer to Barn D across the road. Hopefully, if anyone spotted her Chevy, they'd assume she was attending to a patient there.

She slid down from the cab, shivered, and zipped her hooded sweatshirt. With a pair of Latex gloves stuffed in her hip pocket and her stethoscope draped around her neck, she dumped a few supplies in a white bucket to cover the items in the bottom. Should she be caught, she'd say she received a text about an emergency. If pressured, she'd claim they must have typed in the wrong barn.

Yeah, right.

She picked up the bucket and crossed the road to enter the upper side of Barn A. She tried to act nonchalant. Professional. Relaxed. Just another routine call.

Except her teeth were chattering, and she'd broken out in a nervous sweat.

She made her way toward the center of the shedrow and slipped into the covered walkway that separated Barns A and B, reaching the door to Daniel's tack room. The flashlight from her phone revealed a sign that read, "Private Property. Keep Out." She'd made it. So far, so good.

She lowered her light to a padlocked hasp and hoped it had been left unlocked. A quick yank proved it hadn't. This couldn't possibly be that easy.

She rummaged through the bucket to find the short length of wire and screwdriver she'd stashed beneath the boxes of sterile pads, bandages, and tape. She bent the wire and inserted it into the slot at the base of the lock. The absurdity of the situation struck her. *Dr. Jessie Cameron: Secret Agent.* Maybe she should consider a change in careers.

She worked the wire this way and that to no avail, removed and re-shaped it before making another failed effort. This always worked on TV.

The crunch of tires on gravel alerted her to the approach of a vehicle. The humor of her predicament quickly faded. The makeshift key didn't operate any better with sweat dripping in her eyes.

The vehicle stopped on the road in front of Barn B. Jessie couldn't see the occupants. That meant they couldn't see her either. Two car doors slammed. Muffled voices wafted toward her. Time to forget about subtlety. She dropped the wire back into the bucket and picked up the screwdriver.

The voices were getting louder. They—whoever *they* were—were headed her way. Jessie prayed they'd stop short of the gap between barns, but she couldn't take any chances. She rammed the business end of the screwdriver into the lock and tried to pry it open. It held tight. Adjusting her grip, she tried again. Still, it held. What did they make these things from?

She ventured a quick peek around the corner, hoping the darkness would shield her. Two figures—one tall, one short—walked directly toward her. Her cockamamie story about responding to the wrong barn for an emergency suddenly sounded ludicrous. She ducked back around the corner, protected from their eyes but only if they didn't come much closer. Taking a deep breath, she repositioned the screwdriver. This time, she threw all her weight into it. She stifled a groan as the handle bit into her palm. The door creaked. Gritting her teeth, she gave one more heave. The lock sprung open with a loud metallic clank.

The approaching voices and footsteps stopped. "What was that?" one asked.

"Probably one of the horses rattling his gate," the other replied.

Jessie quietly placed the screwdriver in the bucket and removed the padlock from the latch. Snatching the bucket, she darted inside the tack room and shoved the door shut behind her.

Breathing hard in the dark, she listened. Neither of the voices outside sounded familiar. Nor did they seem to be coming any closer. Jessie slumped against the wall and waited for her heart to stop pounding against the inside of her sternum.

A pale shaft of light snuck under the gap beneath the tack room door. They had turned on the shedrow lights. Through the wood, she heard dull thumps and bumps. All the while, the voices kept up a steady patter. It sounded as though they had opened the feed room door just across from where she hid. A chorus of nickers confirmed her suspicion.

Jessie willed her shoulders to relax. She'd made it in. But how was she going to get out? She pushed the concern from her mind. Time enough to worry about that minor detail later. She dug a black Maglite from the bucket, figuring it would provide better illumination than the flashlight on her phone. She swept the beam around the room. Three bulky Western saddles with wool saddle pads draped over them hung on racks built into the wall. Bridles and breast collars hung from nails next to them. The equipment had the look of years of hard use, but glistened, clean and well oiled.

Jessie swung the light to three plastic fifty-gallon garbage cans with lids secured by bungee cords. She crossed to the cans, unhooked one end of a bungee and lifted the lid. The sweet fragrance of oats floated up into her face. Above the cans, small plastic buckets of vitamins and supplements lined a shelf. Four dusty framed photographs of Daniel and assorted associates, either mounted on a horse or standing beside one, hung on the wall.

She turned and flashed the beam ahead of her. A countertop, cluttered with everything from rusty horseshoes to tools to bottles of fly spray, ran the full length of one wall. She pulled on the Latex gloves, quietly opened a metal cabinet mounted to the wall, and reached inside. A dozen or so packages of Vet Wrap, a box of eighteen-gauge needles, assorted syringes, a plastic tub of Finish Line Kool-Out Clay, two jugs of alcohol, and a square brown bottle of Regu-Mate filled the shelves. She encountered the same supplies in every racehorse barn she'd ever been in.

Jessie started to close the cabinet, but something caught her eye as she swung the light away. She brought the beam back to the cabinet's interior and reached behind the tub of poultice clay. Her fingers touched glass. She pulled out a bottle and aimed the Maglite at the label.

Acepromazine. Exactly what she'd hoped she *wouldn't* find. The date on the label matched the date on the records back at her office. Sherry hadn't been lying.

Jessie held the bottle up to eye level. Although impossible to tell for sure, she guessed that about four cc's were missing. Enough to tranquilize one horse.

Her phone burst into song, startling her. The bottle slipped from her fingers. She grabbed for it, bobbled it, and managed to catch it. Setting down the flashlight, she ripped the phone from her pocket. No longer muffled, the music rang out even louder before she could jab the dismiss button.

Another sound—a soft rumble—drew her attention. The Maglite had started to roll on the not-quite-level countertop. She stretched for it but only succeeded in knocking it to the floor. The lens end struck first with a crack and went dark.

Her pulse pounding in her ears, Jessie stood motionless in the pitch-black room and listened. The voices outside had fallen quiet.

"Did you drop something?" one of them asked.

"No. I think Jacob stomped at a fly."

Jessie closed her eyes in relief.

"I thought I heard a cell phone."

"You sure it's not yours?"

Jessie's eyes flew open, staring into the blackness.

"Yeah, I'm sure. It must be yours."

"I left mine in the car."

The stillness hung in the air like a threatening storm cloud, alive with electricity. Jessie didn't dare breathe.

"You sure you heard something?"

"I'm positive."

Another long silence.

"Maybe somebody left their phone in the barn somewhere."

"Could be. Sounded like it came from Shumway's tack room."

One of them laughed. "Somebody's probably going nuts trying to remember where they left the thing."

"Should we try to find it?"

No. Panic crushed in on Jessie. Why hadn't she braced something against the door?

"It's not our problem. Let's get back to work."

Jessie's knees gave way. She slid down onto the dirty floor and waited for her legs to feel like something other than overcooked spaghetti. She may have escaped one dilemma but knew she was a long way from being in the clear.

Clutching the container of ace in one hand, she fumbled for the flashlight in the dark with the other. On hands and knees, she crawled through the dust, searching through the cobwebs under the counter. In the back of her mind, she recalled her mother commenting on what a clean child she had been. If Mom could see her now.

Her fingers grazed the round barrel of the flashlight, and she clutched it to her. Now all she had to do was get out.

She found her bucket next to the door, pulled a Ziploc baggy from under the decoy vet supplies, and dropped the acepromazine into it. After peeling off the gloves and stashing everything, including the broken Maglite, in the bucket, she pressed a shoulder and one ear against the door.

The voices were still there, but more distant. Were they done? Or were they simply feeding their horses farther down the row? It didn't matter. This was her chance.

She wrapped her fingers around the door handle. With a gentle tug, she swung it toward her. She closed her eyes and offered up a silent prayer to whoever was the patron saint of good-intentioned cat burglars. Opening her eyes again, she leaned out and peered into the walkway between the two stables. The gray dawn cast just enough light to reveal a clear path. She stepped out, snatched the lock from the bucket, and hooked it through the hasp. She hoped prying the padlock open hadn't broken it. With a quick shove, the lock clicked into place. She might just make it free and clear after all.

Exiting the covered gap, she looked around. Only a few sleepy horses with heads hanging over their stall webbings greeted her.

Jessie lugged her bucket down the shedrow toward her truck, feeling the exultation of charging down the homestretch toward the finish line with no one even close to catching her.

Until a white Ford Expedition rolled passed the end of the shedrows. Daniel.

Jessie froze, praying he hadn't seen her.

But the Expedition reversed and swung toward her.

Suddenly, breaking into Daniel's tack room seemed like the stupidest idea she'd ever had.

"Jessie?" Daniel stepped down from the big SUV.

Time to find out how good of an actor she was. "Morning." She hoped her voice didn't sound as pathetically perky as she feared.

He smiled. "What are you doing here? Did you come to join me for a morning ride?"

"Sorry." She held up the bucket and tried to forget what was hidden inside. "I have an emergency, but I mixed up the barns." She threw in an eye roll for good measure.

"Oh." He sounded either disappointed or doubtful. Or maybe she was hearing her own doubts reflected in his voice. "I'm glad I ran into you though. I need to talk to you about this quarantine thing."

"Okay. But I need to get going. I'm supposed to be in Barn F right now." She gave him a sheepish grin.

"I understand. As soon as you get a chance, come see me, okay? Maybe we can have lunch?"

"Sure. That would be great." Lunch *would* be great. If she didn't fear he might have something to do with Doc's death. She started to pass him. *Get to the truck. Just get to the truck.*

He caught her arm. "Wait."

The touch of his hand sent electric shivers through her. Shivers of attraction or shivers of fear? Or both? She couldn't decide.

"Can you at least tell me when you expect the results of the bloodwork you drew yesterday?"

"A minimum of twenty-four hours. With this being the week-end, I'd say Monday, maybe Tuesday."

He didn't appear pleased, but he released her arm.

She moved toward her truck, fighting the urge to break into a run.

"Jessie?"

Gritting her teeth, she stopped and pivoted.

"Are you all right? You look exhausted. And have you been rolling around in the dirt?"

She felt the blood drain from her face. *Smile*. Act normal. She looked down at the patches of dust and cobwebs covering her jeans and sweatshirt and made a feeble attempt to brush them away. "I was—uh—trying to drag the cat out from under the sofa this morning. Guess I need to clean in there."

He laughed. "In your spare time?"

She laughed back. "Right." The laugh and the smile died as soon as she turned away.

She wondered if his eyes lingered on her, watching her go, but she didn't dare look to find out. And she didn't breathe until she had climbed into the cab of the Chevy with the incriminating bucket.

FALLOUT FROM THE NEWS of the quarantine hit the clinic midmorning. Jessie had gotten off the phone with Greg's voicemail when an angry horde of owners and trainers descended. The complaining she'd endured from Emerick while drawing blood turned out to be a mere whimper compared to the onslaught they delivered.

"What the hell's going on with this epidemic?" demanded a tall, rotund man wearing a plaid shirt with pearl snaps straining over his oversized belly. Jessie recognized him as one of the horse owners but couldn't put a name to the face.

His question was greeted with murmurs from the crowd, echoing his inquiry.

"I never said this was an epidemic." Jessie stood just inside the exam area. Her imagination played out a scenario of being mobbed and forced to sprint through the passageway between clinic and spa and out the doors at the far end of the building.

"Then why the quarantine?"

"To *prevent* an epidemic. And so far, the quarantine is limited to Barns K and F."

"So far," said another in the crowd. "But it's bound to expand to the entire track, isn't that right?"

"It's too early to tell."

"What *can* you tell us? You've quarantined two barns with the threat of closing down the track. I think we all ought to just load up and beat it out of here before things get worse."

Jessie raised both hands. "Hold on. What I don't want anyone to do is panic. If you'll calm down a minute, I'll tell you what I know and what I believe may or may not happen."

Another murmur ran through the group. The heavyset fellow with the gapping shirtfront appeared to be the leader, assigned or otherwise. He looked over his constituency and exchanged a comment or two with several of them before facing her. "Fine. Give it to us straight, Dr. Cameron."

She searched for the words that would keep everyone, if not happy, at least less murderous.

"One horse stabled in Neil Emerick's barn has shown symptoms I suspect could be EIA."

"Aren't all horses coming onto track property supposed to be tested for that?" came a shout from the back of the crowd.

"Yes, but the papers are good for a full twelve months. Within that time frame, anything can happen, I'm afraid. A horse could become infected two months—or two weeks—after the test and still carry valid health papers. The testing system isn't failsafe." Especially when a lazy vet bypassed it.

The answer seemed to satisfy the group, so Jessie continued. "Placing the entire facility under quarantine may become necessary if the horse under suspicion and any other horses test positive. At the very least, blood tests will be required of all animals on the property. I know quarantine for everyone isn't something any of us want to think about, and it very well may not be necessary. The final decision falls to the Department of Agriculture. But if EIA is present, it must stop here. You used the word 'epidemic.' That's what we're desperately trying to avoid. A few days of inconvenience is a small price to pay, don't you think?"

The heavyset man folded his arms. "A few days? Is that all it's gonna be?"

"I hope to have the first set of test results Monday. Tuesday at the latest. If everything is negative, then the issue is dropped, and I focus on diagnosing one horse's ailment. If we get one or more positive results, decisions will have to be made. If that's the case, the horses affected will have to be put down, and the rest of Barns K and F will be in quarantine until all the horses continue to test negative after two months. I presume, if the decision is made to quarantine the entire facility, that quarantine will only be in effect until all the horses in every barn test negative."

"But what if they don't? What if it's spread?" This came from a young woman with short pigtails and sad eyes.

Jessie met her gaze. "Then the track will have to be shut down and no one will be able to take their animals off the property until they all test negative for two months." Hearing the grumble of impending revolt echoing through the group, she raised her voice. "But, if you happen to be the owner of one of the sick animals—and it may not appear to be sick at the moment—and you take it out of here now, take it home, put it in your barn or your pasture with your other horses, you risk spreading the virus beyond Riverview. You risk infecting your entire herd. Is that what you want to do?"

The throng grew so silent that Jessie could hear the pigeons cooing outside. Heads began to nod, and little by little the crowd broke up and drifted off. A few people, including the sad-eyed woman, thanked her for her time. Finally, only the big man with the straining snaps remained.

"I'd sure like to know how this horse was allowed to be brought in," he said. Then he turned and left with the others.

Jessie slouched against the clinic's doorframe. For a moment she wished Doc were still alive so she could have the pleasure of killing him herself.

At the sound of approaching footsteps, she lifted her head. Daniel loomed over her, a cup of coffee in hand. "You managed that really well."

With his blond hair disheveled from the spring breeze, he did *not* look like her idea of a killer.

He fixed her with a troubled frown. "Do you really think it's EIA?"

"I don't know. That's why we do bloodwork."

"But you suspect it."

"I do."

He took a sip of coffee. "And what about the quarantine? Do you expect it to close us down?"

She caught his use of the word *us*, as if they were still on the same team. "Like I told them, it depends on the test results."

"Educated guess."

Jessie sighed in exasperation. Everyone wanted her to predict the future. They didn't teach that at OSU. "Honestly, I don't know. I think we should just be patient and see what the lab has to say."

"But you said the entire track might be closed down."

She studied his face. If he had in fact been aware of what Doc was doing, he had to know this could happen. What was he really trying to get out of her? Was he trying to determine how much *she* knew? She gazed into his pale blue eyes and felt a chill at the realization that while she was trying to read him, he was trying to read her.

"Well?" His voice took on an insistent edge.

She'd forgotten the question. "I'm sorry. What did you say?"

"Do you think there's a chance the entire track will be locked down? I need to know." His fingers closed around her arm.

The urgency in his voice cut through her. She longed to offer him some small comfort. Her gaze settled on his mouth, and for a split second she was back at her house after their dinner at Lorenzo's. That fleeting kiss as he said goodnight. Followed by Milt's voice telling her, *Shumway, or whatever his name is, killed a man.* Had he killed Doc too? She clenched her fists until her nails bit into her palms. "There is a chance, yes. But it's too early to worry about it."

"When?" He gave her a gentle shake. "When should I start worrying about closing down the track? About losing everything I own?"

The anguish in his voice made fearing him impossible.

"Look." She brought her hands up between them, hesitated, then rested her palms lightly on the front of his shirt. "I imagine you heard what I told them."

"I did."

"That's really all I know. Guesses, educated or otherwise, will only feed the panic."

His eyes bore into hers as if mining for answers. She held his gaze but sensed a great many of his questions had nothing to do with the quarantine.

Outside, a vehicle rolled up to the clinic door. Jessie looked over Daniel's shoulder to see Greg climb out of the state police SUV. Daniel released her and crossed to the stainless-steel sink and counter.

Greg's gaze shifted between them. "Hey, Jess. Daniel."

Daniel gave a nod of acknowledgment.

"What's going on?" Greg said to Jessie. "I got your message that you wanted to talk to me."

"I did." But alone.

Daniel crumpled his empty cup and tossed it in the trash before turning toward Greg. "You missed the mob scene."

"Oh?"

"It was nothing." Jessie tried to sound nonchalant. "Concerned horse owners and trainers. That's all."

"She handled them like a pro. You should use her for riot control." Daniel grinned as if nothing were wrong.

Jessie marveled at his acting skills.

"Are you okay?" Greg asked her.

"Yes, of course."

"What did you call him about?" Daniel asked. "Have you come up with anything new about Doc's death?"

Was she imagining the ominous tone in Daniel's voice? She looked at Greg, her eyes wide, and hoped he'd be able to read her silent plea. "Nothing new. I just needed to talk to you. About personal stuff."

One of Greg's eyebrows hiked up his forehead.

"The lawyer you've hounded me to get. I wanted to ask you about a few names I've come up with."

Greg's second eyebrow joined the first one. "Really?" He sounded pleased. The bastard.

"Well, you don't need me for this." Daniel stepped between Jessie and Greg, stopped, and looked at her. "Unless you want me to stick around."

"I'll be fine." She hoped her relief didn't show.

"By the way, did you happen to see anyone hanging around my barn this morning when you were there?"

Her mouth went dry. "No. Why?"

"Someone broke the lock on my tack room door."

"Really?" Greg said. "Did they take anything?"

Daniel glanced over his shoulder at him. "I didn't notice anything missing."

Greg pulled out his notebook. "Do you want to file a report?"

"That won't be necessary. Nothing appeared tampered with. No signs of anyone being in there at all. Except the broken lock." Daniel's gaze stayed on Jessie.

"Do you want me to take a look at it?"

"No. Thanks just the same."

Jessie fought to remain expressionless. It had been way too long since she played poker in college. And she was never very good at it. She studied Daniel's face, struggling to read his expression. Apparently, he was a much better poker player than she.

"I'll leave you two to your personal business. Keep me posted about the testing, okay?"

"Absolutely."

Daniel caressed her cheek with the back of one finger and then strode out of the clinic.

Once he was gone, Jessie let out the breath she'd been holding and sank against the doorframe.

"What the hell was that all about? You didn't call me here to talk about lawyers."

"No, I didn't." She motioned for Greg to follow her into the office. "I need to sit down."

Eighteen

"You know, Jess, of all the idiotic things you've done, breaking into Shumway's tack room ranks right up there."

Exasperated, Jessie deposited the tabby, who had been snuggling in her lap, onto the office floor. "I admit it wasn't my finest moment. But seriously. I just told you Shumway may not be his real name. He may have killed someone and served time for it, and Doc was probably blackmailing him. And all you can say is I'm an idiot?" She stood and stormed around the desk to lean against the file cabinets.

Greg remained seated on the sofa, Molly in his lap. "What exactly did you hope to accomplish? You can't verify the drug you found was the same one injected into that horse."

"I hoped I wouldn't find anything. I hoped to prove he'd never taken possession of the stuff in the first place." She'd hoped—and failed—to prove Sherry was trying to throw suspicion on an innocent man.

"Still wouldn't prove anything. What if he'd left it in his truck? Or at his house? Or what if he'd tossed what was left in the trash?"

"Okay," she snapped. "I'm a lousy detective. I get it."

Greg rubbed Molly's black ears in silence. When he spoke again, his tone was softer. "You really care for this guy, don't you?"

She remembered how Daniel had looked in his suit. Thought of the kiss at her back door. God, she wanted things to be different. To be easy. She wanted to look into Daniel's eyes and feel safe in his arms. She wanted a little sappy romance in her life.

Greg's voice sliced through her fantasy. "I really wish you'd let go of your obsession with a murder that never happened."

She wheeled on him. "You still don't believe Doc was murdered?"

Greg hesitated before replying. "I think you're stirring up stuff that could get you into trouble. You're not making a lot of friends over this, you know."

"I can't help the quarantine."

"I know you can't, but it's more than that. Shumway saw you by his stable and now the lock to his tack room is broken. He's not a moron, Jess. And there's everyone else you've been accusing. Whether or not one of them had anything to do with Doc's death, none of them are looking too favorably at you right now. You're poking a sleeping bear with a stick."

He had a point. "So what do we do?"

"What do you mean 'we'?" His annoying grin had returned.

"I mean about Daniel. I have the vial of ace from his tack room. It looks to me like it's missing about one dose."

"Damn, you're good. You can tell just by looking at it, huh? Besides, that vial doesn't mean a thing. How many partially used bottles of tranquilizer do you suppose there are around this track? Twenty? Thirty maybe?"

At least. "But not everyone who has one also has a reason to want Doc dead. Or a past conviction for murder."

The patronizing smile vanished. "I admit that bothers me. Do you know anything at all about his conviction?"

"Just what Milt said Doc told him. And if it got out, Daniel would lose his gaming license." She eyed Greg. "Can't you use your cop database and quietly do some digging?"

"Not if I value my job. It's criminal behavior to misuse law enforcement databases."

"You're kidding."

Greg nudged Molly off his lap. "Nope."

Jessie let out a discouraged growl. She realized she had one more straw to grasp. One more shot to confirm her belief that Sherry was setting Daniel up. Jessie strode out of the office.

Greg's voice trailed after her. "Where are you going?"

She unlocked and opened the medicine cabinet, removed a small brown paper bag marked with the initials *D. S.*, and turned to find Greg had followed her, as she knew he would. "This is the bottle I took from Daniel's tack room."

"You mean stole."

She glowered at him. "I wore gloves when I handled it."

"What do you want *me* to do with it? It's not evidence. If it was, you've destroyed any chain of custody, rendering it completely inadmissible in court."

"Just check it for prints. Daniel's or..." Or Sherry's. "Or anyone else's."

"It's not that simple. A case number would have to be assigned. And since there is no criminal investigation—"

"Because Doc's death was an accident." Jessie made no effort to camouflage her disgust.

"Exactly. I can't run fingerprints without good reason. Not to mention you wanted me to dig quietly. Once they go in the system, there is no 'quietly.'" But he took the bag.

"Then what are you going to do with that?"

"Nothing."

She studied his poker face and wasn't sure she believed him.

"Try to stay out of trouble, okay?"

"I'll try."

"Uh-huh," he said doubtfully as he headed for the door.

By noon on Sunday, Jessie felt as though she was the one carrying a contagious disease. She had all the usual calls for post-workout problems, a couple of hock injections, and one filly with a mystery gash above her eye that required stitches. But there was no jovial banter or small talk on the part of the trainers. Every single human Jessie encountered treated her quietly, professionally, and with a chill that threatened to freeze every water bucket on the premises.

She could only wonder how they would treat her after the test results came in.

The warmth of the spring sun made up for the frigid attitudes on the backside. A perfect day for a drive to the Dodds' farm.

"Thanks for coming out. I know you're terribly busy." No stray wisp of hay or bits of dust sullied Catherine's flawless black jeans tucked into Dan Post boots. Her auburn hair was gathered high on her head in a ponytail that hung down the back of a curve-hugging red tank top.

Jessie made a feeble attempt to brush off her own dusty Wranglers.

"I don't really know what I expect from you," Catherine said. "I guess I hope you'll tell me it's all been a big mistake. That Blue's going to be just fine."

Jessie smiled at her. She knew Catherine was holding onto a dream and could sympathize. Letting go—admitting defeat—sucked.

Catherine led the way into the stable. She lifted a lead shank from a hook on the barn wall and unlatched a stall door. Jessie watched as Catherine fed the chain through the big gray's halter. He followed her out of the stall, jittery but obedient.

Jessie studied the horse. Mexicali Blue was about as nice a piece of horseflesh as she was likely to encounter. She approached him and placed a hand on the broad space between his large, dark eyes then slid the hand up between his small ears, running her fingers through his steel-gray forelock. She touched his jaw, which was the size of a holiday platter, and then traced the heavy muscle of his neck, from behind his jaw all the way to his perfectly sloped shoulder. Not a rib showed beneath his coat. Everything about him was round and hard and powerful.

Then Jessie's gaze dropped to his feet. What a shame. She understood Catherine's frustration.

"It's a pity, isn't it?" Catherine said. "He looks like a gray version of Secretariat. But that damned foot..."

"Let's have a look and see if anything's changed for the better, okay?" Jessie hoped her optimism didn't sound as false as it felt.

"That's why I called you."

"Let's take him out on the cement."

Jessie headed outside to her truck and pulled her portable x-ray machine from the back of the storage unit. Catherine led the gray stallion to the paved apron in front of the barn. Jessie set the console on the ground and uncoiled the cables, watching as Blue tossed his head and nipped at Catherine.

"Cut it out," Catherine scolded the horse. Then to Jessie she said, "Milt told me about the quarantine and the sick horses at the track. With everything going on, I was relieved you agreed to drive out here."

"Actually, it's only one sick horse." So far.

Catherine seemed not to notice the correction. "There's another reason I'm glad you could come. I wanted to talk to you. Privately."

"What about?"

"You know that conversation we had a few days ago?"

Jessie froze. "About you and Doc?"

"Yeah. About that." Catherine shifted her weight from one foot to the other. "I was hoping you could forget what I said. I overreacted, thinking Milt could possibly be sleeping around." She shifted back to the first foot. "I shouldn't have burdened you with my unfounded suspicions."

Jessie went back to plugging in the cables. "I kind of thought that myself," she said under her breath.

"Huh?"

"Nothing. You don't believe Milt was having an affair?"

When Catherine didn't respond, Jessie looked up. Catherine's eyes seemed to be searching the distant hillside for something. An answer, maybe. "I choose to believe he's been faithful to me." She emphasized each word. Jessie wondered which of them she was trying to convince.

Choose to believe. Jessie let the comment hang while she concentrated on tapping her patient's information onto the screen. When she finished, she looked up at Catherine. "What about you and Doc? Do you choose to forget that ever happened too?"

Catherine's voice dropped an octave. "I would prefer if *you* did."

Jessie positioned the digital sensor panel and ordered Catherine to hold it still. "Steady there, old man," she said to Blue and tapped the touch screen to capture the image.

"Look," Catherine went on as Jessie set up the next angle. "The whole thing was silliness on my part. None of it meant anything. But if Milt ever found out about it, it would destroy him, don't you see?"

Not to mention what it would do to their marriage.

"So?" Catherine's voice sounded like a taut rubber band, stretched to its limit. "Are you going to tell Milt?"

"Why should I?" Jessie repositioned the sensor panel. "It's none of my business. Besides, I like Milt. I would never do anything to hurt him. Knowing his wife slept with his best friend would tear him apart."

"You'll forget we ever had that talk?"

"I promise, I'll never tell another soul." Forgetting might be asking too much.

Catherine seemed satisfied. "Thanks. You don't know how much that means to me."

Jessie snapped a second picture. She set up and captured several additional angles without further comment from Catherine. "That does it." Jessie shut down the machine.

Catherine patted the gray's neck. "When should we know anything?"

Jessie hadn't liked what she saw in the digital previews but wasn't about to comment until she had a closer look. "I'll view these as soon as I get a chance and call you later with the results."

Catherine started to lead Blue into the stable but paused and looked back. "Thanks, Jessie. For everything." Then she turned and clucked to the stallion.

Jessie watched the gray's muscular rump as it disappeared into his stall. No sign of a limp, but that wasn't unusual for the kind of break she remembered from the previous radiographs. She had no trouble understanding how Catherine had fallen in love with Mexicali Blue and dreamed of great things with him in her stable. Funny, Jessie thought, how the truth could lie just under the surface, unseen. Unless you knew where to look.

Sunday night had been anything but restful. An emergency farm call from an old client awakened Jessie at three in the morning. Rather than bothering Meryl, Jessie left her makeshift bed in the clinic's office to drive through the pre-dawn fog and pull a mare through a rough foaling. Mother and baby survived.

Two hours later, Jessie was tired, but too wide-awake to sleep on that ratty old sofa. With the office supply website pulled up on her phone, she sat at her desk and began adding items to her virtual shopping cart. It'd been over a week since her laptop had fallen victim to the scuffle with Frank Hamilton, and five nights of fitful sleep on the too small, too uncomfortable sofa were plenty. Long before she began her morning routine, she'd placed an order for two new laptops, a printer, a router, and a futon.

At seven o'clock, she climbed into the Chevy and started her rounds. Paranoia had spread through the backside. Assorted owners, trainers, and grooms flocked toward her truck, waving her down with a non-stop parade of patients. One horse seemed sluggish over the weekend. Another didn't finish his morning ration of grain. Did Jessie think yet another one looked a little on the thin side? When she wasn't holding hands, soothing nerves, or taking temperatures, she was repeating her answer to the question of the day. No, she hadn't received any test results yet.

Jessie intentionally avoided Barn K, certain Emerick was ready to spontaneously combust.

At noon, she stopped at the rec hall for an order of fries. While she waited for it to be filled, her phone rang. The screen showed the call was from the lab. The Coggins tests results were complete. She canceled the order and gave the lab the number for Doc's fax machine, grateful it hadn't suffered the same fate as her laptop. By the time she returned to her office, the old dinosaur was spitting out paper.

Jessie collected the stack and picked up one that had fallen to the floor. Her gaze shot to the bottom of each. The section marked *For Laboratory Use Only*. The box marked *Test Results*. Negative. Negative. Negative.

Then she came to the sixth sheet. The report on the sickly gray. Jessie looked at it. Wiped a hand across her eyes to clear the fog, willing the results to change.

Positive.

JESSIE CHEWED HER LIP as she stood outside Daniel's door. Time to suck it up. She raised a fist and knocked.

"Come in."

Clutching the stack of papers to her chest, she entered his office. His smile faded. "You don't look like someone with good news."

"It could be worse, I suppose." She crossed to where he sat behind his desk and set the pile in front of him.

He pushed them away. "Just tell me."

"The gray tested positive for the EIA virus. All the others tested negative."

"That's good. Isn't it? It means the disease hasn't spread, right?"

"Not definitively."

He studied her, a question in his eyes.

"We can be cautiously optimistic. More than the one positive would have been bad. *Very* bad. As is, we need to keep Barns K and F quarantined. The infected horse will need to be euthanized." She hated that word almost as much as she hated following through with it. "Then we need to test those horses again until they all continue to show negative—"

"For two months," he interrupted. "I remember. What about the rest of it?"

She looked down at the stack of papers. At the pen and paper on the desk. Anywhere but at Daniel's piercing blue eyes. "I have to call the USDA. They'll consider the situation. Between them and the track stewards, a decision will be made."

"Bullshit."

She flinched. "Excuse me?"

"You're the attending veterinarian. They'll follow your recommendation. Bottom line, this is your decision. I know you'd rather push it off on the bureaucrats, but this is just you and me here." He leaned down, placing his palms on the desk. "Tell me. What happens now?"

"You're wrong. I have nothing to say about it. Nothing."

The look in his eyes clearly stated he didn't believe her. "They'll shut me down. Over one horse."

"Not necessarily. Yes, I do think the only possible way to guarantee the safety of all the animals and those who would potentially race here would be to close the track for that two-month period. No one in or out." The muscle in Daniel's jaw twitched. "But I'm aware of what that would do to the track financially. I'm sure the USDA is as well."

"The track? To *me*. It would wipe me out. Not to mention the publicity. My God." He ran a hand through his hair and wheeled away from her.

"I can't help the publicity. That's going to happen either way. But I think I can justify recommending to the feds that they limit the quarantine to the one barn."

He spun, eyes wide, and reached out as if to hug her.

"*If*," she added, before he could do it. "*If* they give my recommendation any credence and *if* all the other horses on the grounds test negative. I want to begin drawing blood as soon as I can round up some help."

Daniel beamed. "Absolutely. Do it. I'll figure out some way to put a spin on it for the media to keep the damage to a minimum."

His idea of damage and hers didn't quite mesh. "All incoming horses need to have their health papers and Coggins tests checked and verified."

"They already are."

"If any of them were signed by Doc, I want the horse barred until new tests are run."

Daniel's lips pressed into a thin line. "Okay."

She gathered the stack of reports. "I need to speak with Neil Emerick and Doug Whitman."

He touched her hand. A tickle of electricity fluttered across her skin. She wished Milt had never told her about Daniel's past. She understood the old *ignorance is bliss* adage as never before.

"I'll go with you," he said.

She started to argue, but he shushed her with a finger to her lips. "It's only right. This track is my responsibility. I should be there."

Nineteen

The scene in Barn K had been anything but pleasant. Emerick vented his frustration by ranting at Jessie until Daniel put a stop to his tirade. At that point, the trainer stomped out of the barn and kicked a plastic bucket of grooming tools, scattering its contents. Doug Whitman sank down onto a bale of straw and buried his face in his hands. Jessie expected him to follow Emerick and leave one of the ashen-faced girls, who worked as grooms, to deal with the task at hand. But to Jessie's surprise, he gathered his wits and looked up at her, tears in his eyes. "When do you want to do this?"

She kept her voice soft. "No use putting it off."

Whitman nodded and climbed to his feet. "I'll meet you there."

Barn F was eerily quiet. No cats prowled the shedrow. Even the pigeons seemed to be avoiding the place. Its lone resident hung his head over the stall webbing, showing no interest in Jessie and Daniel's arrival. Whitman turned the corner at the far end of the barn and made his way toward them.

Daniel put a hand on her shoulder and squeezed. Jessie resisted the urge to lean against him. He'd known about Doc's negligence and could have put an end to it. This wouldn't be happening if he had. She stepped away from his touch.

"Let's take him down to the far end of the road," she said.

Whitman looked stunned. "Can't you just do it here?"

Jessie glanced at Daniel, who answered the owner. "We wouldn't be able to get him out of the stall once he's down."

Whitman thought about it. Any remaining color drained from his face as reality sank in. Without another word, he picked up a lead

219

shank and unclipped the webbing to bring the gray out of the stall one final time.

They led the sullen horse down the shedrow and out into the road at the end of the barn.

Jessie hated this part of her job. It had almost stopped her in the middle of her studies at OSU, but Doc had given her a lecture on the sanctity of life. How death was a natural part of it. And how, as veterinarians, they had the privilege of easing their patients' suffering and of helping them through this passage. For years, she ran Doc's words through her mind every time she'd been called upon to put an animal down. This time, the words rang hollow.

She filled a syringe and moved to the gray's side. She stroked his neck and murmured into his ear as she probed his neck just behind his jawbone until her fingers detected the throb of a weak pulse.

She glanced at Whitman who stood close to the animal's head. "You've never been through this before, have you?"

He shook his head.

"It's going to be fast. Real fast. You might want to step back."

He looked puzzled but did as she said.

She inserted the needle under the skin and felt it pop into the vein. Drawing a breath, she depressed the plunger and injected the drug into the gray's blood. She barely had time to remove the needle when, stiff-legged, he went down. Hard.

Whitman's face was so white he almost looked transparent. He clutched the lead shank in his trembling hands as he stared down at his horse. Tears streamed down his cheeks.

Daniel turned away.

Jessie knelt beside the animal and pressed a stethoscope to his girth. "He's gone." She knew full well he'd been dead before he hit the ground.

Whitman nodded, still clinging to the lead rope.

Her part of the ordeal completed, Jessie left Whitman and Daniel to arrange for someone to pick up the animal. She retreated to her office.

Several calls had gone to voicemail. Checking them, she learned none were emergencies, so she locked the door and curled up on the ratty sofa, hugging Molly close. She longed for sleep, but when she closed her eyes, she pictured Daniel's face. The image faded into the positive Coggins test result and finally dissolved into the dark, mournful eyes of the sickly gray as she stuck him with the needle.

Rubbing her face, she sat up. Molly meowed her displeasure and hopped from the sofa, sulking off to her food bowl. Jessie moved to her desk and thumbed through the Rolodex for the number for the USDA.

As she'd expected, the chief veterinary officer at the Department of Agriculture officially ordered Emerick's barn quarantined. The rest of the track would remain open for normal operation pending further testing.

Veterinary Services was sending a doctor to assist. Still, the prospect of drawing blood from every horse stabled at the track was overwhelming. Her next call was to Dr. McCarrell, the other track vet. After reminding her that he was trying to cut back on his workload, not increase it, he grudgingly agreed to help.

Her third call was to Meryl, who sounded frazzled. "What do you mean, you need my help at the track? I'm busy with your practice here."

"I had a horse test positive for EIA."

The line went silent, followed by Meryl's whispered, "Shit." Another brief silence. "I'll cancel the rest of today's appointments. Be there in half an hour."

She hung up before Jessie could thank her.

Jessie loaded up the Bowie unit in her truck with all the red-stop-pered Vacutainers she had in stock. The crunch of shoes on gravel interrupted her preparations. She looked up to see Sherry.

Hooking her thumbs in her jeans' pockets, Sherry said, "I thought you could use an extra pair of hands."

"I could. I'm surprised you would offer."

She nudged a rock with her toe. "I just picked up my mail. Got my state license. I'm a real vet now."

"Congratulations." Jessie was too tired for sarcasm.

Sherry rolled her eyes. "Lotta good it does me since dear ol' Dad didn't see fit to leave me his practice. Look, do you want my help or not?"

Jessie took a moment to think about it. "I do. Thanks."

"Where do we start?"

"At Barn A." Jessie opened the driver's door and tipped her head toward the other side. "Get in." She turned the key and shifted into gear. "Mind if I ask you a question?"

"Does it matter? You're gonna ask me anyway, aren't you?"

"How could you let him do this?"

Sherry turned on her. "Me? How about you? You knew what he'd been doing."

"Only recently. Even then, I didn't know for sure. The first time, I thought—hoped—it was an isolated incident. But..." She searched, not only for the right words, but for the truth. "I didn't want to believe he could—"

"That he could be so lazy?" Sherry offered.

"That he could be intentionally negligent."

Sherry looked out the passenger window without answering.

"You knew what was happening with the gray. Why didn't you speak up sooner?"

"I wish I could've."

"Why couldn't you?"

"I was in a bind. I needed money. And Neil wasn't going to let me out of it."

"What's Neil got to do with it?"

Sherry turned her back to the door. "Dad used Sullivan's blood for the Coggins tests."

Mighty Sullivan with the bowed tendon. That would explain why Emerick kept the horse at the track instead of resting him elsewhere. It wasn't just the lure of the swimming pool.

"It really was never a big deal," Sherry went on. "The horses were already here at the track. They'd had legitimate negative tests all along. If we'd had any doubts, Dad never would've done it."

Jessie choked. "How can you say that about the gray? He was bought at an auction and brought to the track where Doc fudged the test."

Sherry fell silent, her face pinched in a troubled scowl.

Jessie remembered something else.

"You said you owed Neil Emerick money?"

"No. I owe Butch money."

"Butch? The loan shark security guard?"

"Yeah."

Jessie rolled this latest revelation around in her mind. "And Doc left you money to pay off loans."

"Loan. Just one. He left me the money to pay off Butch. Damn him. He wouldn't give me the money to pay off the jerk while he was still alive."

Jessie wondered how much money they were talking about. "How does Emerick play into that?"

"Neil's been helping me make my loan payments up to now. In exchange, I take care of vetting his horses. And I keep my mouth shut about the other crap that goes on in his barn."

"Like the gray?"

Sherry faced forward again. "It's all gonna come out now. I don't need his money anymore."

Jessie noticed a smug smile on her face.

Sherry caught her looking. "You're a lot like my dad, you know." And then she quickly added, "The good parts of him, I mean."

Jessie shot another glance Sherry's way.

If she was being sarcastic, she didn't show it. "Don't act so surprised. I know I've been an ass. I guess I owe you an apology."

"I've wondered what you had against me. Did you really want Doc's practice that bad?"

"No. Maybe." Sherry huffed a short laugh at her own indecisiveness. "No. I just hated you is all."

"Why?"

"Because my dad loved you."

Not the answer Jessie expected.

"My dad always raved about you." Sherry gazed out the front window. "He'd go on and on about what a good student you'd been. What a hard worker you were. He made me feel like I had to live up to that. I couldn't. My grades were never anywhere near what yours were. I like to have fun. Every time I screwed up, he'd give me the Saint Jessie speech." Her voice deepened to mimic her father's lecturing tone. "Jessie *always* studied hard. *Jessie* never asked me for money. She *worked* her way through school. Why can't you be more like Jessie?" Her voice settled back to normal. "Jessie this, Jessie that. Blah, blah, blah."

Stunned at the outburst, Jessie tried to make sense of it in the larger picture. "Is that why you broke into my house?"

Sherry's head snapped toward her. "What?"

Jessie parked the truck in front of Barn A and turned sideways to observe the young woman.

Sherry's face had reddened. "What the hell are you talking about?"

"You broke into my house the night I went out to dinner with Daniel."

"I most certainly did not. Where did you get an idea like that?"

Jessie wished she had the barrette in her pocket instead of in her desk drawer back at the office. "I have evidence."

"Whatever evidence you have is a lie. I don't even know where you live." Sherry threw open the passenger door and stepped out.

She exhibited the appropriate amount of ire for being falsely accused. Jessie's instincts told her Sherry wasn't lying. Then again, her instincts hadn't been on target lately. If she was wrong, who *had* broken in?

Who had destroyed Doc's files?

"You coming?" Sherry stood in front of the truck. "Or are you gonna let me do all the work?"

Steeling herself, Jessie opened her door and slid down from the truck's cab.

They'd only drawn blood from four of the horses in Barn A when a Pennsylvania State Police Interceptor pulled up next to Jessie's Chevy.

Greg stepped out. "I need to talk to you."

Jessie held up a tube of blood that she was in the process of labeling. "I'm a little busy at the moment."

"Now." His voice carried that stern, no-nonsense tone he usually reserved for the bad guys.

Jessie looked at Sherry, who gave her a dismissive wave. "Go. I'll grab one of the grooms to help me."

"Thanks." Jessie handed her the tube.

As she approached the Interceptor, Greg said, "Get in."

First Sherry and now Greg. Jessie had dealt with more than enough attitude for one day. "What's this all about?"

His voice softened. "Just get in, already."

When she climbed into the passenger seat, he handed her a brown nine-by-twelve envelope. "Hold this." He swung the car toward the stable gate.

"Where are we going?"

"Someplace we can talk without being interrupted." He drove less than a half mile before pulling off in front of a vacant diner.

"What the hell's going on, Greg?"

He turned to face her. "I did some digging into Daniel Shumway."

"I thought you said you'd lose your job."

"Yeah, well..." Greg rubbed his ear. "Believe it or not, I really do still care about you and don't want to see you getting yourself killed. And if anyone asks, Shumway has visited the house and I needed to rule his prints out as our burglar."

Jessie stared at Greg in disbelief. He was being...nice. Not to mention risking his career for her. "Thanks," she whispered. "Did you learn anything?"

"His prints were definitely on the vial you stole from his tack room."

A dull throb settled into Jessie's temples. "And?"

"His real name is Daniel Brice." Greg nodded at the envelope on her lap. "Go ahead. Look at it."

She swiped her eyes and opened the flap with her thumbs.

"Daniel Brice was charged and convicted of murder," Greg recited as Jessie stared at the single-page rap sheet. "Brice was nineteen at the time, served out his sentence, and then proceeded to drop off the map."

The face in the mug shot was little more than a boy—tousled blond hair, eyes that appeared to have been caught in headlights. The jaw appeared sharper, and no weathered creases lined his face. No doubt about it. She was looking at a younger version of Daniel. "That's it? That's all you've got about him?"

"The murder took place in California. I don't have access to their reports. Apparently as soon as he got out of prison, Daniel Brice ceased to exist. My guess is Daniel Shumway emerged in his place."

"Did you find any kind of criminal record for him under the name Shumway?"

Greg pointed at the page in her hands. "That's his entire rap sheet."

Jessie stared at the face of the terrified boy in the mug shot.

"Jess? How do you want to handle it?"

Startled, she looked up. "Me?"

Greg's gaze dropped to his knees. "I know you have feelings for him. If word of this reaches the racing commission, he will definitely lose his license."

"*If?*"

"This is just between you and me." Greg peered at her askance. "I'm not going to say anything unless you tell me to."

Great. Daniel already believed she controlled his destiny with regards to the quarantine and closing down the track. Now this. She studied the face in the photo. Was this the face of a cold-blooded killer? She didn't think so.

Unless he was a very clever one.

Greg shifted in his seat. "What do you want me to do?"

Good question. "I need some time to think about it."

"Fair enough. But will you do something for me? Stay clear of him for now. Don't let on that you know about his past."

"Why?"

"You have to ask? We have no idea what he's capable of, except that he's committed murder at least once. If he's committed murder twice—the second time to keep his secret—you're not safe."

The weight of Greg's words bore down on her. "I thought you didn't believe Doc was murdered."

"What I believe is beside the point. There's no use taking unnecessary risks."

Jessie studied him, wishing she could read his mind. "Greg, I work at the track Daniel runs, and we're in the middle of a crisis with this quarantine. I can't avoid him."

"I realize that. But you can at least manage to not be alone with him."

The prospect of no more awkward dinners at Lorenzo's suited her just fine. But the memory of the kiss at her door flashed through her mind followed by the thought of Daniel the next day, touching her arm, whispering in her ear.

"Jess?"

"You have my word," she said reluctantly. "No private meetings with Daniel."

"Good." Greg sounded satisfied, maybe even relieved.

"I need to get back."

He faced forward and reached for the key. "If you need me for anything, call. And let me know when you decide how you want to deal with this."

How to deal with this? She had no idea. Right now, she almost felt grateful for the overwhelming task waiting for her back at Riverview.

Almost.

Twenty

The area in front of Barn A looked like the parking lot for a veterinarians' convention. Three pickups beside her own, all sporting Bowie storage units, jammed the road. The only human visible in the shedrow was a skinny girl sitting on a rickety folding chair, cleaning a bridle. Jessie cut between stables and glanced at the new padlock on Daniel's tack room door.

The upper side of Barn B appeared to be the venue for the convention. Dr. McCarrell, Sherry, Meryl, half a dozen assorted helpers, and one unfamiliar woman wearing dark-rimmed glasses and a stern expression were spread out down the shedrow.

Meryl spotted Jessie. "About time you got here."

"Sorry I wasn't around to greet you all."

The woman, whom Jessie didn't recognize, handed a tube of blood to Sherry and stripped off her Latex gloves. She approached with an extended hand. "You must be Dr. Cameron. I'm Dr. Leslie Baker from Veterinary Services."

Jessie took her hand. "Dr. Baker. I apologize for my absence."

"Now that you're here, I suggest we get to work. This is a serious matter, and we have a lot of animals to check."

"You're absolutely right."

Dr. Baker pointed out which horses still needed attention. Jessie suggested they break up into teams. Dr. Baker agreed and patted Sherry on the shoulder. "I understand Dr. Malone here just received her license. She seems very capable. I'd like to continue working with her if that's all right with you?"

Sherry beamed.

Dr. McCarrell expressed a preference to work with his regular assistant.

Meryl considered Jessie with mock distaste. "I guess that leaves me with you."

"So it would seem."

They enlisted a pair of young men to help and headed to the next barn.

Meryl tossed a tablet of Veterinary Service EIA lab test forms to Jessie. "What did Greg want?"

Jessie sent a groom into the first stall to halter its occupant and handed the forms to her assistant to fill out. "He wanted to talk to me about the break-in." She could imagine Meryl's reaction to Daniel's criminal record. If Jessie intended to keep his secret, Meryl wasn't the person to confide in.

"Oh? He find out who did it?"

Their second assistant entered the next stall to jot down the second horse's tattoo and markings. Jessie kept her eyes on the Vacutainer she was preparing. "Not yet."

"Greg needed you to go with him to tell you there's no news?"

"Something like that."

"Whatever you say." Meryl gave a skeptical grunt. "I hear Sherry Malone is now a full-fledged vet."

"That's what she tells me."

"What did she say when you showed her the hair clip you found in your house?"

Jessie swabbed the first horse's neck with an alcohol prep before sticking it and watching the blood flow into the vacuum tube. "She denies breaking in. But I didn't mention finding her barrette."

"Why the hell not?"

"I'm saving it."

"For what?"

"For when I need the element of surprise." Jessie removed the tube, then the needle. She held pressure with a thumb to make sure the bleeding stopped. Speaking of the element of surprise. "Turns out Sherry didn't inherit Doc's practice like she expected."

"Oh?" Meryl looked up from signing one of the forms, her dark eyes even darker than usual. "Don't tell me he left it to you."

"No. I suppose it went to Amelia as part of his estate." Jessie labeled the tube while the groom moved to the next stall to hold Meryl's patient.

But Meryl just stood there holding the empty Vacutainer and watched Jessie, as if she knew there was more.

Jessie knelt to place the tube of blood into the plastic carrier. "How would you feel about buying my half of our practice?" she asked and waited for the explosion.

But it never came. Instead, Meryl's expression grew sad. "No." She stepped into the stall.

Not the reaction Jessie expected. Ranting, raving, swearing? Yes. But a flat-out denial? Never. "Excuse me?"

Meryl finished with her horse before replying. "I said no. I can't afford to buy out your practice any more than you can afford to buy this one." She gathered her equipment and brushed past Jessie to the next stall.

Jessie stood in stunned silence. Every argument she had planned, every reason she intended to offer, evaporated like so much morning mist under a hot sun. She noticed the groom, a boy with a bad case of acne, watching her with the same trepidation as someone waiting for a green horse to spook. Realizing her mouth hung open, she closed it and bent to gather the plastic bin containing the Vacutainers. When she straightened, the sight of Daniel leaning against the wall startled her.

The groom turned to see what had surprised her and snapped to attention.

"How's it going?" Daniel asked.

"Slow." She noticed the boy, still rigid as he clenched the lead shank. "At ease, son."

"Sorry," he whispered, and with the reverence one might reserve for a movie star, added, "It's just, you know, Mr. *Shumway*."

She lowered her head to hide her amused smile.

Daniel pushed away from the wall and approached her. "I see you have help. That's good."

Jessie spotted Meryl peering over the top of the test forms tablet.

"Any idea how long this is going to take? When will we know?"

"There are two other vets working on it besides us." Jessie remembered Sherry's new license. "Make that three. Once we've drawn blood from every horse, it'll be at least twenty-four hours to get the lab work done. Maybe longer with this volume. Dr. Baker from Veterinary Services might be able to light a fire under the lab guys, but I wouldn't count on it." Jessie motioned for her assistant to follow her past the stall where Meryl was working. And eavesdropping.

Daniel trailed along. "I just got off the phone with Zelda Peterson. She wants to bring Clown back to the track to get him ready for his next race, but for obvious reasons isn't too anxious to do it until we know for certain."

"I don't blame her." An image of Daniel injecting Clown with ace flashed through her mind. She shook her head to chase it away.

Daniel scowled. "What's wrong?"

"Nothing. Flies." She waved a hand and shook her head again for good measure.

He put a hand on the back of her neck, and she jumped.

"That wasn't a fly." He let his hand drop. "What's going on? You've been acting strange for a couple of days."

She pretended to be intent on watching her assistant as he went into the next stall. "I haven't been sleeping well."

He gave a short laugh. "I know what you mean. This quarantine business is eating me alive. I don't think I've had more than eight hours sleep total since it all started. And I know you're doing everything you can."

His hand settled on the small of her back, and she willed her muscles to relax under his touch. She thought back to their dinner at Lorenzo's. Even knowing about his criminal record, that he had killed in the past and might be responsible for Doc's death, a big part of her felt drawn to him.

"You know what I think?" Daniel's mouth was close enough to her ear that she felt the warmth of his breath on her neck. "I think, when this is all over and settled, you and I should take a vacation. Where would you like to go?"

She closed her eyes against reality and let her imagination take flight. Thanks to her vagabond parents, she'd seen more than her share of the country, but few of the places tourists would frequent. A pristine beach perhaps, with the color of the sky reflected in the water, the sun warm on her bare shoulders. And Daniel at her side.

A horse snorted nearby bringing her back to Riverview Park. She opened her eyes to see the kid with the acne watching them from the stall, clearly afraid of interrupting a private moment. She held up one finger to him.

"That sounds great, but I have to keep moving or we'll never get done."

Daniel stepped back, slipping his hands into his jeans' pockets. "I'll get out of your way. But think about it, okay?"

She met his gaze. God, she wished she didn't know anything about Daniel Brice or that damned bottle of acepromazine. "I already am." She didn't add that *thinking* was as far as it could go.

He turned away. "Keep me posted," he called over his shoulder.

A vacation with Daniel after this was all settled. Jessie sighed, knowing all too well that by the time this was settled, she'd be the last person Daniel would want to spend time with.

BY MIDAFTERNOON, JESSIE and Dr. McCarrell had to leave to make their Lasix rounds. Jessie caught up to Meryl, Dr. Baker, and Sherry after the races and found them still at work. It was well past midnight before they completed the task of drawing blood from every horse stabled at Riverview.

Dr. Baker wasted no time getting back on the road, turning down an offer to grab something to eat. Meryl drove out behind her, and Sherry grunted goodnight before shoving her hands in her pockets and ambling off in the direction of the rec hall.

At the clinic, Jessie discovered several large boxes sitting next to the locked door. She hauled them inside and spent a large portion of the remainder of the night unpacking and setting up her new laptops. The last box contained the futon, some assembly required. After dragging the old sofa out of the office, she slit open the box with her pocketknife, dumped the contents on the exam area floor, and lugged the seat portion of the dismantled futon into the office. She collapsed onto it fully clothed and fell into a deep sleep.

She awoke, groggy and disoriented, to the ringing of her cell phone. Molly had made a nest between her legs and the tabby had draped himself over her belly. She disengaged from her bedmates and grabbed the phone from the desk.

"Jessie, it's me. Catherine." The voice at the other end was irritatingly perky. "Have you had a chance to look at Blue's x-rays?"

Rubbing her eyes with her free hand, Jessie struggled to focus. X-rays? What day was this? She squinted at the clock above the futon seat. Nine fifteen? Crap. She was running a mere two hours late and she felt like she had a mouthful of surgical sponges. "Sorry, Catherine. I put in a late night." Sometime during her short slumber, she'd managed to kick off her boots. She reached out to snag the first one, then the other. "Why don't I call you back in an hour or so?"

"That won't be necessary. I'll be there to see you around noon. Okay?"

The phone went dead before Jessie could reply. She ran her tongue over fuzzy teeth. "Noon," she said to Molly. "Great."

Rounds were light that morning, probably because Jessie was running late and anyone with emergencies would have already given up and called Dr. McCarrell.

By the time Catherine's white sedan rolled to a stop outside the clinic doors precisely at twelve, Jessie had grabbed a quick shower, brushed her teeth, and changed into a fresh t-shirt and jeans. She'd figured out how to upload the radiographs onto the new computer but hadn't had a chance to look at them.

Catherine sashayed into the office in white strappy sandals and a pale blue skirt and jacket. She thumped a purse big enough to hold a small pony onto the desk. "Well? What did you find out?"

"I haven't had a chance to view these yet." Jessie slid into her chair and pulled the file up on the laptop. She scrutinized each picture. She hadn't liked the previews, and the full-sized versions didn't look any better. She motioned for Catherine to come around to her side of the desk and placed one finger on the screen. "You see this?"

Catherine nodded, but from her pursed lips and creased brow, Jessie knew she didn't.

"The fracture is on the articular surface, high on the coffin bone. The prognosis isn't what we'd like, I'm afraid."

Catherine deflated. "I don't understand. I broke my ankle when I was a kid, and it healed up just fine."

"The coffin bone doesn't correspond to the ankle. It's more like breaking your big toe if you were a ballerina. Besides, it's porous, and when it mends, a fibrous union is produced instead of a bony one. That's why the prognosis is so poor on these types of injuries. I'm sorry. I wish I had better news."

Catherine deflated even more. "I do too."

"I have to think Blue was injured before you bought him." Jessie swiveled the chair to face Catherine and leaned back. "I wish you'd had a pre-purchase vet check on him. It would've saved you a lot of money, not to mention heartache."

"But we did," Catherine insisted. "At least I thought Milt did." She sounded less certain. "I guess it doesn't matter now. What's done is done." Catherine picked up her purse. "Thanks just the same. I appreciate you taking the time to look at him."

"I'm sorry I can't offer you more hope. He'll likely be fine for light riding, but no way will he hold up to the stress of training or racing."

Catherine headed for the door, her fashion runway gait a little slower than usual. She paused to cast a weary smile at Jessie. "If only Milt and I had kids, we could use him for pony rides." Lowering her head, she turned and walked out.

Jessie stared at the image on the computer screen. Frustration at not being able to do anything for Blue gave way to anger. Odds were someone had pushed the horse too hard. But who?

She jumped up and charged from the office, racing across the exam area. "Catherine!"

But the sedan was pulling away, and Jessie didn't feel like chasing it. From what she'd seen of Catherine and Milt's working relationship, Catherine probably wasn't the one to ask.

Twenty-One

Tuesday morning passed at a snail's pace. The only chatter was low-key conversation about anything except the elephant that had taken up residence in Riverview's backside. No one mentioned EIA or the word "quarantine" or even the health of anyone's animals regardless of how minor a problem might be. Consequently, Jessie received few requests for her services.

One thing hadn't been affected yet, and that was the racing schedule. Lasix rounds came as a relief, giving Jessie something to do other than play the what-if game. Once she finished with the injections, she headed for the front side. If the evening's emergencies mirrored the morning ones, she might actually catch a race or two.

She stopped at the concession stand, collected an order of nachos with extra cheese, and found an empty picnic table on the deck outside.

Jessie removed her ball cap to let the early spring sun bathe her face. Across the track, the tote board displayed the fluctuating odds for the first race. A tractor dragged a massive rake around the dirt surface. The normality of it appeased her. If she closed her eyes, she could pretend life was equally normal behind the scenes.

From over her shoulder a hand tossed a racing program onto the table next to her nachos. "Hey there, darlin'." Milt swung a leg over the bench as if mounting a horse. He tapped the program. "You need one of these if you plan to hang out over here."

"Thanks." She tried to manage a smile of appreciation, which she was certain didn't make it through the layers of worry. "Is Catherine around?"

"Nope. No Derby prospects running tonight." He gave her shoulder a nudge. "What brings you to the front side?"

Jessie dipped a nacho into the artificially yellow cheese sauce and popped the dripping mess into her mouth. Chewing gave her time to contemplate an answer. As she savored the salt, the crunch, and the tang, the glass doors to the grandstand swung open. A couple dozen racing enthusiasts poured out. From the tunnel, the horses for the first race stepped onto the track.

Jessie swallowed and pointed at them. "That's what brings me here. Same as everyone else. The horses."

Milt shifted to watch the post parade. "It's addictive, ain't it?"

She mulled over the word. "It is." She felt his gaze on her. "Sherry didn't inherit Doc's practice."

Jessie didn't have to look at Milt to know he was smiling. "You'll be staying on then," he said.

She sighed. "I wish."

"What do you mean?"

She thumbed the program open to the first race. "Meryl isn't interested in buying my half of the Cameron Veterinary Hospital. Without that money, I can't afford it."

Milt fell silent.

The horses on the track made their way around the far turn to the starting gate positioned in the chute at the head of the backstretch. According to the program, the race would be a maiden special weight for three-year-old fillies. Six furlongs. And Jessie had treated five of the eight entries for one thing or another. One of the other three had Neil Emerick listed as trainer. A check of the tote board revealed that entry as a scratch.

Milt reached over to reposition the program so he could read it too. "Do you have a favorite?"

"Five of them."

He met her gaze. A slow smile spread across his face. "You get attached. You work on them, and suddenly, you got a dog in the hunt."

She hadn't thought of it in those terms, but he was right.

"Darlin', where there's a will, there's a way. You want Doc's practice, you'll figure out how to make it happen. Hell, I'd loan you the money if I had it."

Which reminded Jessie of what she'd wanted to talk to Milt about. "I saw Catherine earlier."

He looked up from the program. "Oh?"

Jessie told him about the results of the new x-rays on Blue.

"No surprise there," he said when she finished.

"There seems to be some question about a pre-purchase vet check, though."

"What question?"

"I told Catherine I wished you'd had one performed on him, and she thought you had."

Milt lifted his gaze to the track. Jessie followed it. The horses were loading into the gate. "I like that number two filly. She's been in the money every dang time she runs but drops off in the stretch in those longer races. Six furlongs might be the distance for her."

Jessie looked at him. Was he intentionally avoiding the subject of Blue?

He caught her watching him and sighed. "You wish I'd had him checked? Well, so do I. Damn it all to hell. Sure would've saved me a shitload of greenbacks. I could kick myself now. But just look at him. I've seen lameness in horses. God knows I have. See it every day. But there was no sign of it in that old boy. He was sound as they come." Milt shook his head. "It wasn't until later, when Zelda started putting him through some serious workouts, that it showed up. We rested him. He got sound. We ran him. He got gimpy. That's when I called you."

"That's typical of this kind of injury. I told Catherine he'd be fine for some light riding."

"Light riding ain't what we bought him for." Milt picked up the race program and gave it a shake. "Hell, without any kind of past performance record, we can't even get decent money for stud fees."

"He is pretty, though."

"Oh, you bet. He's a damn fine-looking animal."

Over the crackling PA, the announcer proclaimed the horses were in the gate. A moment later, all seven horses broke clean and jostled for position down the backstretch. Jessie used a hand to shield her eyes from the sun. "Which filly was your pick?"

"Number two. Did you decide on one?"

"Let's see." She retrieved the crumpled program from Milt. "Numbers two, three, five, seven, and eight."

He snorted without taking his eyes from the horses approaching the far turn. "I said one. Not five of them."

"And show favoritism among my patients? No way." At least not this time. She strained to pick out the order from the announcer's call, since she couldn't make out a thing from where they sat. No wonder Catherine preferred her box seats with the closed-circuit TV.

Milt reached around and backhanded Jessie's arm. "Here she comes."

As the horses charged down the stretch, Jessie made out the number two filly making a big move up the outside. But the numbers one and six horses battled for the lead closer to the wire. Not her patients. "Come on, baby!" she shouted, adding to the din of the crowd around them.

The horses thundered in front of them and under the wire, the number two filly closing the gap as the number one horse faded slightly. The announcer called a photo finish and ordered, "Hold all tickets."

The roar of the crowd died down to await the official results.

Jessie tapped the program. "Do you have any money on her?"

"No, dang it." Milt gave her a sheepish grin. "Yet another case of 20/20 hindsight."

She thought of the stallion in the Dodds' barn. "Maybe you should try breeding Blue. With his conformation, if he produces some nice babies that grow up to win, it won't matter what he did or didn't do on the track."

Milt removed his cap and wiped the back of his arm across his forehead. "That's a big gamble. Expensive too. I'd rather sell him. Get my money back. Let somebody else feed him for four or five years until his babies prove themselves." A far away twinkle lit his blue eyes. "Maybe some other fool would buy him without having a vet check first. What they don't know, won't hurt me." As soon as he said it, guilt flashed across his face.

"Milt," she said disapprovingly.

"Just kidding, darlin'. Just kidding. You know me better'n that." He winked at her. Then pointed at the tote board. "Look."

The OFFICIAL sign flashed with the order of finish. Two, six, and one.

"I picked a winner." Milt replaced his cap and swung his leg over the bench to stand. "Goes to show you. Even a blind squirrel finds a nut every once in a while." He patted her shoulder. "Later."

"Wait." She caught his arm. "There was one other thing I wondered about."

"What's that?"

"Who'd you buy Blue from?"

Milt winced as if he'd been stung by a horsefly. He looked toward the backside, and his reply was so soft, she wasn't sure she heard it right. "Neil Emerick." Without another word, Milt walked away.

Jessie watched as he merged with the crowd of bettors heading inside to cash their winning tickets. Or place more bets. Or check out the horses in the paddock.

Neil Emerick. She should've guessed.

A LARGE, THICK ENVELOPE arrived by FedEx Wednesday morning while Jessie sat at her new computer, entering reports from the last few days. She stared at the package, turning it over in her hands. Drawing a deep breath, she slit the envelope open with her penknife. The contents, a stack of Coggins test papers, spilled out onto her desk. One by one, she checked the results. With each *negative*, the tension in her shoulders released a notch. By the time she came to the last sheet without a positive finding in the bunch, she'd almost melted onto the floor with relief.

She fumbled with her phone, hastily punching in the number from the business card she'd kept tucked in her jeans' pocket. After conferring with Dr. Baker, Jessie crammed the Coggins papers back into the envelope, tucked it under her arm, and jogged out of the clinic.

Only a few early bird gamblers at the slot machines occupied the grandstand. Jessie hoped Daniel would be in his office. At his doorway, she considered Greg's demand that she avoid being alone with Daniel. She took a deep breath, dismissed the advice, then breezed through.

"Jessie." Daniel sounded pleased to see her, but when he noticed the papers in her hands, his lips pressed into a tight, thin line.

"I thought you'd want to take a look at these." She deposited the envelope on his desk.

"Have you gone through them yet?"

"Oh, yeah."

"And?" He hadn't reached for the envelope as if the mere touch of it might jinx the results.

"They're all negative." She smiled her first genuine smile in days.

Daniel looked apprehensive. "All of them?"

"Every last one."

His lips parted, showing perfect white teeth. The creases that had once been dimples deepened in his face. Both hands curled into fists and he drummed on his desktop. "Yes." He jumped to his feet and came around the desk toward Jessie.

Before she had time to react, he grabbed her and pressed a kiss, hot and hard, to her lips. Blindsided, both her mind and her knees lost their resolve. As she moved to slip her arms around his waist, he released her. She staggered and caught the edge of his desk, clinging to it the way she'd momentarily wanted to cling to him.

"Does this mean what I hope it means?" he asked. "The quarantine will be limited to the two barns?"

"Uh. Yeah." Breathless, she fought to regain her composure. "I spoke with Dr. Baker from Veterinary Services, and she agrees. There'll still be follow-up tests, though."

"Fine. Whatever you say." Daniel snatched her into his arms, and for a moment, she thought he was going to kiss her again. Instead, he swung her around in what she supposed was a waltz. "We have to celebrate."

She pushed away from him before she tripped over her own feet. "Celebrate?"

"Absolutely. Dinner. Anyplace you want. After we give everyone the good news, that is."

"Dinner?" The kiss still lingered on her mind along with its promise of much more.

"Where do you want to go?"

"I...don't know."

"That's all right. You can tell me when and where later." He turned toward his phone. "Right now, I want to call Zelda. She's been waiting for word of when she could bring Clown back."

The fantasy melted away like the last snow of spring dropping into the Monongahela River. Jessie stared at Daniel's back as he placed the call. Could this be the man who drugged Clown, turning the Thoroughbred into a murder weapon?

Was she falling in love with a killer?

BARN BY BARN, JESSIE delivered the owners' copies of the negative Coggins tests. For days, she'd felt like Typhoid Mary. Today, she was greeted with smiles and handshakes and a round of thank-yous.

As she crossed the road between barns, footsteps padded up behind her. She turned to find Sherry jogging toward her. Jessie kept walking, and she fell into step at her side. "I hear the news is good."

"Better than the news I had to deliver to Doug Whitman."

"I bet."

"By the way, I wanted to thank you for helping out on Monday. I really appreciate it."

"How much?"

Jessie stopped short. "What do you mean?"

"How much do you appreciate my help? Enough to take me into partnership with you here at the track?"

Jessie studied her face, searching for some sign she was kidding. But Sherry's eyes were bright and steady. "You can't be serious," Jessie said.

"Why not? I figured you'd buy my dad's practice since he didn't leave it to me. Old Dr. McCarrell wants to retire, so there'll be more clients here than you can handle alone."

"You admitted you hate me and now you want to work with me?"

"Hated. Past tense." Sherry walked a few paces ahead of Jessie, then turned to face her again. "Besides, we wouldn't actually be working together most of the time. The horsemen could pick which one of us they preferred."

From Sherry's grin, Jessie surmised she expected to gain the larger numbers.

It wasn't a bad idea. From what Jessie had seen, Sherry was more than competent. And she knew her way around the racing world. There were, however, a couple of problems with the plan. One being Jessie didn't trust her. The other was the simple fact that Meryl had turned down her request to buy the hospital. Jessie chose to keep both to herself. "I'll think about it." She continued across the road and into the next shedrow.

Sherry kept pace. "Good. I need to start making some money."

"What about your inheritance?"

"I haven't received the check yet. Besides, it's already earmarked to pay off my loan."

"To Butch."

Sherry rammed her hands into her jeans' pockets and lowered her head. "Yeah."

While Jessie had Sherry in a talkative mood, she decided to do some digging. "By the way, do you happen to know anything about a horse named Mexicali Blue?"

Sherry tripped but caught herself. "Like what exactly?"

"Milt Dodd bought him from your friend Neil Emerick but didn't have a pre-purchase exam done. It turns out Blue has a broken coffin bone."

Sherry let out a raspy whistle. "That's rough. Bad injury for a racehorse. Milt didn't have him checked?"

"Yeah."

"That's pretty stupid, don't you think?"

Jessie took the question as rhetorical. "Do you know anything?"

Sherry glanced over her shoulder. Then back to the ground in front of her feet. "Nope. Don't know a thing. Look, I gotta go. You have fun on your mail route." She wheeled and strode off in the direction from which they'd come.

Sherry was lying. She may not want to admit it, but she knew about Blue. Jessie was sure of it. Doc's daughter seemed well versed in the practice of deception. And there was still the issue of the silver and turquoise barrette stashed in Jessie's desk drawer.

What else was the new Dr. Malone lying about?

Twenty-Two

The celebratory atmosphere that had enveloped Riverview's backside was short-lived. Jessie hadn't completed delivering the test papers before owners and trainers, negative Coggins tests in hand, loaded their animals into trailers and headed for the exit.

By the time Jessie returned to the clinic, a line of horse trailers jammed the road from the gate toward the river. The rumble of gasoline and diesel engines and the choking stench of exhaust filled the air. She spoke to several of the men and women behind the wheels of the rigs, imploring them to stay, but the general consensus was to beat it before the powers-that-be changed their minds.

Dinner might not be the festive occasion Daniel had anticipated.

She stood in the shade of the clinic with her arms crossed, watching the exodus. This wasn't what she'd wanted.

Her phone rang. She slipped inside and pressed a finger into her other ear to block the growl of idling engines.

Sherry's voice greeted her. "I need to talk to you."

"Well, you've got me. If you're calling about partnering up with me, take a look around. There aren't going to be enough horses left on the grounds for even one of us to treat."

"Shut up and listen. I know something about my dad's death."

Had Jessie heard right? "Wait a minute." With her finger still rammed in her ear, she hurried into the office and kicked the door closed behind her. "What did you say?"

"I have a pretty good idea who killed him and why."

The air in the office suddenly felt unbreathable. And not because of the diesel fumes. Jessie dropped onto the futon next to the tabby.

She waited for Sherry to continue, but there was only silence on the other end of the receiver. "Hello?" Jessie wondered if they'd been cut off.

"I'm here."

"So tell me."

"Not over the phone. I want to meet someplace where we won't be interrupted. If he finds out we're on to him..."

"Him? Who's 'him'?"

"I told you. Not on the phone. I had an appointment to swim Sullivan this afternoon before the EIA thing came up and never bothered to cancel. Check the book. Did anyone else change it?"

Jessie pinched the phone between her ear and shoulder, yanked open the file cabinet drawer, and fumbled through the contents. She retrieved the book and opened it on her lap. The pool was severely underutilized. The only name on the page was Sherry Malone.

"You're still on for two o'clock."

"Good. No one else will be around the spa. I'll meet you then."

The spa. The pool. *Someone might just give you a little shove, and you might end up taking a swim like old Sullivan here.* "Isn't there someplace else we could meet? How about my office?"

"Not private enough."

"I could lock the door."

An exasperated hiss of air crossed the phone line. "The spa at two o'clock. Be there."

The line went dead. Jessie looked at the time on the phone's screen. One thirty.

If he finds out we're on to him...

Who? Jessie tried to swallow, but her mouth and throat felt as dry as a roll of sterile gauze. She already knew the answer.

Daniel had served time for murder. He had everything to lose if Doc had revealed his secret past. Daniel possessed a bottle of the drug that turned a high-strung, but tractable, stallion into a raging killer.

Molly strolled out of the bathroom, stretched, and sauntered toward Jessie, springing lightly into her lap. Jessie stroked the old cat's velvety head, letting her hand trail down her neck and back, all the way to the tip of her black tail.

There was another possibility. Jessie set Molly down on the floor and moved to the chair behind the desk. She slid open the top drawer and removed the barrette. Evidence that Sherry had been in her house and destroyed Doc's records. What had she been trying to cover up? She was in debt to the local loan shark and needed money that Doc refused to give her while he was still alive. She'd been trying to throw suspicion onto everyone else all along. Butch. Frank Hamilton. Even Daniel.

If Sherry wanted to play this hand, fine. Jessie would go along with it and meet her at the spa. However, Jessie intended to stay far away from that awful green water. She would listen to what Sherry had to say. And then Jessie would throw down the card she'd been holding for the last week. She turned the barrette over and over in her hand feeling the smooth metal and stone against her fingers. It was time to call Sherry's bluff.

At ten minutes before two, Jessie's phone signaled a new text message. She looked at the screen. *Emergency. Barn E.*

With an exasperated growl, she grabbed a pen and jotted an explanatory note to Sherry, ending with, *I'll be back as soon as I can.* After tearing a strip of tape from the dispenser, she jogged through the hallway to the spa and taped the note to the light switch, which she left turned off. Unless Sherry wanted to wait in the dark, there would be no way she could miss the message.

Unlike many of the stables, Barn E was not deserted. When Jessie entered the shedrow, several horses' heads hung over their stall doors. A rail-thin boy sat on an overturned bucket cleaning a bridle. Farther down, Jessie spotted Zelda's groom, Miguel Diaz, dragging a water hose from stall to stall. Neither seemed particularly upset. The boy looked up at her with no expression.

"Did you call for a vet?"

He went back to his work. "Not me, man."

About halfway down the shedrow, Zelda stepped out of a stall, latching the webbing behind her.

Jessie called to her.

Zelda looked in her direction. "Dr. Cameron. How nice to see you. I missed you when you were here earlier distributing the test results. Great news, isn't it?"

"It is. I guess it wasn't you who texted me."

Zelda frowned at the boy on the bucket. He shook his head at her. She turned toward the other end of the barn. "Miguel, did you call for the vet?"

"No, *Senora* Zelda. I did not."

Zelda's mouth puckered to one side. "That's strange."

"Is there anyone else around who might have sent me a text?"

Zelda extended both arms, taking in her two helpers and the entire shedrow of horses. "Nobody here but us."

Jessie dug her phone from her pocket, pulled up the list of messages in her inbox, and opened the most recent. It was short and sweet. *Emergency. Barn E.* She hadn't misread it. This time, she noted the number from which the text had been sent. An icy chill tickled the back of her neck.

Zelda was tapping her chin with one finger. "Maybe we should look around?"

"I don't think that'll be necessary." Jessie strode toward the groom. "Miguel, did you ever find your phone?"

"No, Doctor Jessie." He wrinkled his nose. "I think I maybe dropped it in the manure dumpster."

Zelda joined them and put a comforting hand on her groom's shoulder. "We figured someone's using it to mulch mushrooms right about now."

Jessie checked her own phone one more time before pocketing it. "I don't think so. Someone just used it to text me."

THE CLOCK ON THE CHEVY'S dashboard read two fifteen when Jessie braked to a stop in front of the clinic.

On the short drive across the backside, she'd determined Sherry had summoned her away from the clinic in order to steal or destroy the rest of Doc's records. And, if Sherry had Miguel's missing phone, she'd been the one who'd lured Doc to Clown's stall that night. It all made perfect sense.

But then why make the appointment to meet poolside in the first place?

Jessie bolted from the truck, pounded across the exam area, and slammed through the office door, expecting to find empty file drawers hanging open. Instead, the tabby, frightened by Jessie's abrupt entrance, scrambled from the futon to the bathroom. Molly didn't stir from her napping spot on the desk. Everything else was just as Jessie had left it.

She pulled the door closed and gazed down the poorly lit passageway toward the spa. "Sherry?"

No one replied. For the second time in a half hour, Jessie made the dreaded trek to the pool. The back door remained closed. The lights were still off. Apparently, Sherry hadn't shown up.

Jessie picked her way across the floor, waiting for her eyes to acclimate to the darkness. She reached for the switch. The note she'd left was gone. She flicked on the overhead lights. Once the fluorescent bulbs hesitated, flashed, dimmed, and finally came on, she searched the wall, thinking maybe Sherry had left a note of her own. Jessie scanned the walls and the countertops but found nothing out of the ordinary. She checked the railing around the pool. Nothing.

Except...

She looked again. Not at the railing, but at the water's surface. It shimmered black. The reflection of the overhead lights skimmed across the pool until they hit an obstacle. Something in the pool broke the reflected image.

Jessie edged closer. A cold, opaque veil slid over her eyes. For a moment the world stopped. No movement. No sound. Nothing penetrated the veil that encompassed her brain.

She blinked, breaking the spell and the stillness. The image in front of her snapped into detailed focus.

An oblong pale blue balloon became the back of a shirt inflated with air trapped between the body and the fabric. Resting on top of that blue balloon, making a slight dent in it, was a long braid, once blonde, now dark and waterlogged.

Jessie fumbled for her phone. Fought to control the shaking of her usually steady hands long enough to punch in 911. She had no idea what she babbled to the dispatcher and hoped she made sense. There was no time to repeat herself.

She dipped under the railing surrounding the pool. The phone slipped from her fingers and clattered to the floor. She made a grab for it, but the phone skittered into the water with a soft *sploosh*.

The pool reeled in front of her eyes. Ignoring the vertigo, she raced around the catwalk, clinging to the railing. At the far side of the pool, Jessie let go and dropped to her knees. She reached toward Sherry's body but only snatched at air.

Jessie lowered to her belly. Stretched farther. Gripped the edge of the catwalk with one hand, strained toward Sherry with the other. Still, the body bobbed just beyond her fingers.

She pressed back to her knees. Frantic, she scanned the spa, searching for something—a pole, a rope—anything to extend her reach. A broom leaned next to the door. She climbed to her feet and sprinted along the catwalk toward it.

She didn't see the wet patch until it was too late. In one dreadful moment, her feet shot out from under her. The edge of the catwalk raced up. The impact knocked the wind out of her. Her right leg went over the side. Scrambling, scratching, she fought for a grip on the slick wood.

But the momentum carried her into the pool.

Water closed around her face, her head. The old familiar panic seized her. Just like when she was eight. No one saw her go under that time either. She flailed. Which way was up to air? Which way only took her closer to hopelessness? Was she being drawn to the surface? Or sinking like a stone? Her lungs threatened to explode. Time stalled.

Then her hand struck something solid. The edge of the pool. She clawed at it, desperate for a finger hold on the slimy surface. With darkness enveloping her, she flung one arm upward. Her fingers found the edge of the walkway. She held on.

Blinded, Jessie heaved herself up, gagging and choking. She strained to hook an arm on the edge of the catwalk. Then the other arm. She clung there, spewing foul tasting water. Gasping for breath. Blinking. For a moment, she didn't dare move except to breathe and gather her wits. Her chest burned. Cautiously, she looked toward Sherry. There was no movement. No struggle.

But sometimes drowning victims could be resuscitated. She had to make the effort.

Wheezing, Jessie hoisted herself higher. Braced on her elbows. Grit her teeth as she tried to swing a leg up onto the catwalk. On the third attempt, her heel caught. Struggling against the weight of her water-logged clothes, she climbed the rest of the way up. Her ribs throbbed from the blow to the edge of the walkway. Hugging the rail, she picked her way along the wet catwalk, grabbed the broom, and retraced her steps to where Sherry's body floated.

Jessie extended the straw bristle end toward the blue balloon, which was in the process of deflating. She succeeded. Slowly, she drew the broom and Sherry toward her. But the broom slipped off. Jessie tried again and dragged her closer. Close enough that she tossed the broom aside and caught a handful of blue fabric. She floated the body to the edge of the pool and grabbed her with both hands. Bracing her heels against an uneven board, she lugged Sherry's sodden form onto the walkway and rolled her onto her back.

Years of working on animals had not dulled the basic CPR skills she'd learned ages ago. She checked for a carotid pulse. Nothing. Jessie lifted Sherry's jaw, pressed her lips to Sherry's mouth, and forced two puffs of air into her lungs. Shifted her position and started chest compressions.

"Hello?" came a voice outside the door.

"*In here!*" Jessie called.

She couldn't remember ever being as happy to see anyone as she was to see those men with the paramedic emblems on their shirts charging toward her.

Twenty-Three

Jessie felt as if gallons of the fetid water had gotten trapped inside her head, behind her eyes, and in her sinuses, creating pressure on her brain. Someone draped an old horse blanket reeking of stale sweat around her shoulders. She watched as the paramedics administered CPR and pasted leads for a portable EKG unit to Sherry's torso. Jessie was too far away to hear their whispered comments, but from their glum expressions, she surmised they didn't have much to work with.

They found a bloody gash on Sherry's head. Jessie hadn't noticed it before, too busy trying to get both of them out of that damned pool.

She wasn't sure when Daniel showed up, only knew he was at her side.

Two uniformed police officers entered from the passageway. State Trooper Larry Popovich trailed behind them. The same crew as the night Doc died.

Someone shoved a Styrofoam cup of coffee in her hands. She looked up into Greg's face. She tipped her head toward the other cops and the paramedics. "We have to stop meeting like this."

Greg's expression lacked humor. "What the hell happened, Jess?"

With one hand, she clutched the rank horse blanket around her. She extended the one holding the coffee cup toward the pool and pointed. "I fell in."

"I heard. You look like shit."

She noticed his paint-splattered once-white t-shirt and faded blue jeans. His usually neat, short-cropped hair was uncombed. "So

255

do you." In truth, he reminded her entirely too much of the guy she'd fallen in love with all those years ago.

He snorted a short laugh. "I guess you're all right."

Popovich strolled toward them. For a man only slightly smaller than a mountain, he moved like a cat. He extended one massive paw toward Greg, who grasped it. Then the trooper turned to Jessie. "Twice in one month. That has to be some sort of record for this place."

Jessie released the blanket to shake Popovich's offered hand, and the blanket slid off her shoulders to the floor. She'd forgotten Daniel was there until he bent down to retrieve it. She considered telling him to leave it. The thing stunk. But she realized she was still shivering and allowed him to wrap her in it once again. His arm stayed protectively around her shoulders.

Trooper Popovich produced a pad and pen from his pockets. "If you don't mind, I'd like to ask you a few questions."

She wished the pressure inside of her head would ease up and allow her to think. "Sure." Flanked by Greg and Daniel, she told the trooper about Sherry's cryptic call requesting they meet.

"What did she want to talk to you about?"

Jessie resisted an urge to cast a sideways glance at Daniel. "I don't know. She just said it was important."

"Go on."

"Ten minutes before she was supposed to come here, I got a text about an emergency in Zelda Peterson's barn." Jessie looked at Greg. "But no one there sent it. And when I checked the number the text came from, it was the same one that called Doc the night he died."

Greg shot a glance at Popovich. The big trooper held out his palm. "Do you mind if I have a look at your phone?"

Jessie worked her hand into her wet jeans' pocket. No phone. She fought the fog and the pressure to think. Where was it? She'd used it to call for help.

"Dr. Cameron?" the trooper prompted.

She glanced around and remembered the sickening splash. "I dropped it. It went in the pool."

"Wonderful," he muttered. "Okay, you were at Peterson's barn. Then what happened?"

"I rushed back here. The lights were out, so at first, I thought she hadn't shown up. But my note was gone—"

"What note?"

"I left her a note taped to the light switch before I went over to Barn E, telling her where I was and why."

"Where is it now?"

"I don't know. I told you. It was gone when I returned."

He jotted something in his notebook. "Then what?"

"When I turned on the lights, I saw her floating in the pool. I called 911 and then tried to pull her out, but I fell in."

"You fell? You didn't dive in to get her?"

Jessie thought she detected a note of accusation in his voice. "I can't swim."

She expected him to ask her why not, but instead he asked, "Do you have any idea how the victim got that cut on her head?"

"No." The pressure behind her forehead was becoming unbearable. "I didn't know there was a cut until I heard the paramedics talking."

"You didn't know?" Popovich looked incredulous. "How could you not notice? It was a good size gash."

Jessie liked the tone of his questions less and less. "I was busy."

Popovich thumbed back through his notes. "I understand you and Ms. Malone have had a number of arguments in recent weeks."

Daniel extended an arm toward the trooper. "Excuse me, sir, should Dr. Cameron have a lawyer present?"

Popovich looked surprised. Jessie was pretty sure he wasn't. "Only if she feels she needs one."

"Are you accusing her of something?"

Greg stepped between them. "Hold on now." He turned to face his colleague. "Larry, just what are you getting at?"

He shrugged. "You know how it goes, Greg. I need to find out exactly what happened here this afternoon. A girl is dead. She was supposed to meet your wife. Your wife happens to be the one who found her."

"And pulled her out of the water," Jessie reminded him.

The trooper held up a hand. "Which definitely helps if you want to look innocent."

I am innocent, she wanted to shout. Greg took Popovich by the arm and directed him away from her.

Jessie rubbed the throbbing pain between her eyes. "What the hell is going on?"

Daniel's stony gaze followed the two troopers. "Don't worry about it. Everything's going to be all right."

Jessie wasn't so sure. The suffocating sensation of being in over her head came back. And she was standing on dry ground.

Greg returned without Popovich, who stayed huddled with the officers from the county police department. "They're calling in the crime scene unit."

Jessie repositioned the horse blanket. Besides stinking to high heaven, the thing was getting heavy. "Finally."

He raised an eyebrow at her. "Finally? It's only been what?" He checked his watch. "A half hour?"

"More like two and a half weeks. If you'd investigated Doc's death, this one might not have happened."

He glanced at Daniel who'd stepped away to speak with one of the officers. Greg lowered his head toward Jessie so his comment would reach her alone. "I did investigate." His eyes hinted at more, but Daniel's return kept him from elaborating.

He looked at Greg. "I was talking to your colleagues. They sound like they seriously suspect her."

"I know."

She choked on a sip of the lukewarm coffee.

Daniel glared at Greg. "Then why aren't you over there setting them straight?"

"Wouldn't do any good. I'm not on this case."

The pain behind Jessie's eyes kicked up a notch. "Why not?" She looked at Greg first, then Daniel. Neither of them replied. "Why not?" she repeated, but slower, in case they hadn't understood her the first time.

Greg looked down at the floor. Daniel was the one to respond. "Conflict of interest."

The putrid horse blanket's lining must have been wicking the moisture from her sopping clothes because it felt like it weighed a hundred pounds. She shrugged it from her shoulders. "In other words, the one cop who knows me well enough to know I couldn't have killed anyone is the cop who's not allowed to investigate the case."

"That pretty much sums it up," Greg said.

She stared into the cold coffee in the cup and wished for something much, much stronger than sugar to add to it.

"Once Larry speaks to Zelda Peterson and the coroner narrows down the time of death, you should be in the clear."

"*Should* be?"

"You need to get some rest."

Jessie looked toward the hallway to her office. Somehow, she found nothing restful about the idea of sleeping less than fifty feet from where Sherry had drowned. And where she had almost fallen victim to the same fate.

Daniel must have read her mind. "Pack your things. You're coming back to my place tonight."

Before Jessie had a chance to consider the appealing offer, Greg snapped an answer for her. "No." He gave her that same dark look that suggested he knew a hell of a lot more than he was saying. "You're coming back to the house with me."

She kept her eyes on Greg, but she sensed Daniel tense beside her. "Okay," she said.

Daniel's look of displeasure with Greg turned to one of disappointment aimed at her.

She peeled her gaze from the man who had broken her heart, transferring it to the man who simultaneously beguiled and terrified her. "I'll be more comfortable in my own bed. And Molly will be happy to go home."

Daniel's expression softened. "If that's what you want, then that's where you should be. I guess our dinner plans for tonight are off?"

She tried to swallow, but her throat was the only dry part of her anatomy. "Raincheck?"

"You bet." He took a step toward her and pressed a tender kiss to her cheek. In a growl directed at Greg, he said, "Get her out of here. And don't let anything happen to her."

Greg's gaze followed Daniel as he made his way toward the group of local police. "Dinner? Didn't I tell you to steer clear of him?"

She opened her mouth to explain but was glad when he raised a hand to shush her. After all, she didn't have much of an explanation.

"Never mind." He looked past her toward the pool. She wondered if he was trying to imagine what had happened there. "I'm going to tell Popovich we're leaving. Go pick up Molly and I'll meet you out front."

"And the tabby."

"Right." He shoved his hands in his back pockets and headed for the other cops.

Jessie picked up the blanket and tossed it on a workbench. She looked toward the crowd gathered at the back doors and spotted a new face among them.

Emerick stood, arms crossed, surveying the scene inside the spa. His dark gaze shifted from the pool to settle on her. From the distance, she couldn't quite make out his dark expression. Accusatory? Angry?

Smug?

His chin lifted, and there was no doubt about the smirk that crossed his lips before he turned his back and strode away.

JESSIE AWOKE IN HER own bed with the awful sensation of her head being packed with cotton. More specifically, cotton soaked in water from the pool. She sat up and looked around. Everything was in its proper place, so why did she feel like she had been dropped into an episode of the *Twilight Zone*?

And where were the cats?

Wearing her usual oversized t-shirt, she climbed out of bed and tugged on a pair of jeans. She opened the door—usually she slept with it open, but it seemed inappropriate with Greg in the house—and stepped into the hall.

Apparently, Greg did not share her awkward need for privacy. She peeked inside the guest room where Greg lay on his back, the sheet pulled up to his hips revealing his lean, muscular torso. His arms were crossed behind his head, and he was staring at the ceiling. Molly and the tabby snuggled on either side of him. Peanut lay on the rug next to the bed.

Traitors.

He spotted her and smiled. "Good morning."

She averted her eyes and mumbled an echo of his greeting. After ten years of marriage, it struck her that she was alone in the house with a stranger. Before she had a chance to say something stupid, she wheeled and padded into the bathroom in search of something to relieve her headache.

The medicine cabinet contained a wide assortment of over-the-counter products. Ibuprofen. Acetaminophen. Aspirin. Not to mention ointments, creams, and bandages. Rummaging through them, she located a box of generic decongestant. The expiration date had long since come and gone, but it promised relief from sinus headaches. She popped two, chased by a glass of water.

The mundane process of making breakfast eased the tension created by Greg's presence. Jessie laid out the bowls and spoons while he rounded up the box of cereal and the carton of milk. She made coffee. He poured orange juice. Peanut and the cats ate side by side, although the tabby, unused to the big Lab, kept a cautious eye on the dog.

Greg broke the silence. "You really have to give that poor kitten a name."

Jessie shook her head emphatically. "If I name him—"

"You'll have to keep him, I know. Face it, Jess. That cat isn't going anywhere."

He knew her all too well. "I'll think about it."

Greg shoveled a spoonful of cereal into his mouth and leaned back in the chair, his forehead creased in thought as he chewed. "How about Spot?"

Jessie almost snorted orange juice through her nose. "Are you kidding?"

"What's wrong with Spot?" He feigned deep personal injury.

"Nothing if he was a dog. Or had spots."

"Stripe, then."

"Oh, that's so much better."

He laughed, an easy comfortable laugh. Jessie smiled, the headache and the awkward moment upstairs almost forgotten. Almost.

She rearranged her cereal with the spoon. "Greg, about Daniel..."

The laughter died. He cleared his throat. "What was that about dinner?"

She decided against answering. What part of "dinner" needed to be explained?

"Didn't you hear me when I told you to keep away from him?"

"I heard you. Did you learn anything more about his criminal record?"

"What more is there to learn? He was convicted of murder."

"But there has to be more to it. You said he served his time."

"Yes."

"He wasn't given a life sentence. I mean he was released, right? He didn't escape."

"No, he didn't escape. But not all killers get life. You know that. Prisons are too crowded. Convicts get reduced sentences for good behavior."

"My point is he paid his debt to society. Have you found anything more about him since he started using the name Shumway?"

"No."

"So he's been clean since he got out."

Greg slammed his spoon down on the table. "Jess, you're trying to convince yourself the man is innocent. He's not."

The headache was back. She pressed two fingers into the space between her eyes. "Yesterday you said you investigated Doc's death. What'd you mean?"

"Just what I said."

"Uh-uh. I know you. There's more to it. What'd you find out?"

Greg scowled into his bowl. He glanced at her then returned his full attention to the cereal. "Doc wasn't exactly well liked by the masses."

Jessie leaned back and folded her arms. "If you're afraid you're gonna shatter my illusion of him being a god, you can relax. I've already figured that out."

"In the weeks before his death, he managed to get into several arguments."

Old news. But she kept that to herself. "With whom?"

Greg shot another glance at Jessie but continued to direct his conversation into his breakfast bowl. "Your Daniel Shumway for one. My source wasn't able to say what the argument was about, just that it was animated."

"Who else?"

He looked up again. This time his expression clearly stated he didn't think he needed to go on.

Jessie held his gaze, determined he would.

He sighed. "A guy from security."

"Butch."

Now Greg looked annoyed. "You already know so much, why don't you tell me?"

"No, that's okay. You go on."

He started ticking names off on his fingers. "Sherry Malone. Neil Emerick. Frank Hamilton." Greg held his hand in front of her with the four fingers poised, waiting to include the thumb. "Do you have anyone to add?"

"You've pretty well covered it."

"You could have shared what you knew."

"You kept telling me there was no murder. No investigation."

A muscle in Greg's jaw twitched.

"Did your source tell you what any of the arguments were about?"

"More than one source, actually. And no. They either didn't know or wouldn't say."

"Care to share your sources' names?"

"So you can track them down and pump them for information after I've promised them anonymity? I don't think so."

Jessie picked up her spoon. "Can't blame a gal for trying." She took a bite. "Anything on who broke in here?"

He shook his head. "I've checked all the pawn shops from Chester to Follansbee for your laptop."

A soft tapping on the doorframe between the dining room and kitchen drew Jessie's attention. She looked up to find Vanessa standing there, the one small fist that had been doing the knocking still raised. Peanut abandoned his food, nails scratching and sliding on the floor as he scurried to his new best friend.

Jessie lost interest in her meal too, but for a different reason. Greg jumped to his feet. His chair tipped back, and he grabbed for it, catching it before it went all the way over.

The petite blonde's childlike voice was barely audible. "I hope I'm not interrupting."

Jessie's head throbbed with renewed vigor. "What are you doing here? I fired you. Remember?"

"I'm not here to work. I came looking for Greg." Vanessa gazed at him with those plaintive blue eyes. "I missed you."

Any remaining appetite Jessie had vanished. "You might not have a job, but I do." She pushed back her chair and stood. "If you'll excuse me, I'll be going now."

Vanessa scooted out of the doorway, keeping her head lowered as if afraid Jessie might attack her. Peanut looked back and forth between them.

Jessie stopped to scratch him under the chin. "See you tonight, fella." She straightened and glared down at Vanessa, who was almost a head shorter and still avoiding her eyes. "Enjoy your visit. Because I'm still not giving you my house."

"Jess." Greg apparently didn't approve of Jessie's tone. She started into the kitchen, but he called her name again, this time using his stop-in-the-name-of-the-law voice.

She wheeled. "What?"

He dug in his pocket and removed his cell phone. "You'd better take this until you can get a new one. Since yours is at the bottom of the pool."

Or at the crime lab.

He tossed it to her. "Make sure you get your calls forwarded to it."

Jessie stared at the phone. Part of her longed to wing it back at him. Bounce it off his head. Instead, she curled her fingers around it. "Thanks."

As she paused on the back porch to tug on her boots, she glanced through the window into the dining room. She looked away. And looked back. Vanessa was in Greg's arms. Six-foot-four state cop holding barely five-foot unemployed veterinary receptionist. It occurred to Jessie that in spite of the size difference, they fit. It also occurred to her that her head still ached. But her heart didn't. The realization made her smile. Maybe she'd reached the final stage of grief after all.

Twenty-Four

Trooper Popovich's navy-blue Ford Explorer sat in Jessie's usual parking spot, so she pulled to the side of the clinic and cut the engine. Had Popovich never left? Or was he back again bright and early?

Yellow crime scene tape still hung in the hallway between the clinic and the spa just past her office. That was fine. The last place she wanted to be right now was anywhere near the equine swimming pool.

She inserted her key into the office door's lock.

"Good. You're here."

She jumped.

Popovich stood in the semi-darkness of the roped-off hallway with one hand resting on his sidearm. "Sorry. I didn't mean to scare you."

Jessie thought about reminding him that two vets had recently turned up dead, giving her every reason to be jittery. Instead, she pushed into her office.

He followed her. "I thought you might like to know we've got the autopsy results."

"That was fast."

"Seems Miss Malone's death was no accident."

Jessie dropped into her chair. "I figured as much."

He studied her, sizing her up. A smile curled his lip. "Greg mentioned you think you're Nancy Drew. You believe that old man's death a couple of weeks ago was murder too."

Jessie decided against sharing her suspicions. "I've been told the coroner ruled that one accidental."

"That's right." Popovich's smile faded. "Mind if I take a look around?"

"Why?"

He tipped his head to one side. "Why not?"

She came up with a quick list including the fact her head was about to explode. "Do whatever you want."

Popovich had just wiggled his fingers into a pair of nitrile gloves when Milt rapped on the open door. "Hey, darlin'. What's going on?"

"Ask him." Jessie hoisted a thumb at the trooper.

Popovich flashed a smile. "Just doing my job."

"He's investigating Sherry's murder."

Milt scowled. "Oh?" He swaggered into the room and planted a hip on the edge of the desk. "You okay?"

She pressed her fingers into her eyebrows. "Not in the slightest. I don't suppose you have any aspirin on you?"

"Sorry."

"That's okay. I think I need something stronger anyway."

Popovich, who was opening and closing file cabinet drawers, gave her a questioning look.

"Like antibiotics. I'm working on a good case of sinusitis from inhaling that crappy water."

"That'll do it." Milt swung one leg creating a slow, hollow thunk every time his heel hit the desk.

Popovich straightened from his rummaging. He held the log-book for the pool in his hands. "What's this?"

"That's the appointment book for the spa."

He slipped on a pair of old-fashioned reading glasses and thumbed through the pages. "Looks like Miss Malone had scheduled time to swim a horse yesterday." He peered over the glasses at Jessie. "Where was the horse?"

"In quarantine." When he stared blankly at her, she went on to give him the Cliff's Notes version of the dilemma in Emerick's stable.

"Then why didn't she cancel her appointment?"

"I told you yesterday. She called and said she wanted to meet with me."

"Oh, yes." His tone turned patronizing. "And you got called away and left her a note, which we still haven't been able to locate."

Jessie didn't have an answer for that one.

Popovich set the book on the desk. "Do you mind?" He waved a paw at her as if shooing a fly.

She sighed and vacated her chair, moving to the futon.

Milt followed, taking a seat next to her. He leaned toward her and whispered in her ear. "Any idea what Sherry wanted to talk to you about?"

Jessie thought she noticed Popovich's ears twitch.

Seeing that the trooper's eyes were focused on the desk's center drawer, she mouthed the word, "Later," to Milt. He winked at her and nodded.

"What's this?"

Jessie looked up to see Popovich sitting in her chair, holding the silver and turquoise barrette. An icy stillness settled over her.

"Jessie, isn't that the hair thingamabob Sherry's been yammering about losing?" Milt asked. "Where'd you find it?"

She widened her eyes at him hoping he got her wordless message to shut the hell up.

Popovich made an annoying humming sound. He turned the barrette first one way and then another as he scrutinized it. "That's a very good question, Mr. Dodd. Would you like to tell me what it's doing in your desk, Dr. Cameron?"

Jessie rehearsed her words inside her head, wondering how they would sound to a cop investigating a murder. Speaking deliberately, she said, "Someone broke into my house last week."

"Uh-huh."

"And I found that barrette in with the broken glass."

"Did you know it belonged to Miss Malone?"

"It looked like one she wears."

"Looked like? Mr. Dodd here says she lost it."

"I didn't know that at the time."

"But you thought it was hers?"

"I thought it might be."

He hummed again. "What do you suppose it was doing at your house?"

"I've been wondering that myself."

"You think she had something to do with the break-in?"

His rapid-fire questions exhausted her. "I don't know."

More humming. "I'm going to keep this. And the logbook."

"Knock yourself out." Popovich glowered at her, and she came up with a more respectful reply. "Yes, sir."

Popovich stood up, tucking the book under one arm and cradling the barrette in his palm as if it were some valuable piece of jewelry instead of a cheap, gaudy hunk of costume crap. "One more question, Dr. Cameron. You can answer this one too, Mr. Dodd." The trooper's gaze shifted from one to the other. "Do you have any idea who might have wanted Miss Malone dead?"

Jessie wished she knew. Daniel? She couldn't bring herself to say his name in this context. Not yet.

Popovich cleared his throat. "Besides yourself, that is."

There it was. The blatant accusation. She climbed to her feet and glowered at the trooper. "You find out who killed Doc Lewis and you'll have Sherry's murderer too."

JESSIE LEFT HER TRUCK parked at the clinic and struck out on foot for the front side, hoping the walk might calm her nerves.

Popovich might be putting his money on her as Sherry's killer, but he hadn't arrested her. Yet. Before he had a chance to reconsider, Jessie had to see a man about a horse.

Although it was still only May, the rising humidity was more akin to July. Jessie peeled off her hoodie before she made it halfway across the backside and tied it by the arms around her waist. Riverview was virtually deserted following the EIA scare, so the unmistakable sound of truck and trailer—grumbling diesel engine and clanking aluminum gooseneck—rolling up behind her seemed out of place. What brave soul dared venture onto contaminated soil when everyone else had beaten a hasty retreat?

Zelda waved from the driver's side window of her red and silver rig. Jessie stepped aside and waited for Zelda to pull up next to her.

"Hey, Dr. Cameron. How are you holding up? Terrible thing, what happened to Doc's assistant."

"It was." Jessie shielded her eyes from the glaring sun and looked back at the trailer. "Are you hauling in or out?"

"In. I've got Clown back there." Zelda gestured toward the big four-horse slant-ride. "I wanted to thank you for allowing it."

"I had nothing to do with it." Doc's death wasn't the Thoroughbred's fault. No reason Zelda or the horse should suffer those consequences.

Zelda gave her a knowing smile. "Sure you did. And I intend to make certain nothing else happens like..." She didn't finish the sentence but waved and gassed the truck, leaving Jessie in a wake of dust and diesel fumes.

No, none of it was Clown's fault, so why did Jessie suddenly feel overwhelmed with apprehension?

She slipped through one of the pedestrian gates and jogged toward the track on her way to the grandstand. She stopped at the rail on the far turn to watch two horses in the middle of their morning workout, loping around the oval with exercise boys standing in their stirrups. A hefty man with a rounded back cupped a stopwatch in his hands. Even after the exodus, life went on.

Following the footpath around the outside of the homestretch, she listened to the drumming of hoof beats on the dirt to her left, savored the heat of the sun on her face. For a few brief minutes, all was right with her world.

Inside the grandstand, the squeak of Jessie's rubber-soled boots echoed, but at this hour, the solitude was normal. She crossed the expansive lobby to the offices, stopped outside Daniel's, and hesitated. She'd made some foolhardy moves in her life. This was possibly the biggest. She considered beating a hasty retreat. Instead, she stepped inside.

Daniel was on the phone. He looked up and smiled but not his usual, full-blown boyish smile. He held up one finger and spoke into the receiver. "How long have we been doing business? You know I'm good for it. Just give me a couple weeks to let all this blow over...Yeah? Well, thanks a lot." His smooth voice had turned bitter. He set the receiver down hard in its cradle. Then he leaned back in his chair and ran both hands through his hair.

The distressed look on his rugged face softened Jessie's resolve. "Rough day?"

"You could say that. Creditors don't like to hear the barns are mostly empty. And bettors don't like to hear there are barely enough horses entered to fill a race card."

She wished she could ease his pain instead of adding to it.

He met her gaze. "I don't blame you for any of this, you know."

She licked her dry lips, trying to summon up courage. "Can I ask you something?"

"Of course." He interlaced his fingers behind his head. "Anything."

She drew a breath. Blew it out. "Did you have anything to do with Doc's death? Or Sherry's?"

Minutes felt like long, silent hours as Daniel held her gaze. When he finally moved, it was in slow motion. He came forward in his chair, brought his hands to his desk surface, and broke the silence with a strangled, "What?"

The question didn't require any elaboration, so she continued to wait.

"Why in heaven's name would you think such a thing?"

The words stuck, but she forced them out. "You've done it before."

Daniel Shumway, who'd always seemed larger than life, shrank. "You know." He choked a humorless laugh. With one thumb, he rubbed at a sunspot on the back of his other hand as if trying to wipe away a memory. "That was a long time ago."

"When you were Daniel Brice?"

"Yes." He made a few false starts, but finally managed to ask, "Are you going to report me to the racing commission?"

"Did you have anything to do with Doc's death?" She said it with more force this time.

"Would you believe me if I say no?"

"Convince me." She considered taking a seat in one of the chairs facing his desk. Instead, she opted to keep the chair between them and rested her hands on its back. "Doc found out about your past. He blackmailed you into keeping quiet about him falsifying Coggins test results."

Daniel didn't blink. Nor did he deny her allegations.

"You got a vial of ace from Sherry right before Doc died."

A sad smile crossed his face. "I wondered what you were doing in my tack room that morning."

"And Sherry—" Jessie's fingers tightened on the chair back. "She figured out who murdered her dad and was just about to tell me."

Jessie fought to hold her voice steady. "Did you—" She failed, and it cracked. "Did you kill her?"

The heartbreak in Daniel's eyes cut deeper than any scalpel could. "I thought we had something. I thought you trusted me."

She wanted to. More than anything. But she couldn't block the picture of Doc mangled in Clown's stall or Sherry floating in the pool. She couldn't afford to trust anyone right now.

Daniel didn't blink. "I guess this means you're canceling our raincheck for dinner."

Heat singed her eyes, but she wasn't going to let him see her cry. "I guess so."

Both Daniel's phone and the phone Greg had given Jessie rang at the same moment. Daniel picked his up and swiveled his chair away from her. She yanked hers from her pocket, brushed an arm across her face, and answered.

"Dr. Cameron?" She recognized Trooper Popovich's voice. "I need you to come back to your clinic."

"Why?"

"We've found some evidence, and I'd like your input on it. Now." The line went dead before she could protest.

Daniel was hanging up his phone too. "That was security. A cop just called."

"Popovich?"

"He thinks they have the murder weapon. They found it at your clinic." Daniel gazed at her with the same accusatory expression she'd used on him a few minutes earlier. Only he didn't come right out and ask if she'd done it.

Twenty-Five

Wearing gloves, Popovich removed a pair of hoof nippers from a brown paper evidence bag and waved them in front of Jessie. "Do these look familiar, Doctor?"

"They're mine." Blacksmiths weren't the only ones who owned farriers' tools. On occasion, she needed to pull a shoe from a lame horse.

"You're sure?"

"I'm positive." She had run a band of red electrician's tape around each handle to keep her tools from being mixed up with anyone else's. Now it felt like a damned stupid thing to do.

"Can you explain the blood on the end of them?"

"No."

Popovich squinted as if to study the dark reddish-brown stain. "The crime scene boys got a strand of long blonde hair from them too." He eyed her. "Your hair isn't blonde."

The comment didn't require an answer.

Daniel stood next to her in the dreaded spa. "If you're accusing her of something, I think she'd better have an attorney present before she says anything else."

Jessie looked at him. Why was he standing up for her after what she'd said to him mere minutes ago? She half expected him to shove her into Popovich's vehicle, maybe help slap the cuffs on her wrists.

"Did I say I was accusing anyone of anything?" Popovich's innocent routine didn't work, but that didn't stop him from using it. "We're simply having a conversation. We don't know what the blood and tissue samples we got from these—what are they? Some sort of pliers?"

"Nippers," Jessie said. "Hoof nippers."

"Ah, nippers. Thank you. As I was saying, we don't know what the blood and tissue samples we got from these nippers will show." Popovich returned the tool to the evidence bag. "May not even be human. But I believe we'll find a match to Miss Malone. And I believe our murderer used these to knock Miss Malone into the water. Any thoughts on that, Doctor?"

If she'd learned anything from Greg, it was that she had the right to remain silent. For once, she decided to invoke it.

"Any idea who, besides yourself, might have access to these...nippers?"

Daniel stepped between them and looked up at Popovich. The state trooper stood several inches taller than the track CEO, but at that moment Daniel's presence overpowered the officer's. "Anyone could have grabbed those from that bucket." He motioned to the white plastic pail Jessie used to store her farriers' tools. "This isn't a conversation. It's an interrogation. And you need to put an end to it until she has a lawyer present. Do I make myself clear, Trooper?"

Popovich looked down his nose at Daniel. "Fine." He pointed the bagged nippers at Jessie. "I want to be able to find you at a moment's notice, you understand? Do not make me look for you."

He sauntered out of the clinic, motioning for the remaining Crime Scene Unit guys to follow him.

Alone with Daniel, Jessie restrained an impulse to throw herself into his arms for making Popovich go away. When Daniel turned to face her, his expression made her wonder if Popovich should've stayed.

"I told you they suspected you." His voice took on a hard edge. "You know damned well the blood is Sherry's. He may not have arrested you today, but it's only a matter of time."

Her gaze drifted to the black, glassy surface of the pool, the reflections of the overhead lights, uninterrupted this time. But the memory of that blue balloon gave her a chill, intensified by the cold reality in Daniel's words. She took a step toward the passageway. "Let's get out of here."

He caught her arm. "You need to get a lawyer."

"Don't suppose you can recommend one?" She offered him a conciliatory smile.

"Yes, I could." His expression didn't look very forgiving. "However, I'm going to need him myself, considering what you've accused me of. You're on your own."

Her headache was back, but sinusitis had little to do with it.

"There's something else."

She pressed her fingers into the space between her eyes and squinted up at him.

He lifted his chin, looking down at her with an expression she couldn't read. "I want you off Riverview property."

"Excuse me?"

"You're a suspect in a murder that took place here at *my* track. Pack your things. I'll have someone from security come by at seven and escort you out. The guards will be given orders that you are not to set foot through the gate again. At least until things are settled."

Jessie took a lurching step to the wall and reached out for it. "But—but what about my patients?"

"There aren't any races tonight. I'll arrange to get someone qualified in here tomorrow." Daniel studied her in silence for a moment before speaking again. "I'm sorry, but you haven't given me much choice." He reached across the gulf between them, fingered a loose strand of her hair, and tucked it behind her ear. Turning, he strode across the spa, and ducked under the yellow tape at the back door.

Jessie watched him go, her mind reeling like a roulette wheel. And then the ball dropped. "My God," she whispered to the empty spa. "He really did kill Sherry. Now he's barring me from track property so I can't investigate and prove he's framing me."

Gripping the wall, she staggered in the opposite direction, through the hallway to the office. Her office. Except that it wasn't. And never would be.

OLD MCDONALD HAD NOTHING on Meryl's farm. Half a dozen beef cattle grazed in the pasture next to the drive. A small herd of horses and ponies in the lower field napped in the shade of a strand of willows. A coonhound and a yellow Lab—slightly less rotund than Peanut—offered her a raucous greeting, leaping at the fence enclosing Meryl's front yard. Jessie circled to the back deck where a trio of cats lounged in the fading light. The yelps, squeals, and shouts of a house with three boys and one young daughter in residence filtered through the walls. Jessie rapped on the sliding glass door. The din continued with no change in volume or pitch. Nor did anyone come to the door. She knocked again, louder. This time the house fell silent. The slats in the blind parted, revealing a brown eyeball that widened at the sight of Jessie. The latch clicked and the door slid open with a soft whoosh. Meryl stood there in jeans and a gray t-shirt. "Jessie? Are you all right?"

"Other than being homeless, unemployed, and a suspect in a murder investigation?"

Meryl opened her mouth with the obvious intent of making a smartass remark, but the murder suspect comment sank in. Her expression changed to one of puzzlement. Standing aside, she invited Jessie in.

The interior decibel level had cranked back up to rock-concert levels, and it took a few minutes for Meryl to round up her troop and shoo them outside. "Sorry about that. Hal's in the barn. He can handle them for a while." She motioned toward the kitchen table, piled with papers. "Have you eaten?"

Jessie tried to remember the last time she'd had a real meal. "Not recently."

Meryl gave her The Mom Look. "Sit." She dialed up the flame on the stove and reached for a skillet. "What's this about being a murder suspect?"

Jessie dropped into a solid oak chair and poured out the events of the last couple of days while Meryl cracked and whisked eggs with the efficiency of a master chef. Jessie skipped over the part about thinking she was falling in love with the man she believed to be the real killer. She already knew what Meryl would have to say about that.

As Jessie reached the end of her sad tale, Meryl slid a mushroom and cheese omelet onto a plate and plunked it in front of her. "You're being a bit melodramatic, don't you think?"

"What do you mean?" Jessie shoveled a large forkful into her mouth.

Meryl held up one finger. "You aren't homeless. Just boot Greg's ass out of your house and move back in." She held up a second finger. "You aren't unemployed either. I have a ton of work waiting for you." Third finger. "And you didn't kill anyone, which Trooper Popoholic will soon figure out."

Jessie snorted and grabbed for a napkin. "Don't let him hear you call him that."

Meryl blew a raspberry and withdrew a bottle of white zinfandel from the refrigerator. "Care for a glass?"

Jessie stopped chewing. Ordinarily, she didn't drink, but only because she was always on call. "Depends."

"On what?" Meryl had already removed two wine glasses from the cupboard.

"Can I crash here tonight?"

"Just so you won't have to drink and drive?"

"Just so I don't have to go home and face Greg."

Meryl huffed a sarcastic laugh. "Of course, you can stay here." She sat across the table from Jessie and filled the two glasses. "As for Greg, I already told you what you should do about him. Especially now that the Malone chick is dead."

Jessie winced. Funny. She'd started to have kinder feelings for Doc's illegitimate daughter now that she was gone.

"You still believe she's the one who broke in, don't you?" Meryl swirled the wine in the glass.

"I'm not sure." Jessie traded the fork for the glass of wine, sipped, and let the warm tingle seep into the back of her throat while she considered the question. "No, I don't think she did."

"Why not? And if not Malone, who?"

Jessie set the glass down and went back to picking apart the cheese and egg. "Whoever broke in destroyed a bunch of Doc's files."

"They stole your computer too. Maybe they took it to get the records on it."

"If that was their intention, they failed miserably."

Meryl fingered the stem of the wine glass. "You mean because you back up your computer files?"

"Uh-huh." She'd already retrieved her electronic records. "But Doc backed up his files too."

Meryl stopped with her glass halfway to her lips. "Wait. He only kept paper records, right?"

Jessie took another bite of the omelet. "And a spare set at his house. I'd retrieved Zelda Peterson's folder because I couldn't find Clown's record at the clinic." She realized what she'd just said and set her fork down on the plate with a hard clink.

"What?"

"When Clown's record first went missing, it crossed my mind that Doc's killer might be responsible, but I dismissed the idea because I assumed Doc had just misfiled it."

"Was that record with the stuff that got burned at your house?"

"No. I only had the files from A to H. The backups of those should still be at Amelia's."

Meryl's phone rang. She excused herself and crossed the kitchen to retrieve it from the counter.

Jessie forked down the rest of the omelet while forming a plan of attack for the morning. Could the answer to two murders be in Doc's file cabinet? Around the periphery of her thoughts, she heard Meryl agreeing to something on the phone and not sounding particularly happy about it.

Meryl returned to the table and tossed the phone on top of a pile of papers. She flopped into her chair and slugged down the rest of her wine.

"I gather that wasn't an emergency call." Jessie knew Meryl shared her aversion to the idea of drinking "on duty."

"Not exactly. You have to work for me tomorrow."

"But I wanted to go over to Amelia's and go through Doc's stuff."

Meryl shook her head. "That was Daniel on the phone. He wants me to fill in for you at the track."

Last winter, Jessie had walked into the little diner in West Cumberland and spotted Greg holding hands with a leggy redhead. Having Daniel replace her within hours, and with her best friend no less, may not have hurt quite as much. It was a business deal, after all, not an emotional one. So why was she feeling so damned betrayed?

Meryl reached across the table to give her a gentle nudge. "Hey. If you'd rather I told him to go to hell, I will."

Jessie coughed out a laugh. "No, I know my patients there will be in good hands with you." Then she slammed a hand down on the table, making her fork rattle on the empty plate. "But don't go falling in love with the place. I still might want to buy Doc's practice if I can swing it." She thought about all that had transpired in the last few weeks. "If there's anything left at Riverview once the dust settles."

DROPPING IN ON AMELIA before work was becoming a bad habit. This time, Jessie called first. Doc's widow sounded much cheerier on the phone than during their previous talk.

She also looked better when she met Jessie at the front door. "It's so good to see you, sweetie." Amelia gave her a big hug.

"I should've stopped in again before now."

"Don't be silly. I know what kind of schedule you have. I was married to the man you replaced, remember?

"I could never replace Doc."

"You know what I mean. Come in. Can I get you some breakfast?"

"No, thanks. I already ate." But she ventured a peek into the kitchen and was relieved to see a neat table and uncluttered countertops.

Amelia caught her looking. "I'm doing better."

"Good."

Amelia took a seat on the couch, which was free of blankets and bed pillows. "Please. Sit down." She motioned to a chair.

"I wish I could, but I have to get to work." Jessie decided against mentioning that "work" didn't involve the track today.

"You said on the phone you needed Doc's records."

"I don't know if you heard. Someone broke into my house and destroyed some of the files I had there."

Amelia gasped. "How horrible."

"I think there was something in them the burglar didn't want me to see."

A cloud of sadness crossed Amelia's eyes. "I'd hoped there was another reason you wanted them."

Work or not, Jessie took a seat beside Doc's widow. "What do you mean?"

"I imagine you've heard about Sherry Malone."

Jessie's mind spun through all there was to know. The topic was endless. "What about her?"

"She was his daughter."

Amelia knew after all. Jessie remained quiet, choosing to let Doc's widow volunteer whatever information she wanted to share.

"Sherry wanted his practice. Doc was going to leave it to her in his will. But something happened. Not long before he...died, he changed his mind and left her money instead."

Jessie took her hand. "I know. I wasn't sure how much *you* knew, though."

There was no joy in Amelia's smile. "He didn't think I knew about the girl. But I did. I never agreed with his decision to give her the practice. I think the only reason he planned to do it was to appease his own guilt."

"Why'd he change his mind?"

"I don't know." Amelia patted Jessie's hand. "It's my hope that you'll take it over."

Jessie wondered if she knew Sherry was dead. Or that Jessie was under suspicion. "I wish I could."

"Why can't you?"

Jessie looked around the living room, clicking off the reasons in her mind. Starting with the fact that Daniel had barred her from Riverview property. Segueing to the EIA scare that might bankrupt the track. And ending with the most benevolent reason, which was the only one she shared. "I can't afford to pay you even a fraction of its value."

Amelia's face blossomed into a smile, this one heartfelt. "My dear girl. I want you to have it. What am I going to do with a clinic and all those cabinets full of records? The lease on the building at Riverview is paid through the next two years, so you have plenty of time to deal with that part of it." Her voice turned hard and determined. "I just don't want that Malone woman to get it."

Obviously, Amelia hadn't heard. "Sherry's dead."

Amelia's trembling fingers touched her mouth. "That's awful. Do you think her death is connected to...?"

"Doc's? Yes, I do. That's why I want his records. I want to go through them and find out what someone wants to keep quiet badly enough to kill for."

Amelia's hand dropped to her lap. "By all means. Take them."

Jessie rose and started for the hall.

"Jessie?"

She turned back.

"Keep them. I meant it when I said I want you to have the practice. You're the *only* one I want to see have it."

Jessie nodded and headed down the hallway to Doc's office. Now all she had to do was solve two murders, clear her name, and keep Daniel Shumway out of bankruptcy. Provided solving the murders didn't land him in jail.

Twenty-Six

J essie parked the Chevy in her regular spot between the Cameron
Veterinary Hospital and her house and slid down from the driver's seat. Spring in western Pennsylvania was nothing more than a
battlefield for dominance between winter and summer. A week ago,
Jessie needed to run the furnace. Today, it wasn't even nine o'clock
and already sweat beaded along her spine, gluing her t-shirt to her
skin.

Boxes of folders filled the truck's cab, leaving barely enough
room for Jessie. More boxes packed the center portion of the storage
unit. Loose files had been tucked in anywhere and everywhere. She
itched to dig into them, but with Meryl taking over at the track,
Jessie had a busy day ahead at her hospital.

She watched as one of her clients carried a small plastic crate toward the front door. Meryl had warned her that she had a full slate
of surgeries lined up for the morning, followed by a packed schedule
of appointments. "Welcome back," Meryl had told her with entirely
too much glee.

Choosing to avoid the clamor her staff would raise if she trailed
in behind the client, she headed around to the side door for a less
grand entrance. She lifted a white lab coat from the hook on the wall.
Let the day begin.

Meryl hadn't been exaggerating. The morning was a blur of spays,
neuters, and dental cleanings with a couple of biopsies thrown in.
With only one vet working, all appointments were jammed into the
afternoon hours. There was no time for lunch, even though Jessie's

own kitchen was right next door. She found herself longing for an order of rec hall french fries.

By the time she finished writing a prescription for her final patient of the day, the clock read 7:25. Later than usual for hospital hours. She was beat but kept thinking about the track. The first race was history. Entries for the second should be at the post. Meryl still had a long evening ahead of her.

Exhausted or not, Jessie would've loved to trade places with her. Milt was right. She'd fallen in love with Riverview.

Jessie bid her receptionist and both techs goodnight and headed outside for the first time all day. She immediately walked into a wall of humidity charged with electricity. Black clouds boiled in the western sky.

She opened the passenger door of the Chevy and looked at the mountain of boxes. Meryl wasn't the only one with a long night ahead.

Lugging two boxes, one stacked on top of the other, when a single one would've been the wiser move, Jessie picked her way down the path to her back porch. She braced the boxes between her shoulder and the doorframe as she unlocked and opened the door.

A wide-eyed Vanessa met her in the kitchen. "I thought someone was breaking in again. What are you doing here?"

Jessie staggered past her into the dining room with the boxes. "Burglars generally don't use keys. And what are *you* doing here? Where's Greg?"

"He's working. I'm watching the house."

Jessie couldn't see Vanessa's face, but from the sound of her voice, she apparently took this as a very important job. "Well, I'm here now. You can go."

"Um. I can't. I don't have my car."

Jessie pivoted to catch a glimpse of Vanessa biting her lip. "Fine. Just stay out of my way."

When Jessie hit the bottom step, Peanut came bounding down from the second floor, tail wagging and tongue draped out the side of his smiling mouth.

With no free hand to pet him, she braced herself against his greeting. He bumped into her legs, bouncing as if trying to leap into her arms. "Come on, baby," Jessie cooed and started up the stairs. The dog followed and then proceeded to escort her on each of her eight trips from the truck to her office.

On the fourth or fifth trek through the house, Jessie stopped in front of Vanessa, who had snuggled into the overstuffed chair in the dining room with a book. Molly curled in her lap. "Where's the kitten?" Jessie asked.

Vanessa lifted her head and gave the room a quick scan. "I don't know. He's around here somewhere." Then she returned to her reading.

By the time Jessie carted the last stack of folders down the hill from her truck, she was grateful to have beaten the weather. The wind had kicked up, and the black and gray clouds flickered with lightning.

With the boxes stacked haphazardly around the room, Jessie rolled her office chair out from the desk and found the tabby curled up in the seat. She ran a hand over his pumpkin-colored coat. He awoke with a soft mew and leaned into her hand. She really needed to name him.

After raiding the refrigerator and throwing together a cheese, tomato and cucumber sandwich, Jessie grabbed a ginger ale and carried her makeshift dinner back to the office. With the tabby in her lap, the sandwich and soda at her elbow, she began to sort through the files, beginning with A.

The food didn't last through the Bs. By the end of the Cs, the tabby had relocated to the windowsill to watch Mother Nature's light show. Jessie hadn't found anything questionable. She stood up and stretched. Peanut followed her downstairs where she intended to dig up a bag of chips or something equally unhealthy to keep her going. She found Vanessa in the kitchen—*her* kitchen—sliding a frozen pizza into the oven.

"Want some?" Vanessa asked without much enthusiasm. Jessie imagined the offer had been made only because she'd been caught.

"Maybe later." Jessie grabbed a half-eaten bag of Kettle Korn and a bottle of water and retreated upstairs, accompanied by the rumble of thunder.

She was two-thirds of the way through the Ds when she came across the file marked "Dodd." Pushing the Kettle Korn to one side, she spread the papers out on the desk, studying each one.

Catherine had gone through more than two dozen horses over the last few years in her quest for a champion. Most had come and gone in short order, leaving only a page of notes. One of the thicker packets belonged to the Kentucky Derby aspirant turned lame has-been, Mexicali Blue. Curious, Jessie leaned forward to study Doc's findings.

The first thing that startled her was the pre-purchase exam report, performed while Emerick still owned the horse. The test findings revealed no sign of lameness. That couldn't be. Jessie shuffled the papers and located a set of radiographs. The old film kind. She didn't have a light box in her home office and had to settle for holding the films up to her reading lamp. Hardly ideal conditions for reading x-rays.

Something about the pictures triggered her internal alarm.

The radiographs she'd taken of Blue were on the computer back at the clinic. She had, however, backed them up online. She swiveled her chair to face her laptop and tapped the mousepad. As the screen came to life, another flash of lightning lit up the room at the same time a crash of thunder rattled the windows. Peanut whined and cowered under her feet. The tabby bolted from the room.

And the house fell into darkness.

Jessie stared at the computer—the only light source remaining. She glanced at her router. The green lights that usually twinkled across its surface were now black. So much for accessing her files from her online backup service.

She fumbled for the old x-ray and found it. Then she gazed at the light show outside her window. Storm or not, she knew what she had to do.

ON AN ORDINARY NIGHT, Riverview's final race went off just before eleven. The parking lot would be vacant by eleven thirty. But the storm must've caused a delay. The parking lot didn't empty out until close to one.

Jessie left her truck at the darkened amusement park, adjacent to Riverview. She skimmed the edge of the miniature golf course and stepped over the rickety wood fence separating the two properties. She may have been banned from the track, but if she bypassed the guard shack at the stable gate and avoided the front side security guys, who would know? Dressed entirely in black, she skirted the dirt track's white outside rail.

The wind was picking up again, scattering dust and debris. Lightning flickered in the clouds overhead. Mother Nature wasn't done with her pyrotechnics.

Jessie had spent enough time around the backside to know the strengths and weaknesses of the security measures. An eight-foot Cyclone fence encircled the barn area with the electronically operated arms at the stable entrance. Guards kept a close eye on the padlocked gate next to the rec hall and another that horses and riders passed through on their way between the track and the barns. There were two additional pedestrian gates near the maintenance buildings that security almost always overlooked. Jessie hoped tonight wasn't an exception.

As she neared the empty grandstand, she took a furtive look around. Seeing none of Riverview's rent-a-cops, she darted toward the backside. With the brown envelope containing Mexicali Blue's x-rays tucked under one arm, she hurried along the Cyclone fence to the first pedestrian gate, hoping to find it unlatched. No such luck.

She took another cautious check of her surroundings and hurried past the maintenance buildings to the second gate.

It was locked too. If only she'd thought of a Plan B.

She curled her fingers around the vertical pipes that made up the gate and gave it a frustrated shake. To her surprise, the padlock hit the pavement with a metallic clank. She snatched it and looked around, afraid she'd drawn unwanted attention. All she saw was the flicker of lightning.

Jessie opened the gate wide enough to squeeze through and let it drift shut. She hooked the padlock on the wire fencing next to the opening. Now she simply had to work her way across the backside to the clinic without being seen.

Thunder rumbled to the west. Dawn-to-dusk lights illuminated the backside in patches, leaving long shadows in their wake. Jessie clung to the dark sides of the stables. The soft rumble of a car engine forced her into one of the covered gaps between barns until track security's battered Chevy Cavalier rolled past.

The clinic loomed ahead. Jessie's heart pounded in her ears. *Walk*, she reminded herself. Running would attract attention, especially with the stable gate's guard shack nearby. Better to keep her head down and her pace casual.

She hesitated at the corner of the clinic. The front door was closed. Besides being very much in sight of the guard on duty, she thought of the racket opening it would make. With a slight adjustment in her original plan, she picked her way along the side of the building to the back entrance.

That door was closed too. Remnants of yellow tape fluttered. Jessie grabbed the handle and heaved. With a moan, the door opened.

Jessie paused to allow her eyes to adjust to the dark. A flash of lightning cast an eerie gray burst through the windows, illuminating the cavernous spa and emphasizing the liquid black pit that took up a good third of it. Then it was dark again, and she had to rely on her memory to pick her way to the passage. She clung to the side well away from the pool. When she was almost halfway across, lightning again lit the room and revealed the maw of the hall. She scurried the rest of the way.

Groping the wall, she made her way along the dark passage to the office door. She dug her keys from her jeans' pocket, fingered them until she found the right one, and probed until it slipped into the lock.

Force of habit drew her hand to the light switch, but she stopped in time. The nights spent sleeping in the office had given her a familiarity of the space even in the dark. She scooped up the laptop and headed to the exam area.

The light box cast a pale glow. Jessie snapped the two sheets of film into the clips at the top of it. She opened the laptop, logged in, and browsed through her files until she located what she was looking for. Then she stood back to study the shades of black, gray, and white.

The films on the light box showed a perfectly normal bone structure. The more recent digital pictures showed the thin line where a break had occurred. She was so engrossed in the variations in the coffin bone that she didn't immediately catch the more obvious difference—the radiograph of the sound foot also showed a longer pastern than the other.

The radiographs were from two different horses.

She snatched one of the films off the light box and squinted in the quasi-darkness to read Doc's scribble on the piece of white tape attached to the corner. Perhaps the wrong horse's x-ray had been mistakenly placed into Blue's records. But the film was clearly labeled "Mexicali Blue" and the date.

Doc had misrepresented Blue to the Dodds. He surely knew the horse was unsound. Otherwise, why substitute a different horse's x-ray? Why convince Milt to purchase a lame horse for Catherine?

Then she thought of Blue's past owner and the whole Coggins mess.

Doc was in cahoots with Emerick for more than swapping out blood samples.

Jessie gathered the films and the laptop and switched off the light box. Back inside the office, she dug out the phone Greg had given her and punched in a familiar number.

Vanessa's muffled, sleepy voice answered.

"Vanessa, this is Jessie. I need your help."

"What's going on? Is Greg all right?"

"I'm sure he is. Go to my office. I'll tell you what I need once you get there. Okay?"

Vanessa sounded tired. Too tired to be argumentative. "Hold on." A minute or so passed. "Okay. I'm here. What do you want?"

"Look in the boxes of records I brought home and find the ones for Neil Emerick."

Twenty-Seven

O ver the phone, Vanessa relayed page after page of Doc's notes on Mexicali Blue. Emerick purchased the colt as a yearling. A pre-purchase exam done on the horse showed the youngster had been clean. But following a strenuous training schedule and a couple of impressive wins as a two-year-old, Blue turned up lame, thanks no doubt to the trainer's high-pressure techniques. At that point, Doc radiographed the colt and diagnosed the fracture of the coffin bone.

Jessie was about to thank Vanessa for her help and hang up when she gave a startled cry. Something fell out of the Emerick folder, she said. A note in Doc's distinctive scrawl. As Jessie sat in stunned silence, Vanessa read it to her.

Jessie copied Blue's new radiographs onto a flash drive, which she tucked in the envelope with the old films. Hugging the package under her arm, she made her way back to the gate. The wind stirred a dust devil that swirled up into the halogen light between barns, mirroring the tornadic spiral of Jessie's thoughts.

Dazed, Jessie reached the gate, only to realize she hadn't been paying attention. She was at the wrong one. The one that was padlocked. She swore and turned away. Lightning lit the shadowy side of a nearby barn, revealing a figure ambling toward her. Neil Emerick?

"Hey, darlin'. What are you doing out on a night like this?" Milt stepped out of the shadows, squinting against the wind.

Jessie relaxed. "Snooping. I'm not supposed to be here, remember? Why are *you* still here?"

He gestured over his shoulder. "Flat tire. Had to wait 'til the rain let up to change the dang thing. Got her done and was fixin' to leave when I spotted you sneaking around. What're you snooping into now?"

She touched the envelope clamped against her side and wondered how much, if any of it, he knew. "I figured out who killed Doc and why."

"Oh?"

"Come on. Walk with me. I don't want to be caught on Riverview property. At least not until I can clear things up with Daniel."

"I gather it ain't Daniel that you suspect?"

"No. Neil Emerick."

"Neil?" Milt gave a low whistle that was drowned out by the rumble of thunder. "What'd you find?"

Jessie lowered her head against another gust of wind, shoved her hands deep into the pockets of her hoodie, and revealed what Vanessa had shared minutes earlier. "You know how Neil claimed ignorance about the condition of that gray that started this EIA business? Turns out Neil had Doc do one of his ringer blood tests on the horse before it arrived. But once the gray got here, Doc took one look at it and knew something was wrong. He demanded a real test. Only Neil had Sherry swap out the gray's blood sample for one from Sullivan. When the test came back negative, Doc was appeased for a while. But apparently Sherry had a change of heart and admitted what she'd done." A jagged flash split the night sky and a second later, thunder boomed, shaking the ground. Jessie flinched. Getting fried wasn't high on her list of priorities for the evening. Tracking down Daniel and Greg and getting them to arrest Emerick was.

Milt must have been having similar concerns about the electrical storm. He caught her elbow and steered her under the cover of a shedrow. "How on earth do you know all this?"

Jessie thought about the envelope again. "I called Vanessa at my house and had her go through Doc's records and a note fell out. You know how he documented every detail? Well, he'd written it all out. I'm pretty sure that's why Doc and Sherry fought and why he decided against leaving his practice to her. The last part of the note stated he'd told Emerick once Doc got back from his vacation he planned to go public with everything. The entire scam. Even if it meant Doc lost his own license." A rush of hot tears burned Jessie's eyes. Maybe there really was a part of the man she thought she'd known left in Doc's soul.

Milt leaned against the block wall of the barn, his face in shadows. "Neil had no choice but to do whatever it took to keep Doc from blowing the whistle."

"And Doc must've known if anything happened to him, I would be the one to find his note condemning his killer."

Milt pushed away from the wall and tipped his head to look out from under the shedrow roof at the sky. "Maybe if we make a run for it, we can beat this storm. I reckon you're eager to turn this over to that ex-husband of yours."

"And his trusty sidekick, Trooper Popovich, who still thinks I'm responsible for Sherry's death. Looks like Emerick killed her to shut her up too."

They headed toward the maintenance buildings. When they were almost to the gate, Milt reached over and tapped the envelope. "What's this?"

She stopped and removed it from under her arm. The bad news was going to come out eventually. She might as well be the one to break it to him. "It's Blue's x-rays."

Milt turned to face her. "*Mexicali* Blue?"

She nodded. "I'm afraid blood tests weren't the only things Doc used a ringer for."

Any trace of a smile had vanished from Milt's face. "What do you mean?"

"The x-rays from your pre-purchase exam show a different bone structure than the ones I made last weekend." She sighed. "I'm afraid Doc knew you were buying a lame horse. I'm sure it was another case of him and Emerick being in cahoots."

Milt took the envelope from her, pinching it between his thumb and finger as if it were toxic. "It's all here, is it?"

"I'm afraid so." She strode the last few steps to the gate. "I've been completely wrong about Daniel too. Turns out he had nothing to do with any of it."

"No, he didn't."

Jessie grabbed the pipe and gave it a tug. But it held firm with a clank. She tried again with the same result. The padlock she'd left hanging on the wire was now clipped through the latch and locked. Still clutching the gate, she felt the world inside her head grow quiet. Even the thunder sounded distant, as though she was hearing it through an echo chamber. Milt's words—especially the raspy quality of his voice—stuck in her mind. "What did you say?"

"Daniel didn't have anything to do with it."

She released the gate. Turned slowly to face the man she thought was a friend.

Milt's face was a study in agony. "Neither did Neil Emerick. It'll be nice to pin it all on him, though. The man's a bastard."

The stillness inside Jessie's head exploded. Pieces to the puzzle clicked into place. "The pre-purchase exam. You told me you didn't have one done. But you did." She pointed to the envelope now in his hands. "It was in Doc's records. I mentioned to Sherry that there hadn't been a vet check on Blue. She knew better. That's when she figured it out."

"Dang it, Jessie. If only you'd left it alone. That little gal never would've gotten wise on her own."

A spatter of rain hit Jessie's back, but she couldn't blame her chill on it. "You killed Sherry. With my nippers, so it would look like I did it."

He stuffed the envelope inside his jacket. "I hated to do it. But you made it easy. Everyone knew about the two of you feuding. With you behind bars, you'd have to quit your damned digging. It was the only way I could figure to make you stop. Other than…"

Jessie's breath came slow. "Other than killing me too?"

He looked down at his boots and nodded.

She studied him and tried to stay calm. "Now what?"

"You haven't left me much choice."

She took a quick look around, memorizing the details of her surroundings—details she missed in her everyday dealings in this area. Details she needed if she were to stay alive.

Behind her, the locked gate eliminated the option to escape. The maintenance buildings on either side of her created a wide corridor to the backside. Her best bet was the barns. There were plenty of empty stalls to hide in, thanks to the exodus. Except Milt stood in the way. Her only option, and it wasn't a good one, was surprise.

Jessie drew a breath, steeling her nerves, and charged straight at him with a yell that was half growl, half war cry. Startled, Milt raised his arms in front of him like a linebacker and lunged at her.

But she dodged to her left and threw her right shoulder into his.

The move staggered him. He didn't go down, but she slipped his grasp and sprinted toward the barns.

Just as the clouds opened.

She hoped Milt's age and the bad back he complained about would slow him down but wasn't putting money on it. She raced past the first stable she came to and cut between barns. The downpour soaked through the hoodie. The discomfort didn't bother her as much as the roar of the rain on the pavement and the roofs deafened her to his footsteps. She didn't dare look back. Not yet.

Her lungs burned. She skimmed through and around stables, avoiding any predictable routes. Gasping for breath, she took shelter under the covered gap between barns and collapsed against the wall.

She swiped a wet arm across her face in a failed attempt to brush the water from her eyes. Her ball cap had soaked through before she'd made the turn at the first barn.

Lightning gave her a glimpse inside the shedrow. Nothing moved. No sinister figures lurked. With the stable dark once again, she hugged the wall, feeling her way from stall to stall. An avalanche of thunder rolled overhead. The rumble faded in the distance. Did she hear footsteps? She froze. Listened. But there was nothing.

Another flash revealed an open hay shed, hay stacked almost to the ceiling, directly in front of her.

Jessie dived into the shed, hoping the roar of the rain and thunder drowned out the clunk of her boots on the wooden floor. Her shin hit something. An open bale. She stumbled. Fell into the pile. Scrambling, she reached up and scaled the stack like one of those climbing walls. A bale pulled free, and she almost tumbled to the ground. She caught herself. Paused. Drew a deep breath. And then scurried to the top. Ignoring the chafing hay biting through her sleeves, she squeezed into the space between the top row and the roof and wriggled as far inside as she could.

The rain softened from a deafening roar to a soft hiss against the tin. Jessie strained to hear movement outside, but the only sound was the rasping of her own breath. Chaff stuck to her wet face and worked into her clothes.

Where was Milt?

She jammed her hand into her jeans' pocket and pulled out her phone. Her first instinct was to call Greg.

Except she had his phone.

She punched in another number.

Vanessa sounded frightened when she picked up. "Greg?"

"No, it's me. Jessie." Something beeped in her ear.

"Again?" Now she sounded miffed.

"I'm in a real bind. I need you to track Greg down."

"Why? What's wrong?"

"I don't have time to go into it all right now—" Something out in the shedrow made a thud. Jessie gasped.

"Are you there?"

"Yes," Jessie whispered. She heard that beep again. "Hold on a minute."

She clamped the phone against her chest and listened. Footsteps. Definitely footsteps. Milt was right outside the hay shed. She battled a spark of hysteria. *Stay calm.* The sound stopped. She pictured him peering into the shed. Noticing the mess of broken bales she'd made in her frantic attempt to burrow in.

She heard the footsteps again, moving away this time, fading into the soft rush of light rain on the roof.

Jessie blew out a breath and brought the phone back to her ear. It beeped again. What was that? "Vanessa?"

"I'm here. What's going on?"

"Find Greg. Tell him it's Milt. Milt killed Doc and Sherry, and now he's trying to kill me."

"Oh, my." Vanessa's little-girl voice shot up an octave.

"Tell him I'm at Riverview and I need him *now*." No response. "Hello? Hello?" Jessie gaped down at the dark screen and dead phone. That's why it had been beeping.

How much had Vanessa heard before the phone cut out? Did she hear the part about Jessie being at the track? Did she hear the part about telling Greg she needed him? And if she had, Jessie wasn't Vanessa's favorite person these days. Would she even bother to make the effort?

Taking a long breath, Jessie listened again, hearing nothing.

She couldn't depend on Greg to come to her rescue. She needed to get out of this on her own. It probably wouldn't be long before Milt came back.

She crawled to the front of the haystack. Looked out and saw nothing. She swung one leg over the edge, then the other, and dropped to the floor, landing with a soft thud. At the front of the shed, she waited for another flash of lightning. It came and disclosed an empty shedrow. She stepped from her safe haven, jogged to the end of the barn, and stopped before turning the corner.

She needed a better plan than just darting from shedrow to shedrow. The gates were all locked, and she doubted she could scale the chain fence. Maybe she could get back to the clinic and lock herself in the office. But if Milt couldn't find her in the barns, he would likely head there and lay in wait for her. With a little luck, she could sneak past the clinic. Make a run for the stable gate. Scream like bloody hell and hope the guard reached her before Milt did.

She peeked around the corner to see if anyone was there. Nothing. Relieved, she gathered her courage.

Something scraped behind her. She wheeled.

The back of a shovel.

Searing pain.

And everything went black.

Twenty-Eight

A low moan filtered into Jessie's consciousness. It took a few seconds to realize the sound came from her own throat. Her face throbbed. Her sinus headache must be back. When she raised a hand to her left cheek, pain sliced through her head.

She opened her eyes. Blinked. Tried to figure out where she was. Rafters and a bare light bulb. Sounds crept through the haze. Rustling. Then a stomp followed by a snort. The smell of manure and damp straw.

"Wake up, darlin.'"

Jessie turned her head. Bad idea. The movement sent a glitter of razor-sharp stars dancing across her eyes. She squeezed them shut and held her breath until the pain subsided. When she opened them again, the source of the familiar drawl swam into view.

Milt stood over her holding the halter of a big chestnut. Jessie struggled to prop herself up on one elbow. The man and horse began to spin around her. She collapsed back into the prickly bedding. "Ow."

"I'm really sorry I had to whack you like that, but I should've done it long ago. Might've knocked some sense into you."

She forced her eyes open and concentrated on clearing her vision. And her thoughts.

The horse Milt was holding had his ears pinned back, and his eyes were ringed with white. A cold weight crushed the breath from her as she recognized the stallion. *Clown.* Milt's other hand, encased in a Latex glove, hung at his side, closed in a fist. He noticed her looking and uncurled his fingers, revealing a syringe.

"Ace?"

Milt offered her a smile that appeared genuinely sad. "Damn it all to hell, Jessie. I hate that it's come to this. You just wouldn't leave it alone."

She swallowed a hard, dry lump in her throat. "You're going to kill me the same way you killed Doc."

"It worked before. There's nothing to keep it from working again."

"Two of us dying the same way? No one's going to believe it's an accident."

"Doesn't matter. No one's gonna suspect me. You've given me the perfect scapegoat." Milt tipped his head back and chuckled. "Neil Emerick. That son of a bitch. I was never sure how much of the scheme to dump that worthless piece of horseflesh off on me was Neil's idea and how much of it was Doc's. This way they'll both pay. I'm much obliged to you for finding all that evidence against him."

She had to ignore both the pain in her face and in her heart if she were going to survive this night. Keep him talking. "Can you explain something to me?"

"What's that, darlin'?"

"You've been after me all along to take over Doc's practice. Why? If you didn't want me digging into his death, why not just encourage me to leave?"

Milt rubbed his chin with the back of his gloved hand. "That was a mistake. You see, I honestly liked you." The sad smile was back. "I thought you'd be a nice addition to this second-rate operation." The smile turned to a snarl. "And I wouldn't have to worry about you screwing my wife."

"You knew."

Clown tossed his head and almost broke free. Milt tightened his grip on the lead shank. "Whoa, son." He looked at Jessie, but she could tell he was seeing something else. "I suspected. Then that weekend...the weekend Doc and Amelia were supposed to be leaving for Hawaii...I was away at a symposium out in Harrisburg. I decided to come home early and surprise my beloved wife. Only I was the one who got the surprise. They were so wrapped up with each other, they didn't even realize I was there. Do you know what it's like to walk into your own home and find your beautiful wife in bed with your best friend?"

"Actually, I sort of do know."

Milt's eyes snapped back to focus on her. "I guess you do, don't you?"

"Only with me, it was my husband holding hands with a total stranger in a diner." The irony of exchanging tales of heartbreak with a man who literally held her life in his hands wasn't lost on her. But she needed to give Greg time to get the message and come to her rescue.

Milt had said he honestly liked her. If she could appeal to that side of him. Keep him from injecting the drug into Clown. She might be able to talk her way out of this.

"And now," Jessie continued. "Now, he's sleeping with a little blonde twerp who worked for me."

"It sucks, don't it?"

"It does. At least I had the satisfaction of firing her." Jessie forced a grin. It hurt like hell in more ways than one, but she hoped the pain didn't show.

"And I had the satisfaction of watching Doc die." Milt's voice could have frozen water buckets in July. He looked at the syringe.

Her breath caught. Keep him talking. "Something else I don't understand. Why did Doc fake the x-rays on Blue?"

Milt lifted his head. Once more Jessie had the feeling he was looking back in time. "He knew I was strapped. Catherine and her ponies. It's not a cheap hobby, you know."

Jessie nodded.

"I was in debt up to my ears. Buying horses. Feed. Training bills. Money pouring out and none coming in. But it was the price of keeping Catherine happy."

Jessie thought maybe it was the price of keeping Catherine. Period.

"My dear friend Doc finds this big ol' boy. Mexicali Blue. Bloodlines out his ass. Now my wife thinks Doc is the best thing since sliced bread for finding her this horse. Except then the horse goes lame. But it ain't Doc's fault. Oh, no. He's still her hero. And I'm left paying for it." Milt looked down and kicked at a mound of manure. "I think that was Doc's plan all along. Ruin me. Then he could ride in on his white steed and take my Catherine away from such squalor."

The stall fell silent. Milt, the picture of a broken man, gazed into space.

Clown broke the silence. He snorted and pawed the straw bedding dangerously close to Jessie's legs. She drew her knees in. Startled, the stallion flung his head up, taking Milt with him.

"*Stop that.*" Milt jerked the halter.

"It seems like an odd way to kill someone." Jessie kept her voice soft, not wanting to spook either the horse or Milt. "I mean, how could you count on Clown killing Doc?"

Milt considered the question before answering. "To tell you the truth, I'd have been happy if all Doc got was busted up real good. But he was so damned distracted with his vacation plans that he let ol' Clown kill him."

Doc's vacation. "It could have been me." Jessie shivered. "What if I'd have shown up instead of Doc? You had to know I was supposed to be filling in for him."

"That old cuss wouldn't miss a call until Amelia had his ass in the seat of the airplane." Milt's face softened. "But if you had shown up, I was right there. I'd have been Sir Lancelot coming to your rescue. I never wanted to hurt you, darlin.'"

"You watched him die."

"I did."

"Milt, you keep saying you don't want to hurt me. Don't do this."

The agony etching his face gave her hope. "You wouldn't listen to me. I kept trying to get you to leave it alone. Just let it be an accident. Even your idiot husband kept telling you that." Milt shook his head. "I wish to hell you'd have listened to us. Now I have no choice."

She opened her mouth to argue, but he held up a finger to shush her.

"There's no other way. You'd have to tell what you know. It's just who you are." He flipped the cap off the syringe with his thumb.

Jessie swallowed down the panic. "You removed Clown's records from the file cabinet in the office."

"Yep. You were digging into this boy's history." He nodded at the horse. "I figured as long as you didn't find out about his reaction to the drug, you'd drop it. How the hell did you get your hands on them after I got rid of them?"

"You didn't know? Doc kept backup records at his house."

Milt pressed his lips into a thin, flat line. "Dang."

"Why did you break into my house?"

"You know why." He rubbed Clown's neck—the spot he intended to inject.

"I get why you burned the records." She had to keep him distracted. "But why bust up my stuff?"

He chuckled. "If all I did was get rid of evidence, it would've been too obvious, don't you think?"

Jessie longed to check over her shoulder in hope of seeing Greg, or even Popovich, standing outside the stall but doubted anyone had received her distress call. And she didn't know how much longer she could keep this up. "What about the cats?"

"Pardon?"

"My cats. You locked them in the closet."

"Them danged cats." Milt rested his elbow on Clown's withers. "That black and white one kept getting under my feet when I was rummaging through your office. I tossed her in the closet to get her out of my way. But then she started yowling so loud it about drove me nuts, so I got the other one out of the cage and put it in there to keep her company. I suppose I could've shut her up permanently, but like I said, I never intended to hurt you. Or your kitty cats. I just wanted to scare you into backing the hell off."

"And you planted Sherry's barrette."

Milt held up one finger. "Don't think I don't know what you're doin'. But you're just delaying the inevitable. Enough with the chitchat." He looked up at the stallion who was standing quietly despite the curled lip and worry lines around his eyes. "It's time for this to all be over. That scum Emerick will take the fall. And no one will look at me twice." He moved his right hand, the one holding the syringe, toward Clown's neck.

This was it. When Milt turned his attention away from Jessie, she looked toward the stall door. Instead of a simple stall webbing or grate, the bottom half of the split door had been closed and probably latched. Before she could make a move, the steel toe of Milt's work boot caught her in the ribs. Her breath whooshed out of her as if he'd given her the Heimlich maneuver. The pain threatened to cut her in half. She hugged her knees and groaned.

"Don't make this any harder on yourself than it has to be." Milt's voice had turned stone cold. He'd released his hold on the horse to kick her, and Clown cowered in the stall corner. Milt turned his back on Jessie and approached the stallion. He grabbed the halter with his left hand. With his right, he slammed the needle into his neck and rammed the plunger home.

Jessie judged the distance to the stall door. She turned back just in time to see Milt's boot coming at her ribs again. Blocking out the searing pain screaming through her body, she rolled toward the foot and caught it in her arms. With one hand on the heel of his boot and the other clutching the toe, she twisted.

He roared in a mixture of pain and fury and crashed into the straw beside her.

She made it onto her hands and knees. Milt caught her around the waist and heaved her away from the stall gate. She rolled over him, landing between him and Clown. The chestnut stallion hunched back into a corner to avoid stepping on the humans in the middle of his stall.

Milt lunged for the door. Jessie scissored her legs around his. He tumbled onto his side and struck out, only succeeding in thumping her thigh. At this point, one more bruise didn't matter. Jessie released her legs' vice-like grip long enough to draw one back and let loose with a kick to his groin. She wasn't close enough to land a crippling blow. But it was enough to curl him into a ball and elicit a string of foul language.

A different kind of roar drew her attention. Clown no longer cowered in the corner. A thin film of sweat darkened his coppery coat. His eyes looked more crazed than frightened. The drug had hit his bloodstream.

Her peripheral vision caught movement. Milt was on his knees. Clenching both fists, he swung at her. She rolled away from him, and he caught her shoulder instead of her face. Thrown off balance, he toppled onto her.

Jessie tried to wiggle out from under him. His fingers found her throat and squeezed. She fought to pry his hands free. Tiny flash bulbs began going off inside her eyes. Sound became muffled. She could hear a primordial bellow, but it seemed miles away. Suddenly Milt's grip loosened. He screamed. Instinctively, she rolled and found her way to her knees.

Clown had Milt's shoulder in his teeth. The horse began shaking him like a dog worrying an old sock. Milt's arms flailed. He kicked at the horse.

Jessie scrambled toward the stall door. Somehow, Milt broke free. She heard him behind her, clawing his way on all fours. He grabbed Jessie's ankle. As he tried to climb over her, she kicked at him with her other foot.

But it wasn't *her* foot that made contact. Something cracked like a tree limb snapping in a storm.

Milt shrieked and crashed facedown into the straw. Jessie caught a glimpse of Clown's drug-addled eye and one hoof pawing. It must have nailed Milt's leg.

God, Jessie thought. This was how Doc died. She didn't want to go this way. She didn't even want Milt to go this way. The only way to stop it from happening was to get out of the stall. Find a pitchfork or something—anything—to hold the crazed stallion at bay.

She made a lunge toward the door.

But Milt once again caught her ankle. "Jessie, help me."

She flipped onto her back. Sat up. Grabbed a handful of Milt's shirt fabric. Dug her heels into the straw. And heaved. But it was like trying to drag a sack of lead.

A shadow fell over them. Clown reared behind Milt, blocking the light from the bare bulb. The stallion's front legs raked the air. And then drove forward. Jessie saw what was coming but was powerless to stop the inevitable. The hooves caught Milt's back and slammed him into her with the force of a truck.

The deep-throated growl coming from the horse was unlike anything Jessie had ever heard before. Clown hunkered back onto his haunches and reared again. The blacksmith lay still, no longer holding onto her. Jessie managed to wrest free of him just as the horse came down, battering his front hoofs into Milt's motionless body. The crack of bone and the sickening thud of metal shoes against flesh filled the stall. The coppery stench of blood curdled Jessie's stomach. As the horse reared a third time, she made it to the closed stall door and clawed her way up the wood. The stallion drove down on Milt one more time.

Jessie reached over the door and fumbled for the latch. Straw rustled behind her. From the corner of her eye she saw the big chestnut. His head snaked out in front of him as he advanced toward her. In two more steps he'd be on her, but she couldn't watch. She had to find the damned latch.

Her fingers did not touch the steel bolt, but she heard it scrape, metal-on-metal. The door swung open, and she tumbled into the aisle. Strong hands dragged her from the stall. The door slammed behind her. She heard and felt the impact as Clown crashed into it and let loose another blood-chilling scream.

Jessie's rescuer knelt beside her and helped her to sit. She raised her head and stared into Daniel's pale blue eyes.

"Milt," she whispered. "Help me save Milt."

"It's too late." Daniel's voice was soft. "There's nothing left to save."

Jessie choked back a sob. "How did you...?"

"Vanessa called me. She said you phoned and were in trouble. She couldn't track down Greg, so she called me instead."

Jessie closed her eyes, grateful for the ditzy blonde's remarkable memory for names and phone numbers. At the same time, Jessie wished she could close her ears to the thrashing going on inside Clown's stall. Wished she could close her mind to the memories of the last few hours. The last few weeks. When she opened her eyes again, Daniel was watching her. "I'm so sorry," she said.

In the distance, the wail of sirens merged with Clown's screams.

Daniel took off his coat and bundled it around her. "There's nothing to be sorry for."

She glanced at the stall. The same stall where Doc had died. And now Milt. "You're wrong. There's everything to be sorry for."

Twenty-Nine

The icepack felt delicious against Jessie's face, quelling the fiery daggers stabbing into her cheek and eye. If only it could numb her brain.

"You're gonna have a hell of a shiner."

She looked at Greg with her good eye. "You think?"

Jessie sat sideways on the gurney inside the ambulance. Greg perched on the edge of the jump seat across from her, resting his elbows on his knees. They both turned their heads to look out the open back doors.

The sight was too déjà vu for Jessie. The road below Barn E was jammed with police cars, lights flashing. The coroner's van had pulled in a few minutes earlier. From where she sat, she couldn't see them wheel the cot into the shedrow. Couldn't see them bring the bagged body out. She didn't need to.

She'd already given statements to two uniformed officers as well as Trooper Larry Popovich. He'd had the nerve to hint that she was the one who drugged the horse, so she wasn't exactly thrilled to see the big trooper show up in the ambulance doorway. He sat on the bumper step, and the vehicle rocked slightly from the additional load.

Greg shifted to face his colleague. "Larry, don't you think you could cut her some slack?"

"Relax, Cameron." The trooper pulled a paper bag from his pocket, snapped on a Latex glove, and removed a cell phone from the sack. "We found this in the blacksmith's truck."

Jessie looked at the phone and then back at Popovich. "Is that...Miguel Diaz's?"

"Uh-huh. Apparently, Mr. Dodd found it and instead of turning it in to lost and found, used it to call Doc Lewis and then 911 after watching Lewis die. And he texted you. Those are the last three numbers in its log." Popovich dropped the phone back into the evidence bag and peeled off the glove. "By itself, it doesn't clear you. But I've talked to Vanessa Yarnevich." He shot a glance at Greg before turning his full attention back to Jessie. "And one of the county detectives spoke with Mrs. Dodd. They both confirm your story."

The numbness had leeched out of Jessie's skin, leaving her face throbbing. She squished the chemicals around in the plastic sack to find the coldest spot and pressed it to her cheek. "Catherine must be devastated."

Popovich crossed his arms. "The only thing I still don't get is that hair clip in your desk."

The one thing she hadn't been able to get Milt to clear up. She didn't need him to. "Milt planted it at my house so I'd think Sherry was behind the break in." Jessie huffed. "Turns out Sherry's the one who pieced it all together. He killed her before she had a chance to tell me." Jessie looked at Popovich. "Or you."

Daniel appeared at the rear of the ambulance. It was the first Jessie had seen of him since the ambulance arrived. His face and voice remained stoic. "Are you okay?"

She looked down at her boots. *Okay* was about the last word she'd use to describe how she was. She'd lost the man who'd been closer to her than her own father only to find out she hardly knew him. Now she'd lost another man she'd thought was a good friend after discovering she'd been even more wrong about him. Milt had killed Doc. And nearly succeeded in killing her. Yet, on top of all that, she ached at his death. "I'm just peachy."

Popovich rose. The ambulance lifted with him. He reached in and slapped Greg on the knee. "I'll catch you later." He pointed a stubby finger at Jessie. "Stay out of trouble." Then he disappeared around the side of the vehicle.

Daniel's gaze shifted from Jessie to Greg and back. "Seriously. How are you?"

Jessie lowered the icepack. From the reactions she'd been getting, she gathered the shovel had left a mark. "According to the paramedics, I probably have a concussion. They're pretty insistent I let them transport me to the hospital."

"I think that would be wise." Daniel motioned for her to put the icepack back.

She complied without argument. The cold felt so damned good.

He stepped back. "Call me if you need anything." He turned to Greg. A look of understanding flashed between the two men. Daniel gave him a nod. To Jessie, Daniel said, "I'll be in touch." And then he was gone.

Greg gazed out the doors. "He's not a bad guy."

"No, he's not." There was someone else she'd been wrong about. "Speaking of not being so bad, I need to talk to Vanessa."

Greg's gaze snapped to Jessie. "Why?"

"To apologize. And to thank her."

"Oh?"

"She saved my life tonight. If she hadn't called Daniel, there would be two bodies for the coroner to deal with."

"I'm not so sure about that. Daniel said you were halfway out of that stall already when he arrived. He says he just caught you as you came tumbling out."

She looked out of the ambulance. The flickering blue and red light show reminded her of a colorized version of the storm that had long since blown over the mountains to the east. "Daniel was being kind."

She could feel Greg's gaze on her. "I think he's rather fond of you."

Jessie choked out a laugh. "Let's see. I threaten to close down the track, basically throwing him into financial ruin. Then I dig up a past he's trying to put behind him. Not to mention accusing him of two murders. I'm sure 'fond' isn't the word he'd use."

"He might not, but I would."

"Anyway, tell Vanessa thanks for me."

Greg met and held Jessie's gaze. "I will." He started to get up and thunked his head on the storage cabinet over the jump seat. "Dammit."

Jessie extended the icepack toward him, but he waved it away, gave her a weak smile, and climbed out of the ambulance.

As she watched him go, it occurred to her that maybe—just maybe—she and Greg might make it out of this mess as friends.

Epilogue

Jessie padded barefoot down the stairs of her house, a pair of scuffed Mary Janes clamped to her side by one elbow as she attempted to slide the post of one of her pierced earrings through the hole in her lobe. She hadn't worn the things since her dinner with Daniel.

She crossed the center hallway into the living room where Molly lay on the sill of the newly replaced front window. The tabby crouched next to the sofa, his rapt attention riveted on something black in front of him. A spider. He drew one paw back and batted it.

Jessie left him to his prey and headed toward the dining room. The earring back slipped into place on the post just as someone pounded on the back door. She glanced at the mantle clock. Who the hell could that be? She was going to be late.

After dumping the shoes in the middle of the floor, she crossed the kitchen and peeked out the windows of the enclosed back porch.

Daniel waved.

She hadn't seen or heard from him since that night two weeks ago at the track.

"I hope you don't mind me just dropping in like this," he said when she opened the door. "Are you going somewhere?"

Jessie smoothed away some nonexistent wrinkles from the front of her sleeveless sweater and glanced down at her black jeans. Not quite the attire for Lorenzo's but a step up from her usual faded blue jeans and t-shirt. "I have an appointment."

"With the doctor? You look great." Daniel motioned to her cheek. "The swelling has really gone down."

"And greenish yellow is a better color on me than the old purple and blue. But no, not the doctor." She stepped back and tipped her head to one side, inviting him in. "I'm meeting with my divorce attorney."

He feigned shock. "Really? I'm surprised."

She started to close the door but hesitated when she caught sight of the smallish red SUV parked on the hillside. "Where's your Corvette?"

"I sold it. And the Expedition."

She shut the door behind him. While the contractor had been there fixing the window, he'd repaired the door too. It closed and stayed closed.

Jessie followed Daniel through the kitchen to the dining room where he turned toward her. "Money's been tight lately."

"But your 'Vette? You loved that car."

He shrugged. "I'll own another one when the situation improves. I'm working on some investments to turn things around. What about you? A divorce attorney?"

"I've put it off long enough. I'm moving on. I've had to accept Doc wasn't the hero I always believed him to be. And Milt—" Her voice caught. Daniel reached a hand toward her, but she shook her head. "I'm still having trouble accepting that Milt was responsible for Doc's death. And tried to kill *me*. But I'm working on it."

Daniel studied her, his eyes narrowed.

Jessie lowered into a chair at the table. "At least one good thing came out of the ordeal. After sleeping here those few nights, Vanessa discovered she doesn't like the dark and quiet of country life, so she's not lusting after my house anymore."

"That's great." He pulled out a chair and sat next to her.

Silence fell over the room, broken only by the steady *tick, tick, tick* of the mantel clock. Jessie wasn't sure how to broach the subject of her future employment with the man she'd accused of murder. She studied the backs of her hands, but the answer wasn't there. Finally, she drew a deep breath and lifted her gaze to find him watching her. "I...wanted to talk to you. About Doc's practice at the track."

Daniel leaned back and crossed an ankle over a knee. "What a coincidence. I wanted to talk to you about that too."

She wondered if that was a good thing or a bad thing. "Okay. You first."

He shook his head. "You brought it up."

"But a lot of it's up to you. I mean, the last we talked, you banned me from Riverview property."

"No. The last we talked, you were violating that ban and nearly got yourself killed."

"True." She cleared her throat trying to dislodge the lump stuck there.

"For the record, I've lifted the ban."

She relaxed. A little. "Then, if it's all right with you, I'd like to take it over. Doc's practice, that is." She detected a hint of a smile on his face. "After I meet with the attorney, there's a young vet coming here to look at the hospital. He's interested in buying us out. And even if he doesn't, Amelia's agreed to let me make payments. Plus she's made me a heck of a deal on it."

The hint of a smile turned into a full blown one. "Yes, it's all right with me. It's what I've wanted all along, remember?"

"But a lot's happened since then. Things are so bad you had to sell your cars. If it wasn't for me and the quarantine—"

"The quarantine isn't your fault. It's part of the mess you inherited from Doc." All traces of the smile vanished. "And me. I have to claim my share of responsibility in the matter. I should have put a stop to it the minute I found out instead of letting Doc manipulate me. I was afraid of losing everything I've worked for. And now, it still might happen." He huffed a short laugh. "You sure you want to come back to Riverview? You might be climbing onto a sinking ship."

Now it was her turn to smile. "I don't believe that. From what I've seen, you can handle whatever adversity comes your way." She grew serious. "Did you really kill a man?"

He traced an invisible pattern on the tabletop. "A long time ago, I did. Yes."

She reached over and put her hand on his to stop the doodling. "What happened?"

A melancholy smile spread across his lips. "Maybe I'll tell you about it someday. Not now."

Jessie gave his hand a gentle squeeze. "I'm sorry. I've been burned quite a few times lately by blind trust. I don't have it in me to do it again."

He met her gaze, considered her words, and nodded. "The short version? I was in college. And in love. A man...a fellow student...raped my girlfriend. His parents were rich, so he got off, which only emboldened him." Daniel took a ragged breath and shifted his gaze away from Jessie, looking over her shoulder. "He started harassing her, stalking her. I only meant to scare him. To make him stop. I never should've taken that gun." His voice broke.

As did Jessie's heart. "I get it. You don't have to say anymore."

He lowered his eyes.

Time to change the subject. She leaned back. "What's going to happen to Clown?"

Daniel's expression relaxed. "Zelda decided to retire him to stud on her farm and doesn't plan on moving him anywhere ever again. That way she can keep a better eye on what drugs get shot into him."

"Good. She called me right after I got out of the hospital. Told me if I wanted her to, she'd have him put down. But I don't see the sense in it. Milt was the murderer, not the horse. Clown was simply Milt's weapon of choice."

Daniel uncrossed his legs and leaned toward her. "By the way, you should come over to my place. I've got something I'd like to show you."

"Oh?"

Daniel grinned. "I bought Mexicali Blue. Catherine's selling out and moving to Kentucky, can you believe it? Guess she figures she'll be closer to her dream, physically at least. She made me a hell of a deal on the horse."

"But, Daniel, you know he's not sound."

"Doesn't need to be. I'm offering him for stud. I know what you're going to say. He's not proven. But I'm looking at it as one of those investments I mentioned. I may pick up a few mares of my own. See what happens. I've got that big empty barn."

"That's a pretty risky investment for someone who's just sold his Corvette to make ends meet."

"Maybe that's what I'll name his first offspring. *Risky Investment.*"

Jessie laughed. "It's got a ring to it."

Just then the tabby skidded through the dining room, claws scratching, scrambling to find traction against the wood floor as he made a less-than-graceful turn and charged into the hallway, chasing some imaginary creature.

Daniel chuckled. "What was that all about?"

"Since his hip has healed, he's turned into a maniac. If there isn't something real to hunt, he chases shadows. I'll never have to worry about mice as long as he's around."

"Looks like we both have a knack for picking up strays." Daniel slapped the table with his palm. "Speaking of good names. Hunter," he said. "There's your name for him."

"Hunter?"

Daniel smiled. "He's a tabby. Tab. Tab Hunter."

"Huh?"

"Oh, great. Make me feel like an old man. *Tab Hunter*. He was a huge star—back in the fifties and sixties."

"Never heard of him. But I like the name. Hunter it is. Looks like I have to keep him now."

"One other thing." Daniel fixed her with a puzzled gaze. "You said you have a vet who's interested in buying 'us' out. Us?"

"Meryl and me. You don't know?"

"Apparently not." He looked like he wasn't sure he wanted to.

Jessie grinned. "Meryl's selling her half of Cameron Veterinary Hospital too. She's taking over for old Dr. McCarrell. But he's agreed to stay on until I'm cleared to come back to work."

Daniel's shoulders sagged in mock defeat. At least Jessie hoped it was mock. "Are you telling me," he said, "that both of you are going to be practicing at my track?"

She gave him a smug smile.

"Look at all the trouble just one of you caused. I can't begin to imagine the headaches *two* of you will give me."

Don't miss out!

Visit the website below and you can sign up to receive emails whenever Annette Dashofy publishes a new book. There's no charge and no obligation.

https://books2read.com/r/B-A-TPUN-EZUMB

BOOKS READ

Connecting independent readers to independent writers.

Also by Annette Dashofy

Death by Equine

Watch for more at www.annettedashofy.com.

About the Author

Annette Dashofy is the *USA Today* best-selling author of the multi–Agatha Award-nominated Zoe Chambers mystery series. She and her husband live on ten acres of what was once her grandfather's dairy farm in southwestern Pennsylvania with one very spoiled cat.

Reach out to her at www.annettedashofy.com

Read more at www.annettedashofy.com.

CPSIA information can be obtained
at www.ICGtesting.com
Printed in the USA
LVHW110013010622
720183LV00021B/285